Muhsin Al-Ramli

THE PRESIDENT'S GARDENS

Translated from the Arabic by
Luke Leafgren

MACLEHOSE PRESS
QUERCUS · LONDON

First published in the Arabic language as *Had–a'iq ar-ra'ays* in 2012
First published in Great Britain in 2017 by
MacLehose Press

An imprint of Quercus Publishing Ltd
Carmelite House
50 Victoria Embankment
London EC4Y 0DZ

An Hachette UK company

This book has been selected to receive financial assistance from English PEN's
PEN Translates! programme. English PEN exists to promote literature and our
understanding of it, to uphold writers' freedoms around the world, to campaign
against the persecution and imprisonment of writers for stating their views, and
to promote the friendly co-operation of writers and the free exchange of ideas.
www.englishpen.org

A CIP catalogue record for this book is available
from the British Library.

ISBN (TPB) 978 0 8570 5678 8
ISBN (Ebook) 97808570 5679 5

10 9 8 7 6 5 4 3 2 1

Designed and typeset in Collis by Libanus Press
Printed and bound in Denmark by Norhaven

To the souls of my nine relatives
slaughtered on the third day of Ramadan, 2006

And to all the oppressed in Iraq
May the deceased forgive our bitter grief and rest in peace
May the living do their utmost for the sake of peace and tolerance

CHAPTER 1

Sons of the Earth Crack

In a land without bananas, the village awoke to nine banana crates, each containing the severed head of one of its sons. Along with each head was an I.D. card to identify the victim since some of the faces were completely disfigured, either by torture before the beheading or by something similar after the slaughter. The characteristic features by which they had been known through all the years of their bygone lives were no longer present to distinguish them.

The first person to notice these crates alongside the main street was the dull-witted herdsman, Isma'il. Curious, he approached without dismounting from his donkey. The donkey's image was inextricably tied to Isma'il's in the minds of the people because of how long he had ridden it – sidesaddle, both legs hanging down on the same side – as though the two of them shared one body. As soon as Isma'il saw the bloody heads inside the boxes, he slid off his donkey and bent close, poking at them with the end of his staff. He recognised some of the heads. All traces of sleep fled his eyes as he rubbed them to make sure he was not dreaming. Then he looked around to confirm he was in his own village and not somewhere else.

The last silver light of dawn was filling the street. The shops on either side were closed. The sleeping village was calm and still, apart from the crowing of a rooster and the barking of a distant dog, responding to another dog in some yet more distant corner. In that moment, Isma'il felt liberated from the ancient sense of guilt that had pursued him in nightmares ever since, as a boy, he cut out the tongue of a goat that had annoyed him with its bleating when he was braiding a wool belt for Hamida amid the solitary silence of Hyena Valley.

In that same moment, Isma'il's tongue recovered from its paralysis, and he began screaming at the top of his lungs, causing his donkey to jump, his flock of sheep to freeze, and the pigeons and sparrows to launch from the treetops and rooftops. He kept yelling without realising what he was saying, and his cries seemed to resemble the bleating of that goat whose tongue he had cut out and grilled. He kept yelling until he saw people rushing towards him from some of the village houses – then all the people from all the houses, after the alarm was raised over the mosque loudspeakers.

And if Abdullah Kafka had spoken about this incident, he would have said, "It was on the third day of the month of Ramadan, 2006. According to ancient history, that was when a strange amorphous blob with a giant body and a small head, called America, came from across the oceans and occupied a country named Iraq. Historians make clear in some footnotes that the people of that time had hearts that were primitive in their cruelty, savage hearts, like beasts of prey. As a result, among the injurious relations they had with each other were such dishonourable deeds as assault, terrorism, wars, invasions and occupations. In those remote times, the heart of humanity was sunk in darkness. It wasn't a darkness of intellect or vision, such that man was unable to cogitate upon the murder of his brother man. Rather, it was much worse, in that he might actually follow through with it."

This is how Abdullah Kafka would see and speak about everything that happened, describing it all as ancient, lost, dead history. The present and the future did not exist at all for him. There was only the past, and all of it was black. Some of it died irrevocably and did not return, and the rest of it was repeated later, in a time that other people called the future.

Thus for all the years since his return from captivity in Iran, Abdullah Kafka, that prince of pessimists, had been content to sit on the same chair in the corner of the village café from the moment it opened its doors in the morning until it closed after midnight. Sipping cups of bitter coffee and glasses of tea black as ink, he would smoke a *nargileh* absent-mindedly or just listen in silence. He returned greetings with a nod of his head or a gesture with a hand that still gripped the smoking nozzle of the water pipe. If he spoke, or rather, if he was forced to speak, he would go on speaking interminably, or he would be satisfied with a comment of no more than a few words.

So it was one spring when they informed him that the river had flooded. It overflowed its banks and covered the fields and gardens, carrying off the nearby huts and mud houses and unearthing the hillside cemetery to scatter the bones and skulls of the dearly departed. Abdullah Kafka did not say a thing. Ignoring the alarm of those bringing the news, he continued puffing on his water pipe as people ran in every direction before him. He said nothing until Isma'il the herdsman came in, petrified and howling, because the flood had swept away his animal pen and carried off ten sheep and one of his goats. He was sobbing as he described how his goat had floated on the surface of the water, brown with flotsam and mud. It was bleating and looking at him, as though in supplication, and Isma'il could do nothing to save it because he did not know how to swim.

Isma'il's despair filled the café: "The water is rising. It's creeping towards the rest of the village! It's the end! It's the Day of Judgment and the end of the world!"

At this, Abdullah Kafka cleared his throat and asked him calmly, "And did the water rise so much that your goat's back touched the sky above us?"

"No," Isma'il said.

Abdullah said to him, "Then this is nothing. But would that the end had come and brought the heavens down to the earth." And he turned deliberately back to his pipe and went on smoking.

As for this morning, when they informed him that the head of his lifelong companion Ibrahim was among the nine, Abdullah replied, "It is finished! He has attained his rest. For this time he has truly died, leaving us to the chaos of fate and the futility of waiting for our own deaths, we the living dead."

Abdullah fell silent and remained motionless apart from the rise and fall of his chest with each breath. He sat frozen there for several moments. Then he began to smoke and smoke. And for the first time, the people saw tears stream from his unblinking eyes. He did not wipe them away, and he did not stop smoking.

When the news reached the third member of their lifelong

brotherhood, Sheikh Tariq, he felt faint and all but collapsed. He sat down quickly, propping up his spirit – so as not to kill himself – by reciting the many religious sayings he had learned by heart and which were always on the tip of his tongue. He wept and asked God's forgiveness; he wept and cursed the devil so as not to be driven to despair; he wept and wept until the tears wet the edges of his red, henna-dyed beard.

Questions from the onlookers saved Tariq from succumbing to an even longer bout of sobbing. "What do we do, O sheikh? Do we bury the heads on their own, or do we wait until we come across their bodies and bury them together? They were killed in Baghdad, or on the road to Baghdad, and now Baghdad is a chaos choking on anonymous corpses, buried explosives, car bombs, foreigners and deceit. It might be impossible to find their bodies."

Tariq said, "It's best to bury the heads, and if their bodies are discovered later on, it's not a problem for them to be buried with the heads, or separately, or in the place where they are found. Our sons and brothers are not better or more venerable than the prince of martyrs, Hussein, grandson of the Prophet, whose head they buried in Egypt or Syria while his body stayed in Iraq. Make haste to bury the heads, for the way to honour the dead is to bury them."

Only Qisma, the widow who became an orphan that early morning, opposed them and wanted to keep the head of her father Ibrahim unburied until his body was found. But she resisted in vain when the men refused and rebuked her, saying, "Hold your tongue, woman, and cease this madness! What do you know about such things?"

They pushed her away to where the women were gathered, many of whom were surprised at Qisma's stance since they knew she had not always seen eye to eye with her father. Nevertheless, as was her wont, Qisma refused to give in and began planning her next steps. Only her fat neighbour Amira supported her and wanted to do the same thing, to preserve her husband's head in the freezer until they located his body.

Each head had a story. Every one of these nine heads had a family and dreams and the horror of being slaughtered, just like the hundreds of thousands slain in a country stained with blood since its founding and until God inherits the earth and everyone in it. And if every victim had a book, Iraq in its entirety would become a huge library, impossible ever to catalogue.

Sheikh Tariq said, "Do not wash the heads, for they are martyrs. A martyr is not washed before being buried because he is purified just as he is. His wounds will exude the scent of musk on the Day of Resurrection."

As the last rites were being performed for the heads, Tariq approached the head of Ibrahim and fell upon it, hugging it to his chest and kissing it so hard that his embrace scraped away the scabs formed by dirt and congealed blood that stopped up the wounds and the veins in the neck. The blood drained from it afresh and stained the front of the sheikh's white robe, his hands, and his beard. They gently pulled him away and wrapped the head in a white burial shroud to match the others, which they buried together in a line. In the end, they dug complete graves the length of a normal man, not the size of a child's, even though they lowered only the heads into their depths.

Abdullah Kafka did not attend the funeral but stayed at the café, smoking. No-one blamed him, even though all the people of the village knew the strength of the bond that had existed between these three men since childhood, such that they were called by various epithets, all of which played on the idea of three – "the eternal triad", "the happy threesome", or even "the three butt cheeks in the same briefs" and "the triple balls" and so on – because they would almost never be seen apart until destiny separated them in the days of the Iraq–Iran War. But the most widely used name was "sons of the earth crack". That name had a story, which was itself a testament to the strength of their early alliance.

It went back to the early years of their boyhood, the days when they would swim in the Tigris during the burning heat of July afternoons, quarrel with the girls bathing and washing clothes near the shore, hunt at night for the sand grouse sleeping in the nearby deserts, root out snakes and jerboa from their holes to break off their teeth, and drive off the wolves and jackals. When the Bedouin herdsman Jad'an spotted them near his tent, he did not recognise them, even though he knew nearly all the villagers on account of his living there with his family and his flock of sheep for one month each year, right after the harvest. He asked Abdullah, "Whose son are you?" And because Abdullah did not know his real father, he was quiet for a moment and then said, "I'm the son of the earth crack." Jad'an turned to Ibrahim and Tariq with the same question, and they gave the same answer out of solidarity with Abdullah. At that, the Bedouin fell silent for a while, stroking his beard as if in thought, and said, "Yes, we are all sons of the earth crack. The earth is our mother, all of us. Out of her we are born, and to her we return."

Jad'an ruffled their hair affectionately and invited them to his tent to taste "the best butter in the world", as he called it, which was the butter of his wife, Umm Fahda, and to drink some of the milk from her village. The invitation pleased them to the same degree that it filled their souls with fear and trembling, for this was an unexpected opportunity for Tariq to see Fahda, daughter of Jad'an and Umm Fahda, inside her tent, instead of making secret rendezvous with her between the sacks of harvested wheat and barley or among the flock of resting ewes. Did her father know what had been going on between them, and was his invitation nothing more than an ambush to trap them and do God knows what to them? Stories of Bedouin cruelty and betrayals were notorious, especially when connected to questions of honour.

Jad'an later told the story to the village elders as they sat together, drinking their morning coffee. They all burst out laughing and praised the boys' solidarity and fidelity to the ideal of true friendship. The story circulated widely, just as everything said in the village reached every ear, even when whispered in confidence. From that time the name "sons of the earth crack" became commonplace.

Abdullah wasn't lying when he said that he was the son of the earth crack, for that is what he knew at the time, as did everyone else. But now, nearly fifty years old, he was the only one who knew the origin of the story. The mayor's wife, who had tarried in life until he returned from the long years of his captivity in Iran, had told him the truth of the matter.

He alone knew that she was his grandmother, and that the dull-witted herdsman Isma'il was his maternal uncle. His story was like something out of the old melodramas from India, so it was no surprise that he was known for defining life as "a Hindi movie".

About himself he would say, "I am a victim and the son of victims. I am the son of the murdered going back to Abel, and I'm surprised not to have been killed yet." Then he would add, "The logic of my ancestors' history stipulates that my death be connected with love. Perhaps my failure to bind myself to the one I loved is what has come between me and my death. Or else that failure itself is my true downfall . . . Perhaps I am the final sentence in this volume containing the family tree of the murdered."

Abdullah did not clarify to anyone the true secret behind his allusions. And no-one asked him for any explanation since they were used to such pronouncements, which they called his "philosophising". The inscrutability of these sayings usually baffled them, and people would interpret them as they pleased or else forget about them entirely. Abdullah did not disclose the secret even to his lifelong friends despite their implicit mutual pledge to secrecy. In turn, they too carried secrets in their breasts that they resolved would remain confined unto death. Everybody has a secret, maybe more than one, which they decide not to reveal to anyone. Sometimes because it is shameful, embarrassing, or painful. Sometimes because they do not find the right opportunity to announce it: the secret's time has not yet come, or else it has passed, and its revelation no longer carries any meaning or importance.

Abdullah was raised at the hands of good parents who loved him as though he were the fruit of their loins. If he had been a girl, they would have named him Hadiya, "gift", because they believed he was "a gift from above". Abdullah's parents said that repeatedly throughout their lives.

Salih and Maryam's small mud house was at the very edge of the village, on the side of the hill by the river. One spring dawn, when the white of the first approaching light scattered the last remnants of the retreating darkness, Maryam awoke as usual and went out to the square mud stall that rose as high as the shoulder of someone standing beside it. At a distance of sixty steps from the door, it was situated in the furthest part of the dwelling's courtyard, right above a deep crack in the side of the hill. This crack had been made by a torrential rain many long years before, and Salih had put it to good use as a toilet, which they called "the pit".

Previously, Salih and Maryam, like everyone living on the outskirts of the village, used to do their business in the river valley, the thickets, or out in the open after nightfall. With the crack, Salih did nothing more than construct the mud wall, and since it cost him nothing, he chalked it up to his own ingenuity. You only had to spread your legs to either side of the crack and squat down, then expel your excretions into the mouth of the dark opening, waiting to hear the sound of its fall, hidden in the depths far below.

Some suggested this crack was an old well, reopened by the rain. Others said that perhaps the hill contained ancient ruins, for when digging wells or kneading mud to build their houses or make a bread oven, people often found urns, bracelets, earrings, tablets, belts, swords, and armour made from brass, gold and silver. They would give anything made for women as gifts to their own wives and keep anything made for men as ornaments to put on the walls of their reception rooms. They used the urns – after dumping out the bones and washing them – to cool water or pickle vegetables. As for the ceramic tablets, which had drawings and inscriptions scratched upon them, these they used as door-steps, or to reinforce door frames, or as part of a window, or under the legs of beds or wardrobes to fix their balance.

That morning, before Maryam went inside "the pit", she saw a bundle of cloth propped up against the wall next to the entrance, near the outer opening of the crack. She was startled and put her hand to her mouth, then to her breast. As she calmed down and took a deep breath, she reached her hand out cautiously to the top of the bundle and slowly drew back the edges of the cloth. She was terrified to see the face of a newborn baby, asleep. She ran back to the house and shook Salih until the entire bed shook with him. He woke up and asked what was wrong. Maryam stuttered as she pointed outside, "A baby – a baby – the pit – a baby!" And if it were not the case that Salih had never before seen his wife in such a state of bewilderment, he would not have hurried outbarefoot and in his pyjamas.

They carried the bundle inside and set it down. They kept looking at each other in silence, their unspoken thoughts hanging in the air. "Salih," Maryam said at last, "do you think it is a gift from God in return for our patience? Is it an answer to our prayers?"

"I don't know," he said. "But what could have brought it here? I'll go to dawn prayers at the mosque and ask if anyone has lost a baby."

He got up and made his way to "the pit" in order to perform the ritual purification. He walked around the structure twice as though looking for something – perhaps another baby. He squatted inside and strained but only gas came out. He washed and went back to put on his clean robe. He stared at the face of the child and said, "Please check – is it a boy or a girl?"

Maryam uncovered the infant with trembling fingers and burst into tears. "It's a boy!"

Salih went out as though a wind were at his back – and a second wind pulling him from the front. As soon as he arrived at the mosque, he told Sheikh Zahir, the imam, what had happened so that he could inform the congregation. Contrary to Salih's expectations, Zahir was not surprised, a response Salih put down to the sheikh's sophistication, the breadth of his knowledge, his equanimity and the firmness of his faith.

After the prayers, the imam addressed the people, asking them about the matter. Given that no-one there had lost a baby or heard about anyone losing a baby, Zahir said, "Let those who are present inform those who are absent. Tell all the people of the village. And if no-one claims the child and establishes his paternity within three days, then the infant belongs to Salih and Maryam. It is undoubtedly a gift from the Lord of Creation for their patience, their goodness and their faith."

Everyone agreed, and indeed, it warmed their hearts on account of their affection for Salih. At first they hoped, then they said, and in the end they believed that the matter truly was a miracle, God's recompense to the good and patient couple.

Salih's face could not hide the tears gleaming in his eyes. And as soon as he found himself outside, he hurried home, carried along by the same gale at his back. Beaming, he came in to where Maryam was waiting and said, "It really is a gift, Maryam, just as you said! And if it had been a girl, we would have named her that, 'Hadiya'. But now, we'll name him . . . we'll name him Abdullah, after my father, who died dreaming of a grandson to carry his name."

Maryam was about to trill with joy, but Salih stopped her, even though the force of his own exultation would have made him trill had he known how. "Not now," he said. "Wait another two days, and at that time we'll slaughter our bull and hold a huge feast for everyone. A party with dancing, just like a wedding. Then you can trill all you want."

And so it was.

CHAPTER 2

The Lives of the Ancestors, or, A Secret Understanding

Tariq, son of Zahir, the imam of the mosque; Abdullah, son of the earth crack, who became Abdullah, son of Salih; and Ibrahim, son of Suhayl the Damascene: these three were born in successive months in the year 1959. Ever since they first crawled and played with naked bottoms in the dirt near their mothers – who gathered together in the evenings around the bread ovens or in front of their homes to chat and exchange gossip, which they regarded as a science – they were inseparable, parting only to sleep under their parents' roofs. Even then, they would sometimes spend the night in each other's home if they had stayed up too late or if one of them was angry with his parents.

Together they came down with the measles, and together they got better. Together they learned to walk, swim, hunt sparrows, train pigeons, steal watermelons and pomegranates, practise their aim with arrows and with rocks, play football and hide-and-seek, and compete at the high jump. Together they entered school, defended each other against bullies, and studied for exams out in the fields or at night in one of their bedrooms.

Beyond the common name by which the people knew them, "the sons of the earth crack", these three gave each other nicknames to use among themselves, names adopted from some characteristic behaviour or trait. These names quickly spread among the people, just like everything else that was said in the village, even if the original source or reasons were unknown.

Tariq was the most meticulous with regards to his appearance, and the most passionate about reading and girls alike. They called Tariq "the Befuddled" because he would always show childlike amazement upon encountering any new thing or idea, no matter how banal, and he enthusiastically embraced any idea or ideology, even if he forgot his enthusiasm the next day. It was no surprise, therefore, that contradictory inclinations roiled within him until in the end he became devoutly religious. It was Abdullah who gave him that epithet, always calling attention to Tariq's passionate reactions. "Take it easy!" he would say. "What's wrong with you, always so befuddled like a dimwit?"

For his own part, it was Tariq who gave the name "Kafka" to Abdullah in the days when he was amazed to discover Franz Kafka and burned through everything written by and about him. That was because Abdullah was typically attuned to the blackest side of any idea or situation, and even when he laughed, a deep and firmly rooted sadness appeared in his eyes. There is no question that uncertainty about his real parents played a part in that. And if Tariq had kept reading foreign authors his whole life instead of being diverted to the religious books his father had left to him, he would have named him Abdullah Beckett, given that Abdullah's face started to resemble the fiercest photographs of Samuel Beckett in all his creased dejection. Sharp wrinkles covered him until he resembled the crumpled skin of a flayed animal, or the ground when the water has receded, and it dries and cracks. But Abdullah liked the nickname Kafka very much, especially after Tariq told him about this literary man's melancholy and his obscure relationship with his father, and Abdullah took the name with him throughout life.

As for Ibrahim, who had the strongest body of the three and was the kindest and calmest, they called him Ibrahim Qisma, "Ibrahim the Fated", because he accepted every report and every accident with an astonishing equanimity, always repeating afterwards, "Everything is fate and decree," or simply, "It's my fate." In the same way, for the sake of variety, they gave him the nickname Abu Qisma, or "the father of fate". And he actually did give his daughter this name later on. If he had fathered a boy instead of his daughter Qisma, it would not have been out of the question to choose a related masculine word, Naseeb, meaning "decree", as Ibrahim himself explained one bantering evening, happy in the presence of his two closest friends as they reminisced. It was Ibrahim's fate to be his parents' firstborn son and the oldest brother to a crowd of siblings, a fact which demanded sacrifices that redirected the course of his entire life.

Their fathers had been friends too, even if their friendship had involved an element of collusion and an acceptance of the need to coexist, however possible, in a small village. Hajji Zahir, father of Tariq the Befuddled, was remarkably intelligent and clever, always smiling, and the only blond-haired man who lived there. Stout around the middle, his belly and his beard both shook whenever he laughed. He had studied at a Qur'an school in Mosul and afterwards returned to become the teacher in their school and the mosque imam. He liked food, women and jokes.

Zahir married three times. Tariq was the son of his second wife, whom Zahir had met during a visit to a neighbouring village to attend a wedding that ended before it began when the groom was killed by the revolver of the bride's cousin, who had wanted her for himself. Zahir came through that bloody night the clear winner, for the cousin, after killing the groom, put the pistol to his temple and pulled the trigger. Thus, before the consummation of the marriage, the bride became a widow on her wedding night.

The parents clamoured around the bride, and the gathered assembly erupted in turmoil amid overpowering perfume and dinner tables piled high with meat, rice and stew. The bride clawed her fingernails into her face as she lamented her ill fortune. Her father was about to kill his brother, the father of the murderous cousin, while the father of the murdered groom was about to kill the dead murderer's brother-in-law. Bloody intentions mixed with the blood already shed in the marriage courtyard until the people imagined they would soon be up to their knees in it.

No-one knows how Zahir magically calmed the opposing sides and dissolved the strife with quick handshakes mediated by Qur'anic verses, sayings of the Prophet, and decrees of the imams, which pacified the raging souls and satisfied everyone. It may have been that all of them, deep down, hoped to arrive at any solution that would prevent them from being swept along by their rage to uncertain ends, in which they too were either killer, killed, or fugitive. Zahir convinced them that the solution lay in the sister of the murderous cousin paying the blood debt by marrying the brother of the murdered groom. As for the bride, who was widowed, and whom it was likely no-one would ever marry again on account of her being an ill-fated omen of calamity, Zahir declared, "I will marry her."

So on that night, Zahir returned from his visit to that village with a bride of his own having been invited to her wedding. He married her and brought her home, still in her gold necklaces and perfumed wedding gown – even if her face was scratched and the dress was stained with drops of her blood. And that same night, Zahir was able to make her forget everything that had happened, such that she awoke the next morning happy and smiling. He employed an abundant supply of caresses and kept her laughing with witticisms and amusing stories that sprang from his expertise in the comings and goings of men – and even more, those of women. And she bore him sons and daughters, including Tariq the Befuddled and his sister Sameeha.

Zahir loved feasts. He loved being alive, and in all things he lived a charmed life. The only exception was his excruciating death, after he and his friend the mayor were struck down by a strange disease and suffered horrible pain for an entire year. They watched festering ulcers cover their bodies as the illness peeled away their skin and ate their flesh down to the bone. They died on the same day, disintegrating in their putrid sickbeds.

Tariq resembled his father in many ways, but according to the testimony of everyone from his father's generation, Tariq had the kinder heart. He studied at the same school as his father, after it had been changed to an institute of Islamic law. His father, Zahir, was one of only four people who knew the identity of Abdullah Kafka's real parents.

As for Suhayl, the father of Ibrahim Qisma, he seemed to come straight out of one of the tales of the ancestors: slender, short, strong – or "strong-boned", as they put it – missing his nose, always smiling, playing, or cracking a joke, with a sharp eye and a sharp tongue, passionate about smoking. He preferred the cigarettes he rolled himself with such remarkable speed that no-one could beat him in a cigarette-rolling contest. After a challenge and an entire night dedicated to this activity, Suhayl reached the point where he was able to roll seventeen in a single minute. He never failed to offer his cigarettes to anyone who sat and talked with him, even if that person did not smoke. When they were younger, Zahir had given him a silver cigarette box, but Suhayl seldom used it. He had no need for it as long as he could roll a cigarette in the same time it took to remove the box from his pocket, open it, and take one out.

Although cigarettes were Suhayl's greatest pleasure, he had other pleasures and other abilities that the women would whisper about. Some of the reports originated with Suhayl's blind wife, who used to think that all men had what hers had, a member as long as her forearm. She would have gone on thinking that had one of the women not surprised her with an amazed groan, first out of envy, then out of amusement, and commented, "So that's what made you blind, Umm Ibrahim!"

The woman said it as a joke, obviously, for Umm Ibrahim had been blind since birth. It was perhaps precisely because of her blindness that Suhayl the Damascene had married her, since no woman with the power of sight would ever have consented to marry him, given his small stature and a noseless face with its two yawning holes. The rest of the nose had been eaten away, leaving behind mere traces like the foundations of a collapsed mud house. The sight of smoke coming out of those holes was extremely amusing, and if the village had not got used to this sight, they would have split their sides and died laughing. Likewise, the story Zahir invented for Suhayl had a sobering effect, transforming this strange nose from something ugly into a source of pride, a badge of honour and bravery reminding everyone of Suhayl's participation in the War of Palestine in 1948.

He and Zahir had been young men, part of the Iraqi armed forces who passed through Damascus and crossed the south of Lebanon to Palestine. They were travelling together in the same army unit and standing in the same spot when an artillery shell exploded behind them. Zahir wet his pants, and Suhayl fell down from laughing so hard at him. Meanwhile, in his violent fear, Zahir lay flat on his stomach and couldn't stop trembling and crying hysterically. This made the Turkish commanding officer pour upon him the harshest epithets of abuse and contempt before relegating him to the rear.

Ten days later, a boil appeared on Suhayl's nose. It grew quite large and began to fester on account of the filthy conditions, the infrequency of washing, and the absence of any medical attention, which, even if it were readily available, would have been dedicated to the wounded and not to treating the boil of a midget soldier who was no larger than his boil, as one of the male nurses put it. It itched, so Suhayl kept scratching it, and both skin and soft flesh peeled away under his fingers. In the end, the nose had festered so much that when they got back to Damascus, the medics there were unable to do much besides amputate the dangling remnants and disinfect the nose socket to prevent the mangy inflammation from eating away the rest of his face.

Zahir kept Suhayl company in the hospital through all this. Afterwards, in the markets, Zahir would gaze, sighing, at every local Levantine woman who passed by, while Suhayl wrapped his face up to his eyes, embarrassed about his calamity and mourning his lost nose. Zahir made fun of him in the café when he found him lifting the veil to insert his glass of tea to drink. "With that face veil," he said, "the people will think you are a woman. They'll think you're my wife!"

Suhayl was furious and dragged Zahir by the collar out of the café and into a deserted side alley, swearing he would kill him if he did not stop making jokes and laughing. Zahir reminded him that it was Suhayl who laughed at him when he wet his pants and was humiliated by the officer in front of everyone, mocked as a weakling, more cowardly than a woman. "Maybe God cut off your nose as a punishment for making fun of me at the lowest point in my entire life."

They both fell silent until they calmed down and went back inside the café where they finished sipping their tea side by side without a word. Then they made their way back to the camp.

They had no choice but to agree on what they would say when they returned to their village. Zahir was the more eager about this, for a man wetting his pants out of cowardice was more humiliating than losing one's nose to a boil amidst army camp conditions. So he racked his brain on the desert road heading home until the solution crystallised in his mind. As they stopped to camp for the second night, he pulled Suhayl aside under the shade of a solitary tree. Without even noticing what type of tree it was, he said, "Listen, Suhayl. We have to make a solemn and eternal covenant between men that each of us will protect the other and take his friend's secret with him to the grave."

Suhayl nearly made a biting comment at the mention of the word "men" in Zahir's statement, connecting it to his pants-wetting when the shell exploded. He thought it best to overlook that and asked, "How?"

"We'll tell the villagers that your bravery was the main reason Damascus was saved from falling into the hands of the enemy."

These words knocked Suhayl back a step in surprise. "What!? What is this nonsense? Listen, Zahir," Suhayl continued after a pause. "This is the second and final time I will warn you not to mock me. And if you do, I swear to God Almighty I'll slit your throat and leave your corpse to rot in the desert."

In other circumstances, Zahir might have commented on the word "rot", making reference to the decay of Suhayl's nose. But as it was, he was eager to calm Suhayl down and make him understand what he was thinking. "Oh no, Suhayl! Just a minute, brother. I'm being serious, believe me!"

"How so?"

"We'll tell them that the officer chose you on account of your bravery and your small, light body, which perhaps wouldn't set off the landmines. He sent you on a reconnaissance mission at night to spy on the enemy's front lines. You performed the mission expertly by slipping through and listening in just as a Syrian spy was explaining to the Israeli general that, by following secret and scarcely defended paths, he would be able to cross over to Damascus with minimal losses and surprise the Arab armies from behind. And because you couldn't bear this spy's treachery, you lost control of yourself and opened fire, killing him. As you were making your escape, they sent a volley of gunfire after you, and one of the bullets carried away your nose."

"Hmm, no. No. Let's leave out the story about killing the spy and find something else."

"Fine. We can say that their guards discovered you. You fought them hand to hand, blades flashing in the dark, and one of their bayonets sliced off your nose. But you were able to escape and get back, making them realise that sneaking up on Damascus was no longer possible because the Arabs would reinforce the paths."

"No . . . no! Who would believe a story like that? And how in good conscience could we claim for ourselves a fake heroism after we've seen with our own eyes men fighting like lions and becoming martyrs through the real thing? What's more, surely the people will know the truth from the radio reports."

"Listen to me – what matters as far as we are concerned is that they are simple villagers. I'm certain that they'll believe the story. Leave it all to me. You'll see. What's more, we'll tell them that the Syrians called you 'the Damascene' as a way of showing you gratitude and honour, bestowing upon you the name of the city that was saved thanks to you."

"Do you really think that would pull the wool over their eyes?"

"Of course! Trust me – you'll see. Then, if someone asks us why they didn't hear anything like this on the radio, we'll tell them that delicate political matters and military secrets like these are not announced publicly. And that's not all! Indeed, we'll also say that the governor of Damascus asked to meet you and threw a magnificent party in your honour. He offered you any house in Damascus you wanted to live in, granted you Syrian citizenship, and promised whichever girl you desired to be your wife. But you humbly refused all that, saying you were just doing your duty. You said you'd be content to receive the title 'the Damascene' as a memento of the honour, and that you preferred to live in your own village among its people, who are your people."

"Oh, you devil! Where do you come up with all these ghastly ideas?! Well, yes, O.K. But let's drop this business about the house and the wife."

"No, Suhayl! Adding that will heighten your position in the eyes of the villagers – especially the women – when they know that you preferred a mud house among them to a palace in Damascus, and that you preferred to take a wife from among the daughters of the village rather than the most gorgeous beauty of the Levant. Believe me, I know what I'm talking about! Trust me, brother."

"And what will we say about you?"

"About me we'll say – and of course, the lion's share of this is on you – that I would ignite the zeal of the soldiers with my orations. I was the first to shout '*Allahu akbar*' at the beginning of each attack, and I would lead the charge, waving the Iraqi flag, or the Palestinian one. What do you think?"

"No! No, let's leave out this business of the flag and be content with the rest."

"Fine. We're agreed?"

"Yes, agreed."

They shook hands and embraced, but that was not enough for Zahir, who said, "Come, let's swear on the Qur'an to confirm what we've promised each other."

"But we have no Qur'an!"

Zahir took a piece of paper and a pen out of his pocket and wrote the short *sura* about God's oneness – only four verses long – three times. He said, "The prophet said this *sura* is equal to a third of the Qur'an. So repeating it three times is equal to the whole thing. Put your hand on it and swear."

So Suhayl put his hand on the paper and took the oath, followed by Zahir. They spent the rest of the journey home and their three days in the camp in Mosul reviewing and modifying the details, weaving them together, memorising them, and practising their recitation until it all became a real part of their memories and they almost believed the story themselves.

CHAPTER 3

Ibrahim and his Qisma

Qisma wavered a long time: one step forward, two steps back. But in the end, she decided to go to the house of Abdullah Kafka. He was the only one who could help her carry out her intention of searching for her father's body. He was her father's closest friend, and to him alone had Ibrahim revealed the secret of those days when everything was crashing down around them. She remembered what her father said to her one time: "Tariq and Abdullah are my closest friends, but I love Abdullah more." Abdullah also had no family or work to hold him back, and he was not afraid of anything, not even of death itself.

In these ways, Qisma shored up her conviction that the decision to approach him was sound, despite the doubts and rumours, followed by scandal, that would result if a young widow were seen entering the house of an unmarried man in the furthest corner of the village. But she had not wanted to broach the issue with him in front of the villagers, the very people who had dragged her away on the burial day and rebuked her, together with fat Amira. And given that Abdullah sat at the café most of the time, from when it first opened in the morning until it closed after midnight, she had no choice but to seek him out at dawn. It was not easy for her to take such a risky decision.

But, in any case, it was not the first of its kind in her life.

She passed bitter nights of broken sleep, when hot tears of sorrow for her father alternated with racing thoughts of what she wanted to do. Then she made up her mind to proceed. She was not sure why she carried her baby with her, still sound asleep. He stirred uneasily but did not wake up as she pressed his head into her shoulder as though tucking in a corner of her shawl. Perhaps it occurred to her that bringing him would dispel doubts should someone happen to see her, or that she could somehow protect herself with him. Or maybe she thought Abdullah would feel more sympathetic when he saw the little sleeper, even though she knew his wrath at the name of the baby. Her husband, a native of Baghdad, had wanted his son to bear the name of the President out of admiration for him. At the same time, the name was a type of insurance against any doubts regarding his own loyalty to the Leader. Or maybe he chose the name as a way to ingratiate himself with his superiors, a method adopted by many other strivers. For what else could he do, being an officer who truly loved his military identity and was sincerely devoted to his superiors, from the generals to the government officials? He admired the President, with whom, about whom, and for whom he dreamed, fantasising that he himself would one day become president, with all that power in his hands.

Would Abdullah agree to go with her to the burning city of Baghdad to search for one corpse amid thousands, when he was the one who had not stirred from his seat in the café to attend the burial? Would he tell her what she wanted to know, more about her father, when he was the one who remained silent nearly all the time? She kept returning to these questions as she tossed and turned in bed, recalling everything she could about her father and suffering pangs of guilt for having fought with him and abandoned him for many years even though she was his only daughter.

At the same time, she was impelled by the challenge to prove to everyone that a daughter, too, is worthy of carrying her father's name and can defend his memory; that it is not only the male child who bears the father's name and continues his line, as those people thought who said, "He who fathers only daughters is no father at all!"

She realised now, more than ever before, the extent to which her father Ibrahim had suffered on behalf of his parents and his siblings. And also for her and because of her, especially now that she was a mother and a widow, like him, who, as a father and a widower, had refused to marry again after the passing of her mother, both to spare her a stepmother who would harass her – and for the sake of the secret.

Ibrahim had wanted to talk with her about everything, but her young suitor had swept her away. And her desire for a different life, to be like the others, and her egotistical preoccupation with herself and nothing more, had prevented what she heard from being preserved in memory. Intentionally or not, she had avoided hearing the details he told her about his life. She had not wanted her memory to serve as a new storehouse for the contents of his – she wished to have no memory at all. During the years of living, studying, and getting married in Baghdad, she had wished to expunge every recollection of childhood and bury the truth that her parents were poor, simple villagers.

Meanwhile, Ibrahim's sole consolation was telling things. Specifically to her, for she was his only daughter, the extension of his own memories and the memory of him. Otherwise, all that he was would dissolve and vanish, and nothing frightens a man more than that. He would eagerly seize every opportunity to tell her stories. Sometimes he would repeat the same ones and go into detail, occasionally even crying or laughing as though he were reliving that which he related.

This earnest desire, visible in his eyes, had forcibly left a part of his memory within hers, even though it was in the form of scattered pictures. Anointed by a sense of regret, she began trying, after his death, to gather these stories, to recall them, to repeat them to herself and to hear them in her own memory this time. She realised there were many holes in her father's biography, many gaps in her knowledge of him, which she needed to fill with the help of others if it were to be complete, or at least as complete as it could be.

And deep down, she decided to tell her son, too, when he got older, about his grandfather. She now saw him as a hero, even if heroism was no longer esteemed in a country where heroes and traitors, humanity and savagery, sacrifice and exploitation were intertwined, and everything mixed together amid battle smoke, chaos, blood and destruction. True heroism lay hidden in self-denial, and that is primarily what her father Ibrahim had practised throughout his life with a remarkable patience and submission. She had found those qualities so detestable that she searched for the exact opposite in her husband. But now, as a widowed mother in her mid-twenties who had returned to the village, she began to see things in a different light. "With all its blows," she said to her neighbour Amira, "life teaches a person to understand better the meaning of life."

As soon as Ibrahim had finished primary school his father put a stop to his education and the dreams Ibrahim held for it. Ibrahim never forgot that morning, when he had not yet reached the age of fifteen. After the diplomas were awarded in the school courtyard amid the clapping of some students and the crying of others, Ibrahim embraced his friends Tariq and Abdullah, overjoyed at their results.

Then Ibrahim took off, running home to show his diploma to his father. Or rather, to share the good news of his success, as his father could not read or write. As usual, he would stare at the piece of paper, uncomprehending, looking for red lines under numbers that he would be told were the official grades. Then he would point a finger at his name and say, "This is my name . . . isn't it?" He knew by heart the shape of his written name from the days of military service when he had recognised it as a drawing and wrote it as a drawing, without understanding the letters or knowing how to pronounce them.

Ibrahim's father said to him, "Congratulations, my son." He handed back the diploma and said, "Sit. Well, you have become a man, and we must talk together like men."

Ibrahim sat down in front of his father, confused at his tone, in which he sensed a blend of reverence and earnest affection that he had never before observed in him.

His father cleared his throat and lit a cigarette from the butt of the one he just finished, exhaling its smoke up through his nostril holes as he said, "Listen, Ibrahim. You've now learned to read and write, and that's enough. So it's time to leave school and start working. I need you, for as you know, the burdens of providing for the family weigh heavily upon my shoulders, out there on my own, and you are the eldest of your brothers. You have to help me. Sowing the field and tending the livestock is more than my energy allows, so I need you with me. At the same time, we also need to think about getting you married next season, or the one after. Just like every man, I too want to see my grandchildren before I die."

Ibrahim said nothing, so his father asked, "What do you say?"

Ibrahim still said nothing. He just inclined his head and gave a little nod as a sign of assent, or rather, a sign of obedience. Then he went off in a very different state from before. Moving slowly and dragging his feet, he left the house, the square, and the village. He went off towards the hillside overlooking Hyena Valley, looking for his friends there, where they usually sat. He found Abdullah alone, trying to bore through a small, snow-white stone, from which he said he would fashion a necklace to give his future beloved. Ibrahim sat beside him without a word. Abdullah felt the weight of his silence, and he tried to break it by showing him the stone and saying, "I'm trying to file it away a little on this side to make it look like a heart. What do you think?"

"My father wants me to abandon my studies."

"What did you tell him?"

"I can't refuse his wishes."

"So it goes."

"But I had hoped to keep going until the end. Now you and Tariq will be in school while I'm in the field or with the animals. I don't like to be separated from you."

"Don't worry. I'll quit school with you."

"What! What about your parents?"

"They won't refuse anything I ask."

When they told Tariq what was going on, he too wanted to leave school to be with them, but his father would not allow it. This made his subsequent studies merely a formality insofar as he cheated on his exams and skipped lessons to keep the other two company, going out to look for them in the pastures with the cattle or in the fields where they sat on the edge of the irrigation canal to eat watermelon and talk.

In Tariq's eyes, as Abdullah and Ibrahim carried their hoes, sickles and shovels – cigarettes in the corners of their mouths, turbans wrapped around their heads, the edges of their robes tucked into their broad leather belts to reveal powerful legs sinking in the mud – they did what men did, and it all provoked envy in his soul. As a way of compensating and expressing his manhood in the face of their manly appearance, he would talk all the more about women and his adventures with girls. He would sometimes goad them into races to see who could come the fastest. They would hide themselves in the thickets, facing each other in a circle, and then spread their legs and uncover their penises (or their "sparrows", as they called them) and "One . . . two . . . three!" they would start jerking themselves off until they saw someone's sperm spurting out, and he would be the winner. Usually, Tariq was the fastest, but as he lay in bed he would envy the size of their cocks, Abdullah's in particular, which was the biggest and blackest on account of his dark skin. Abdullah was also the first to grow pubic hair, beating them to that sign of manhood.

Of course, these competitions did not go on for long. They were growing up, and their friendship changed with their interests and concerns. That is why, when they reminded Tariq about the stories he told of his relationship with the Bedouin girl Fahda – about whose love he used to brag, describing her enormous breasts that moved freely under her robe like two rabbits, or how he would hug her, resting his head on their softness or touching them through the wide neck of her dress and making her groan with eyes closed as soon as his fingers reached her erect nipples – he would confess that she smelled like the sheep and would say, "It's as though you were embracing an ewe, brother!" And they would laugh.

As soon as they reached eighteen, Abdullah Kafka and Ibrahim Qisma were called up to perform their compulsory military service. Tariq the Befuddled's student status protected him from that duty, and he felt empty and alone in their absence. He sought an escape by filling his time with more independent reading that went beyond his textbooks. He sought himself in literature, ideas and ideologies, wandering from the furthest left to the furthest right: communism, socialism, existentialism, nihilism, surrealism, mysticism and fundamentalism.

Meanwhile, Abdullah and Ibrahim were inseparable. Their journey to the Ghazlani army base in Mosul was their first trip to a city. The harsh military training was, in their eyes, just an athletic exercise and a way to get to know new people and places, different foods and different ways of doing things. As far as they were concerned, it was all a delightful opportunity to explore life far from the eyes of parents and the village and its traditions, which seldom gave way to anything new. They always stood together in the drills, they slept in the same tent, and in the evenings they left the camp to take four-hour strolls through the markets of Nineveh province.

After six months of training, they were given the same classification – infantry – and transferred together to a military unit in the south, in Hilla, where they became acquainted with the remaining ruins of Babylon, as well as with new types of fruit, new styles of singing and dancing, and new ways of life. After that, they were transferred to Basra to guard the Umm Qasr port, and they saw the sea for the first time. Their military service carried them from the north to the south and back again to their village during their monthly leaves. It brought them to many cities and villages, and put them up for a night in Baghdad, which they passed in one of the cheap hotels of Martyrs' Plaza, also known as "the Square". It made them better acquainted with their homeland than had the maps, pictures and anthems in their schoolbooks.

While on leave, they would tell Tariq about what they had seen and learned. He, in turn, told them about what he was reading. He gave them titles to bring for him when they passed by the city bookshops. Likewise, he would recommend something he liked or a page-turner for the road or for nights in camp and their long hours keeping watch. Just as every transfer was a new discovery for Abdullah and Ibrahim, for Tariq every new book was a journey into a different world. Such was the day when he became acquainted with the works of Kafka, which he considered a great discovery. It was at the pinnacle of this craze for everything Kafkaesque that he had given Abdullah his nickname. He told them all about Kafka, about the depth of the melancholy found in his novels, and his difficulties with his father. As a result, Abdullah accepted this name all the more easily as he felt an affinity with his own soul, especially in relation to problems arising from the uncertainty of his parentage.

Their monthly leave from duty kept them tied to life in the village. After a year and a half of military service, Ibrahim learned while on leave that his family had chosen a bride for him. The young woman was a relative, the daughter of one of his mother's paternal cousins, and he did not know her well. His mother had suggested her, and his father had confirmed the choice, thinking the blood ties would make the bride obedient to a blind mother-in-law and a good helper when it came to the house chores. Ibrahim, as usual, did not object. He requested marriage leave, which was forty days, and they got married. His parents set aside the biggest and best room in the house.

Soon afterwards, Abdullah's adoptive father, Salih, passed away from heart failure. Exactly twenty days later, Maryam died out of sorrow for him. Their deaths were a cruel blow, bequeathing Abdullah a rich inheritance of sorrow, depression and pessimism. At that time, a hatred for fate and its caprices began to grow inside him. He suddenly found himself alone in the house, and he took little pleasure in his trips home – still less once Ibrahim began spending his furloughs with his wife.

It was here that credit goes to Tariq for making Abdullah a guest in his house. He put him up in his own room, among his family, which is how Abdullah got to know Tariq's sister, Sameeha. He fell in love with her from the very first glass of tea she served him. They would steal glances at each other, their eyes communicating without their lips saying a thing. The whole affair frightened him at first since she was the sister of Tariq, the friend who trusted him and made him a guest in his home. For that reason, he was determined not to reveal anything to her. Instead, he tried to master his desires and his emotions so that his face would not betray what raged in his heart.

Sameeha blushed furiously whenever Abdullah visited during his leave. She took more care in combing her hair, painting her nails, and dressing as elegantly as she could. She moved more energetically, a permanent smile fixed upon her face, often lost in thought. She would wake up early and wait for Tariq and Abdullah to rise so she could make them breakfast herself. She was bolder than Abdullah and more eager to see him as often as possible. She sometimes created opportunities to brush his shoulder with her own. This behaviour made Abdullah feel awkward and put him in a difficult position morally; it deepened his silence and contributed to his chain-smoking.

Nevertheless, he took part in everything and felt that he was a member of the family. At night, he and Tariq would converse back and forth until the small hours. Even after Tariq went to sleep, Abdullah would stay up reading his books. Between one page and the next, he would stare through the window at the stars, thinking of Sameeha, whose every breath he would sense as she slept in the next room. He knew the sound of her footfalls as she moved between the living room and the kitchen. Indeed, he could almost smell her perfume, hear the rustle of her dress, feel the beating of her heart, and see how her hair spilled across the pillow.

When it came time to pick the cotton, he was sure her glances were following him. Sameeha did not let any opportunity pass to get close to him and brush their fingers together when they poured their palm-leaf baskets into the burlap sacks. Once, she timed it carefully to match their trips to empty the baskets, and when they were alone, she quickly reached out her hand to squeeze his with a tenderness that pressed his heart and shook him to the core.

He submitted to her hand while embracing her with his gaze. He looked deeply into her eyes with an expression of pleasure and torment, as though his eyes were two birds about to tumble from their nest in his face and take their first flight – into her face, the open air, the horizon, paradise. The constricted words in his chest nearly made him weep.

She understood all that. She read it and heard it and loved him all the more. "Me too," she said to him, without having heard a word.

He looked around to make sure no-one saw them as he stammered in confusion, "And I ... Very, very much ... but ..."

"We will get married."

"Ah, yes!" he groaned. "Yes, there's nothing I want more. But let's wait a year, until my military service ends. Then I'll never have to leave you."

That is how they declared their love for each other and came to a decision in their very first conversation. After that, his life had meaning. Every moment was filled with daydreams of Sameeha. They did not tell anyone about their love but began meeting in secret so he could smell her perfume, feast his eyes on hers, and embrace her slender, supple waist. He was afraid she would break between his arms when he crushed her to him, as though wanting to pull her inside his chest.

He decided abruptly to return to his own house. He no longer felt his solitude and isolation so long as he was thinking of her. Indeed, he began seeking out this delicious isolation all the more in order to think about her and to savour the details of his few memories with her.

He gave her the necklace with the white stone that he had pierced and shaped by hand into a heart. Using a heated piece of metal, he had etched the first letter of her name on one side, and on the other, the first letter of his own. She was as delighted with it as if it were a real jewel. "I'll keep it safe to wear with my white dress on our wedding day," she said.

Abdullah said, "For the wedding, I have to give you gold, just like every other bridegroom."

She said, "This necklace is more precious to me than gold and will always be my most beautiful gift."

He began renovating the house during his monthly leaves, having neglected it entirely following the death of his parents. He repaired the doors, cabinets, and windows that were falling apart. He changed the curtains, rugs, pillows, and cooking utensils. He imagined Sameeha keeping him company in his solitude and filling the place with splendour, picturing how she would sit here, how she would walk or stand there, holding this and touching that. Instead of asking for her hand in marriage while living under her parents' roof, he thought it better to move back to his house and wait a respectable amount of time before venturing to return and ask for the engagement.

Every evening since the death of his parents, the mayor's wife, Zaynab, would drop by his house when he was there, bringing him pitta bread along with cooked meat, rice, soup and grape leaves. She would help him by sewing pillow corners that had come unstitched or the buttons of his clothes, which she insisted on washing for him. She spoke to him with extraordinary tenderness, calling him "my son". The extreme sincerity of her tone and the way she watched over him like a mother was such that in his depths he felt it truly was so.

Everyone knew of this lady's generosity and goodness. Of all the mayor's wives, it was she alone who stayed with him, putting up with him and bearing all his children. He had married her young and poor from one of the Kurdish villages, and in her first years she did not know a word of Arabic. The mayor would speak to her in Kurdish, a language he knew well on account of his long relationships and business dealings with the Kurds, which he had inherited from his father. Zaynab quickly learned Arabic in the dialect of the village, and just as quickly she became one of them.

It was no surprise that the mayor's family took care of those in need given that he was the richest man in the village. His fields were the largest, his livestock the most numerous, and his business ventures unceasing because he was the one who bought the village's harvest and sold it in the cities. Several people worked in his service, including dull-witted Isma'il. Isma'il's parents had been refugees, and the mayor built them a small mud house, which was handed down to Isma'il and his sister after their parents' deaths. The mayor had built the house next to his own, without a wall in between, and he entrusted Isma'il with the tending of his sheep and goats, as well as the sheep of anyone in the village who was willing to pay Isma'il for that work. The mayor treated the two orphans like his own children, even though he profited more from their labour than he did from his own children, whom he pampered and never burdened with any task. The mayor and his lifelong friend, Tariq's father Zahir, were the ones who paid the costs for Isma'il's dull-witted sister to marry one of the distant villages, as the people phrased it. In doing so, the mayor earned everyone's respect. Anyone in need sought recourse to him, and in the reception room of his house all the village's conflicts were resolved.

Zaynab would shower Abdullah with the most extraordinary tenderness. He always expressed his gratitude and left her the key to his house when he returned to his military service so that she might keep an eye on things in his absence. She used to tell him, "You must get married, my son." He would respond, "I will, as soon as I finish my military service." She supported his decision and expressed her readiness to help him with everything he needed, such as a dowry and planning the wedding. She assured him, "Choose whichever girl in the village you want, and I'll make the engagement happen, no matter who her father may be."

He took her hand and thanked her, saying, "This promise I accept, Umm Jalal."

What no-one expected was that war would break out in 1980. A war that would last eight years and sweep away many dreams and destinies.

CHAPTER 4

Ever More War

Abdullah and Ibrahim were calculating the few days remaining until the end of their military service, counting them up and crossing off each day on a calendar as soon as the sun rose. They spoke about the rapture of freedom they would feel back in the village, the projects they would undertake, and the sons they would father. Each promised to give the other's name to his firstborn son, laughing as they went on to say, "Only the first name, of course!" meaning Abdullah, and not Abdullah Kafka; and Ibrahim, not Ibrahim the Fated. They sipped tea, legs hanging over the edge of the watchtower guarding Basra harbour as they looked at the distant ships out at sea. They forgot about the weapons strapped to their backs and about their duty to keep a lookout, refreshed by the April breeze, cardamom tea and their dreams.

That was the last time they sat together at ease, for the harbour, the camp and the entire country soon sounded the alarm and burst into tumult. War was declared against Iran, and instead of being released from military service according to schedule on their birthdays, birthdays became a day of conscription for many others – both young and old.

At that time, they recalled distant, foggy memories from their childhood about what the adults had called "The War of the

North", which had taken place in the mid-sixties when the Kurds rebelled against the government in Baghdad. The elders of the village had asked the Bedouin Jad'an what he had seen of the war in his wanderings, and he related stories filled with pain, injustice, exile and death. The only thing left in the memories of the village youth from that war was the sight of the first dead person they had seen in their lives. It was the corpse of Sergeant Nawaf stretched out in the courtyard of the mosque. The adults were praying over it. They carried the body on foot to the cemetery and buried it without changing its military uniform, stained with dirt and blood. Then they went home in silence.

Like everyone else, Abdullah and Ibrahim hoped and expected the war with Iran would end at any moment through the offices of some intermediary. After a few hours, that day or the next, they would be rejoicing at the news on the radio. Later, they began hoping for the war to end within a matter of weeks, then months. Then a year passed, during which their martial destiny brought them to more than one theatre of war.

During this time, Abdullah confessed to Ibrahim his love for Sameeha. Ibrahim was the first and only person Abdullah told about it, fearing he would die without breathing a word of the passion that stormed in his breast. He talked to Ibrahim about his love with delight and anguish, as though he were discovering her, or discovering himself, and he recounted their earlier promise to marry as soon as he was released from military service. "But it's the war, my friend. It's the damned war, as you see."

Ibrahim advised him to marry right away, and not to count on the end of the war, "for it might never end. Or you might die before it's over. Here I am, waiting and expecting a baby, as you know, so that if I die I'll at least have left behind a descendant."

He was speaking of his daughter Qisma, who was born after the first year of the war had passed and was already two months old when he first saw her, because the war prevented him from taking his regular leave. When he came home, he was surprised to find a baby smiling up at his face. They laid her in his arms and said, "This is your daughter, and she still doesn't have a name. We call her 'baby', waiting for you to name her."

"Qisma," he said.

He did not indicate whether he was merely repeating his habitual expression, "fate", or whether he was naming her. But they quickly seized upon the word and considered it her name even without waiting to confirm what Ibrahim meant. The name stuck. Apart from how closely it matched his vision of reality and how he approached life, this name made the one by which Ibrahim had been known in jest since childhood come true. In all truth and earnestness they could now call him Abu Qisma, "Father of Qisma", having long called him Ibrahim Qisma, which could literally mean "Ibrahim, son of fate".

As for Abdullah, the refusal of Sameeha's father to grant her to him in marriage fell upon his soul as a blow equal to the war itself. Without warning, a firebomb had fallen upon the threshing floor of his dreams, and he turned to Zaynab for the help she had promised. Zaynab assured Abdullah she would take the matter on her own shoulders. She spoke with Sameeha secretly to be sure of her wishes, discovering that Sameeha's passion for Abdullah was no less than his for her, and that Sameeha had long been waiting for the moment of their union. Zaynab then spoke to her husband, the mayor, and the mayor spoke to his friend Zahir, Sameeha's father, when the three of them were alone in the reception room, as usual, after the rest of those attending the night's festivities had departed.

"I can't," Zahir said, "and you two alone know why."

Zaynab said to him, "But he's our son, as you well know."

"It doesn't matter. And in any case, he's a bastard."

After a surge of anger, Zaynab wept and pleaded with him. She sought the mayor's help in persuading his companion. But the mayor did not insist on the matter. He understood his friend's position, and deep down he agreed with Zahir, thinking that he would have done the same. He would not have married any daughter of his to a bastard. In the end, after secretly reaching an agreement with the mayor through a glance, Zahir sought to soothe Zaynab's anger and tears by saying, "Give me a couple days to think it over."

When news of this disappointment reached Abdullah, he thought he might strengthen his position by speaking with his friend Tariq and asking him to use influence to persuade his father. What Abdullah did not know – no-one but Zahir did – is that when Tariq took his father aside, he urged Zahir to hold fast to his refusal, requesting he never marry Sameeha to Abdullah.

Zahir was surprised and asked about the reason, given that Abdullah was his son's closest friend. Tariq replied, "Exactly. I know him better than anybody else. He is a depressed and lazy person who doesn't like to work. It's true that he's a good man, and he owns a house and a field that he inherited from his adoptive parents. But we cannot rely upon him such that we'd feel secure regarding the future of my sister and her children by him. What's more, we are from a respected family lineage, while his origins are unknown. Even though I have loved Abdullah as a friend, I love my sister more."

Tariq went on at length to urge other justifications as his father listened. But the real motivation for his position was something entirely different, a private and personal reason, which he kept to himself. Something petty, which he could not reveal to anyone. In this, he was not the only member of the human race to defend a position with justifications that differed from their true motives. Not unlike wars supported with placards proclaiming weighty, moralistic words when the true, shameful reasons are very different.

"They've broken the boy's heart," Zaynab said. "May God break their hearts, the wicked bastards!"

She wept as she tried to persuade Abdullah to choose someone other than Sameeha, any girl he wanted, but he just bowed his head in refusal and returned to a renewed depression and sorrow. His isolation and loneliness only increased when military orders separated him from Ibrahim, sending each to a different sector of the front: a different unit, a different battalion, and a different fate. They parted in tears, hanging on to each other's neck until the officer scolded them and ordered them to stop: "Quit bawling like women! You're men! How can you cry like this? You ought to be ashamed of yourselves. Come on, let's go. Come on!"

In May 1982, at the Battle of Khorramshahr, Iranian forces

took thousands of Iraqi soldiers prisoner, including Abdullah Kafka. Of course, no-one in the village knew anything about the battle or what happened to Abdullah. Just that he did not return for his scheduled leave. Meanwhile, the government broadcasts spoke only of victories, and the official television stations showed only enemy corpses, enemy prisoners, and demolished enemy vehicles. What is more, there was no news or notification letter to be sent to his family since Abdullah did not actually have any parents.

Zaynab pleaded with Ibrahim to make enquiries, which he was already intending to do on his own. He had to cut short his leave to search out Abdullah's military unit. When he found it, Ibrahim learned that the entire unit had been wiped out in the Battle of Khorramshahr, every last man killed or taken prisoner. They did not know the fate of any individual soldier since the bodies were left there on the battlefield. So they gave Ibrahim a piece of paper indicating Abdullah's status as "missing in action".

Ibrahim gave this paper to Zaynab, who took it as a confirmation of what her heart told her: that Abdullah had not died but was still alive. She pleaded with the mayor to listen secretly to the Iranian broadcasts in the middle of the night, to a special programme in which Iraqi prisoners introduced themselves and offered a short greeting to their loved ones, followed by further statements praising the Islamic Republic of Iran. They did not hear Abdullah's voice, even though they listened to hundreds of jumbled iterations of this programme over hundreds of sleepless nights. Zaynab began visiting fortune-tellers, showering them with gifts so they would reveal the unknown to her. She never heard about a famous fortune-teller in the surrounding villages without going to see her. All these women would assure her that Abdullah was alive. Indeed, they even claimed to be able to see him, saying, "He has a beard now. Very sad, locked up in a raw prison with hard conditions. But his health is good, and he hasn't been injured."

Zaynab did not stop her regular trips to Abdullah's house to clean it, even though her visits became less frequent as time went on. But she continued to cry for him in his house, or in hers, or under the sea-urchin tree in the cemetery.

As for Sameeha, her parents forced her to marry a cousin. She did not love him, but they ignored her objections. Forty days after the wedding she fled, but her parents sent her back after beating her until she was bedridden. After a year, Sameeha gave birth to his daughter. Ten days after giving birth, she fled a second time, leaving her daughter behind. So they beat her and returned her once again, wrapped up and carried in a blanket. But she repeated her flight as soon as she had recovered her strength. Yet again they beat her and were going to bring her back, but shortly before doing so, they were met by a delegation that delivered Sameeha's daughter along with the divorce papers. Sameeha's husband would no longer put up with the scandal of a wife who was always running away from him: he could not bear the disgrace in the eyes of the people.

Sameeha sighed with relief and remained in her father's house. She raised her daughter, content to endure all the hostility of her family's behaviour towards her, which she preferred to life with a husband whose very breathing disgusted her to the point of loathing. Yet she failed in the long struggle to submit to her lot like so many women and forget Abdullah. She could never forget him.

Over time Sameeha's family became used to her and her child's presence, and her relationship with her brother Tariq gradually began to resume its former warmth. She would borrow novels from his library, even though she did not read any of them through to the end.

Ibrahim urged his wife to treat Sameeha well and keep her company, particularly in the first years of her isolation, when she was besieged by her family's censure and mistreatment. He sometimes bought clothes and gifts for the two children, his daughter Qisma and Sameeha's daughter, which he would secretly send along to her with his wife. He would also provide her with some financial assistance. His wife said that Sameeha's daughter looked exactly like her mother: "It's as though she were a miniature copy of her in everything, Ibrahim!"

It cut Ibrahim to the core – patient Ibrahim, submissive in war and peace – that he did not beget any children besides Qisma. This led his father to hasten the marriages of Ibrahim's siblings, who began bringing him grandsons whose names he forgot over time because there were so many of them – and because he was getting old, because illnesses racked his body, and because too much smoking had ruined his lungs.

In order to conceive again, Ibrahim's wife sought recourse with the old women and their folk remedies, either medical or magical. Ibrahim secretly visited the city doctors. They all confirmed that the cause was with him, and that his sterility resulted from the different weapons used during the war: nerve gas, germ warfare, chemical weapons. He had been transferred up and down the long front over eight years of war, witnessing the deaths of hundreds whom he had known, the ruin of cities, humanity, livestock and plants, the madness of fire and iron. He submitted to his destiny, obeying his commanding officers, never going A.W.O.L. even for a single day, never shirking in the performance of any task assigned to him. Thanks to this diligent service and his good behaviour, he rose to the rank of master sergeant and acquired an expertise in weapons, hunger, fear, bloodletting and death. But he became yet more expert in his ability to adapt and be patient and endure. Submission to his destiny, no matter what came his way, filled his spirit with a remarkable equanimity and strength.

After hearing what the doctors told him, Ibrahim remembered soldiers telling stories about rumours of sterility caused by chemical weapons or by walking in front of the night-vision equipment used by lookout posts, tanks and armoured vehicles, all of which emitted radiation called infraviolet or ultraviolet – he no longer recalled the exact terminology – that was invisible to the naked eye. Of course, he informed no-one, not even his wife, about all that, nor about his repeated trips to the doctors. He kept refusing appeals from his brother and father to marry a different woman whom fate and chance might bring his way. He always replied by pointing to his daughter: "I have my Qisma, and she is enough for me."

When the war ended, Ibrahim was released from his service. He got out in one piece, without any physical wound, just the horrors he had seen and lived through. But he looked older, tired.

He allowed himself to treat the first month of his freedom as a holiday, during which he did nothing but eat, sleep and bathe. "I'm dirty and sleep-deprived," he said, "with a weariness that has been stored up for years."

He had no desire to talk about the war. He wanted to forget the details, or at least set them apart from his life. He would pile them up in some corner of his mind, at least for a time. But he occasionally told his wife love stories he had heard from other soldiers, often when urging her to keep in touch with Sameeha. He himself had never tasted the love they described. His relationship with his wife, whom he had only met on their wedding night, was a relationship of affectionate coexistence and companionship, something different from the anguish he saw in the faces and words of lovers. He felt he was in the presence of something significant, something he had to work out. When he saw how much they suffered, he was relieved that he did not feel passion like that. But when they reminisced about an untroubled hour or a meeting, or about small, happy details that were transformed in their souls and their words to the critical moments of life and gave their poems and songs an enormous significance: just in those moments, he wished he had experienced love like that, at least for a day. And thanks to the romantic stories of the soldiers, he was better able to comprehend the anguish of his friend Abdullah. Indeed, he came to understand it fully, just as he came to feel Sameeha's pain, even though he had never spoken with her.

He witnessed soldiers crying as they stared at pictures of a sweetheart taken out from their wallets, hidden among their money and I.D. cards. Love helped some find courage and survive the perils of war. Love led some to place themselves in the line of fire when their beloved betrayed them or they quarrelled. They lost themselves when they lost their love, and by means of the war they would find a cheap and easy path to suicide. He saw some soldiers who, after experiencing life at the front, would obtain freedom from the army by exposing an arm or leg to the enemy lookout so it might be pierced by a sniper's bullet or blown off by a shell. Some of them would search with their feet for a landmine, and when the foot was blown off, you would see them screaming in pain and smiling at the same time.

Among those whom Ibrahim knew and developed a close friendship with was Ahmad al-Najafi, a veteran of many years in the trenches. They shared their dry bread, their blankets, and cups of tea in the cold. Ibrahim went with Ahmad to visit his family in Najaf. Ahmad's father was dead, and his mother ran the household in the absence of her three sons, all caught up in the war. Ahmad was the youngest, and his two older brothers were both married and had children. They all lived together in one house sheltered under the mother's care. At night, she would stay up late to pray and intercede with the Lord to preserve her sons, and during the day she laboured in the house and looked after her grandchildren.

Ever since he was young, Ahmad had loved a neighbour's daughter, who grew up to become a beautiful university student. As Abdullah had done, Ahmad made an agreement with her to put off their marriage for a while, and then longer still, in the hopes that the war might end, or until she finished her studies. But the death of his brothers in the war suddenly placed him in a bitter situation when his mother implored him, sobbing, to do what so many others had done and marry his brothers' widows. She was afraid they would remarry, as was their right, and the family would disperse with the children lost. Taking him by the hands, his mother cried and said, "Please, my son! The preservation of the family and the house is in your hands alone."

Ahmad resisted. He ran off and wept, but the eyes of his brothers' small children, the sorrow of the two widows, his mother's listlessness and her beseeching, and pressure from society's system of values forced him to give in. It was not easy at first since he thought of his brothers' wives as his own sisters. They were older than him, and living together in the same house meant they had taken care of him: feeding him, washing his clothes, cleaning his room. But he got used to his new situation by force of habit in their new roles and through the children they bore him. Yet he had lost his beloved, who, along with her family, had refused Ahmad's marriage proposal. In this way Ahmad ended up with two wives and responsibility for a large family. He cried on the breast of Ibrahim, and Ibrahim comforted him, saying, "It's your fate and your destiny, brother. Every creature has its own inescapable lot and portion in life."

Ibrahim used to imagine that true love could only be like the love he felt towards Qisma. When he came to understand what lovers felt, he empathised with their anguish and told his wife, "It's a remarkable thing, Umm Qisma, this love. May God hold every lover close to his heart!"

When his wife asked him about his friend Tariq's numerous

romantic escapades, he commented, "Tariq makes this kind of relationship a profession, not a deep, true love. You remember what I told you about the first of them, the Bedouin girl."

They laughed, and Ibrahim went on to tell her about Ahmad al-Najafi: "One afternoon, we were taking our siesta in the bunker. We woke up in terror when we heard a bullet go through the ceiling. We found Ahmad screaming, holding one hand with the other. Blood and bits of flesh and bone were splattered across the tin roof ceiling and on our faces. The hole where the bullet had passed through the palm of his hand was small, and the exit wound on the back of the hand was bigger. We could smell gunpowder and smoke was coming out of the muzzle of his rifle. We knew at once that he had shot his own hand. He was crying as he said, 'My mother is sick, and two of my children as well. My family has nothing. I have to go back to them.'"

The investigation determined, of course, that Ahmad had done it to himself. They were used to this sort of thing, and it was something that the military code punished. So they treated his hand and put him in prison for six months. Fortunately, the bullet had not severed any nerves or done any lasting damage. It was just a hole that quickly healed and left a scar. Ahmad submitted once again to the injustice of his military life until the end of the war, when he and Ibrahim were set free from the same unit on the same day.

At the end of his month of rest, Ibrahim began thinking about how to organise his life afresh, or rather, to start living. The field was the obvious place to start. He joined in working it with his brothers and their families, some of whom lived on their own in new houses. By force of tradition and custom, the first house, called "the Old Home", was set aside for the eldest brother.

Very soon a broader scope of work was opened to him when a letter from Abdullah arrived, delivered by the International Committee of the Red Cross. Like most such letters, it was succinct and carefully worded. Abdullah explained that he was still alive and was being held prisoner in Iran. His health was good, and the only thing he lacked was cigarettes. He granted Ibrahim the right to profit from his house and field in whatever way he saw fit, and if it happened that he should die, he left everything he owned to Ibrahim's daughter Qisma.

The arrival of this letter was a cause for celebration, and they invited the whole village to a feast. Zaynab decided to slaughter her biggest bull for the occasion, but Ibrahim and Tariq insisted on helping with the costs and the organising. The village celebrated, and everyone perused the letter, including those who could not read or write.

Afterwards, Ibrahim started renting Abdullah's house to the schoolteachers sent out to the village from the city, and he worked to get the field ready for planting again. He kept the accounts with the utmost exactitude, ordering his wife to hide away Abdullah's share – his "portion", as he put it – in a safe place in their bedroom where no-one's hand would touch it. She hid the paper money he gave her in a box containing her simple jewellery – necklaces, bracelets, rings, and earrings of gold and silver – some of which she had inherited from her mother and the rest of which were wedding gifts.

As for Ibrahim's friendships, his bond with Tariq was of

course the strongest, and the two of them spent entire weekends together. They were not together more because Tariq worked during the week as a teacher in one of the distant villages, having completed his studies at the religious institute in Mosul. His grades in school did not qualify for anything higher than that institute, and the choice was also in keeping with his father's wishes.

According to his habit of adapting to any given situation, Ibrahim began observing the norms required by social custom: consoling the sick, burying the dead, visiting neighbours to congratulate them on births and marriages, taking part in the crop harvest, and things like that. He was content in the security this way of life provided, feeling that his village, peaceful and gentle – and indeed, forgotten – was the most lovely place in the world. Playing in the evenings with his Qisma was magical. When she laughed with delight, he felt all his present cares and the weariness of the past fall from his shoulders like someone stripping off a robe heavy with mud. He felt a cleanliness and a lightness, as though his fingers were touching the honey of life every time he touched her.

What he had not taken into account was that Iraq would invade Kuwait on 2 August, 1990, and that the drums of war would beat again, louder this time, with a greater violence and cruelty.

CHAPTER 5

The Storms of Destruction

The village, the country, and the entire world woke up to a shock: Iraqi tanks in the streets of Kuwait City at dawn. And if Abdullah Kafka had been in the village café at that moment with the men circling around the television, mouths agape, he would have said, "It's no more surprising than the first shit of the day. The world is a jungle. Always has been. Any animal might pounce and tear apart any other at any moment. There are no surprises – animal behaviour is entirely predictable. People always do the same stupid things and then call them surprises, no matter how self-evident and obvious. Just like they say a person changing his mind is a surprise, or they say someone dying is a surprise, as though he hadn't actually been waiting for death from the moment he was born!"

The government conscripted everyone of Ibrahim's age, as well as those younger and older. They cut short his rest and forced him to leave his daughter just when she had become as close to him as could be. He had to abandon his field in the middle of the planting season and report to his former army unit, following orders that were announced on the radio.

The journey weighed on his spirit. A chaotic fog swirled in his mind, and he could not think clearly. A muddled confusion, shards of anxiety, a choking grief, a vast unknown: it was like being trapped in a nightmare. He reached his unit headquarters and entered it as naturally as if he had left just the day before, not almost two years ago. It was as though peace were the exception, a dream, while war was the customary state of affairs.

In this whirlpool where the real and the imaginary swirled together, what was truly present? What was seen and felt and lived? What was lived without being seen or felt? Ibrahim was brought back to reality when he ran into Ahmad al-Najafi. They threw themselves upon each other in the warmest embrace. Each played the role of fireman, wrapping his arms around the other to pull him out of the inferno. This meeting, comforting intimacy amid the rough press towards the coming unknown, eased the brutal shock that came with returning to that hateful place.

Getting registered and equipped only took a few hours. And before they knew it, they found themselves just as they used to be, in their khaki uniforms and equipped with pistol, AK-47, ammunition belt, helmet, bayonet, water canteen and a gas mask in its special bag, sitting in the column of trucks that set off in the noontime blaze from Camp Rashid in Baghdad for the south, the broiling heat and choking humidity increasing the further they advanced towards the bottom of the country, the further they penetrated into the desert, the deeper they plunged into the war.

Ibrahim and Ahmad passed the time by exchanging stories of what they had accomplished and experienced during the last two years. Because the road was long, they drew out the details and repeated them until their tales brought them a confidence and a closeness, a union of their identities and spirits, forged in an atmosphere of unreserved brotherly affection.

Only the racket coming from the younger soldiers riding with them in the back of the truck interrupted their side-by-side whispering. One of the men would start to sing and the others would join in, either singing or clapping. Then one or more would volunteer to dance in the middle. Or they would exchange the latest jokes – sexual or irreverent – and they would all burst out in hysterical laughter. Indeed, all their movements and tones of voice betrayed this same hysteria, though no-one alluded to the war, politics, or the fate awaiting them.

If they passed a village and saw a young peasant woman, they rained upon her whistles, catcalls and flirtatious remarks that were more frightening than flattering. It would end with some of them making crudely explicit remarks as they pulled away and she receded into the distance, perhaps muttering that they could go to hell. But if it was an old woman they encountered, or a group of old women, the soldiers would raise their voices together with some snippet from a familiar military hymn or popular song from the radio, twirling their rifles in the air in place of the traditional dancing staff. The poor old woman would raise her arms to the sky and beseech the Lord to preserve these poor young men. Perhaps she would also cry, for certainly she would be a mother or grandmother, like so many of the broken-hearted, wearing black in mourning for one or more lost sons. She would recede further and further in the distance, a black spot against a horizon of black earth, until she was swallowed up by the swirling dust or a desert mirage.

Over the months of the occupation, their unit's home was the desert, near the Saudi border. This annoyed the youngest soldiers because they had heard about the army divisions in the cities enjoying the luxuries of electricity, air conditioning, water, plentiful food and plunder. They heard about officers and soldiers getting rich by stealing gold, jewellery, cars, appliances, furniture, and whatever they wanted from markets, government buildings, and private houses. Moreover, their loved ones visited them and returned home with whatever they could carry.

Their unit, on the other hand, had only the burning sun and the sand, not to mention a face-off against the amassed armies of the world, against a scarcity of water, the burning of hot winds and a desolate horizon. They had to dig trenches for themselves and sow the dunes with landmines whose locations they would forget the next day on account of terrain that seldom showed any distinguishing features. This went on until Ahmad al-Najafi grew upset in Ibrahim's presence after hearing about others getting rich off plunder, given that he had been supporting his family through his labour as a mechanic in an old workshop in Najaf's industrial district. "How will I feed all these mouths now?!" he asked.

Ibrahim replied, "I see it as a sign of God's favour upon us that He did not send us to the cities to tempt us to feed our families through ungodly theft as He did those others."

Ahmad kicked his heel into the side of the sand dune they were sitting on that evening and said in frustration, "The war has stolen my life, so why shouldn't I steal from it?"

Ibrahim wrapped his arm around the shoulder of his companion to comfort him and said, "Everything is fate and decree. Who knows what will work out better or worse in the end? For as the Qur'an says, 'Maybe you hate something, and it is the best for you, and you love something that is worse – God knows, and you do not.'"

Ahmad was not fully satisfied with Ibrahim's words, and he threw himself back on the cold evening sand, letting out a hot, weary sigh as he said, "I'm sad this time, Ibrahim. Sa-a-ad. There's a hollow feeling in my chest. Maybe it's anxiety. Maybe it's fear. I don't know exactly, but my heart hurts and it knows there's worse to come."

Later, after the defeat and the chaotic, disastrous retreat, Ibrahim remembered this speech of Ahmad, and he said to himself, "Dear God above! There really are people whose pure hearts warn them of their fate, who sense when their end is nigh." He wept then. He would weep many bitter tears for that memory, one which would affect his life and even the nature of his death.

Aircraft began their incessant bombing, day and night. The sand rose like surging fountains, with smoke billowing darkly above their heads. One traditional method of camouflage they used was to build counterfeit artillery pieces, tanks and other conspicuous installations out of tin or cardboard. Meanwhile, they smeared the real things with mud and hid them in dugouts between the sand dunes, in ditches and under brambles. They used motorcycles, camels and carrier pigeons to transmit their messages since radio signals would be intercepted, given that the adversary, composed of the armed forces of nearly thirty nations, had the most modern technology as well as the most highly developed training and weaponry. Though at the end of the day, no matter how advanced the weapons deployed, the main goal of war remains the same: for one side to kill the other.

On 24 February, 1991, the allied forces began their land assault, setting off from the sands of Saudi Arabia. The desert, which had been abandoned for centuries, was transformed into a sea of fire and iron. The scene was nothing short of apocalyptic, revealing the power of this small creature, man, to change the face of the natural world in a shocking and awe-inspiring way.

Throughout eight years of war against Iran, Ibrahim and Ahmad had never seen a battle like this. The skies rained down hell, the earth vomited it back up, and near Al-Jahra, north-west of Kuwait City, the simple Iraqi soldiers who resisted fought in despair and died. Thousands of others abandoned the trenches waving every white thing in their possession – handkerchiefs, turbans, papers, plates, underwear – as a sign of surrender. Injured soldiers cried for help as the sand entered their wounds and filled their screaming mouths. As soon as the roaring machines that sprang out of the shimmering desert arrived at the front line, they began to cut the white flags down with bullets and crush the bodies of the wounded beneath tyres and tracks.

When Ibrahim and Ahmad saw what was happening, they slipped away along a shallow valley between the dunes towards the rear bunkers, which they found transformed by the bombs into pits filled with shredded bodies, limbs scattered in every direction. They came across the motorcycle of one of the letter carriers, whose disembowelled corpse lay nearby with the bag still hanging round his neck. They got on and followed animal trails and the small paths combed into the sand dunes by the wind. When they turned to look back, they could see iron creatures ploughing through the trenches and burying dozens of Iraqi soldiers alive. Their cries for mercy rose even above the roar of the iron and the sound of hidden mines exploding in the sand.

Every other unit they came upon in the rearguard was retreating in chaos without waiting for official orders to fall back, which were not announced until the next day. After some indeterminate time and distance, the motorcycle ran out of fuel. They got off and abandoned it, along with their rifles and ammunition belts. Content to keep only their pistols and water canteens, they picked a direction and began running to get away however they might.

They travelled as far as they could that night. During the day they rested or continued walking in the shade of foothills and thorny shrubs, or they dug into the sand to hide. They did not know exactly how much time had passed. Perhaps two days and two nights? But at dawn they spied the international highway connecting Kuwait and Basra. It looked like a gypsy's clothesline, swarming with long lines of cars, military vehicles, various kinds of carts and thousands of people, both soldiers and civilians, everyone fleeing as fast as possible. Some had driven their vehicles off road in order to get around the others. There were some whose cars had broken down and were negotiating however they could with the closest car, cart, or any other object that was moving down the road and had room for them, room for hope. There were those who had met their end and those who waited.

This column of humanity and machinery was so long that Ibrahim and Ahmad could not make out its beginning or its end. They intended to catch a ride with someone or hang on to the side of any vehicle that offered itself, but before they got there, formations of aeroplanes – among which they recognised the giant American bomber, the B-52 – arrived and began pouring lava upon the travellers.

What they saw was a true hell in all its horrors. In their entire lives, they had never seen, nor would they ever see again, an event as terrifying as this, a madness incarnate. Severed body parts and scraps of metal were scattered amid tongues of flame and the thunder of explosions. The road was transmogrified into an explosion of fire, smoke, limbs, blood, destruction, ashes, death. It was a highway of death, on which and around which everything that moved was ground together in flames.

They stayed where they were, stretched flat on the ground, looking down at this terror and scarcely believing what they saw. Ahmad said, "It's a depravity for them to kill people as they retreat and surrender!"

Ibrahim said, "It was depravity to invade our brothers and our neighbours."

Ahmad said, "You know we aren't the ones who did that, and that anyone who refused was sentenced to death."

The road became a thread of molten lava stretching through an empty, desolate land. Ibrahim and Ahmad kept saying it was the end of the world. Only a few people escaped: those who were some distance off the road, those whom the bombs missed, or those whom chance spared.

Whenever the air attacks lessened as the planes came and went, the two of them continued towards Iraq, parallel to the road but some distance away. At nightfall when the bombing ceased, they were getting closer to Iraq and found thousands of corpses, burned and charred, on both sides of the road. They searched in the darkness for water and something to eat and found a little without too much trouble. They encountered many others doing the same thing, and they banded together to continue the journey. Other groups joined as well, but there was no talking apart from constrained murmurs and curses. Some wanted to cry, while others wanted to save the wounded. Some were trying to start the vehicles that had not been too badly damaged. When the throng swelled into a crowd, they knew they had reached the border crossing of Safwan. Ibrahim and Ahmad traded their pistols for cheese-and-tomato sandwiches. After a wait and without remembering exactly how, they crossed the border into Iraq.

But the hell of the bombardment continued over the heads of those retreating even on the road inside Iraqi territory. They were travelling in the direction of Basra when a plane rained death upon them. Ibrahim and Ahmad threw themselves to the ground along with everyone else, and Ibrahim saw Ahmad about fifty yards to his right falling and crying out with a bleeding hole in his belly. It was only a fleeting glance before what seemed like a mine exploded underneath him. Ibrahim lost consciousness even before knowing how he was injured, as though the bombs had gone off inside his head. He was only aware of the colour yellow, a colour which burned in his head until it turned to black and he was melting like a drop of butter on the hot sand. His body seemed to fade ever further into the distance, or else it was seeping into the sand or the sea, into the smoke or non-existence. He thought he was dying, and he focused what remained of his mental faculties on the face of his daughter and the voice of his father.

When Ibrahim opened his eyes, he felt a violent thirst. His body was in a pile of other dead bodies, as though the land were no longer big enough to contain them all. He raised his head and looked to the left. Not far away, two dogs were eating a human body. He swung his gaze the other way. Another dog with the head and face of a human was coming towards him. He tried to get up but could not. One of his arms had fallen asleep underneath him. The dog with the human face calmly approached him among the corpses, and the monstrosity of the sight terrified him. When the dog turned away, Ibrahim realised it did not have human features, but rather it was carrying someone's severed head in its jaws, the face turned forward. The dog carried the head away. Ibrahim turned to the right and began calling, "Ahmad! Ahmad! Where are you, Ahmad?" He did not know whether the sound could be heard or whether the cry choked up within him.

Away at a distance, behind the two snapping dogs, he spied three youths riding on donkeys. They dismounted and bent down, searching among the corpses before returning to their mounts. They are real people, he said to himself. No, they are angels. He called out at the top of his voice, not knowing whether anyone could hear him. He could not feel his legs: another corpse was on top of them, or else they were buried in the earth or gone altogether. A nightmarish weight crouched upon his chest, suffocating him with a paralysing weakness. But he kept calling to Ahmad and the three boys. He was still screaming "Ahmad!" when he lost consciousness a second time.

CHAPTER 6

The Journey of a Single Step

Ibrahim opened his eyes and found himself in a strange bed, in a strange house. He was a stranger in a strange land, a strange world. A woman's face was looking down into his own. She reached her hand out to his forehead and smiled gently. He felt as though she were his mother, with the obvious difference that she could see and was not blind, given that she was staring directly into his eyes.

"Where am I?" he asked.

She said, "You're home, my son. You are in Zubair. Praise be to God for your deliverance!"

"And Ahmad?"

"He is coming now."

"I'd like some water."

"Just a little since you're wounded." She took a nearby container, dipped her fingers, and wet his lips, letting a few drops drip from her fingertips into his mouth as though he were a sparrow. Then she wiped his face with her wet hand.

The cold of the water invigorated him. From the corners of his eyes, tears ran down either side. He said, "What happened, ma'am?"

"This is war, my child. This is the madness and evil of humanity.

The catastrophe continues, and we have no idea when or how it will end."

As she was saying this, a young man in his mid-twenties entered, his head draped with a *keffiyeh*. His body looked strong and vigorous. He said, "Well, mother, how's it going?"

She moved aside from where she had been sitting, allowing him to look down at Ibrahim's face. "This is my son, Ahmad, who saved you."

Reaching up to shake his hand, Ibrahim said, "Thank you, brother. For a moment back there, I thought you were angels."

The mother remarked, "They certainly are angels, true friends indeed, those who save the wounded when everyone else is focused on saving himself."

"And my friend Ahmad?" Ibrahim asked. "I saw him fall close by me. He may have been wounded in the stomach."

"I don't know, brother. There were only three of us, on donkeys. We saved perhaps nine or ten. Then we urged two good men who were staying in the hospital to go out to the road and save more. It was a huge risk to take a car out there."

Ibrahim began describing his friend Ahmad and where he fell in case the other Ahmad would remember anything about him. But the young man could not recall any specific details – the ground had been so covered with corpses it was hard to spot the living among them: "We were watching for movement, breathing, things like that. As for you," he added, "I had passed you by, but I heard someone behind me calling out 'Ahmad, Ahmad' in a weak voice that gave me goose pimples. I thought it was someone who knew me, someone I knew. So I came over and picked you up. You were calling out with your eyes closed."

Ahmad smiled and went on. "I thought you were calling me. Who knows? It was God's will. You truly were calling me. When I picked you up, I only found light wounds on your body from small pieces of shrapnel, but your right foot was just dangling, barely connected to the leg by a strip of skin. So I cut it off and bandaged the stump with my shirt. Then I took you to the hospital."

That was when Ibrahim realised he had lost his foot, and that the horrendous pain he thought had been the explosion of a landmine underneath him was a shell that had crushed his bone. The young man went on talking in order to comfort him.

"You may have been the luckiest of the wounded. Many had fatal injuries, and there were others who begged us to kill them to put an end to their suffering. Of course we didn't do that, but you saw the piles of dead men yourself. All of us who saw it – no matter how badly hurt – we all know how lucky we were."

Ibrahim said, "How long have I been here?"

"About two days. One in the hospital and another here."

"Is there some way that I could check on my friend Ahmad? Could I call the hospital or his family?"

The young man smiled bitterly. "What are you saying, brother? Which hospital are you talking about? There's nothing left besides the name. Just about everyone there fled, and people have stolen the beds, the chairs, and the equipment, everything. Nothing remains apart from a few doctors and nurses who preserve what's left of conscience and mercy, carrying out their moral duty as far as they are able. Meanwhile, the wounded lie on the floors in the rooms and hallways, and the tiles are covered in blood. In any case, all the telephone lines have been cut."

Ahmad began describing for Ibrahim the chaotic situation: "They're still bombing everything – military camps, bridges, communication stations and towers, power plants, water treatment facilities, government buildings, police stations, businesses, houses – everything, just everything. The prisons have been opened and the inmates set free. They've taken up the weapons of the police, as well as the guns left behind by the army. Killing, chaos and looting are rampant. The banks were robbed. Museums, too, and universities, schools, hospitals, all government agencies and offices, and even the schools. Many of the buildings were set on fire. Some of the bombs hit the markets. You can't imagine it! Corpses fill the streets.

"There has been a determined uprising against the government everywhere. They say it was sparked suddenly when people saw a soldier returning from the disaster in Kuwait who was brave enough to piss on a big picture of the President in one of the city squares. Then he riddled it with bullets. The regime has collapsed entirely in the south, and there are reports that it has fallen in the north as well. They say the tyrant and his entourage are packing suitcases with everything they've stolen and are getting ready to flee. They're killing government employees, policemen, and soldiers according to their religious and ethnic identities. In the square in the city centre, I saw a group strip some women naked, douse them with gasoline, and set them on fire. You don't know who is killing who or why. The cities have been transformed into labyrinths of savage ghosts."

"But why do they continue the bombing? Didn't Iraq

announce an unconditional surrender and retreat?"

"Yes, but foreign forces are still entering Iraq and destroying everything. The worst of it is that the people, our countrymen, are taking advantage of this destruction. Some of them are like wild beasts set free from their cages."

Ibrahim tried to picture the scope of the devastation, even though in reality it was far greater than he could imagine. "How awful!" he murmured. "What are you saying, brother? This means the country is finished."

"A tragedy," the young man replied with fervour, choosing his words deliberately. "But take comfort! The people are suffering, but they will never submit. These are the birth pangs of revolution."

"Revolution!"

"Yes. But unfortunately it lacks direction. The uprising by the common people and the truly oppressed was lost amid the havoc wreaked by infiltrators. With my own two eyes, I saw armed foreigners in the streets. They were with Iraqis jabbering away in some foreign language. As you know, Iraq didn't leave any significant forces to secure the rest of its borders, and at a few places on the border with Iran, as soon as the guards retreated or were killed, well . . ."

Ibrahim shuddered at hearing the mention of Iran, as though in a single moment that entire long war he had experienced was replayed in his mind.

Ahmad noticed the tension distorting Ibrahim's face. "I'm sorry, brother," he said. After a pause: "I saw corpses being eaten by dogs in the markets."

"I too saw dogs eating bodies. It's as though the age of dogs has arrived."

Ahmad's mother entered, carrying a crutch that she offered to Ibrahim, saying, "This crutch belonged to Ahmad's father, may he rest in peace. It's for you."

"Of course, you'll just use it in the beginning," Ahmad said. "Later on, they'll make a new foot for you. Medicine is advanced these days, and that sort of thing is easily done. The wars have left behind so many amputees that Iraqi doctors have become experts at fashioning new limbs. I heard somewhere that the number of handicapped people in Iraq has exceeded a million."

Ahmad would sometimes be gone for the whole day and come back only as evening fell. If he stayed out into the night, his mother would become anxious and start pacing back and forth. She relieved her fear by talking about him to Ibrahim, just as he told her about Qisma. She told him how she had tried to convince Ahmad to get married. He refused. Books and university friends had won him over. "He has married the cause," she said.

Later on, when Ibrahim asked Ahmad about what she had meant, he replied, "The cause of Iraq."

"Don't you see how everyone stakes his marriage claim upon her?"

"You said it yourself, 'everyone stakes his claim.' But I'm not an opportunist or a plunderer. I'm a native son of the country – we're the real thing."

For more than two weeks, Ibrahim would learn from Ahmad what was happening in the outside world since from his bed he could not hear anything besides the rattle of bullets and continuous explosions. The fighting was so frequent that it became the natural state of affairs, and it felt strange whenever it stopped. People would wonder about the reason for the silence and ask each other what just happened.

As for the official news, he heard it on a small radio that Ahmad provided to keep him company, but the broadcasts would make him dizzy with their contradictions. On top of that, they spoke about leaders and politicians more than about what was happening on the ground around him and how the people were faring. So he had to rely on Ahmad for information.

"Some people call it a revolution, but the government says it's mob violence," Ibrahim once began. "What do you say, Ahmad?"

"It is a genuine uprising of the downtrodden, and I'm playing my part. But unfortunately, various opportunists are diverting it from its course and corrupting it. Many people, Arabs and non-Arabs, are vying to control the movement. The Americans have withdrawn from the south, abandoning to their fate all the people who rose up. By retreating just when the government was about to fall for the final time, the Americans gave a green light to the regime to crush the people, and now they've gathered up what remains of the army and the Republican Guard to launch devastating raids against all the cities and villages that revolted. They're bombing schools, houses, mosques and mausoleums, killing without mercy. The bodies in the streets outnumber those buried in the communal graves. Many people have been separated from their families. Some sought refuge with the American forces in order to be taken with them. Some families fled across the borders to neighbouring countries, and others were forced by the regime into exile or placed in isolated desert camps. The regime and the Americans – they're no different in what they do to the people!"

When Ibrahim decided to travel back to his family, Ahmad and his mother tried to dissuade him due to the ongoing chaos and the dangers of the road. But Ibrahim said he was better now: the stump where his foot had been was healed, and he could walk with the help of the crutch. Moreover, his family was no doubt sick with worry, and there was no way to let them know how he was doing since the telephone lines were still down. In any case, even if they were repaired, there were no telephones in his village.

Ibrahim wanted them to give him their address and telephone number so he could visit them in the future and thank them properly for saving his life. Ahmad refused, saying that he had not done it for the sake of recompense. But when Ahmad was away, Ibrahim kept asking the mother until she repeated the address and telephone number enough times that Ibrahim learned them by heart, even though he was terrible at memorising numbers. He could not remember any apart from the year he was born, 1959, and even then he did not know the exact month or day. The only other numbers he had memorised were Abdullah Kafka's Red Cross I.D., the address of his friend Ahmad al-Najafi and this new one.

Ahmad and Ibrahim set off for Baghdad in the car of some trustworthy friends who were heading there to search for one of their brothers, about whom they had had no word since the beginning of the war. Ahmad told Ibrahim, "Once we get to Baghdad, it's up to you to work out your own way from there."

Ahmad gave Ibrahim some of his own civilian clothes and a little bit of money. Meanwhile, the mother gave him a bag containing three plastic containers filled with food she had cooked, some pitta bread, and a bottle of water, saying, "So that you'll have some provisions on the road. Greet your family and kiss your daughter Qisma for me."

On the road, Ibrahim stared out the windows on both sides, noticing how the scenery had changed around him: the land, gardens and houses he had come to know through all his military travels appeared emptier and darker, older and sadder. They informed him that black rain poured from the sky because the clouds were weighed down by smoke from Kuwaiti oil wells, which the Iraqi forces had set alight before retreating. There was also smoke from the fires around Baghdad and other large cities in a vain attempt to impede the vision of the warplanes making raids.

The military checkpoints scattered along the length of the highway would wave them through without demanding any papers or identification when Ibrahim lifted up his leg, amputated at the foot. As they passed near Najaf, he urged his companions to make a detour for a few minutes to the house of his friend Ahmad. But they refused: "There's no time, and travelling in the cities is very dangerous now."

He did not press them, for deep down, he was not really sure he wanted to make the visit, nor was he convinced it would do any good. What would he tell them? That he and Ahmad were together for months and all through the retreat, but then he just lost track of him? Would he say that Ahmad was injured or dead? And if he was injured, why hadn't Ibrahim tried to save him?

Why had he abandoned him? How? At the very least, he should have confirmed that Ahmad was dead or alive, or determined the spot where he fell.

The situation kept tormenting Ibrahim, especially since he could not forget the pain felt by Zaynab, Tariq and everyone who loved Abdullah Kafka when he brought them the news that Abdullah was missing. What does that word mean anyway? "Missing". He would never forget Zaynab's face as her hot tears fell. It was so hard that he wished in that moment he could have placed Abdullah's body in her hands. That way, she would see him and cry, and her heart would know for certain he had died. But for Ibrahim, together with the paper in his hand, to tell her Abdullah was "missing" was a worse torture, insofar as it cruelly suspended her between hope and despair on a thread that was neither reinforced nor cut. Every moment of waiting was a slow torture, and all her thoughts scattered into confused absent-mindedness.

Ibrahim did not want to experience the same thing a second time with the family of Ahmad al-Najafi. He did not want to shirk his duty, of course, but he just could not endure the encounter, and feelings of guilt were tearing him up inside. He had a strong sense of his own inadequacy and failure, a disappointment in himself that he had never before experienced. In those moments when the weight of the rebuke grew heavy on his soul, it was enough to make him wish he had died with Ahmad.

In Baghdad, they dropped him off at the Alawite Garage bus station, where they found some cars heading north. Ibrahim shared out the remaining food and thanked them warmly, expressing his hope that they would succeed in finding their brother.

On the road, his new travel companions spoke about what had happened in their region: "The Kurds rose up too, as you know, and all the government's control over them crumbled. We came here looking for our relatives. Some of us fled Baghdad to relatives in the countryside because only the small, secluded villages are safe now. They don't have anything that would tempt the government to steal, and no power to suppress. It's true that some people attacked the schools and clinics, and stole chairs, tables and medical equipment, but the thieves returned those things the next day seeing as they didn't benefit from them at all. In addition, everyone knows everyone else in the villages, so the people's disgust at what they had done outweighed the value of the stolen goods."

They told Ibrahim that all the villagers who were able to, both soldiers and officers, had fled and returned home. They listed names of people he knew so he would believe them. Otherwise, who could ever have imagined an officer running away when the penalty just for being absent or late in reporting for duty was death? What would it be for desertion?

"Things have spiralled out of control, brother, and nothing is more common than death. A man's death these days means as much as pissing in the sea. There's nothing to be gained! That man loses himself and his family pays the price. So the real hero now is he who knows how to preserve his own life and limb until the storm has passed."

CHAPTER 7

Sick and Besieged

Ibrahim made it home. He asked about his brother Wadih, the other soldier in the family, and they informed him they did not know anything, just that his unit had been in Kuwait. Besides Wadih, there were many young men from the village about whom there was no news.

"Do you know anything?" they asked.

"No."

His brother's young wife held him and cried before going to sit in the far corner to cry some more. Ibrahim's father embraced him from his seat. Weakened by sickness, fear and old age, he had lost weight, and it was hard for him to stand unaided. Ibrahim smelled his father's characteristic odour of cigarettes, familiar since childhood. His blind mother began touching the end of his leg and had difficulty imagining him without a foot, a foot she had known and measured with her fingers as it grew. She cried not to find it.

The face of Ibrahim's wife radiated joy at his return, and were it not for the tears of Wadih's wife nearby, she would have let out a trill of joy. Meanwhile, his daughter Qisma embraced him. Or rather, he embraced her. She pulled away and gave him an odd look, regarding his leg with its missing foot like a dirty walking stick stretched out in front of him. The other siblings wanted to slaughter a ram and hold a feast to celebrate Ibrahim's return, but their father said, "Put it off for a few days until Wadih returns. Then slaughter a bull and make it a real feast." Ibrahim agreed with his father on the matter.

After the villagers had finished their congratulations and dispersed, his father remarked with a smile, as they were drinking perhaps their tenth glass of tea, "I lost my nose in one war, and you lost your foot in another. I don't know which is preferable, losing a nose or a foot. In any case, anything is better than losing one's life."

Ibrahim did not repeat what he had done at the end of the previous war, when he allowed himself a month of nothing but eating, sleeping and bathing. The pain in his leg was intense, but he did not show it in front of the others, taking extra care with his parents, who were suffering intensely on account of Wadih, whose absence became a tangible presence among them, dominating their lives. It was there in their actions, tone of voice, glances, and the long silences that passed between them. This absence somehow pervaded even the air they breathed, and each day the sorrow of Wadih's young wife renewed its hold on them.

Ibrahim had to get used to a limp and to his new life in the company of a crutch. The pain cut him to the quick, but it was nothing compared to what he experienced when he noticed that Qisma was avoiding him. He sensed that she felt lukewarm towards him and was keeping her distance.

His friend Tariq was always visiting to renew their intimacy, sometimes accompanied by one of his small children. Tariq had not gone to the war, because he was a schoolteacher and a mosque imam. He also had connections in Mosul, and the order for his conscription was first delayed and then resolved with him being assigned guard duty over one of the government agencies in the city, a duty he quickly dispensed with when he saw the entire system collapse and everyone abandoning their posts to return home. Tariq still dressed well, looked healthy and well-fed, and talked and joked as he always had.

Every time Ibrahim's father saw Tariq he would say, "The spitting image of your father, may he rest in peace."

Tariq would reply with a laugh, "Yes, but he was a better man than me in that he married three times, whereas I spend my evenings with just one wife. In any case, one woman is enough because she ties you around her finger like a bull around the irrigation pump. Ah, how marvellous the days of bachelorhood when I could wander freely among the women like a bee among the flowers!"

Ibrahim made it a joke of it: "Aren't all the flowers you smelled enough for you? But not just smelled – didn't you also pluck them and throw them away?!"

"Well, can someone addicted to sweetness get his fill from a single taste of honey? Then, by God, away with you! As one of these flowers, are you also counting against me a girl like Fahda the Bedouin?"

The two of them burst out laughing and slapped each other's hand. "Believe me," Tariq replied, "it was like hugging a ewe or a she-goat. The smell was enough to choke you, brother!"

Ibrahim's father asked what they were laughing about, and

they told him the story. He laughed with them, praising Fahda's father Jad'an, who would spend one month each year outside the village before moving on. Suhayl's feeble laughter was interrupted by a fit of coughing as a thread of smoke escaped from the gaping holes of his nose.

"Has there been another letter from Abdullah?" Ibrahim asked Tariq. "Any news about the captives in Iran?"

"Nothing new, Abu Qisma. People focus now on the fate of new prisoners, and they forget the old."

When Tariq noticed the spasm of sorrow that flashed across Ibrahim's face, he hurried on to other subjects, trying to entertain him with unusual anecdotes. "Listen to this," he began. "A true story and no joke. A soldier returned home and found his old mother crying, deeply distressed. She had been watching T.V. and listening non-stop to the Iraqi radio stations, which described our victories day and night, the abominable defeats we inflicted upon the enemy. He said to her, 'Why are you crying, mother? The war has ended, and here I am, home safe and sound.' And the mother said, 'I'm crying for the poor Americans, for if we've experienced all this destruction as the victors, what must they have suffered in defeat?'"

It was precisely during this gathering that Qisma's affection for Ibrahim began to falter. She was sitting near the door beside her mother, who did not stop pouring tea. Qisma was watching her father, but she watched his friend Tariq even more. As she compared the two, new feelings she did not fully understand were stirring in her soul. She liked Tariq with his elegance, his pungent cologne and his loud bursts of laughter. She liked his abundant self-confidence as one story followed another, each joke funnier than the last, as he talked about his many acquaintances, about the city, and about things she did not completely comprehend, things related to religion, heaven, angels, politics and books. He filled the air with a vivacious spirit that did not leave awkward silences to be filled with the same old phrases. Likewise, he treated his son, who was younger than she was, in a manner that resembled friendship. Tariq asked the child's opinion about what he said, about the tea, or about his wishes, or he would seek his help to confirm some detail. And the language with which Tariq addressed him differed not at all from the language he used with adults.

Qisma found nothing like that in her father. He seldom spoke, was deeply sad, and submitted to her grandfather with blind obedience. He always treated her as though she were a small child, never put on cologne or wore elegant clothes, and exhibited a quietude that was excessive to the point of tedium. On top of all that, here he was with just one foot, his right leg stretched out in front of him like the stump of an old tree, a crutch at his side.

Qisma was unable to turn her gaze from Tariq except to cast rapid, critical glances at her father. In that instant, she wished that Tariq were her father and that she were the one sitting beside him and leaning against him, or even sitting in his lap as he stroked her hair from time to time. Then she would be stronger, more vigorous – indeed, more beautiful. Or so she imagined. Later on, she began wishing she would grow up quickly, to become an adult with an adult's strength and freedom, an adult like Tariq and not like her father, from whom she began to keep her distance. It was not exactly disgust she felt, but rather a type of coldness and separation. She kept out of his sight and avoided his company.

Of course, Ibrahim was not capable of understanding it in this way, but he did sense her coldness around him, her silence and evasions. He tried to get closer to her by being softer, gentler and more meek, displaying a kind of self-abasement in her presence, but Qisma's distaste only increased when she sensed his weakness, confusion and indecision. As usual, Ibrahim continued to rely on his patience and left the matter to run its course, even as the need to address new events began to turn his focus away from it.

Qisma had celebrated her tenth birthday, and the nipples on her chest were growing restless, like mushrooms at the beginning of April when they rise and push against the crust of the earth.

After two weeks had passed, an unfamiliar car entered the courtyard with a coffin tied to the roof. The driver, a young man with dark skin, powerfully built, got out to confirm the address. Then he set about shaking hands. He lowered his head and said he wished he were not meeting them under these circumstances. He said he was Wadih's friend from Karbala, and that Wadih had been killed at Basra during the events following the retreat. He bowed his head in tears as the group in front of him burst out in loud weeping and Wadih's wife fainted to the ground. Meanwhile, father Suhayl led the young man by the arm to the reception room, struggling to maintain his composure. For the most part, he succeeded, even though he was trembling and water flashed in his eyes behind the two pillars of smoke rising from his nose holes. Old age presented itself as a plausible explanation for his trembling, rather than the weight of this loss.

Ibrahim joined them, leaning on his crutch and against the walls. Meanwhile, their neighbours and all the others who had hurried into the courtyard after hearing the commotion took charge of lowering the coffin and setting up the funeral tent and comforting the mourners. The third brother, together with his friends, gave directions.

In the reception room, the young man gave details about how Wadih had died at his side. He had not wanted to abandon Wadih's body, no matter what the cost, so he brought it to his home in Karbala for a night, then to the village. He told them about their close friendship, about the good character he had observed in Wadih.

Listening to the young man's story, Ibrahim felt sick on account of not having done the same thing for his friend Ahmad al-Najafi. He had not brought anything, not even news, to Ahmad's family. He felt shame and a sense of smallness before this young man, who exemplified nobility, manliness and humanity. Ibrahim expressed his indebtedness, as did his father, though his father's words contained greater maturity and wisdom.

It was a situation that would continue to trouble Ibrahim's conscience for the rest of his life. When he thought about it, he kept trying to understand how it was that some people on this earth could save his life, and others from the same earth had killed his brother. Naturally, in order to resolve this contradiction, he relied on his stance regarding fate, destiny and eternal decrees, and on the fact that no two people are the same even if they come from the same house. But he was never able to understand this distinction in a clear and definitive way, nor did repeated reflections on this matter allow him to crystallise his position.

So it was that after about a year, he revealed to Tariq what was torturing him, asking his friend to accompany him on a trip to the south. Tariq agreed, and they took a car to Najaf. However, they found a different family in the house. Ibrahim was informed that Ahmad's family had been torn apart when his mother died of grief over her last son. The two remaining women sold the house and divided the profits, and the current residents did not know where each of them had taken her children: "It's said that they may have married again, or returned to their families, or moved to some other village or city. We don't know for sure."

They went to a café, where Ibrahim remained silent as Tariq went on at length about the nature of this world, citing precedents from both ancient history and the recent past, concerning similar situations and some that were even more wretched. Yet Ibrahim kept his head bowed, as though not giving his full attention or not listening at all. This continued until in the end he began to cry. Tariq embraced him, and then told him to go and wash his face with cold water in the bathroom.

Ibrahim did so and then came back to sip his tea. He said, "I have another request for you, Tariq."

Tariq said, "Ask what you wish, Abu Qisma. I'm at your service."

"I want us to go to Zubair, to the house of the people who took me in and saved me. On the way we can buy them gifts. I want to thank them."

They had lunch in an inexpensive restaurant next to the café, and then they went to the market and loaded the car with bags of rice, sugar, flour, a large tin of olive oil, and several yards of cloth for both men's and women's clothing. Then they set off in the direction of Basra.

When they arrived at the house in Zubair, a woman in her thirties opened the door. An infant was holding on to the edge of her dress. Ibrahim had never seen her before, and, confused, he began asking her about the young man Ahmad and his mother, describing them to her. She opened the door fully and invited them inside. There, in a small reception room that Ibrahim knew well, and which he saw had not changed a bit, the woman offered them tea. She told them she was Ahmad's sister, and that Ahmad had been forced to flee to Iran after the uprising had been suppressed. Afterwards, the government expelled their mother to Iran as a suspected Iranian sympathiser. The daughter was allowed to remain in Iraq because her husband was a long-time employee in the provincial government, and because he was the descendant of a famous Baghdad family.

They gave her everything they had brought, and Ibrahim asked her to convey his greetings and his eternal gratitude to her brother and mother if she was ever in touch with them. Then they set off, returning to the village. They passed the time on the road by reminiscing, discussing Abdullah Kafka, and reflecting on life in their village, both past and present, recognising that it had not suffered the way the cities had. It seemed that the blessings of living in a village were more fully apparent during crises and wars.

Then Tariq surprised Ibrahim by broaching a subject he had long been preparing. "Let me ask you about something," he began. "Something Uncle Suhayl, your father, asked me to bring up with you. Namely, that you marry the widow of your brother Wadih."

Ibrahim refused immediately. "No! Impossible," he said in dismay. "I can't do that. She's like a sister to me."

"But she's not actually your sister. And you are not the only one who has done this sort of thing in the best interests of the family, as you know."

"No! No, I can't! It has never even crossed my mind. I'll always feel that she's my sister. I always have and I always will. What's more, she's young. She can marry a man her own age and have a better future, a better life."

"Your father thinks that your marrying her would be an honour to her, to her family, and to your brother. He thinks she is an admirable young woman who has become an important part of the family. It would be hard on you all if she had to leave. What's more, she might bear you a brother for Qisma."

Ibrahim insisted, adding further justifications: he had grown too old for something like this; Qisma was enough of a legacy for him; he did not want to hurt the feelings of Qisma's mother by marrying another woman, seeing as she had been his companion for so many years, through the good times and the bad. He ended the discussion by saying that he would speak to his father and try to convince him that he was right to refuse the proposition.

But he never alluded to his sterility, a matter he hid from everyone.

Ibrahim was surprised that convincing his father did not prove as difficult as convincing Tariq, for his father seemed less eager to prolong the conversation. Suhayl was no longer as stubborn and controlling as he used to be, always insisting on his own way. He had grown very feeble, skinny and pale. His voice had changed, becoming lower and weaker. He was a sick old man. Pain in his throat and oesophagus harassed him. There was a growth in his neck, and swallowing – even just his saliva – had become difficult and painful. He was no longer able to eat solid food, so they prepared different kinds of soup for him with minced meat and vegetables in the broth. Whenever he spat out the saliva that gathered in his throat, it was mixed with blood. It was as though he had already taken his leave of this life, and he no longer felt the desire to organise it according to his will. So he set off with his walking stick to the house where the parents of Wadih's widow lived. In a weak voice, he explained the situation to them, making a brief and deeply apologetic speech. After that, they took back their daughter and married her to one of her cousins.

The following years brought nothing but hardship thanks to the economic siege laid upon Iraq and the resulting scarcity of food, medicine, money, paper and iron. And compassion. The international sanctions hurt the common people most, even as they consolidated the government's power, since the government controlled the circulation of the few materials entering the country, distributing them as they saw fit. Its partisans became stronger at the expense of the vanquished majority.

Ibrahim was no longer able to work in the fields, either his own family's or Abdullah's, and the entire burden fell upon his other brother, his brother's wife and Umm Qisma. His brother gave Ibrahim hints about how weary he was, hoping that he might be relieved from working Abdullah's field at least, but Ibrahim implored him to endure. In the same way, he urged his wife to be patient, and he tried to take part as much as he could, even if it just meant being present while they worked. After two years of consultations and bureaucracy, his turn arrived, and one of the specialist hospitals run by the government made him an artificial plastic foot. He wore it on the end of his leg like a boot, and it took more than a little time to get used to. But in the end, though he was still clearly lame, he was able to get around better and could even walk without a crutch.

On one of his many visits to the hospital, Ibrahim had insisted that his father go with him because of his declining health. Swallowing anything – even taking a breath – caused him pain, and the amount of blood in his saliva was increasing. The doctor informed them that he had cancer of the mouth, larynx and oesophagus, and that it had spread through his entire throat and reached the trachea and windpipe. He told them that it was mostly down to how much he smoked, so he had to quit immediately. At the same time, his treatment would require doses of chemotherapy and, ultimately, a surgical operation to remove the larynx and oesophagus. He would breathe directly through a hole in the skin above the chest.

"Of course, it will be hard for you to speak. Actually, you

won't be able to speak at all after the operation," the doctor said. "It's imperative you come back for treatment soon."

Ibrahim's father made no reply to the doctor, who provided them with a list of the steps that had to be followed. But after they left the hospital, Suhayl told Ibrahim, "There's no need for all that, my son. The little bit of life left to me isn't worth all this care and treatment, not to mention the expense it entails. And I'm not going to stop smoking. When smoking has been my lifelong companion through sorrow and joy, how could I abandon it, just because I'm going to die?"

Ibrahim tried to convince him, but his father had made up his mind and was content. He was resigned to his fate, refusing to buy the medicine he needed. At a time when the sanctions made medical supplies scarce, he said, he preferred it to go to someone younger and in greater need of it. And thus, he gradually began moving, speaking and eating less and less. Calmly folding in upon himself in a corner of the reception room, he waited for death until at last it arrived.

Ibrahim's hardships did not cease with his father's death, for his blind mother had become an old woman too, far advanced in years, and she required care and assistance, not least when she went to the toilet. Ibrahim's wife would accompany her for that.

For her own part, Umm Qisma had also become more pale and thin. She was utterly exhausted from her work, and would collapse into bed at the end of the day and sleep like the dead. The paler she became, the more Ibrahim worried for her. He asked her to go to the doctor – she might have diabetes or jaundice. Not wanting to impose any more burdens upon him, she refused, insisting it was just fatigue. But her condition did not improve, and, alarmed by her extreme weakness and ghost-like pallor, Ibrahim took her to the hospital in the city.

The lab did an E.S.R. examination of her blood, coming back with a very high number of 120, which meant she had blood poisoning. The hospital took samples from the lymph nodes under her armpit and in her neck. When the lab performed an analysis, they discovered that she had cancer of the lymph nodes as well. And thus began the odyssey of her treatment. Every twenty-one days, Ibrahim would make her swallow a dose of chemicals with her food. During the examination that took place ten days after every dose, they would make another analysis of her blood. They observed that the E.S.R. numbers measuring the contamination in her blood had dropped to between 60 and 70, and the doctor informed them that the chances of a successful treatment with a full cure were as high as 40 per cent. Fearing death, Umm Qisma cried every night. "We'd continue the treatment even if the chances of recovery were one in a hundred," Ibrahim told her.

Umm Qisma was overcome by a wave of vomiting and diarrhoea after every dose she took. The doctors ordered her to stop working and continue her treatment – despite the exorbitant costs, which required Ibrahim to work even harder in the fields. He also took care of some of the domestic duties of the household, with occasional help from Qisma. Ibrahim's sisters, who were married and lived apart from them, took turns visiting to help with the chores and cheer up Umm Qisma.

Life went on. Ibrahim adapted and got used to it just as he always did, with endurance, patience and self-denial. Their hardship became a routine, a way of life that continued for years without any change – until it was interrupted by the return of Abdullah Kafka.

CHAPTER 8

Kafka's Return from Captivity

No-one in the village would ever forget that scene. Everyone present laughed and cried for five minutes when Abdullah Kafka arrived and embraced Ibrahim the Fated and Tariq the Befuddled. Their three heads came together in the middle of the crowd as though they were whispering to one other, their arms circling around each other's shoulders. Their hands alternated between patting and pulling the embrace tighter. The shoulders of this triad shook, one moment in laughter and the next in tears, and if one of the three lifted his head a little, it was only to kiss the others. All of the women present, and some of the men, wept to see it. They waited for this moving embrace to disentangle so they could take a turn at greeting the one who had returned from captivity after nearly twenty years.

"Here they are," someone observed. "The sons of the earth crack together again."

"The sons of the earth crack have come back to their own mothering earth," another replied.

After the long embrace with his two friends dissolved, Abdullah was told that Zaynab, blind and walking with a cane, was on her way to see him, guided by one of her grandsons. Abdullah set off immediately, leaving everyone behind. A group led him down the path towards her, and there, in the middle of a narrow alley, they cried again to see Zaynab embrace Abdullah, the two of them weeping together.

Zaynab inhaled deeply at his neck and chest, and her trembling fingers explored his entire body. She threw down her cane and held Abdullah's face in her hands, crying out, "My son! My baby, my son! Oh, my sweet child, not a waking moment passed that I did not think of you and weep. I lost my sight since it did me no good in your absence." Her fingers touched his beard. "Is it white?" she asked.

Smiling, he supported her with one arm, pulling her head close with the other hand to kiss her brow. "Half and half," Abdullah said. "White and black."

That evening, a great party was held in the courtyard of Abdullah's house, bigger than any wedding and bigger than the party Salih and Maryam hosted when they found Abdullah as an infant. Two calves were slaughtered, donated by Ibrahim and Zaynab, along with a fat ram contributed by Tariq. All the women of the village took part in the cooking, and everyone was invited. Dozens of rugs and carpets were laid out in the courtyard. Abdullah sat in the middle with the two blind women, the oldest members of the community, either side of him. Umm Ibrahim and Hajja Zaynab did not stop touching and kissing him from one moment to the next. He reflected on the fact that sitting between two blind people was like sitting between the two darknesses of birth and death: Abdullah had become accustomed to finding symbols in everything.

After everyone had finished eating and drinking tea, and the dishes and glasses had been cleared away, there was an outburst of clapping, trilling and laughter.

"What's happening?" Zaynab asked Abdullah.

Forcing himself to smile and clap along while he lit another cigarette from the one gripped between his teeth, Abdullah said, "It's poor Isma'il, that good herdsman. He's dancing in the middle with his staff as though he were mad, making everyone laugh at him."

As her eyes welled over with tears, Zaynab said, "Oh, dear God Almighty! Blood truly knows its own. The heart knows its own and yearns for it."

"I don't understand, Aunt Zaynab."

She wrapped her arm around his neck and drew him so close her lips touched his ear. "I'm not your aunt. Isma'il is your real uncle. And me, I'm your grandmother."

Zaynab sensed Abdullah's confusion and drew him close once more to add, "Don't think I've gone senile in my old age. The only thing that has kept me alive this long, when everyone else from my generation has died, is that I was waiting to tell you the truth and find some peace. Listen, my son, come and find me as soon as you can, tomorrow or the day after, so I can tell you everything. Everything."

From Abdullah's silence, Zaynab realised the shock her words had provoked. Perhaps they were rash, but she knew she could no longer endure in silence. She quickly changed the subject: "I tried every which way to find a wife for poor Isma'il, but no-one would marry their daughters or sisters to him. They said he was dull-witted and could scarcely look after himself. In truth, he never thought about the matter himself. It never crossed his mind, and I don't think he knew what marriage was until . . ."

She fell silent for a moment and then said, "It's you who must get married now. Sameeha is divorced, if you still love her. Otherwise, choose whomever you want."

"No, I don't want to get married. I'm past all that, and it too has left me behind. I just want to rest. Only rest."

"Listen, my son. You are exhausted now, and you have tonight's festivities ahead of you. I'm exhausted too and have to go home. Don't forget to visit me as soon as you can. You absolutely must. I'll tell you the truth – your truth – known only to me and the Lord of the Universe."

"Yes. Yes, I'll be sure to."

"You know, I've just realised something. No-one dies without wanting to or submitting to it deep down. You have to start accepting the idea of death, expecting it and waiting for it. I'm the proof of that. I decided not to die until I'd seen you again. And now you see that I am the last one alive of my generation." She caught herself and added, "Ah, and this other old blind woman, good Umm Ibrahim, who comes next in age."

"The opposite is also true. Sometimes taking the decision to die is a victory over the anxiety of waiting for it." She did not hear him, and he went on, "For my part, I've realised that when you're content with the meaninglessness of all things and the equality of all things, the equality of being alive or dead – that's when the oppression and torments of life lose their power. Understanding that leads to freedom, and even if this freedom comes from the absence of life, it's all the same to you."

"From your words, it's as though I can see your face and your eyes. I see that you are speaking from fatigue and age." And to make a joke as she struggled to get up, she said, "Look! I'm more spry than you!"

He got up too, helping Zaynab to her feet and passing her the cane. They embraced, and suddenly, from between the legs of those crowded around, the young grandson stepped forward to lead her away.

The noisy celebrations continued past four in the morning. They trilled and performed the *dabka* and other dances to the rhythm of drums, traditional flutes, tea and laughter. One by one, they came up to Abdullah to shake his hand, exchange greetings, and congratulate him on his safe return. Some of them tried, more than once, to get him to join the *dabka*. They took him by the arm and pulled him into the circle. His protestations and reluctance were in vain, and he was forced to join in out of politeness. He would take a few steps and say, "As you can see, I don't know how. But then, I'm a bit tired."

So he went back to sitting and smoking. He felt entirely estranged from this world and these people. He knew some of the faces, which he found had aged greatly, but most of them were unfamiliar. There were some he had last seen as children who were now adults, and dozens of children who had been born during his absence. He failed in most of his attempts to identify them, frequently mistaking sons for their fathers. He would say, "Isn't this so-and-so?" And they would tell him, "You don't know him? This is so-and-so's son. Don't you remember?"

He appreciated these noisy celebrations on his behalf. He

appreciated their goodness and generosity. But in truth, he did not want any of it, and nothing at all meant anything to him. He longed to be alone in some corner, or in some land free of people, all by himself. He was accustomed to silence and isolation and dead time, for even though his entire existence was contained within himself, time had no place there. There was no meaning to the movement of things. Things themselves held no meaning, nor did whatever produced the movement of time. He grudgingly endured this noisy goodness of theirs. He understood it. He had no choice, given that they, for their part, would never understand him – which is why he had to practise understanding them. Even if now and for ever after, he would resolutely preserve for himself the privilege of returning to the private freedom of his depression.

When they asked him to describe the years of his captivity in Iran, he made very clear his reluctance to do so and would only say, "To put it briefly, it was worse than the most horrible nightmare. The best thing to do is forget it and move on, don't you agree?"

And of course, the questioner, who was essentially kind and courteous, would confirm Abdullah's words: "Yes. Yes, of course! It is better to forget. Forgetting is a great blessing from God. Consider it past and done. Begin a new life! The important thing is that it's over, and that you've returned safe and sound, praise God!"

That phrase, "praise God", was repeated many times over. He had heard it so often during his years of captivity that its meaning was entirely lost to him.

When the gathering began to disperse, everyone carried home what they had brought: rugs, carpets, pillows, dishes, spoons, glasses, and so on. Ibrahim and Tariq offered to spend the night with Abdullah, if he wished, but he thanked them and said, "You have done so much. You are both tired, and so am I. Go and get some rest. We have the coming days ahead of us. I'll be going to sleep too."

But he was not able to sleep, for as soon as he closed the door of the house behind him, he began looking around. He could not find a single thing that had been moved from its place. It was just as he had left it, though things had become worn and faded: the curtains, the bedding, the pillows, and even the wood of the cabinets, doors, and shutters. Zaynab's care, and after her Ibrahim's and the tenants', was evident: they had left everything clean and tidy, just as it had been.

Abdullah found his body reinhabiting the landscape of memories he had ruminated upon through many long years of captivity. Here he had played when he was young. Here he hid. Here he slept on the lap of his mother Maryam, as she stroked his hair in front of the warm stove. Here he played chess with his father Salih. Here, here, and here . . .

Abdullah put out the light and lay down on the bed without getting undressed. He lit a cigarette in the dark and listened to the empty silence inside himself. He smoked one cigarette after another, lighting each from the last and delighting in the abundance of cigarettes and the freedom to smoke so many, when for so long during the years of his captivity, it had been a struggle – marked by insults, humiliation and robbery – to get just one. He wanted to fill the room with smoke, to transform it into one big cloud, or into a huge cigarette with him in the middle, such that normal breathing would become a kind of smoking.

The silence outside. The smoke within. The emptiness in his mind. Nothing at all. Despite everything, Abdullah did not close his eyes but continued staring into the darkness. He kept staring until the darkness was cut by a line of dawn that crept between the two wooden panels of the shutters. He contemplated the waves of visible smoke along the slowly growing thread of light, the kind of light he remembered from so many sunrises under so many skies.

It went on like this until he heard the sound of irregular foot-falls in the courtyard outside. He got up and put an eye to the gap in the shutters. He looked outside and saw Ibrahim putting rubbish left behind from the night's festivities into a bag he carried: cigarette butts, empty cans, bones, scraps of bread, napkins. Abdullah noticed that Ibrahim limped as he walked. One of his feet made a solid thud when it hit the ground while the other made no sound. Abdullah continued watching Ibrahim for a moment, comparing him to the image so often and longingly recalled during his captivity. Abdullah found him to be older, more tired, and his back had started hunching somewhat at the top. But in his face, Abdullah saw the same gentleness and kindness. It was as though his spirit were formed from a material that did not change with time. Abdullah felt a greater love for him, and the affection churning in his breast struck him so hard he nearly burst into tears. He took a deep breath to ease the pain in his heart and headed to the door to go out into the courtyard.

"What are you doing, Ibrahim? Leave it, man!"

"I'm so happy you're back that I couldn't sleep. So I came to be near you and started cleaning up to give myself something to do."

Abdullah took the bag and the broom out of his hands. He set them aside and led Ibrahim away. "Leave this for now, brother. I couldn't sleep either. Come on, let's make some tea."

Before they went inside, Abdullah asked, "Why are you limping?"

"I lost my foot in the last war. This is an artificial foot."

"Ah, no!"

"I'm fine. Thousands of others lost their lives."

As soon as they entered, the wave of smoke struck Ibrahim. "What's going on? Is something burning?"

Abdullah laughed. "No! No, this is the smoke from my cigarettes. I was taking revenge – or else compensating – for a smoking drought that lasted many years."

"No! Abdullah, you have to quit! It's bad for your health. It's deadly! It can cause throat cancer and lead to a painful death."

"I know, and I don't care. Dying hasn't frightened me for a long time. As far as I'm concerned, life and death are all the same."

"Fine. You make the tea, and I'll keep cleaning. Then bring it to the courtyard and we'll drink outside."

The kitchen was full of food from the night before. Abdullah took a piece of cheese, some butter, and two pittas, which he arranged on a large tray along with the pot of tea and two glasses. Then he brought a small rug from the living room and went out to join Ibrahim. They sat close to the earth crack, its mouth still gaping. It had not changed at all except that its rough edges had become smooth.

Ibrahim told his friend everything that had happened to him in his absence. He told him about the years of the Iraq–Iran War, about the war in Kuwait, about Ahmad al-Najafi, his new foot, his wife's illness, the death of his brother Wadih, the death of his father. He went on to describe at length the suffering brought about by his father's illness, emphasising the coughing, the bloody spit and the difficulty in swallowing and breathing. After every other sentence, he insisted again that Abdullah quit smoking.

Once more Abdullah asked him to drop the subject – smoking was his only pastime and pleasure. He said he understood Ibrahim's father, and if the same thing happened to him as happened to Suhayl, he would adopt the very same stance, preferring to die in the company of cigarettes rather than preserve a life of illness and medicine at the cost of quitting. In an attempt to stem Ibrahim's exhortations, Abdullah concluded, "On top of that, look at your wife. The poor woman doesn't smoke, and cancer has struck her too."

"But that's a different kind," Ibrahim said. He fell silent.

Abdullah tried to soften the impact of what he had said, resorting to his friend's habitual style of persuading others: "Don't you see, smoking had nothing to do with it. Everyone has his lot in life. Everything is fate and decree."

"Yes," Ibrahim echoed. "Everything is fate and decree."

Then Ibrahim took a small cloth bag, stuffed full, out of his pocket. He opened it and carefully removed a stack of papers covered with schedules, numbers and notes written in what Abdullah recognised as Ibrahim's awful handwriting. When Ibrahim opened the bag to pull out a second stack of stamped receipts, Abdullah noticed the bag was also full of money. Ibrahim pushed it over to Abdullah, saying, "Speaking of our lot in life, this is yours. In these papers you'll find everything recorded from the time I started working your land after your letter arrived. These are the receipts for buying the seed and the fertiliser and for selling the crops. Here are the receipts for renting out the house. And these—"

Abdullah interrupted him as he took the stacks of papers and receipts from his hand. "Enough, Ibrahim! You don't have to give me the details. There's no need to document anything at all. You're my brother, and I'm indebted to you beyond what I'm able to express."

Abdullah tore up the papers with the notes and threw them in the crack without even looking at them. He pushed the bag of money into Ibrahim's hand once again.

"And all this is for you. It's yours, for you and your hardship. I didn't do anything to earn it. It's enough for me that you looked after my land and my house in my absence and kept them from wasting away through neglect."

"No! No, this rightfully belongs to you. I only did my duty. Besides, I have already deducted the wages for my labour."

"All this is for you, for the work you did. It belongs to you, and you need it more than me. The government gave us some money when we arrived, and I'll also be collecting my pension. As you can see, I don't have many expenses and no family to spend my money on. Take it! It came to you, and you have a greater right to it than I."

When Ibrahim insisted and would not take the bag, Abdullah opened it and grabbed what he thought was roughly half of the dinars, put them in his pocket, and handed the rest of the money over.

"Fine. Then we'll split it. Like this, without being exact. Take this at least, if only as my contribution to the cost of Umm Qisma's treatment. But my gratitude and the debt I owe you – that can neither be measured in money nor repaid with words."

At that, Ibrahim wrapped Abdullah in a strong embrace where they sat, repeating words of thanks. "You are my brother, Abdullah. I'm with you in everything, now more than ever as you establish your new life."

"I know, Ibrahim. Don't worry! My life is arranged just fine as it is. I don't have any specific ideas or projects or plans."

"No? How come, brother? What about marriage and starting a family? What about the field?"

"No marriage and no family. But as for the field – you continue to manage it, just as you've been doing."

"As you can see, I no longer have the strength for it. My brother takes care of that. I share in a little of the work with him, together with some of the administrative details. He complains about the heavy burden because the work in our field falls on his shoulders too."

"Then find me whoever you want from among the villagers to take charge of working the field, in whatever way and at whatever salary you see fit. You know more about these things than I do."

"But..."

"Enough, Ibrahim! As far as I'm concerned, what I have is sufficient for me, as long as I can afford cigarettes and food. I don't have desires, ambitions, or any other dreams. I have no need for anything at all. I don't have any problems or headaches, and I don't want any. All I want is peace. Yes, Ibrahim, just peace."

Before Ibrahim could make any reply, a car pulled into the courtyard and stopped nearby. Tariq got out in the full elegance of his traditional village robes. He threw his arms in the air with a joyful shout, and the scent of his cologne reached them before he did. With the sun just beginning to rise behind him, Tariq approached and greeted them, clapping Abdullah on the shoulder. "Aha!" he said to Ibrahim. "You've beaten me to him! Why didn't you tell me, you bastard!"

They cleared a space for him beside them on the rug. Tariq sat down, and after gazing at the crack nearby, he laughed with joy. "Haha! The sons of the earth crack finally reunite as a family." He added with a wink, "And you know how I love cracks of all kinds!"

They all laughed, and Ibrahim said affectionately, "Our befuddled friend. He still philosophises just as he used to."

Tariq added, "But unfortunately, Abdullah, to this day I still only possess one crack. What do you think about all three of us searching out new cracks to refresh our beds? We'll all get married on the same night and throw a huge wedding feast!"

"Here's your tea, Tariq. Have you had breakfast?"

Tariq had turned the earlier atmosphere on its head, their new-found cheer reinforced by the delightful warmth of the morning sun and the hot tea. He put his hand on Abdullah's shoulder and said, "Listen, I've brought the car so we can give you a full tour. We'll show you the whole village – where we played as children, the river, the fields, everything. Everything!"

For the rest of the morning until noon they traced the alleys between the houses. "This is the house of so-and-so. Do you remember him? This is a new house, belonging to so-and-so, son of so-and-so. So-and-so married so-and-so, and now they have five children. So-and-so became a widow. Her husband was killed on the last day of the war, when they announced the ceasefire with Iran, then she married so-and-so, and now they have three children. This is the house of so-and-so. His bull gored him and he died. His oldest son married so-and-so, daughter of so-and-so. This mansion belongs to Munthir, son of Hajja Wahida. He took up smuggling with the Kurds and became rich. This shop belongs to Hajji Radi. Do you remember how we used to buy our sweets, balloons and crayons here? It hasn't changed at all, has it? He died, God rest his soul, and now his daughter runs the shop. She's pretty and has large breasts – would you like to see her? This is Jabar's house, and these three beside it are the ones he built for his sons. All of them share one courtyard since he wanted to keep them under his wing."

They told him about many people: those who had died, who were killed, who had got married, who had had children, who had become rich, who had become poor. And when they went out to the land, he realised how much the village had grown and changed. They took him to the hills, the valleys and the wells, the places where they would hunt pigeons, sand grouse and jerboa in their youth. "This is where the Bedouin Abu Fahda would set up his tent. Do you remember him? Haha! You remember Fahda, don't you? He hasn't come back to the village for years – a tragedy!"

Abdullah noticed that even the hills, the valleys, the steppes, and the wells had changed. He felt that they had become smaller than he remembered them, more decrepit, more lifeless, more ordinary. They brought him up once more through the village and went down between the fields towards the river. They greeted everyone they passed, the men and women working in the fields, the herdsmen and the children playing. They told Abdullah, "This is so-and so," or "The son of so-and-so," or "This is so-and-so, the wife of so-and-so, son of so-and-so," or "That woman isn't married."

Abdullah saw a skinny, bearded man with dishevelled hair and a dirty robe. It seemed he was insane, sitting there with his butt on the ground, leaning against a mud wall. He scratched his head and his armpits in turn. His face was not unfamiliar to Abdullah. It was as though he knew him but could not remember who he was. He asked the other two about him, but they changed the subject without reply and went on pointing at things and pouring out more information.

"This is Daoud's field. Last year, strange worms descended on his crop, poor man. And this is Dari's field. Indeed, all of this is his. It's bigger because he bought the neighbouring field from Mas'ud when Mas'ud married a woman from Mosul and moved there. This is our field. Let's get a couple of watermelons . . . Here's your field. Do you want to get out to take a look at it?"

"No, it's O.K. I can see it from here. Let's go to the river now."

Abdullah felt a new sense of exile, for he found that everything he used to picture in his mind during the years of captivity had changed utterly. The trees, the rocks, the earth, the sky, the air – they were all different. Everything had changed, and he did not know what to think about the scenes he used to summon so often to his mind's eye. Where were they? What meaning did they now have? Where had those places gone? Had he kept himself alive by imagining a reality that had no basis in reality? Those deeply rooted memories – where would they all go now?

The answer to these questions, or at least the solution that would bring him peace, was found in his sense of futility, nihilism, meaninglessness and the equality of all things. And what did it mean anyway? Everything seemed so strange, unreal, ephemeral. His existence and his non-existence amounted to the same thing.

Yet when they reached the river, he felt that the water alone was still as it had always been. Yes, even though the banks, the thickets, the roads, and the bluffs were different, the water was unchanged, and his heart throbbed for it in a delicious way. They stopped the car on the riverbank. The sun was in the middle of the sky, straight overhead, and Tariq suggested they swim and play with the watermelons in the water, just like they used to do on those distant afternoons when they were young. They stripped off their robes. Scars criss-crossed Abdullah's back from floggings and beatings, and when he saw the comprehending sorrow in the eyes of Ibrahim and Tariq, he remarked, "Some of the gifts the Islamic Republic gives its guests."

They slowly entered the water. Soon, they were shouting happily and playing as though they were living those ancient moments again and had never grown up. The water was the same, and so were they, with their delight and their laughter. The difference was time, which flowed through them and over them, through and over everything.

They tossed the watermelons back and forth to cool them down. "The difference is that these watermelons aren't stolen," Tariq said. "I don't know why, but the stolen ones tasted better!"

After about an hour of swimming, they climbed out onto the river bank. They found a wide stretch of sand shaded by willow and tamarisk trees and sat on a plastic tarp Tariq brought from his car. They opened the two watermelons with blows of their fists, just as they used to do once upon a time.

In that spot, they asked Abdullah to tell them about his years of captivity. He did not really want to, but he thought it was necessary, at least with his two friends, given that they had told him everything that had happened to them and to the village. Perhaps he could unburden himself of this matter once and for all. He would concisely narrate whatever he could. But only to them, and if they wanted to convey it to others, they could do so. In fact, he might send anyone who pestered him with questions their way, because he, personally, did not ever want to bring it to mind again.

And so it was that he began to tell them his story, seated there around the cold watermelon on the cool, shaded sand.

CHAPTER 9

Guests of the Islamic Republic

"As you know, the Iraqi army penetrated deep into Iranian territory. At the same time, the front was extremely long, and there weren't sufficient forces to cover it all. That was one of the fatal military mistakes that cost thousands their lives. The only thing our government cared about was announcing some victory on T.V., even if those victories were illusory or lacked any real value, things like reaching some mountain summit, descending into some valley, sweeping away an unknown village, or merely crossing an empty desert. The Iranians exploited those advances and surrounded Iraqi units to take huge numbers of captives, while our foolish government continued—"

Tariq interrupted him. "Let me stop you there, Abdullah. I advise you not to speak like this! You know what I mean. We are friends here, and we have complete trust in each other, but take care not to speak like this in front of others. I only say this out of fear for you. You know what I mean."

Abdullah smiled bitterly. "Yes. Yes, I know what you mean. Rest assured that I have no desire to talk about anything with anybody, especially not about this."

"No, no, brother, go on. I only meant to warn you."

"Well! I used the word mistake, but actually, every war is a mistake – no, a crime! As far as I'm concerned, existence itself is a mistake. Or at least, my existence in this world is."

Ibrahim and Tariq exchanged a knowing glance as Abdullah went on.

"Anyway, we realised we were completely surrounded, with bullets and bombs raining down on us from every direction and from the sky above. We were falling one by one in rapid succession, and our ammunition had run out. We realised it was futile – suicidal – to continue the fight as there was no doubt the only result would be our complete annihilation. So we surrendered.

"Legions of Iranians encircled us, swooping down like ravenous lions pouncing on confused rabbits. Firing bullets into the air, into the ground, and into any of us that moved, they raced each other to be the first to lay their hands on us. They beat us and took everything we had, plundering our watches, rings, and wallets, everything in our pockets, and some of our clothes. Some of them traded their boots for the ones on our feet when they saw ours were better. We couldn't have been more terrified, and they couldn't have been more elated. They were celebrating, filling the air with their shouts and cursing at us in Arabic. Some of them took pleasure in kicking us, beating us with their rifle butts, spitting in our faces. I couldn't understand how it was possible for a human being to be that happy just because another human being is terrified and trembling in his grasp. Later, I realised that the cruelty of man is more barbaric than any other creature.

"They forced us to march for hours until we reached their rear lines. There were hundreds of us, though with nearly every step, our number would decrease by one. For the most trifling reasons, or even just for the fun of it, for the insane recklessness of power in the human soul, they would finish off the wounded with a merciless bullet to the head. Otherwise, they would just let them bleed to death, leaving the corpses to lie where they fell.

"Once we arrived, we were arranged in a wide circle. They chose one of us at random and tied his arms to two cars. The cars started driving slowly in opposite directions until the man's body burst apart. Anyone who cried out in protest had the same thing done to him. They repeated this with three or four of us, until some of us began passing out. I've never in my life seen such a horrific way to die.

"They ordered us to sit down, and they came around with water for us to drink. Then their bearded general selected five of us. He ordered the driver of a bulldozer to make a trench in the middle, and they threw the five of them in the trench. Their pleas for mercy would have moved even a heart of stone. They silenced those cries by burying them alive in the dirt. My friend Behnam, a Christian doctor from Qaraqosh, burst into tears. He and I made an effort to stay close to each other throughout all this.

"They wanted this to be a warning, to frighten us more than we already were after everything that had happened since the first shock. And of course, they succeeded. Though we were men, we were more afraid than children – terrified like rats in a flood, worse than a chicken in the jaws of a jackal. I knew deep down I was a dead man: it was only a matter of time. That's why the humiliations, the beatings, the hunger and the torture no longer mattered to me. I considered myself a man condemned, with an indefinite stay of execution. All the pain I endured, and each additional hour of life that I won by means of it, was only a further annoyance. None of it was real, as I saw it. The whole affair was only the nightmare of a restless night. Any moment, it would end in a deep sleep, and I would finally rest.

"They tied our hands behind our backs and blindfolded us. Then they loaded us in military trucks to be transported. When they pulled the blindfolds off our eyes, we found ourselves in a city, parading down a wide street in a convoy. People were crowded on the sidewalk and looked down from balconies, windows and rooftops. They were cheering and pelting us with rocks, empty bottles, knives, shoes, rotten eggs, bags of garbage, and whatever refuse they had at hand. Some of the truck windows broke and many of us were injured. The filth splattered us, and our blood flowed in the truck beds. Some of us were dripping blood onto the street.

"They brought us to a military base outside the city. They offered us pieces of dry bread and a few mouthfuls of water. Then they sat us down under a large shelter with a tin roof. Up in front was a wide, raised platform, covered with carpets, chairs, banners and microphones. After a while, a group of men mounted it. In the middle was a bearded man wearing a turban, whom we recognised as the man in charge, while the others were assistants, guards and his entourage. We were told he was the Director General of Internal Security. He greeted us and began to address us in a calm, relaxing voice, with words of welcome and reassurance.

"'Welcome!' he said. 'Be welcome among your brothers! We know that you were forced to fight us. We here do not consider you captives or even call you by that name. Rather, you are the guests of the Islamic Republic, and you will be treated according to the principles and morals of our glorious revolution.'

"He went on at great length in this reassuring manner. So when he stopped and indicated that whoever had a question should ask it, one of us naively took it upon himself to raise a complaint. 'Sir, do you know how many of us were killed without cause between the time we were taken prisoner and now? Why, when we do not treat our prisoners like that?'

"Suddenly, the features and tone of the man in the turban changed entirely, and he began to yell furiously, his beard shaking with thundering emotion until the amplifiers screeched and whistled: 'Silence, you insect! You dog, you unbelieving godless pig! You have a lying tongue and it deserves to be cut out!' Without warning, guards violently picked the man up over our heads and dragged him away. We never saw him again.

"The next morning, they transported us to Tehran in a train with the shades lowered and taped shut. They brought us to a big camp called Takhti Stadium, which originally had been a sports ground named after one of their famous boxers. There, they divided us up and put us in various large halls. They gave us each a blanket, a bowl, sandals and a special prisoner's uniform. Despite the size of the rooms, they were not big enough for the great number of people – a hundred or more – they put in each one.

"There was one toilet stall in the far corner. Unfortunately, after all the pushing and shoving, Dr Behnam and I ended up in front of the toilet door, meaning we were forced to inhale the odour of noisy farts and the nonstop splattering of shit. Sometimes in the middle of the night, people would trip over our feet as they made their way to the toilet in the dark. We clung to each other as we slept, with one of our blankets covering us and the other spread down on the ground to ward off the damp.

"After a few days, we noticed some unfamiliar faces among us. They were Iraqis, like us, and they acted like prisoners, but there were small things that were different. They wouldn't reveal the names of their division, their brigade, or sometimes even their battalions, and they didn't recognise the names of our generals or know about other matters inside Iraq. We realised they were people the Iraqi government had previously expelled on the pretext that they were of Iranian descent and must be Iranian sympathisers. Since the first day, these exiles had been slipped in among us as spies to distinguish officers from soldiers, discover our military specialities, which province, religion, or sect we belonged to, who held a position of authority or supported the ruling party, and gather any information they could about the military and society in general. After we'd identified them, we spread the word in whispers amongst ourselves, taking care to avoid interacting with them.

"They sent us men from the security forces, the secret police, and the religious government, as well as those we called the 'zealots', who lectured us daily. Among them was a fat creature named Abu Zulfa, who told us, 'I bring you good news! The war will only end with the liberation of Iraq, when we free the final resting places of our holy imams from your grasp, you infidel dogs. Then, at last, they will be in the hands of true believers. For as you know, there can be no peace with the tyrants that rule you.'

"After that, they began dividing us up and setting us apart based on the districts where we were born, our religious affiliations, and our views on such things as the war and the regimes in Iraq and Iran. We tried to avoid talking about anything related to politics or religion, but they were relentless. There was another inspection, and they tore up every photograph they found, whether of relatives or friends, or sights within Iraq, even just pictures of the bank of a river, a palm tree, an ancient building, or a statue.

"I asked my friend, Dr Behnam, to teach me about Christianity because I had claimed to be a Christian like him in order to save myself from their examinations. For his part, Behnam wasn't devout, but he taught me some of the general principles he knew. They grouped us with the unbelievers. The pressure on us was lighter than on the others in the beginning, but they quickly began to torture us like the rest and force us to utter the two professions of faith, to conduct the ritual prayers, to memorise the Qur'an, to pray for the ayatollah of their revolution, and to repeat the slogans of their republic, in the hope that we would eventually convert.

"They isolated us completely from the outside world. No radio, no T.V., no newspapers. Instead they brought us more and more religious books and pamphlets written by their ayatollah until they had established a private library inside the camp.

"The camp was widely known as 'the Cage'. I would have preferred something different, since a cage implied that we were animals. I have become convinced, however, that man's evil, bestial nature far outweighs his humanity. Deep down, every man hides a primitive wild animal, kept in check by society. But that animal escapes as soon as some emergency weakens the warden – like a power cut, for instance, or the chaos of war.

"They would count us at the first light of dawn, something they repeated four times a day. Under the supervision of those whom they called 'evangelists', they forced us to attend lectures, prayers and readings of religious books. These evangelists were religious men who came from Iran, Iraq, Pakistan, Lebanon, the Gulf and Afghanistan, and would scourge us every day with their sermons, their fables and their stories and names from the past until we began to know them by heart. They showered the most glorious praise upon the Iranian regime and, by contrast, cast the dirtiest insults and curses upon ours. They would also broadcast these things on the camp's loudspeakers.

"Abu Zulfa visited us most often, and one evening, after we returned to the hall from one of his lectures, Behnam whispered a grumbled complaint in my ear. 'My God, brother! They are killing us with this . . . this glorified dickhead.' That made me laugh, and I somehow managed a riposte. 'With his beard and turban, he actually looks like your uncircumcised penis!' We burst out laughing until everyone in the hall turned to look at us. That was the first laughter to escape any of our lips since we had become prisoners.

"After that, we began to see more smiles and hear more laughter, more sarcastic comments. That first laugh was like a revelation – it spread an air of relaxation and eased the weight of our oppression. We – Behnam and I, that is – would look at each other and smile every time Abu Zulfa was mentioned. Don't be offended, Tariq! We were referring specifically to this Abu Zulfa and not any other bearded man wearing a turban.

"Behnam took the sermons seriously and read with real intellectual curiosity. At night he would whisper to me his doubts and his critiques of what he had read during the day. He would talk to me and ask me questions since he didn't dare reveal his thoughts to the teachers. One of the things I remember him saying was, 'They have created an entire religion based upon historical events and things that took place after the Prophet delivered his message and died. It's history and not a religion, brother. If you separate everything that is actually religion from what is history, all these books and theses of theirs burst like a bubble.' I replied, 'You did that with Christianity too.' He thought for a while and agreed. 'Yes, you're right. It seems that all religions are like that.'

"I, on the other hand, read differently. To be more precise, I didn't read in any real sense of the word. I would stare for hours at the shapes of letters and words, contemplating these strange and astonishing symbols that spoke in silence. I would imitate them. I would imitate the books, the writing and the letters by speaking in silence. I would think of who had created them, how and when, where his bones now lay, and what meaning they had for him. I imagined the worker who arranged the letters in the printing press; I imagined his family situation, his anxieties, how his boss made him suffer. I thought about the paper: how it became paper, what tree it was from and what kind of life that tree had, what shade it gave, which sparrows visited it, the weather it had endured. What I mean is that things like this would stray into my mind while reading. And when I actually did read, I would turn the pages searching for words and expressions that were new, strong and solid in their composition. I took more interest in contemplating the beauty of their rhetoric, their sound and style, than in discerning their meaning. I used that to strengthen my abilities with language in order to communicate with myself more effectively.

"They forced us – even the Christians – to take part in the ritual of weeping, pounding our chests, and slashing our foreheads during the festival of Ashura. Of course, as a way of applying pressure, they withheld food, water, sleep, cigarettes and all of life's daily pleasures from those of us who refused to accept their theory of the imam's absolute leadership. We got used to that deprivation.

"Those who responded positively got the lion's share of food and drink and were treated better – rewarded with additional cigarettes and blankets. They even began putting them in charge of tasks inside the halls and the camp, such as food distribution, managing the library, organising the ritual washing and prayers, keeping lines orderly, and taking charge of the halls, as well as acting as intermediaries between prisoners and the guards and camp administration. These people were classified into ranks. Some of them were called 'guides', and above them were the 'guides superior', followed by '*dazban*', whatever that meant. Little by little, they were given a mandate to exercise the captor's power over the prisoners, and before you knew it, they had authority within the camp – some of them even took on the role of evangelist itself.

"As for all the rest, they were the 'misguided', the secularists, the unbelievers, and the partisans of our regime's infidel ideology, even if they fasted and prayed, lining up to face Mecca just like the others. A torrential flood of propaganda came our way about the snow-white purity of the Iranian people, depicting Iranian society as the utopia that poets, philosophers and prophets had dreamed of. They formed the ideal city, the model for correctly executing divine law.

"Every evangelist in the camp would be surrounded by a group of hypocrites, sidling up and seeking something for himself. They conveyed information to our captors about all our movements and our whispered conversations.

"Meanwhile, they were starving and tormenting us, mentally and physically, using our fear and our desire. I was sometimes forced to wash someone's socks or underwear for the sake of a few cigarettes. The punishment for anyone who resisted became progressively worse. They would make us stand barefoot on hot rocks under the summer sun, and during the winter we'd stand out in the snow. Or they would dunk us in cold water, beat us with canes, starve us, make us crawl over concrete on our hands and knees, put us in solitary confinement and lash us with whips and electrical wires. This was on top of the shameful relentless insults. I can't tell you how many of us died under that torture!

"At the same time, they were forming a sort of regime among their new prison followers, calling these groups the 'penitents'. These people were permitted to rule over us, and they became even more cruel and violent towards us than the Iranians themselves. The penitents were allowed to leave the camp, take part in public celebrations, attend Friday prayers in the nearby prayer halls or at the mosque, and to meet with important figures in authority. Visits to the religious mausoleums were organised for them.

"These people began to erase their past lives and enter a new one. One example was a young man named Majid, from Karbala, who did not waver even when it came to punishing his own father, who was imprisoned with him. As Majid put it, 'I want only the best for him, but he insists on the path of disobedience.' With my own eyes, I saw Majid twist his father's ears and then use pliers to crush them, ignoring his screams of pain.

"Some of them were more fanatically committed to the theory of the Guardianship of the Jurist than the Iranians were. They denied their past entirely, creating in themselves a personal history that was more in line with what they now believed and the purity of their new ideas. They planted in their souls a seed of hate for their original country and everything connected to it. You would see them refer to the toilet as Baghdad – farts were the national anthem and dirty sandals the Iraqi flag. Some of them became obsessed with everything Iranian, even the air, the cats, the dogs, the trees, the flies and the rubbish bins.

"They would go out for intensive training sessions at the Varamin Camp, to the south of Tehran. This camp was overseen by a converted officer named Ahmad Abd al-Amir, who would observe everyone's behaviour to be sure of the sincerity of their conversion. Afterwards, they would be sent to the front line, and in this way, some of them took part in battles such as Haji Homaran, Halabja and al-Faw."

"In all of history, there's never been anything like it!" said Tariq.

"On the contrary, this has been going on every day since the time of Adam and his two sons."

"I mean a huge brainwashing operation like this, such that prisoners would go on to fight against their own country."

Ibrahim broke in. "I know Tariq, Abdullah. What he means is that he has been reading more history than anything else lately. Don't pay any attention to him. Continue your story, I beg you!"

CHAPTER 10

Death Rock

"Some of the penitents who were successful at putting pressure on the rest of the prisoners were transferred to other camps where there was greater resistance. They called this transfer a 'conquest mission'. Those of us who had not converted were expelled to camps with worse buildings, worse facilities, and more cruelty.

"As for me and Dr Behnam, our lot was Fort Samnan, a camp surrounded by barbed wire in a valley rich in iron deposits. The surrounding landscape was completely bare, desolate. We didn't see even one tree. There were no birds in the sky, and no animals, just spiders, spiny lizards, scorpions, snakes and strange insects. Every now and then at night, we would hear the howls of distant wolves echoing through the mountains around us.

"They split us up, eight to a tent. We were crammed so tight that it was hard to sleep. On hot nights, we'd sleep half outside the tent, while on cold nights, we'd huddle together so close we were almost embracing each other. Whenever the food supplies were delivered late – which was most of the time – our meals would consist of a single spoonful of rice. Or else they would gather up any grass or plants they found growing in the cracks between the rocks and boil it with a little oil, salt and onion to make a strange soup that made our intestines run with diarrhoea until we got used to it. We rejoiced when spring came because we found a variety of plants, some of which we recognised, whereas in summer and winter we were wracked with hunger. The best part about being there was that we were further from the daily observation of the Iranian secret police and the exiles from Iraq, some of whom had been appointed officers.

"The commander at the camp was named Faraj Allah, 'God's Delight'. This officer was heartless. He had spent his entire life, ever since the time of the Shah, working in prison administration. When conditions deteriorated to a hellish degree that could not be endured, we asked for a visit from the International Red Cross, but they refused, calling it an infidel organisation. They also didn't want the name and number of each prisoner to be recorded because that would make them responsible for us later on.

"One day, when we realised they would keep killing more of us so long as no-one had a record of who was there, we informed Faraj Allah that we wouldn't cooperate or receive more visits from the secret police or the evangelists until a Red Cross delegation came to see us. We kept refusing and went on to stage a demonstration. They put it down by sending squads of soldiers into the camp. We fought back with rocks, tent stakes, and our bare hands. They killed some of us and wounded many more. Faraj Allah warned us he would execute whoever did not obey his commands, and he ordered everyone who participated in the demonstrations to be punished. They tied our arms and legs to bedposts and beat us with whips and canes, or with rough electrical wires that were stripped at the end and separated into four copper claws. The blows would number somewhere between eighty and a hundred, but the person being beaten would faint after the twentieth, blood oozing from his back. They beat us in front of the other prisoners to teach them a lesson.

"Of course, our conditions didn't improve. On the contrary, things got worse. Ah! I hate even to recall the details of that ordeal. Illness and disease broke out. They continued the transfers, taking some of us to other camps and bringing in new prisoners. These transfers were a way for us to get some news, hear stories, and learn the names of the other camps and what they were like. We learned there were camps in the Khorasan Mountains, and that the worst by far was called *Bast Sank* or *Sanke Bast*, which means 'Death Rock'.

"Death Rock was a legendary underground prison. Those who entered its depths never saw the sun. Its prisoners were tortured with the most brutal techniques imaginable. Fingernails and teeth ripped out, limbs and genitals crushed. They also tormented them psychologically, even as deliberate neglect caused illnesses to fester and allowed scabies to eat away their skin. Abu Jamal al-Baghdadi, who was transferred to our camp, told us about that. He had been taken captive in the district of Shush in March 1982. Abu Jamal said, 'It truly is a rock of death – a well, a tunnel descending to the netherworld, a gate to hell.'

"Meanwhile, other prisoners told us about other camps, such as Warak Makhsus, Barnadak, al-Dawudiyya, Karkan, Manjil, Sari, the Palace of Fayruza, Barujund, Camp Hashmateh and Dazban. There was also Camp Jirjan, which is the one that the Red Cross wanted to inspect. The Iranians hurriedly exchanged the prisoners there with ones loyal to Iran, and the Red Cross delegation was surprised to find that they refused to receive them. When the delegation finally did enter the camp, a violent quarrel erupted between the prisoners. Shots were fired, killing some prisoners and wounding two members of the delegation. The Red Cross called on the United Nations to form a committee to investigate the facts. After this – but before the investigatory committee arrived – the prisoners were swapped with others to hide what had happened.

"Our second demonstration – staged four years after the first – was larger. They responded with bullets and killed Diyah, Ali, Nayif, Yaacob, Zankana and poor Abu Majid from Karbala, who had become old and feeble. As for the wounded, we treated them in our special way. Dr Behnam extracted the bullets with a spoon, and he was forced to stitch the wounds with a needle we used to patch our clothes and with threads that we pulled from our nylon socks. They denied us food and water for three days. That's when the officer Faraj Allah returned from his holiday. He ordered that the camp be surrounded and for them to open fire on us with rubber bullets while he yelled over the loudspeaker, 'You unbelievers! You will die here like dogs! Know that instructions have been sent down to us to reduce your numbers by twenty-five per cent!'

"They prevented us from going to the toilets. We couldn't even leave the tents to relieve ourselves on the ground outside. People were fainting out of hunger, thirst and exhaustion. On the fourth day, soldiers attacked. They beat us mercilessly with clubs.

They broke two of my ribs, and . . . and they killed Behnam. Dr Behnam, my friend."

Abdullah fell silent and bent his head as his throat tightened up. Tears came to Ibrahim's eyes, and Tariq murmured words of consolation and religious piety. The silence lasted so long they thought Abdullah was not going to resume speaking, but after a while, he took a piece of watermelon to moisten his throat. Then he lit a new cigarette, taking a deep drag through it as though he had not been smoking the whole time. He continued:

"After Behnam's murder, the weight of my captivity doubled, and my inner death deepened. My spirit dispensed with speaking and listening – with everything – and I began to isolate myself. I wouldn't sleep for days on end, and at other times I would sleep like a dead man. I didn't join anybody in anything. I didn't pay attention to what went on around me – nothing could hold my interest. It was as though I was sealed inside a stone coffin. I shared a smile, a sorrow, or a word with no man. It was as though I had lost all perception, such that at times they would call *me* Death Rock."

Then, with a playful turn, Abdullah remarked, "Of course, Tariq, they were unaware of the name you had given me, Kafka." Abdullah's companions smiled at that. Tariq put a hand on his shoulder and then embraced him. Abdullah went on:

"Behnam was the only one who ever called me by that name, for he knew Kafka. He had read his works and read about his life, and he would talk to me about him sometimes, so much that I liked Kafka more through Behnam's words."

"They say Iran is a beautiful country."

"So they say. The views I had of its landscapes truly were beautiful."

"They say its women are very beautiful."

"I wouldn't know. I did not see any woman, not even a picture of a woman, for nineteen years."

Abdullah had trouble getting these words out. Ibrahim sensed his distress and said, "Let that go, Tariq. Can't you leave your jokes out of it, at least when we are talking about such tragic things? Well, what else, Abdullah?"

"Some of us read the Qur'an intensively, conducted the prayers, and called upon God to bring a visit from the Red Cross. And in fact, a delegation came to us. Among its members I remember there was a Swiss doctor and a number of psychologists. The delegation had a private plane, and its pilot was blessed with diplomatic immunity that allowed him to land in any camp he wished. We heard the plane's descent without any warning. Trills and shouts of joy rang out as prisoners called the good news to one another. The delegation entered the camp, and we received it with the best welcome we could put together, which they were not expecting. There were some among us who spoke English, so we informed the committee what had happened to us. We told them the number and names of those who had been killed – with bullets, with clubs, under torture, or due to illness.

"When the Iranian escorts tried to enter, the head of the delegation – the Swiss officer – asked all of them to leave, and they left! We felt a wonderful moment of freedom, and like children gathered in front of a father who has just returned from a journey, we began vying with each other to recount the details. One of the things they told us was that the Iranians had informed them that this camp was reserved for the mentally ill. We quickly wrote our testimony for the delegation, using the time and paper available. Then we presented them with a video recording that we had filmed with the cooperation of one of the Iranian guards who resented the regime. He was from the province of Khuzestan, and the government had executed his father. He secured a small camera for us, and we used it to film many scenes of torture, and even some shots of solitary confinement. The delegation was astonished. Actually, they had a significant amount of detailed information about our camp, and as soon as they entered they asked about some prisoners by name, including Dr Behnam, Sami and Hamza Azuz and Professor Salim al-Wahib. They recorded each of our names and told us to write letters, as brief as possible, to our families and loved ones. That was when I sent you that single letter. The officer heading the delegation said to us, 'I want to go to the prison they call Death Rock. Where is it located?' Abu Jamal al-Baghdadi and others who knew gave him the information.

"At the end of the visit, we conveyed to the delegation the punishment we would receive after they left. They only nodded their heads as a sign that they expected that. And in the final moments, some of us told the delegation, crying, 'Greet our beloved Iraq on our behalf! Kiss every grain of its dirt for us!'

"I didn't say a thing, and I didn't kiss the ground or the flag even when we returned, as the others did. I saw through everything, and I thought how strange were the fanatical commitments people feel towards ideas or things that others create to control them, even to the point of dying or killing for its sake. When I look at the flag of any country, I see nothing more than a scrap of cloth devoid of any colour or meaning. In Iran, the streets were filled with pictures of their leader. Here too. Both sides claim the truth and the right, and they both try to cram the heads of the unfortunate masses with these ideas – or else they cut them off. How is it that a person is not satisfied with what occupies his own head, such that he strives to take possession of others'?

"There are so many things I wonder about. Where do the pains of torture go after the torture ceases? And what exactly is the stuff of torment and suffering? What does the executioner think about in his quiet hours? What is the meaning of all this pain? Why? What does the killer think when he remembers his victims? How can people put so much effort into all these atrocities just because someone else holds a different opinion?"

"What befell the penitents afterwards?"

"Their fates were varied. Some were killed and buried along the front, or in the cemeteries of Qom, Mashhad, or Zahra's Paradise. After the ceasefire, a number of them went out to integrate into Iranian life. Some went to the countryside to marry village women and find work. They were granted refugee I.D. cards. Some of them bore children and settled in Iran, abandoning their past for good. Some of them remained deep in the mire of politics, moving about among the ranks of the opposition with a practised opportunism. Some of them entered Iraq in 1991 after the Iraqi army collapsed in Kuwait. A group of the penitents contacted the U.N., using their Red Cross numbers, and they acquired asylum in other countries. There were some who wanted to rid themselves of the heritage of their 'penitence', and they organised a private escape to different countries around the world, where they put forward petitions for asylum as Iraqis. And some of them continue to this day working as organisers, politicians and military men on behalf of Iran."

"Are there still prisoners, even now?"

"Yes."

"Did many return with you?"

"There were nearly three hundred in our group, most of whom were considered missing in action. We were handed over at the Muntheria border crossing. The guards were lined up on both sides, each carrying their country's flag. The Iraqis clapped and cheered as we made our way with slow, halting steps. Some of our families were there to receive us with tears and trills of joy after two nights waiting out in the open. Some prisoners were seeing their children for the first time. One member of our group had been captured in the third year of the war, two weeks after his honeymoon, and the reception he had from his wife and daughter was deeply moving.

"In order to give a different picture of how they had treated us, the Iranians made a big show in front of the journalists by having some of their officers carry disabled prisoners when handing them over to their Iraqi counterparts. But actually, all of us were suffering from some malady. Some of us had lost our sense of hearing. Others had lost an eye or had gone blind. Some of us had tuberculosis, others cancer, others had scabies, while others had inflamed bowels, and so on. Apart from the two broken ribs, I have a chronic slipped disc in my back.

"The Iraqis gave us a pile of money, fifty thousand dinars, saying that it was a gift from the exalted president. Some of us were overjoyed, thinking we had become rich since – the last we knew – dinars were each worth more than three dollars. We were quickly disappointed when we realised the magnitude of the devastation that had befallen the country and saw that the scales had shifted, so much so that a single dollar now buys more than a thousand dinars. I immediately spent a quarter of what I received on cigarettes.

"The Iranians gave each of us a small prayer mat and a pair of shoes. The shoes are for you, Ibrahim, and the mat is for you, Tariq. For as you know, I don't accept any gifts."

"Your safe return to us is the only gift we need," Ibrahim said. "And your being in better shape than many who came back. Some of them burst into tears merely at being reminded of their years in captivity. Do you remember the crazy man with the beard you asked us about? That was Sabry, son of Hajji Rada. They brought his parents a charred and disfigured body, saying that it was their son. The family buried it and conducted the funeral rites. After a time, one of his brothers married his widow to preserve her and his nephews. Suddenly, after fifteen years, Sabry came back to them. His brother couldn't bear the situation and killed himself. As for Sabry, the poor guy, when he learned what had happened, the shock made him lose his mind."

Tariq said, "A cousin of a friend of mine from Hamam al-Alil was a fighter pilot. His plane was shot down in Iran at the end of 1981. No news about him reached his family, and he was classified as missing in action for a long period. But in 1998, information reached us that he was a prisoner. Imagine, after seventeen years! A year later, he was released to us. The unfortunate man did not live much longer. He came down with tuberculosis and died two months after arriving. Some people say they had jabbed him with thallium."

They went on telling him stories about many prisoners who had returned with the hope of showing him that he came out better than they had, but Abdullah asked them to stop, seeing as he knew and had lived through things yet more cruel and horrible. At that, Tariq said, "Let's go, then. I told my wife to prepare a special lunch of sand grouse. Do you remember the days we would hunt and grill them out in the desert?"

CHAPTER 11

The Sea Urchin

Abdullah was not able to sleep even though it was his second night in the village. He needed more time to adjust to his new situation. He did not sleep the third night either, since every time the pressure bore him down and he nodded off, he saw whips flying at him and would jolt awake, sometimes even leaping to his feet, thinking he had to get out to the morning prisoner count. Or he would feel Behnam's elbow jabbing him in the ribs.

As soon as he realised he was at home and not in the Cage, he would immediately splash cold water over his face and hair. He would open the windows and doors and start smoking, preferring not to sleep over seeing images from the past years in his dreams. He decided to remain in the house for as long as it took to get used to it. He would find himself dozing off at noon even though the door and windows were open and a bright light shone into the room. So he decided to embrace his ability to sleep during the day and not at night. That is how he started staying up late in the village café until it closed its door after midnight.

On the morning of the third day, someone knocked on the door. Then he heard Ibrahim calling him, and he shouted back, "The door's open!"

"Yes, I see the door's open!"

"So come in then!"

When Ibrahim entered, Abdullah asked, "Can I make you tea?"

Ibrahim said, "No. I brought the farmer who will put your land to work. I advised him that half would go to him, and half to you. Does that suit you?"

"Yes, yes, certainly. But enough! You make the arrangements with him as you see fit, and I will agree."

"He's an excellent and hard-working young man, of good character. You can put your trust in him entirely. He also needs this work in order to provide for his siblings. He is Anwar, the son of poor Sabry. You know Sabry, the crazy prisoner you saw."

"Ah, yes, Sabry." Abdullah was silent for a moment, then added, "Yes, yes, enough! I told you I agree."

"But don't you want to see him?"

"There's no need for that as long as you've arranged everything with him."

"You have to see him, at least so that you'll know who he is. He may need to ask your opinion on something in the future, or else bring you your share. He's here."

"Here?"

"Yes, in the courtyard."

"Why didn't he come in with you?"

"He's shy. You go out to him."

Abdullah went out and saw a young man in the middle of the courtyard, perhaps eighteen or a little older, tall and thin, with his head down and hands clasped in front of him. Abdullah greeted him. The youth hastened to come a few steps forward and timidly shook Abdullah's hand, saying, "Hello, uncle!"

Abdullah said, "Welcome! Please come in and drink tea with us. Come in! And there's no need for you to call me uncle. Call me Abdullah, or address me with 'O Kafka' and nothing else."

The young man came in and sat on the edge of the rug beside Ibrahim. Abdullah offered him a cigarette, but he said, "I don't smoke."

Abdullah felt a liking for the young man and sought to discern from his features – though his glances were mostly directed at the floor – the magnitude of his dejection. He went out to prepare the tea, and when he brought it back, he noticed the remarkable harmony between Anwar and Ibrahim, as though Anwar were his son. Indeed, he even sensed a similarity between them. They seemed to understand each other, united by a contented submission to fate.

In this way, his confidence in the youth deepened greatly, and as he offered him a glass of tea, Abdullah said, "Are you satisfied with what Abu Qisma has told you? Regarding your share, I mean?"

He said, "Yes, if you also agree."

"I agree. And you are completely free in what you do and what you plant. How many siblings do you have?"

"Seven."

"And you are the eldest?"

"Yes."

Later on, when the young man had left, Ibrahim said, "Just he and one sister are Sabry's children. As for the other six, they are from his uncle who married his mother, the uncle who killed himself, poor man."

Later that day, not long after noon, Abdullah was reclining in the living room alone. He had finished what remained of the cold tea and lit a cigarette. He was waiting for sleep to overtake him, even if just for a little, but thoughts of Sameeha kept him awake. He was still thinking about her just as he had through all the years of captivity, when he never once fell asleep without recalling her face or woke without her being the first thing on his mind.

Abdullah thought about how he had not shared with Ibrahim and Tariq the thing that most occupied him during those long stretches of time. He did not explain that for most of the hours he had spent in captivity, he had replayed over and over, without ever growing tired of it, the details of each memory with Sameeha: her smile, her glances, her smell, her voice, the touch of her hand, her embrace, her kiss – which had been the only kiss of his entire life. He did not tell them that it was only the memory of her that had kept him alive. After young Anwar had left and Abdullah was alone again with Ibrahim, he wished to ask: Had she come with the others on the night of the homecoming party? Was she here, and I didn't recognise her, Ibrahim?

Suddenly, he heard someone knocking on the door. He started up to a seated position, swallowed, and said, "Come in!"

After a moment of silence, the same soft knocks were repeated. He said in a louder voice, "Come in! The door's open."

But there was another period of silence, and afterwards, the same knocks yet again. Abdullah got up. He found a child of about ten years old standing there, twisting his fingers together nervously. "Who are you?" he asked.

"I am Samir. Grandmother says, 'Come and have lunch with us.'"

"And who is your grandmother?"

"Zaynab."

Then Abdullah remembered his agreement with her, recalling that this child had been her guide to his house and had sat beside her.

"Now?"

"Yes, now. We have killed a chicken for you, and my mother cooked it with okra and tomatoes."

"Fine. Wait one moment."

"And garlic too. My grandmother loves garlic. But I don't like it."

Abdullah went inside to adjust his clothes. He washed his face, combed his beard in front of the mirror, and put two packs of cigarettes in his pocket. Then he went out. He began walking beside the boy in streets covered with smooth stones, hearing their crunch under his feet. He looked at the houses on both sides. Only a few of the mud houses remained, and in their place, many concrete ones had been constructed, some on top of the foundations of earlier mud houses, and others beside them, or even butting up against them to form an integrated unit. Of the homes he had known, only a few remained.

The child outpaced him by a few steps sometimes, and for a moment Abdullah wanted to take him by the hand and be guided like Zaynab. How would the child's hand feel? What would it be like to walk hand in hand with him? But he quickly put away that thought and tried to fill the silence with questions to keep the young boy from getting too far ahead.

"You told me you don't like garlic?"

"I don't like it except when it's cooked."

"Me neither. What is your name?"

"Samir."

"Is your father at home too?"

"No."

"Where does he work?"

"In the oil refinery in Baiji."

Abdullah could not think of any other questions, so he resumed his silence and contented himself with the sound of the crunching stones and with looking around. In the end, they entered a wide-open space that he recognised immediately as the grounds of the mayor's house. The big eucalyptus tree still stood in the middle. A trellis covered in grapevines circled around it, casting shade on a huge water cistern made of clay. The livestock corral was in the far corner, behind a new plough attached to a big tractor. So, they still had a tractor. Next to the corral was the house of Isma'il the herdsman, just as it had been, one room with mud walls. In the other corner, he recognised the storerooms for crops, where the mayor used to conduct business. He saw the large scales in their familiar place, even more rusty than before. In the centre was the balcony of the house, the wide entrance, and the big doors, which had been painted blue – he remembered them being grey. To the side was the door leading to the reception room – what they used to call the divan.

Abdullah saw a number of boys and a woman coming out to receive him. Hajja Zaynab appeared in the door to the divan, leaning on her cane and calling out a loud welcome. She looked like bliss incarnate, and she squeezed his neck tightly, just as she had done on the first night. Zaynab led Abdullah into the divan, which he found more luxurious than he remembered. There were expensive chairs and couches lined up along three of the walls, with magnificent carpets and many pillows spread out in front of them on the floor.

On the wall facing the door hung a large black-and-white picture of the mayor. It had been taken in his youth and showed his thick moustache as a deep black. Below the picture were two crossed swords and, between them, a shield with three shining silver studs sticking out like flowers.

Without removing her arm from his as she walked slowly beside him, Hajja Zaynab said, "Sit on the couch, if you'd like. But I prefer to sit on the rug, and I'd like you to sit with me."

So he did, saying that he too was accustomed only to sitting on the floor. She sat beside him and reached out her hand, searching for his face. Her fingers read the details of his features and in the end she said, "You haven't shaved your beard yet? Perhaps you would look younger and more attractive without it. Oh well, whatever makes you happy! That's the important thing. By the way, I know a little Persian from my childhood days in Kurdistan. But maybe it's better to forget all that."

Abdullah could not recall having eaten a more delicious meal in his entire life than the one he had there. As a result, he ate with an appetite he did not know he had, going from dishes of rice with almonds and raisins to grape leaves stuffed with okra, tomatoes and garlic cloves, from pieces of grilled chicken to salad and milk in a clay jar. After that, they brought him several glasses of cardamom tea, which combined with the smoke of his cigarettes to make him feel more pure than he ever had before.

Grandmother Zaynab asked him whether he was bound by any appointments or had any work to do that evening, and when he said no, she said, "In that case, we need a car to carry us up to the cemetery."

Without asking her why, Abdullah said, "We can send one of the children to Tariq. He wouldn't be slow in coming."

"No," she said. "We need someone else."

She fell silent for a little. She called one of the boys, telling him to go to their neighbour Abu Muhammad and ask him to bring his car because his grandmother needed it for an errand. After a few minutes, they heard a car horn honking in the courtyard, and she said to the children, "Invite him to get out and have some tea with us."

Abu Muhammad entered and shook hands with Abdullah. He kissed the head of Hajja Zaynab and sat next to her. As he sipped his tea, Zaynab told him, "We want you to take us to the cemetery, just me and Abdullah. You'll leave us there and then come back for us when the sun sets."

When they got out of the car and were alone, Abdullah looked around while Zaynab leaned mute on his arm. In her wisdom, she understood the need for silence in a moment like this. It was as though she saw Abdullah as he gazed in every direction from that distant elevation: the hilltop, the slopes, the valley, the horizon, the fields, the sky, the village. Scenes from his childhood as a boy, playing in these spots, passed through his mind. He knew every stone and tree here. He did not know what to think about this thing or that, or whether any of it had any real value or not. When Abdullah noticed how long he had been standing there without a word, he said, "The cemetery has got very big."

The old woman replied, "Yes – the village too. The dead multiply and so do the living. I don't know why God created so many people! Wouldn't half as many have been enough? The Most High has his wise reasons."

She fell quiet, and then, to break him out of his silence, she resumed speaking conversationally: "Me, I know more of the dead than I do the living. All of them have gone. Only Umm Ibrahim and I are left. As though I were a foreigner, a visitor among the living."

Abdullah said, "The cemetery is many times as large as when I last saw it. It covers nearly the entire hill."

"Yes. That's why they think it necessary to start a new cemetery for the village. They agreed on the big hill on the east side, but up until now, no-one has wanted to bury departed loved ones alone up there, saying they want them to be with the rest of the family. So I volunteered to be the first. I told them to bury me there. Just between ourselves, I don't want to be in the same place as the mayor in death having shared a home with him in life."

Her tone as she uttered this last sentence dripped with contempt. Then she became serious again and said, "And now, do you recognise the old cemetery? Do you see it?"

"It's the part over there, in the middle of the hilltop."

"Do you see the sea-urchin tree? Do you remember it?"

"Yes. It too has got much bigger."

"Take me to it."

No-one knew exactly who had named it the sea urchin, but that name had become popular early on, even though none of the villagers would have seen the sea in their lives. It was a low, broad tree with thorns, resembling an olive tree. Its leaves were a bright, shiny green all year round. The tree was spiny, but it did not look like any other plant with thorns that they knew. Year after year, it sprouted delicate yellowish pods. Abdullah remembered how they used to suck on the pods when they were young. The flavour was a mix of sweetness and burning acidity, like that of lemons. But when the pods got big, they dried out and fell, scattering their seed – or else they themselves would scatter the seeds. But no other tree like it ever grew, so the sea urchin was always alone, slowly getting bigger.

This tree was one of the most prominent features of the village, and people wove stories and songs around it, because it grew precisely at the head of the grave of the man called "the martyr" because whoever died by drowning was considered a martyr. Young people called him "the martyr of love", and they made covenants of faithfulness to each other there underneath the tree. This man was the father of Isma'il the herdsman. He had raced to his wife Najda, who was washing clothes in the river when a wall of water took her. He tried to save her but instead drowned with her when they were swept away by a wave to the middle of the deep river. Afterwards, they found only his body, which had come to rest between two boulders on the far shore south of the village. They buried him here, and the mayor adopted his two dull-witted children, Isma'il and Zakiya. Some said that this thorn tree growing by his head was an apology from the water for what it had done to the two of them. But others said it was proof that he came from the water people. Perhaps the truth of the matter is that they named it the sea urchin as a memorial to his death by drowning, nothing more. Still others said that it was the soul of his wife, which came from the water and grew here because it did not want to be separated from him. People recalled that the two of them had loved each other deeply, and that their love had a long history.

When they reached the sea urchin, Zaynab said, "Take me to the right side of the martyr's grave. Do you see a difference between the space on the right and the space on the left?"

"Well, maybe a small one. There are some plants on the right side, some stems and traces of dry, broken grass that look like they have been planted here. As for the left, it's like the rest of the ground on the hill, covered in stones."

"Come, sit with me on the right, but not exactly on that planted spot."

He led her a couple of steps, and after he had cleared the ground under her feet of rocks and twigs, they sat down. The leaves of the sea-urchin tree hung down above them like a roof. The tree extended until it covered a quarter of the space above the grave. Its leaves were so thick that its branches were only visible from below.

"Listen to me, my son," she said. "I want you to strengthen

your heart and fortify your faith with certainty in God's wisdom and his will to determine our fate."

He felt the weight of that moment, which went beyond anything he had previously experienced. He stopped looking at the thorn tree, the cemetery, and what was around him, focusing his attention on Zaynab's face and especially her mouth, in which there remained only a few rotted teeth.

"How often I have imagined this moment!" she said. "I have waited for it, and I didn't die because I was waiting for it, waiting for you."

She laid her cane down beside her. She was sitting right up next to him, with her leg resting against his, their knees touching. She reached her hand over towards him, searching for his until she found it. She held it tightly, then she stretched her other hand and spread her fingers on the open space between them and the martyr's grave. "Here lies your mother. Your real mother, who gave birth to you from her womb. This is her grave."

She swallowed and squeezed his hand harder while stroking the ground tenderly with her other hand.

"She was Zakiya, and this martyr is your grandfather, Zakiya's father. Isma'il the herdsman is your uncle."

Of course, she did not expect a comment or question now. She imagined the impact of her words, which had caught him unawares. So she went on speaking herself. And despite the calm of her tone, she appeared like someone yelling. He saw tears flow from her eyes, and he realised that she was pouring out words she had been holding inside for years.

"These people are your family on your mother's side. As for

your father's family, the mayor and I are your grandparents, and your father is my eldest son, Jalal."

Zaynab fell silent. Drops of saliva had appeared on her lips from the wide gaps between what remained of her teeth, and she wiped her mouth with an old handkerchief she took from the pocket of her shawl. She said, "From now on, this matter is entrusted to you alone. It's your secret. Yours. You are free to reveal it to whoever you wish, whenever and however you wish. I've never told it to anyone, nor will I ever do so, except if you ask me to. I will tell you everything, everything I remember, and you can ask me whatever you want. It broke my heart that you didn't know. I used to think that my heart would be made whole when I told you, but now as I'm telling you, I feel it will be shattered all over again."

CHAPTER 12

The Secret of the Scandal that Was Not

There, atop the hill in the middle of the cemetery, under the splendid evergreen sea urchin, the air was clean, and the evening sky was a peaceful blend of white and yellow light. Everything looked beautiful and still in such a light, and from that distance, the walls of the houses in the village looked like faces reflecting it back, with black windows for eyes. The light pierced the diaphanous shadows on the valley slopes. Birds soared in flowing circles, not looking for anything, just playing in space, as though watching and listening to the two of them. Voices of distant herdsmen carried from the green fields below.

The calm of the universe that evening was stunning; even the graves looked beautiful, content and assured. As though life – or the universe itself – were a big tent that paid no heed to what happened in it or what was said, including that which Zaynab spoke of to her grandson Abdullah:

"Your grandfather, the mayor, was a young man when he inherited the position of village elder and mayor following the death of his father, who, in his turn, had been mayor and village elder his entire life. It was said that your grandfather was the first child born here when the village started with three houses in this spot. He inherited vast lands too, along with sheep, cows, the wagon and the plough. And the prestige. He was good at managing all that. He put others to work in his fields and watching over his livestock, while he spent more and more of his time travelling and conducting trade in crops, tobacco and weapons. The Kurds were among those to whom he sold weapons. That's how he got to know me, I got to know him, and we got married. I was a young orphan at the time. Like you, I never knew my parents. My grandmother took charge of bringing up my brother and me until she died. Anyway, the details of my former life are not important. But you can take them as an example, if you like – I too grew up without parents, and now you see how large my family has become!

"When I came here I didn't know a single word of Arabic, nor anything about life except a few household tasks – cooking, baking, sweeping and washing clothes. The mayor had married twice before me, but there hadn't been any children. So our first son was the object of all his love and affection. I was the one who insisted that he be named Jalal, after my brother, who went to fight in the mountains when he grew up and never came back. I was told he was killed there.

"The first people I met in this village were your grandparents, the parents of your mother and her brother, Isma'il. They were young, and never in my entire life have I seen a love like the love they had for each other. The mayor told me they weren't from here and had arrived from a distant village one year earlier. 'We are aliens, seeking sanctuary among you,' they had said, asking protection from the mayor since they were fleeing a tribal difficulty. They had married against the wishes of their families, who were now threatening to kill them.

"The mayor welcomed them and gave them a spot next to the house, where they built a single room out of mud to live in – the room in which Isma'il now lives. Your grandmother was a paragon of beauty! Her name was Latifa, and your grandfather, this martyr of the water, was named Nasir. He was constantly moving and never stopped smiling. He didn't miss a single moment he could be with Latifa. He cared for her and treated her in a way that no woman in the village had experienced. As a result, they provoked jealousy in every other woman and provided a vision for their dreams. The men laughed about Nasir and called him cowed, even if deep down they envied him on account of Latifa's beauty and refinement.

"They were very happy. Nasir worked with the mayor in his fields and herded his livestock. Latifa washed clothes and carpets for the villagers whenever their wives became pregnant or sick. She was older than me and looked after me with patience and affection. She was my first and maybe my only friend. She showed me how to dress in these Arab peasant clothes, and she taught me Arabic. She repeated words to me tirelessly and patiently as though she were a mother.

"They bore twins and named the boy after the mayor, Isma'il, as a way of thanking him. The girl they named Zakiya after Latifa's mother, who Latifa told me was the daughter of an Ottoman pasha who fell in love with a peasant, Latifa's father. Latifa's mother ran away with this peasant and married him. Her father's men kept searching for the two of them until they found them and burned them alive, taking their daughter – Latifa – to her grandfather's palace. I remember her laughing – may she rest in peace – as she told me, 'I've repeated my mother's story. Not on purpose, of course, but for the sake of love. I felt my mother's blood burning inside me. They told me I was very like her, in every way, not least in my stubbornness. Perhaps I also wanted, somehow, to avenge my mother or triumph over the pasha for her.'

"From their birth, Isma'il and Zakiya were very small, like ducklings without their fuzz. They were always sick, and their minds developed slowly. Their parents cared for them day and night, caressing them the way water moves around a bowl when you carry it. They never left them alone and tried to work at different times so that one of them would always be with the two little ones. On the first day they couldn't avoid working at the same time, they left the twins with me. That was the first and last time, since they never returned. How often I recall those moments of parting, as they said goodbye to the two babies in my arms! They would take two steps away and then rush back to gather them to their breasts, smelling them and kissing them. They repeated their detailed instructions to me time and again, as though they were setting off on a distant journey, as though they had some inkling that it would be the last time, though they insisted they'd be no more than a few hours. But they didn't come home, and they never will, not until the Day of Resurrection.

"It's said that Latifa was doing the washing as usual on the shore under the bluffs where Nasir was working in the fields. He would look down at her from atop the steep embankment from time to time, joking with her and singing songs of love. He would frequently sing to her in his melodious voice, strong and sweet and sorrowful, a voice that could make the stones weep. When people asked him to sing at weddings or in some field, he would say, 'I only sing for Latifa, and if you want me to sing, ask her permission and bring her in front of me.' Latifa would give her permission, laughing, and they would bring her to sit in front of him. Then, with all the people listening around, he would sing a song, never taking his eyes off her, and she not taking her eyes off him, as though it were only the two of them. I've seen a woman like that twice, and it is a sight that is impossible for anyone to forget.

"It's said that when he was looking down at her one time, he saw the current pulling her away along with a big carpet, so he jumped down the bluff and threw himself after her, still wearing his clothes and shoes. The water dragged him out to the middle of the fast-flowing river. A sudden wave enveloped them, and it was not ordained that even the closest farmers could do anything to save them.

"Afterwards, they came across his body, but found no trace of her. Undoubtedly, he would have wanted to remain lost with her in the river, in a shared watery grave, or else she would have wanted to be with him. But at least one of them remained behind with their children. Your mother, Zakiya the martyr, clings here to her father, the water martyr, lying in peace. They did well to bury her here. Oh, my sweet child, how they wronged her!

"The two children remained in our care as though they were our own. They were quiet and good, but also slow. They were late in making sounds, learning to walk, their first words, and learning in general, which they didn't do well. They stayed like that, always developing slowly. Isma'il, you know. He's now an old man, and even so, he is more of a child than an adult. God has His reasons for His creation! As soon as he was old enough, Isma'il began going out to help the shepherds, and then he became the shepherd of his own flock. Zakiya helped me with the household chores and was responsible for things like washing her own clothes and her brother's.

"Zakiya was with me in the house most of the time, while Isma'il lived out in the room that had been their parents' house. During the day, Zakiya would go there to clean and tidy things up, and at night she would sleep in the house with us. It went on like that until they reached sixteen or so. I don't remember when exactly, but Zakiya became a fine young woman with a full bosom, and she had much of her mother's beauty. But she sometimes went about all dishevelled, not taking care of her hair or clothes or doing anything to adorn herself. If she hadn't been slow, the men would have fought each other to marry her! I looked after her as best I could – bathing her and changing her clothes – and one day, I suddenly noticed that her belly was bulging. At first, I thought it was normal since she had always been a bit chubby. But after I had observed her closely, and later when I felt her, I realised she was pregnant, maybe even in her third month. I informed the mayor of my suspicions, and he told me, 'Confirm this with her in your own way. You're a woman – you know how to do it.'

"I chose a moment when she was in a good mood and took her away from the children she was playing with in the sand. I always used to tell her, 'You are all grown up now! Don't play with the little children!' But as you know, she was still a child at heart and in her mind, even if she had a woman's body. Anyway, I took her aside and began to ask her questions: 'Has someone been embracing you, some man or boy? Has one of them been touching you here?' – pointing to her breast. 'Have they been doing anything like this, or like this?'

"She hesitated at first. But when I employed a certain amount of compassion and more persuasion, combined with a little pressure, she suddenly surprised me by innocently confessing and describing the pleasure she experienced: 'Oh, yes! Jalal loves my breasts very much. He tells me I'm pretty and uses his tongue to play with my nipples. He says it's a game he likes, and I say I like it too. He says, "Don't ever tell anyone about this – this is our secret, just you and me." He gives me candy and money, and if I refuse, he doesn't give me anything.' 'And does he put his hand here, and does he . . . ?' 'Yes . . . yes . . . yes, oh yes!'

"Oh, what a tragedy has befallen you, Umm Jalal! What a scandal! I ran to the mayor and told him. Dear God! It was as though I were splashing his face with boiling oil. He went crazy and kept asking me if I was sure, which I confirmed. 'Prove it!' he said. 'Give every detail!'

"It was dusk then, just as it is now. Jalal wasn't home. He used to get dressed up and put on his father's cologne to go out for the evening. It was said he had had flings with more than one of the young women in the village – the beautiful ones, that is. That delighted his father's sense of masculinity and made him spoil Jalal all the more. When he came home from his trips, he would always bring Jalal more cologne, clothes and new shoes. He gave Jalal money, spared him every kind of work, and just wanted him to continue his studies. But it would never have occurred to him or to anyone else that Jalal would interfere with poor Zakiya! The two of them were brought up together like siblings! Leaving aside the fact that she didn't look after herself and was a halfwit. Maybe that's precisely what led him to do what he did with her. Who knows! They were adolescents, and God has His reasons for His creation.

"We had a secret room, a cellar or basement – whatever you want to call it – six feet long and six feet wide. The mayor had dug it under our bedroom to hide money and weapons. Never very much, three or four chests, but whatever was valuable and secret. The door leading to it was very small and hidden by a long mirror – I'll show it to you – and no-one ever knew anything about it.

"The mayor waited until everyone was asleep. When it was past midnight, he told me, 'Go to Jalal. Wake him quietly and whisper that I want to talk to him about something important. Then bring him to our bedroom here.'

"I begged him to reason with Jalal and not to hurt him, for I knew the mayor's nature. I said to him, 'He's a child!' He said, 'What kind of child would seduce an innocent girl!' Sparks flashed in his eyes and so much rage burned within him that if he were faced with a ferocious lion at that moment, he could have torn it apart with his bare hands. 'Calm yourself,' he said, but I couldn't. I kept insisting and pleading until he exploded, throwing recriminations in my face, saying it was all the result of the deplorable way I raised my children. He said the responsibility of watching over them and knowing what they were doing fell upon my shoulders since he was usually away. In a moment of rage, the mayor was just like everyone else, casting blame about, usually on the person closest. 'No!' I protested. 'It's because you spoil him!' Of course, it wasn't the time for debating things like that. He ordered me to go, and if I didn't, he would go himself and bring back a handful of Jalal's long hair. The mayor had never liked Jalal's long hair since he didn't consider it manly. However, he let it go seeing as this was a fashion among all the young men at that time.

"When Jalal entered our bedroom, he was rubbing his eyes, half asleep. The mayor closed the door behind us and spoke to Jalal in a voice that was remarkably controlled and calm, though I knew he was suppressing a terrible rage. He said, 'You are my eldest son, and I want to show you something important.' He removed the mirror, which opened up like a door. Behind it was a door made of two thick pieces of iron and wood, followed by stairs leading down below our room to another door of wood and iron. Of course, the boy's drowsiness evaporated when he saw that the mirror was a door and behind the mirror was a locked door. The mayor opened it and said, 'Go in.' Jalal bent his head and entered. I went to follow him, but the mayor pushed me violently back and shut the door behind them. I sat on the bed, sobbing silently.

"Then I remembered he had twenty pistols down there that he intended to take to the Kurds on his next trip. My heart sank – I was sure he would kill Jalal. I hurried over and put my ear to the cellar door. I didn't hear anything that was going on or what they said, of course – it was for that very reason that he made the double set of doors. But the keyholes and the tiny gaps under the door brought me the sound of muffled blows, like a stone falling to the muddy bottom of a deep well. I heard what seemed to be screams, but they seemed far away, as though coming from behind a mountain. I decided I would scream and pound on the door if they were inside for too long. Even if it was only a single minute, it seemed to me an eternity of terror. When the mayor came out, panting and with dishevelled hair, his hands and clothes were stained with blood. I burst into tears. 'You killed him? You killed my boy?' The mayor said, 'If only I had. But I will. I'll kill him, this disgrace of a son.'

"I plunged into the cellar, stumbling and falling down the stairs without really noticing, until I found myself at the bottom beside Jalal. He had lost consciousness and was swimming in his own blood, his clothes torn, with bruises covering his body and blood dripping from his wounds. I held him to me. He was breathing, thank God. I wasn't able to carry him, of course, so I hurried up to bring water and rags – anything to treat him with. I found the mayor washing in a basin and changing his clothes. 'He acknowledged it,' he said. 'He confessed his crime. This disgrace, this bastard!'

"Then he passed me the keys and said, 'Listen. I'm going now to Sheikh Zahir to seek his counsel on the matter. You, wash your son. Even if you washed him in all the seas of the world, it would not be enough to cleanse our shame. And don't you dare tell anyone anything. Don't you dare let him leave! If you do, I'll kill you.'

"Zahir was the mayor's friend, and they knew each other inside and out. The mayor couldn't go a day without seeing him, and they would usually travel together. They shared secrets, laughter, business, memories, everything. To give you an example, among the secrets that Zahir told the mayor was the story of him and Suhayl the Damascene from the days of the war in Palestine, despite his vow to keep it hidden. This happened when they were enjoying an evening of drinking and one story led to another. Zahir made us swear not to reveal it to anyone.

"The mayor returned within an hour, accompanied by Zahir. I had done what I could to wash Jalal, change his clothes, apply a compress to all his bruises, and bandage his wounds. I didn't know if any of his bones were broken, so I tried to move him as little as possible. He looked like a corpse – oh, Jalal, apple of your mother's eye!

"The two of them went into the divan. The mayor had calmed down somewhat. Zahir said, 'Can I see the boy?' I looked at the mayor, waiting for his answer. I didn't expect him to let anyone know about the cellar, but it appeared he had already revealed this secret to Zahir. Or maybe it was Zahir's idea in the first place, and maybe Zahir had his own private cellar in his house too. Who knows? The mayor gestured for me to accompany Zahir while he remained in the hall. On our way, I asked Zahir not to let the mayor hurt Jalal any more, for I knew the influence Zahir had over him. He said, 'Don't worry. It was a fit of rage, but now it has passed.'

"In the cellar, Zahir took a bag with two bottles of medicine out of his pocket. One was liquid, perhaps a disinfectant or something like that, and the other was an ointment. He began pouring the liquid on the wounds to clean them, and he rubbed the ointment into the bruises, which were turning blue. He said, 'Do this once every day.' He rolled Jalal's body over, repeating religious phrases. Then he said, 'There are no broken bones, thank God.' At that moment, Jalal breathed deeply and painfully. Zahir went on to say, 'Don't be afraid. He'll heal quickly and be just as he was.' Then he left us. I put the two bottles on one of the chests and followed him out.

"In the divan, the mayor told me to make them tea, and when I returned with it, I found Zahir telling the mayor that this incident was the whispering of the devil and the devil's impetus to strife, for Satan causes strife between a man and his spouse, between a father and his son, and between a human being and himself. Zahir went on to say that the mayor had to act rationally, just as he always did when settling the affairs of the people. The mayor said that if he were to handle this situation like those of the villagers, that would mean making it public, along with the punishment and the resolution. Zahir told him that every problem had various solutions, and that all he had to do now was calm down and find the appropriate one.

"All this time, the mayor continued expressing his sense of shock, saying he couldn't bear the hideous shame, which would forever stain his reputation and the reputation of his family and his line. Zahir began citing numerous similar stories, either from history or from his experience, with their equally numerous solutions. 'For instance, you could marry them,' Zahir suggested. 'And then the problem would be solved.' He looked at his watch. 'I have to go now, but I'll see you tomorrow.'

"After he went, the mayor and I remained silent, not knowing what to say. But I could see he had regained his composure. Then he told me to bring blankets for him to sleep there in the hall. I did so, and from that night up until the day he died, he slept there and didn't once spend a night with me in our bedroom. Just as he never again looked upon Jalal.

"A hard week passed by, during which Jalal got better and began sitting up, moving, eating and talking. The mayor said nothing to me but, 'Make very sure the boxes are locked.' As for Jalal, he felt a deep sense of guilt and regret. He cried and wanted to go to his father, or for his father to come to him, so that he could apologise to him in person, kiss his hands and feet, and beg his forgiveness. He loved his father greatly, and knowing that he had disappointed him tore him up inside. I told him that if he wanted to flee, I'd let him, but he refused, saying, 'I'll do only what my father tells me, only what seems right to him, even if he wants to kill me.' Indeed, Jalal thought about killing himself. I calmed him down and told him he had to be patient, that his father would reconcile and forgive him in the end, but that he was angry now, and he was right to be angry.

"We didn't say anything to anyone. We told the rest of the family that Jalal was travelling to visit his uncles in Kurdistan for a few days and would be back. A week later the three of us, the mayor, Zahir and I, were staying up again to discuss the matter. The idea was to arrange their marriage, and the mayor and Zahir told me to go to Jalal and inform him. The surprising thing was Jalal's absolute refusal. Of course, he was a young man in the prime of his youth, and he couldn't bear the idea of marrying Zakiya when the most beautiful girls of the village were dreaming of him, and when people considered the two of them to be siblings. Zahir went down to persuade him but didn't succeed. Jalal answered that he would kill himself if we forced him to do it. The mayor was about to take his turn and go down and beat Jalal like before until he agreed, but Zahir prevented him, saying, 'You can't compel him to get married. And then, even if we married them, the child would still be a bastard because he was conceived out of wedlock. What's more, people would talk when they saw Zakiya give birth seven months after the wedding. The whispers would start: "See how the mayor led this poor orphan to his son like a ewe to the ram." We have to think of something else.'

"Once more, our spirits were unsettled. Confusion circled around our heads, and the mayor's anxiety mounted. Our thoughts kept going around in circles, searching for some way out. The two of them sifted through religious law and common law, traditions and precedents, suggesting various possibilities. 'We'll cause her to miscarry,' proposed the mayor, 'and the baby will fall out.' 'Haram!' Zahir cried. 'By this point, the foetus has a spirit, and God has breathed a soul into him. Killing him would be a crime. And if we are able to punish his parents for the sin they committed, what is his sin that we would punish him?'

"They kept at it until, in the end, it was decided that Jalal's punishment was to be disowned having been beaten and whipped. He would then be expelled from the village, to return only after many years or never at all. Zakiya would be hidden and held in isolation from the eyes of the people until she bore her child, and then she would be punished. But it all had to be done very quickly and secretly to prevent any scandal and to preserve the mayor's reputation. They described it as the kind of impurity to ward off, not just conceal. 'God has commanded us to purity!' is how they put it.

"I suggested that Jalal be sent away to my relatives in the town of Ranya in Kurdistan. That way we could visit him and be reassured about how he was doing. Jalal could also continue his studies, and after he had spent a few years there, he could return. But the mayor insisted that Jalal be sent away out of Iraq entirely and never return. He neither wanted to see him nor hear anything about him for the rest of his life. He asked Zahir to take Jalal the next night and hand him over under the cover of darkness to friends of theirs on the border, Kurdish smugglers of weapons, goods and people. They would take charge of smuggling Jalal into some neighbouring country – 'or to hell!' as the mayor put it. After that, Jalal would manage his own affairs, 'or else let him die like a mangy dog! Tell him never to come back, never to write us letters or try to get in touch with us. Tell him to forget us forever, as we in our turn will forget him. Starting tomorrow, we will no longer think of him as our son.'

"How often I cried and begged at that time, but neither tears nor pleas availed me anything. I spent the whole night hugging Jalal, crying and counselling him. He cried only because his father didn't want to see him or bid him farewell. Have you seen how men are? How much cruelty they have? The two of them were only thinking of themselves, and not about us – me, Zakiya and you, the unborn child.

"Zahir carried out the mission to the letter. He set off in his car under cover of night, taking Jalal along with the twenty pistols the mayor had been hiding. They didn't neglect to take advantage even of that hard moment for their business dealings! They told people that Jalal had gone to finish his education in Russia. After that, we never learned anything else about Jalal, and people gradually forgot about him after various reports reached us, scant and contradictory. I don't even know where they came from. Among them were that Jalal had crossed the northern border to a neighbouring country – Syria, Iran, or Turkey – went to Germany, got married, and settled down there. Others said that he died in a car accident in Paris, or that he drowned in the Straits of Gibraltar, attempting to sneak across from Morocco to Spain. Still others said he became a religious man in Iran. He went to Afghanistan and was killed in the civil war. He made it to Colombia, joined the militants and achieved a high position among them. He was a drug-dealer in Brazil, a magistrate in a Dutch village . . .

"The threads of the story were lost to me – or perhaps I got lost among the reports and no longer knew which of them I ought to believe. Indeed, my heart, which always kept telling me that you were alive, told me nothing certain about him at all. The mayor forbade me even to mention Jalal's name or to cry over Jalal in his presence. As far as the mayor was concerned, it was as though he had never existed.

"Nevertheless, the mayor did confess to me, in a moment of weakness before his death, that he never forgot Jalal and more than once cried over him in secret."

CHAPTER 13

Life in the Cellar

"As for Zakiya – during the first few days after Jalal left, the mayor removed two of the chests from the cellar and left the third there, empty. He also installed a concrete basin in a corner as a bath. He instructed me to make up a bed for Zakiya in the cellar, saying that the empty box was for her clothes and other necessities. He told me to take her down and keep her there, to look after her until she bore her child. Meanwhile, he and Zahir made it known that they had married Zakiya to a Bedouin in the Ramadi desert. People considered that arranging a husband and a family for this sick orphan was a charitable deed since they never imagined that anyone would agree to marrying her.

"The confinement was hard on Zakiya. It was a tight space with no windows and nothing to distinguish between night and day. She was isolated and saw no-one apart from me. Zakiya was a child, used to moving around and playing with the rest of the children. Adjusting to this situation cost her and me a great deal. I entertained her – and misled her – with stories. I taught her weaving and embroidery, and I urged her to make use of the long hours to prepare clothes for her coming baby. I taught her how to make dolls, and I played with her at length until I myself was carried away, delighted with a pastime that had been forbidden to me in my childhood. We made entire families out of reeds. We would take two reeds – the thicker one, about as long as a hand, formed the trunk; another, shorter and more delicate, which we tied on in the shape of a cross, formed the arms. From a piece of old cloth, we cut clothes for the dolls, and we drew faces for them with a stick of kohl. We created an entire world to replace the one outside. Each doll had a name, a job, a family, a house made out of cardboard boxes, and so on.

"Meanwhile, poor Isma'il kept asking about Zakiya and looking for her, even after they told him about her marriage. He would go to the places where Zakiya used to play or sit, and he would wait there silently, lost in thought, for long periods. His body began wasting away out of extreme longing for her, and given that no-one spoke to him about her, he was forced to repress the pain of her absence as he pretended to forget her. He became less cheerful. The first days of her disappearance were extremely trying for him. Then, little by little, he too accepted her absence in silence.

"I spent all the time I could with Zakiya. I hardly left her alone except when she was sleeping. The only way to do that and still be seen in the outside world was to reverse day and night in her mind, which was possible since she could no longer tell them apart. So she would sleep during the day and wake up at night. For my part, I trained myself to steal a few hours of sleep at dusk and dawn.

"I took her out of the cellar two or three times, just to the bedroom, not outside, and only when the mayor was away. It was when I found her in a panic, suffocating and sobbing. At those times, I let her walk around my room. She kept going in circles, taking big steps, relishing that movement as a rare blessing. Or else she would stretch out on the wide bed and roll around to feel its softness, happy like a duck in water.

"She would tell me about her dreams and her nightmares. She would talk to me about Jalal with pleasure and longing, sharing details about their relationship – things I am embarrassed to recall – and what he would say to her. I sensed something in her. It was as though she loved him without knowing what that feeling was called. She didn't have any idea about love in the way people understand it. But she certainly felt it, and she expressed it through the stories she told, in her gestures and in the tears she shed, now distraught and now happy. I, in my turn, would talk to her about Jalal – about his childhood and everything I remembered.

"In this way, I experienced again the deep longing I felt for Jalal, especially since no-one apart from Zakiya would mention him in front of me. Some of the neighbours would ask me about him, and I would claim that the mayor kept in touch with him through messages and letters – he was doing well, was keeping up with his studies, things like that. I would answer in as few words as possible, most of them cryptic and evasive, and then quickly change the subject.

"I didn't talk to Zakiya at all about the outside world. Instead, I created a new world through stories, dreams and dolls. When she asked me about her brother, Isma'il, I told her he was doing well and sent his greetings. I said he was very busy because the flock he tended was getting larger, with his share of sheep and goats increasing – he now had twenty ewes and twelve goats, all of them his own property. 'And he says that after you give birth, you and your child will be his equal partners in this flock, and you'll have lots of butter, wool and milk.'

"Fortunately, for both her and me, the birth was natural and easy. It happened at night. That is, during the day, as far as she knew it. I took care of everything myself, and when you let out your first cry, still covered in blood, I held you to my breast and wept, while she sank into a remarkably deep, long sleep.

"The next day, when I put you, all clean, on her breast and taught her how to feed you, she gave an innocent gasp of delight, 'Ohhh! This is my son! What's his name?' I said to her, 'Give him whatever name you like.' 'Jalal!' she said immediately, then followed that with, 'No, no, Isma'il. Or Jalal. What do you think?'

"She saw I wasn't happy with either name. In truth I didn't want her to honour the names of the two men who had hurt her – the mayor and his son – even though I knew she was referring to her brother Isma'il. So she said, 'What then?'

"'No,' I said. 'In my opinion, no. Because we have a Jalal, and we have two Isma'ils. The best thing would be for you to think up a new name for him because he is new too. A name all his own, I mean.'

"She thought for a while, and then shouted, 'Qamar!'

"'Yes,' I replied. 'That's a beautiful name for a beautiful baby. Qamar, *the moon* – he is your Qamar and mine.'

"As a child, she had loved staring at the moon, especially on summer nights when we slept outside, on the roof or in the courtyard. She keep gazing at it, sometimes talking to it and singing to it until she fell asleep. In this way, she had named her smallest doll, the one she loved the most, Qamar. She would talk to it, change its clothes, and choose her favourite dolls as its parents and siblings.

"The mayor wasn't one to ask about the details of our lives during the pregnancy, but with no questions asked, he did provide us with everything I requested – medicine, clothes, food, and anything unusual she developed a craving for – things like that. When I informed him about the birth, he asked nothing besides the sex of the child. I hastened to tell him it was a boy. He didn't ask me his name. He kept swallowing painfully, in obvious distress. I know him, and I know the bitterness that passed through his mind, torn between compassion and longing on the one hand, and what he considered to be his inevitable duty on the other.

"Your birth transformed our life in the cellar into a new world, a living world. A beautiful world, even. It was no longer stifling or boring like before. Indeed, we forgot the boundaries of our narrow walls. We forgot the problem that was the reason for our being there as we began talking to you and caring for you. We never stopped watching over you, staring at every movement you made. Zakiya's happiness was more complete than mine, for whenever I paused to think, I remembered the reason we were there and what might happen afterwards, at any moment. And when I remembered Jalal, my son, who didn't know anything about his own son – just as I knew nothing about him – a sour, hot wave of sorrow would well up from my heart of hearts and catch in my throat. But it wouldn't flow out as tears. Instead, I remained lost in a bitter silence until Zakiya shook me out of it by calling my name and pointing out some movement you made.

"After ten days, the mayor asked me about Zakiya's health. I informed him that she had recovered completely, and he said, 'In that case, prepare to put a final end to this disaster.'

"My heart trembled, my mouth dried up, and I asked in a stammer, 'What? How? I mean, what have you come up with?' He replied, 'Sheikh Zahir and I have decided that she will receive her punishment for what she has done. As for the baby, it will proceed to its destiny since it has committed no sin.'

"'But she too has committed no sin! She's mentally incompetent!'

"'The law does not protect the ignorant.'

"'What do you mean? What are you going to do?'

"'Listen, woman,' he said in a tone of forceful rebuke. 'You don't understand these matters. They rely upon tradition, legal customs and principles, and religious law. It is for us men to decide them and take care of things with a minimum of scandal and damage. As for you, you just need to obey. And don't you dare, don't you dare open your mouth to utter a single word to anyone about this matter, for if you do, I'll cut out your tongue! Do you hear me?'

"There was nothing for me to do then but fall on his hand, kissing it, crying and begging him to put off the matter, if only for a few days at least, for the sake of Zakiya and me, and more so for the sake of the child who needed his mother. The mayor was silent for a long time, and I could tell that he had either been moved or was persuaded. 'Fine,' he said. 'I'll consult with Sheikh Zahir.' Then he went out.

"When we saw each other the next day, he did not refer to the matter at all. Nor did I ask him about it, and when I saw that the days were passing without any sign of action, I told myself that they had put things off or had found some other solution and abandoned what they had agreed upon. I was torn between hope and anxiety.

"More than once I was tempted to take Zakiya and the child with me and flee during the night. But how? And where? I thought of Kurdistan, from where I had come, but I didn't actually have any immediate family members there, not even one. My relationships and memories had all but faded away, seeing as I hadn't ever returned after getting married as a young girl. Things had undoubtedly changed and they had surely forgotten me. My memory preserved only confused and scattered pictures about a hard childhood and brief moments of tenderness with my grandmother before she died. I no longer even knew how to get there. My entire life was here now, and it was as though I had been born in this village. At the same time, I was feeding my own hopes that things would take a different turn somehow, and I was inclined to abandon the idea of flight since it was no sure thing. Sometimes, I dreamed that Jalal had returned suddenly, having found his place in the world, and that after seeing his child, he found a solution – such as agreeing to marry Zakiya, if only as a second wife. That way, I would be with my son, my grandson and Zakiya, who was also my daughter, for it was I who had caressed her as a baby.

"After two weeks of silence from the mayor, I was growing more anxious each day. I found myself alone for a moment with Zahir when the mayor went to the toilet during one of their evenings together. I hurried to ask Zahir what they had agreed upon, and he replied, 'We decided to delay the matter for a month. There's only two weeks left, so fortify yourself, Umm Jalal, with wisdom and with patience.'

"I immediately leaped to his side and began kissing his hand and interceding with him. Had I been in my right mind at that moment, I never would have been able to do it. My heart is what made my kisses and my tears leap out. I pleaded with him. I entreated him in the name of his children and his honour that he find a solution that didn't harm Zakiya or her baby, and if he couldn't, that he at least persuade the mayor to put things off for a second month after the end of the first. The man was surprised, disturbed, embarrassed, and he pulled back his hand from me in alarm. He was afraid the mayor would suddenly come in and find us like that. So without thinking, he immediately promised to do it. 'Swear it, in God's name!' I said, and he took the oath.

"They put off the matter until you were exactly two months and ten days old. That's when the accursed night fell. By that time, Zakiya had learned many of the details of caring for a child, and her heart had opened up to love as far as humanly possible. I'll never be able to forget her joy when she saw you smile for the first time. I was arranging the clothes in the chest when she cried out to me, 'Aiii! Come quick! Come quick! Qamar just smiled! My God, I saw him smile!' These smiles were unintentional, the involuntary kind that every baby makes. But she clapped and wept in the depths of her joy.

"At first, she would press her entire breast against your face so that she nearly suffocated you. I taught her how to suckle you from the side. Things like that. You were her whole life. She sometimes asked me about Jalal, and I told her what we told everyone, that he went away to study. I embellished my lie, saying, 'He'll return when he gets the news we sent him.'

"Once when I came into her room she said, 'I want the three most beautiful feathers from the tail of the most beautiful rooster.' I didn't ask her why but just brought them to her the next day. Two days later, she showed me a beautiful cap she had made for you by cutting off the corner of one of the cloth bags and embroidering it. She attached threads on either side to tie it under your chin. On the peak, she had attached the three feathers, and over the forehead, she had hung her silver necklace, which she inherited from her mother. You looked stunning wearing that cap, like a royal peacock. When you turned your head, the necklace jangled and the feathers were a bundle of colours floating in the air like a rainbow. Every day, she kept adding a new detail and more beautiful embroidery, as though the cap were a never-ending work of art. It is the most important thing I've kept in the box till this day. If you'd like, I'll give it to you, together with the box. Tonight, as soon as we get back."

Zaynab fell silent. She sighed deeply and continued: "Ah, my God! I never thought I would reveal the events of that night to anyone. That night, which has suffused with pain all the nights that followed. I didn't imagine I would even tell you – but I will.

You are now a man and have seen horrible things. This is the first and last time I'll narrate those scenes, etched in my mind and heart like open wounds.

"It was perhaps three in the morning when the mayor came to me. He was more tense and brusque than I'd ever seen him. 'Listen carefully,' he ordered in a sharp and frightening tone. 'Put a veil and a blindfold on Zakiya and bring her immediately. Tell her we are taking her to a delightful surprise, and that she must do everything we say. Do you understand?'

"I realised that the moment I had been dreading had now arrived, and that no word or action on my part could do any good. Even if I could find some way to resist, the mayor, when he was in that state, would not hesitate to strike me, or even kill me.

"Somehow, in some indirect way, I started trying to do or say something to distract him. I didn't know what exactly, whatever I could to keep him talking for as long as possible. So I stammered, 'And the child? She'll refuse to go anywhere without him, not even for a single moment. She's desperately attached to him.'

"'Well, fine. Bring him too. Absolutely nothing else.'

"'And me,' I said. 'I have to go with you too because if she is veiled, the child might fall from her hands, or it might cry, or she might ask for me or need me for something.'

"The mayor was silent for a moment. Then he said, 'The important thing now is that you do as you're told. Bring her to the car quickly and without any commotion, and then we'll see. Sheikh Zahir and I will be waiting for you. Come, come quickly.' And he went out.

"I knew he would seek his friend's advice on the question of my accompanying them. When we got to the door of the house, the open door of a car was only a step away. The mayor motioned with his hand that we should get in the back seat quickly. I guided Zakiya and sat her in the car. I put the child in her lap and then pointed at my chest to say, 'Do I get in?' He gave a sign that I should, so I did. The mayor reached out and closed the door without a sound, giving it a strong push to confirm it was latched. The windows were shut, and Zahir was behind the wheel. The car started moving.

"The moon was full in the sky above. If only Zakiya could have seen it! She kept silent, just as I had advised her, holding you in her arms and squeezing you to her chest. Her leg was pressed up against mine to be sure I was beside her, just as I'm doing now with you, as though I want to make sure you are there.

"The village was still. A strange calm had settled on everything, giving the crunch of the car wheels an almost tangible presence. The pebbles and earth grinding together was like fingernails scratching paper. I felt it on my skin and shivered, the hairs on my arm standing on end. Outside the village, the universe was empty, like a hollow chasm. Nothing but the high, climbing moon, with darkness all around it and around us. Little by little, under its light, the scene resembled the dawn as the black outlines of the trees became visible on both sides of the path. But beyond, the blackness stretched out until it gripped the far horizon, and the horizon beyond that.

"Zahir broke the silence by asking Zakiya how she was. 'I'm fine, uncle,' she replied. 'Repeat after me everything I say,' Zahir instructed. Then he began reciting prayers, confessions, Qur'anic passages and religious expressions like the declaration of belief in God, contrition before him, and an affirmation of the inevitability of death, while she repeated everything he said. Then I found he was giving her the words that were dictated to someone at death's door or who had already died, and an even sharper pain made my breaths come short. My voice choked within me, and I couldn't speak. It went on like this until I noticed the car was climbing the cemetery hill. It stopped at the top, here beside the sea urchin, which was much smaller at that time than it is now.

"They got out and told us to do the same. The mayor opened the trunk and took out what I thought at first were two crutches and a box. I later realised that the box was a pillow and the two crutches were a rifle and a shovel. Zahir led us forward a few steps until I saw a long trench, this very one here, next to the grave of the water martyr. 'Put her in,' he said.

"I didn't know what to do. I couldn't believe what was happening, telling myself it was just a nightmare that would end at any moment. Or that if it were real, then it was a dervish ritual or some magical treatment, for I had often heard stories of insane people being cured in cemeteries. Zahir led Zakiya over and made her step down, directing her in a calming tone, gentle and pious. 'Turn like so,' he directed. 'Stop here.'

"He made her stand in the middle of the grave, and he took out a piece of white cloth from under his arm. When he unfolded it, it was in the shape of a white bag – a funeral shroud, which he put over her head. She looked like a ghost standing in the centre of the grave. Suddenly, he wrapped a rope around her body. The mayor helped him tighten it. Zakiya became frightened when she felt how tight her bonds were. She began to squirm, trying to free herself, but the mayor shouted in her face to stop moving, which she did. She stood there, panting and sobbing, and Zahir said to her, 'Be brave, my daughter. We're doing this for your own sake, for the sake of your soul. It will only take a few moments, and then it will all be over, and you'll find yourself in a more peaceful world.'

"The full moon in all its radiance was shining directly in front of her, and I found myself saying, 'At least let her see the moon.' When she heard me, she thought I was saying your name and cried out, 'Yes! I want to see Qamar, I want to see Qamar!' I hurried forward and pressed you up against her veiled face. My head nearly knocked into hers when I stumbled. I kissed her, crying. She was crying too. The mayor yanked my arm, pulling me back several steps, almost dislocating my shoulder, and then pushed me down to the ground as I wept.

"After that, I saw them gathering rocks, and they began stoning her. She screamed as she fell to the ground, knocked flat in the grave. When she raised her voice again, they looked around for the pillow and the rifle, and I knew they were going to shoot her. The last thing I saw was Zahir holding the pillow and the mayor with the gun. I got up, still carrying you, and began to run, fearing what they might do to you. I went down the side of the hill as fast as I could, thorns scratching me and rocks cutting my feet. Down and down, I was nearly flying as I descended in a series of falls. I heard Zakiya's stifled cries receding in the distance. Then I heard the explosion of a muffled shot. Her voice was cut off and there was silence. Then a second shot, clearer, echoing. I stumbled and fell, pressing you tight against my chest, and rolled for some distance until a boulder standing in the bottom of the deep valley brought me to a stop.

"I don't know how long I stayed there trying to quiet your crying. I didn't notice the bruises and cuts I had received. I was resolved either to save your life or to die with you. I kept telling myself that somehow it was all just a nightmare. I implored God's protection from Satan, beseeching him to end it all and let me wake up. Suddenly, I saw the car moving through the valley with the mayor walking ahead of it. The headlights blinded me as the car drew close. The mayor approached and lifted me to my feet, while Zahir got out and pulled you from my clinging arms. I wasn't strong enough to stand, so the mayor supported my weight, half leading and half carrying me, until he put me in the car. All this time he kept reproaching me. 'Are you crazy? What are you doing? Enough! It's all over now.'

"The mayor took you in his arms for the first time. Zahir, sitting behind the wheel and driving, said to me, 'This is better for her soul, sister. It's better to receive punishment for your sin in this transient world than for God's eternal torment to fall upon you in the hereafter. Believe me, she'll thank us in the life to come. You are a believer – resign yourself to God's decree. Be patient and submit to God's wishes and the fate he bestows.'

"This was their crime. They knew perfectly well that what they had done was not from our religion. I didn't say anything. My body was shaking. I caught my breath and wiped away my tears as a sharp pain throbbed in various parts of my body. It felt as though my bones had been shattered and my skin torn. My clothes were wet with blood – I could taste it in my mouth.

"When we reached the house, the mayor said, 'Come on, get out. Go directly to your room. And don't you dare, don't you dare raise any commotion. I'll be back in a little while.'

"Before I got out, I reached over to take you in my arms, and he said, 'Enough! Forget this child. We'll provide him with parents to care for him. Come on, get out. Clean yourself. Perform the ritual washing and the prayers so you can calm down and go to sleep. Go!'"

CHAPTER 14

A Childhood Preserved in a Military Chest

Abdullah did not interrupt Zaynab with a single word. She had expected he would have questions, but he did not, and his silence was as heavy upon her as the weight of her years. She felt this silence and listened to him drawing and exhaling the smoke of his never-ending cigarettes. Having grown accustomed to calculating the time internally, or else by sensing the light, she knew the sun had either set behind the mountain or was just about to. Her intuition was confirmed by the sound of Abu Muhammad's car horn from the bottom of the hill or possibly halfway up the slope.

Before Zaynab got up, she asked Abdullah again whether he had any questions. Did he want her to show him the cellar and give him the box of his things, including the rooster cap? Did he want her to stand beside him and declare to everyone the truth of his lineage, while she in turn would set aside for him his share of the inheritance?

But Abdullah did not say a word. In silence, he helped her up. As she heard the crunch of dried vegetation under their feet, she told him, "I used to come here to tend the flowering shrubs I planted on her grave, but I stopped when I lost my sight."

He supported her arm with one hand as he handed her the

cane with the other. The two of them descended with slow, cautious steps as Abdullah matched his stride to hers. When they got down to the car, he helped her in and sat next to Abu Muhammad in the front seat, not next to Zaynab as before.

After the car set off, Zaynab tried again to break the silence, asking Abu Muhammad about the health of one of his children. Abu Muhammad kept up the conversation with her, describing the harvest that year, mentioning the imminent marriage of his eldest daughter, and going on to recount how one of his cows had broken its tether in the night and eaten so much from the stores of barley that it made itself ill. When they took it to the vet, he told them to give it Pepsi to drink. So they bought an entire case of Pepsi bottles, which they poured into a bucket and forced the cow to drink by plunging its nose in the bucket. The cow had begun mooing out long, gassy burps, which caused the children and the neighbours to collapse in laughter. The two of them laughed as well, while Abdullah's face remained serious, as though he had not heard a thing.

Zaynab and Abu Muhammad kept talking and laughing until they entered the village. Abu Muhammad asked whether he should take them both to Hajja Zaynab's house, where he had picked them up, or whether he should take each to their own house. Zaynab asked Abdullah if he would accept her invitation to dinner. "No, thank you," he said. Her tone hinted at something more, asking whether he wanted to finish the conversation with her, whether he had anything to ask her or a response to her concluding questions. But his answer in the negative made clear to her that volcanoes were bubbling up inside him. She could not divine their exact nature, but she knew without a doubt they were there. So she said to Abu Muhammad, "In that case, take Abdullah to his house first, since it's closer, and then you and I will go on together."

As soon as the car stopped in front of the gate of his courtyard, Abdullah got out silently and moved quickly to the house. He went in and shut the door behind him. He sat in a corner, bringing his hands to his head. "I'm unable to cry," he said aloud to himself, but then he asked, "And why should I cry?" He did not turn on the light but remained in darkness, frozen, squeezing his head between his hands. He had no specific thoughts, but the vague impression simmering inside was that he was about to vomit or burst out yelling.

Abdullah lit a cigarette. He smoked one after another until he calmed down a little. Then he got up and turned on the light. His body was tired, but his mind was wide awake. He stood in front of the pictures of his adoptive parents, Salih and Maryam. Looking at them, he said, "You were deceived, just like me. You lived a lie, like me. The sons of bitches tricked you. The murderers!"

He repeated a quotation by a French philosopher, trying to remember his name: Sarir, Sarar, Sarsar, Sarter, Sarsary? Something like that. He smiled, thinking it strange that he wanted to recall a name at a moment like this. He remembered how Tariq would sometimes quote that philosopher: "Hell is other people." Abdullah took a breath and said, "But no, the two of you were not deceived at all. You needed a son, and just like that one came to you. Why should you care how, who his actual parents were, where he came from, or where he was going? Damn it all! Each of us will believe anything that gives us a reason to keep going, some consolation to help us endure this existence. We all want some illusion to persuade ourselves that life has meaning."

He headed to the kitchen to make tea. A light passed through the shutters, and a car horn sounded outside the gate to the courtyard. He opened the window and saw Abu Muhammad get out and open the gate. He called to Abdullah without turning off the car's engines or lights. Abdullah went out to meet him.

Abu Muhammad gave him a chest and a key and said, "Hajja Umm Jalal sent this to you. Listen, brother Abdullah. If you need anything, don't hesitate to ask. You are one of us."

Abdullah thanked him and went back inside, carrying the box. He took a look at it: a military chest, made of strong wood painted khaki and green. How often he had worked with such boxes during the war! He hated them. Why had one followed him here after all these years? When would he be done with them and everything connected to them? Why were war's symbols constantly pursuing him?

He put the chest in the middle of the room and brought over the teapot and a cup to sit beside it. He stared at the box, inspecting it. It was the size of a suitcase, with numbers and letters that told him it was an ammunition case for mortar shells. How had it come to this out-of-the-way village? What was it doing here? The lock that had been added was big and old-fashioned, the kind used for shop doors.

He took the key out of his pocket. He had no desire to open it, and for that matter, why should he? What did it matter to him, these useless things from a childhood he did not remember, left by a mother he had never known? That person had no place in his life, and suddenly he was told, "You have a mother named Zakiya, and she named you Qamar. Her story goes like this ... and she was murdered!" He threw the key on the chest and went on sipping tea, ruminating over his cigarettes and his thoughts.

He hated this military chest, and he did not want it to stay there with him in the house. He'd smash it or burn it, just like they used to do along the front to cook with the wood, make tea, or feed the fire. He'd destroy it and throw it in the earth crack. And what about the contents? Why had she sent it to him, this grandmother of his? Why had she told him that story? For a moment he felt hatred for her. All the affection she had shown throughout his whole life had been nothing more than an attempt to assuage her feelings of guilt. Yet what was her sin? She was a victim just like him, and she too had suffered greatly. "She waits her whole life to cast the burden of this painful memory from her shoulders onto mine! Do I need more pain? Then she asks me if I want her to reveal my origins and publicly acknowledge me as family, with a share in the inheritance! They deny me when they're alive, and they recognise me in death? They kept quiet during their lives, covering up their crimes of rape and murder. They didn't want to recognise their shame or be reminded of it. And now they want me to carry this shame publicly instead of them!"

Zaynab had said, "God punished them in this world, and he will punish them in the hereafter too for what they did." She had told him how the deaths of the mayor and Zahir had been a true torture. A strange disease had come over them: each began to scratch at his skin, which festered and became mangy; they scratched all the way down to the bone. This went on for a whole year, each one rotting in his bed. Ointments did nothing for them, nor doctors, magic, or dervishes. One of the Iraqi folk doctors told them they had drunk from the same water, and God knows how, or what this water was, and what was in it. The stench became as unbearable as their sufferings, while their flesh stuck to the sheets, and flies swarmed around their festering wounds and peeling skin. Their condition was so disgusting that even their worst enemy would have been pained to see it.

Zaynab had said it was God's punishment. "And how does this punishment of theirs benefit me?" Abdullah asked himself. "What is my sin that my entire life should be a punishment?" He did not know now whether he loved Zaynab or hated her. He did not know what was going on inside him. Nor what, exactly, he was supposed to do. He was all the more convinced that his depression and nihilism were justified, and an obscure pain crushed his soul like an iron weight.

He spent that night alone in the company of a military chest. Nothing inside but dead things, accustomed for their part to isolation and darkness. Alone, and nothing to show for the long years of his life's journey but these dead things. A beginning and an end which now came together . . . in nothing. So what is the meaning of all the suffering in between?

He recalled what his grandmother had told him more than once: "My life is a Hindi movie." He imagined the details she related. Then he tried to picture a face for his mother from the features of Isma'il the herdsman. What was her voice like? he wondered. Her smell? Her smile? Would his life have taken a different path had she lived? Would he have received the sincere tenderness he needed? And what about his father? Where was he now? Had he married and fathered children in some foreign land? Did he resemble the mayor? When he was young, did he look like the mayor in the picture hanging prominently on the wall of the divan, with all his coarseness and his hawkish expression? Or did he resemble his mother, Zaynab? Why had he not asked her all these details? Yet why should he ask her? What use was it to know all that? Strong emotions gripped him. He kept coming back to imagining his mother, much more so than his father. He felt almost no desire to know anything at all about that man. He felt nothing towards him, for at the end of the day, what was he but a long-gone rapist, the pampered son of a rich father who had turned his lust on a poor simple-minded orphan and then left. What meaning did it have that this person was his father, whether he wanted it or not?

He imagined his mother's suffering and how everyone had deceived her before going on to kill her, shrouded, bound, and blindfolded. When all she wanted was to see the moon or her child, they struck her down with stones they had blessed and shot her dead in a trench dug to be her grave!

For a moment, he wanted to take revenge on both of them, along with all the offspring and property they had left behind. He would dig them out of their graves. He would smash their bones to piss and shit upon the shards before scattering them in the dung heaps. As for their children and grandchildren, he'd carry off one each night, wrap them in a shroud, tie them up with a thick rope, and tell them the story. After that, he would rape them.

Then he would stone them, execute them, and bury them in some unknown place. He would keep going until he had finished them all off. Then he would burn their fields and their houses. He would leave this accursed village and country in search of the principal rapist, Jalal, to do the same to him. Then he would leave. Just leave. He did not know where. Perhaps he would leave this bestial world entirely, once and for all, and through his own end put an end to the lineage of this corrupted bloodline.

Such was the cycle of Abdullah's emotions. When a wave of burning anger rose in his soul, he would quickly shake it back out of his head. That sort of thing was just a passing thought with no root in his nature, nothing he could commit to. He hated cruelty and fled from it. How often he had wondered about the secret behind this impulse to cruelty in men's hearts and about the hidden pleasures and grim fantasies their cruelty fulfilled. He thought he should try to forget the whole thing, put it behind him, push it into the dark cellar of the past as though he had never seen it or known anything about it. He would treat it as he did his years of captivity. Forgetting it and burying it away as though it had not been, as though he did not know the truth of his story . . . But now he knew and it was impossible to erase that knowledge. Then let him pretend not to know! Let him hide it, or leave it behind.

Abdullah could not find his way now to any final decision. His internal dialogue brought more questions than answers. He had been born in an underground prison cell, confined in a cage, and he went on to spend nearly twenty years, the prime of his life, in another captivity even more cruel.

"The prisons of this existence, from its beginning till its end – if it ever ends. What is it all for, oh you who are so free? A prisoner from birth, I am driven from prison to prison. After the freedom of nonbeing, what sin of mine merits this? What right have they over me? Why? Is this what some people, like Ibrahim, are able to call fate? What is fate? And why exactly did my fate have to be like this? What great crime have I committed? Why? Why?"

He wished then he had someone there with him to talk to, someone to help him absorb this swarm of questions, raining down like arrows, someone to provide answers, or even just to echo back his questions. "What might someone else say about this situation? How would they understand it? What would they observe? What questions would they pose? What would their answers and their attitudes be?" But how could he even be thinking like this when he was a refugee, fleeing the company of others? Weren't other people hell itself? His entire situation was made by their hands!

"I don't want anyone! I don't want to know anything about anyone, including those who brought me into this world! Everything outside myself, everything other than myself – it all means nothing to me and doesn't affect me in the least. Why don't they just leave me alone? Leave me to my isolation, my depression, to the peace of solitude, which I long for. Is that too much to ask? Why is it that every time I indulge them patiently, hoping they'll leave me alone, they find new ways to intrude upon my life?"

He calmed down somewhat and lay back on the floor where he was sitting. He struck his forehead with his fist, gently at first and then harder. He stroked his beard. When he closed his eyes, the strain of sleep deprivation made them feel like two stones cutting into his eyelids. He sat up again. He took the key off the chest, examined it, looked at the lock, and then threw the key back down. He lit a cigarette as rage fired up inside him again. His fluctuating, contradictory moods, shifting from one moment to the next, meant he needed to talk to someone instead of just tormenting himself with an inner dialogue. He wished Sameeha were with him now so he could tell her everything. All this pain connected to his ancient, lonely love for her, a longing that had taken root and extended vines inside him, so long had he cultivated it within. Root and vine, it had grown within him like the sea urchin in the cemetery.

He would tell her. He wished she were talking to him now. He would share it with her and no-one else. That is, if he decided to share what burned inside him with anyone. What would he say? What would she think of him when she knew he was illegitimate? What would her attitude be towards her father when she learned that he was the one who had killed Abdullah's mother? Would she be ashamed? Angry? Would she apologise? Would she try to understand her father and make excuses for him? Or would she begin to hate her father, and would this hatred strengthen the love she and Abdullah felt for each other? But Abdullah did not hate. He despised hatred and found no meaning in it. Hatred was just another burden on the soul. He wanted peace, nothing more. Just peace.

Abdullah saw the first light of dawn stealing through the cracks in the shutters. He wiped his face with his hands and resolved to get rid of the military chest. He would take it, still locked just as it was, pour some oil on it, light it, and throw it, still burning, into the earth crack, along with everything inside. But he suddenly found himself changing his mind. He opened the lock, and as soon as he raised the lid, an ancient and dusty smell struck his nostrils. He reached inside: old baby clothes, dolls made from reeds, a silver necklace, handkerchiefs, and the cap with its three feathers and embroidery. He examined it with trembling hands, following every thread with his finger, and put it on his head. He felt as though the absent hand of his mother were touching him. He took it off and smelled it; he kissed it. He swept up everything from the chest into his hands and brought them to his face. There was an obscure smell, a mix of old clothes, dust, wood. And something human. He imagined what it was: a suckling baby, the milk it nursed on, a breast, a neck, fingers. The smell of a mother. The smell of his mother. Zakiya.

A need for tenderness flooded Abdullah's soul: the need for a woman, for his mother; for a kind and compassionate human touch, for a hand and fingers, for the feel of living human skin, for a breast, rising and falling with each breath; for a person, for his mother; for crying, for weeping. Abdullah burst into tears and fell to the floor, sprawled out on the carpet. He buried his face in the pile of old baby clothes and handkerchiefs that carried his smell. He cried like a baby until he could cry no more. Utterly exhausted and lying there, he fell into a deep sleep that lasted two whole days.

CHAPTER 15

A Night of Tea Over the Embers

Someone knocked on the door. Abdullah raised his head. It was dark outside, but inside the house the lights were on. More knocks on the door. Tariq's voice was calling his name. He got up and shouted, "Yes, yes, just a minute!" He hastened to carry the scraps of his childhood, which he had been lying on like a pillow, to the bedroom, and threw them on the bed. Tariq was still knocking and calling. Abdullah came back and opened the door to find Tariq, with Ibrahim in tow, and he beckoned them both inside.

"What's wrong with you, man? Sleeping? Only the chickens sleep at this hour! Are you actually a chicken?"

"Yes, I was sleeping. Please, have a seat. I'll wash my face and be right out."

Abdullah felt a deep sense of ease, an ease of a particular quality. He washed his entire head, dried off, and combed his hair and his beard in the mirror. He noticed that smiles came easier to his face; his eyes were wider and clearer. He went out to the other two and asked, "What time is it?"

"What time is it! It's nine in the evening, my friend. Are you alright?"

"Yes. It seems I've slept for a long time. I'm a little hungry. Will you eat anything? Can I make you some tea?"

"Eat whatever you like, and afterwards make us the tea. We ate at the funeral tent."

"The funeral tent? Who died?"

Ibrahim turned to Tariq and said, "Didn't I tell you he didn't know? Otherwise he would have attended the burial for sure."

Tariq addressed his words to Abdullah: "I'm so sorry for your loss. Hajja Zaynab passed away yesterday evening."

"What?! I was with her for all of yesterday evening."

"No, my friend. You were with her the day before yesterday. That's what Abu Muhammad told us. He said she sent him with a chest for you. Is this the chest here?"

"Yes." It was only then that Abdullah realised he had slept for two days.

The chest was still open in the middle of the room. Ibrahim lifted the cover and swung it into place. Surprised, he inspected the box from every angle.

"It's a military chest! A crate for mortar shells. How – what is it doing here? How did it get here?"

Tariq asked, "What was in it?"

"Nothing important. Some things from my childhood. She had been storing them at her house. She said she took them for safekeeping during my absence, when she came to clean."

Meanwhile, Ibrahim kept examining the box, feeling it over on every side as though it were a great discovery. "My God! But how?"

Abdullah brought the teapot and his empty, sticky cup to the kitchen. Meanwhile, Tariq told Ibrahim how the mayor traded weapons, and how his father had been the mayor's business partner. They still had military chests and such things in their house too.

From inside the kitchen, where he made himself tea and nibbled at the piece of bread in his hand, Abdullah continued speaking with them through the open door. "The poor woman. She didn't complain of anything. How did she die?"

"She died as all God's creatures do. They say she went to bed in the usual way, and when she was late to appear in the morning, they tried to wake her but couldn't. What were you two doing in the cemetery?"

"Nothing. It was just a visit. She said she hadn't gone there for a long time. Neither had I, so we went together to spend time with the departed."

"Glory be to God! It's as though she knew her time was coming and went there to say goodbye. We buried her on the hill that will be the new cemetery from now on, just as she wanted."

Ibrahim followed Tariq's words by saying, "It's often said that people can sense the approach of their death, and some even receive something like a message in their sleep, a foretelling. Especially the pure of heart, and she was a good woman. May she rest in peace."

"She loved you very much, Abdullah. As though you were one of her own children. Ah, if you only knew how she cried during your absence and how often she asked about you!"

"Yes, I know."

"She was good to everyone. As though she were a true native of the village. On top of that, she was the only woman who could put up with the mayor. Without her, the mayor might have been an entirely different beast, perhaps even the sort who eats human flesh and throws the bones to the dogs."

When Abdullah returned from the kitchen, he found Ibrahim still squatting beside the chest, examining it, feeling it over, getting so close he might have been smelling it. He asked Abdullah, "What will you do with it?"

"I don't know. Get rid of it. Smash it or burn it. I don't want any military things in my house."

"Yes, let's burn it and make tea. The embers of this wood are amazing, the very best for cooking and making tea. We used to do that during our army days."

This idea appealed to them all. They took the box out to the courtyard, smashed it, and gathered the wood into a shallow hole. They sprinkled some kerosene from one of the lanterns over the wood and set it on fire. Then they placed three medium-sized stones within the fire to form a tripod for the teapot. They brought out two small rugs to sit upon around the fire. In that atmosphere, surrounded by the still night with the glowing embers and the flames dancing between them, a kind of joy stole into their spirits.

Their conversation, guided by a sense of affection and human connection, as well as a feeling of security, touched on other people, themselves, their memories, and whatever topic their words led them to. Using tongs, Abdullah lifted embers from the fire to light his cigarettes. Ibrahim recalled the few good moments he had known during the war: soldiers from different villages and cities, exhausted and far from their families, coming together to make tea and drink it slowly as they talked about the girls they loved, sometimes singing, dancing and laughing together. That had been a rare and special pleasure.

They came back to Hajja Zaynab more than once, and from her they passed on to the mayor, and spoke of the intimate and special friendship between the mayor and Zahir. Tariq said to Ibrahim, "My father was also good friends with yours. They took part in the Palestine War together."

"Yes, but they weren't as close as Zahir was with the mayor."

"As for your father, Abdullah, he was . . . he was not as close to them. A good man, a peaceful man. He spent his life going between his field, his house and the mosque."

For an instant, it occurred to Abdullah to tell them the truth he had learned. But he abandoned the idea. He thought it better to hide the matter and forget about it – perhaps for ever. Having slept soundly for all that time, he felt a sense of tranquility, a pleasant lightness. He did not want to trouble his soul by going over that dark and painful history again.

Abdullah seemed less depressed and more cheerful. He even laughed out loud a few times, which made Tariq think to himself that this might be the moment to propose the idea that kept running through his head, namely, that Abdullah marry his sister Sameeha. Sameeha – together with her daughter – still lived with Tariq at home, silent and withdrawn, refusing all offers of marriage. She always seemed to be alone, no matter how many people bustled about her. Abdullah too, for his part, lived alone. Like her, he seemed silent, depressed, lonely. So why not let them be depressed together? It would be perfect if they came together, got married and kept each other company – together with Sameeha's daughter – for the rest of their allotted time. That way, Tariq would also be freeing up another room in his house, which he could offer to one of his ever-expanding brood. Or he could make some money by renting it out as storage space. And he would free himself of the expenses associated with Sameeha and her daughter.

But the most important consideration was his wish to atone for something buried in his soul that had pained his conscience since youth: his secret role in persuading his father to refuse Abdullah's marriage to his sister. Tariq was a grown man now. He had matured and changed, and his understanding of things was different. As a result, every time he thought about it, he felt guilt – shame, even, and a sense of his own stupidity, to recall his hidden motive for doing it, which he would never, ever, be able to share with anyone. It was too embarrassing to think about even on his own! How could he admit that his refusal was down to seeing Abdullah's massive, dark cock when they were adolescents and jerked off in front of each other to see who could come the fastest, in those days when they used to talk about sex, the village girls – their breasts, legs and bums – and what it might be like to marry each of them. It was intolerable even to imagine Abdullah doing with his sister all those things they talked about. That big dick going in and out of his sister's . . . How could he tell anyone what had been in his head at that time? He justified it by telling himself that he had been young, just an adolescent, while now he was a different man.

Among the twisting threads of the conversation, Tariq tried twice – with Ibrahim's support – to draw Abdullah onto the subject of marriage. But Abdullah quickly deflected the topic with vague comments that suggested a complete lack of desire, or else he would simply not respond and leave the issue hanging there. They read in his reaction more of a refusal than an acceptance, and given the way Abdullah changed the subject to ask about their own families, they concluded that the idea did not interest him much, that he did not want to talk or even think about it.

Tariq expressed his constant desire to marry again, even though he had no problems with his first wife. Something inside him from an early age made him feel the need to have more than one. Whenever he considered this urge, he remembered his father, who had married three times.

Ibrahim then shared the mounting troubles brought by his wife's illness and the costs of her treatment, which were beginning to weigh him down. She could no longer help work the fields. Upon hearing that, Tariq mentioned that he would help him look for some source of income outside agriculture. He suggested there were jobs in the city suitable for Ibrahim's handicap, which would allow him to avoid the costs of travelling there for the chemotherapy every twenty days. Tariq told him about a friend in Mosul whose brother was in the inner circle of the President of the Republic. This brother had helped many people find work, good stable jobs, both civilian and military. Tariq urged Ibrahim to bring him all his documents – his medical reports and so on – from the various hospitals, as well as all the papers that confirmed his participation in the two wars, the medal of valour he received, and documentation of losing a foot in the last war, along with a petition explaining his position as the breadwinner for a large family and the medical reports about his wife's condition. Tariq would give these to his friend, who would pass them then to his brother. Perhaps he would provide a charitable disbursement from the government or else arrange a suitable job for Ibrahim, which would be even more profitable.

"Just give me all these documents, reports and papers," Tariq said in conclusion. "I'll write the petition in my style. Hey, you know how eloquent I can be, don't you? Then I'll keep working on my friend until he brings your case to his brother. Well, what do you think?"

Ibrahim's eyes were wide open with great interest, as though he were listening through them. He turned to Abdullah, trying to read his expression and get his thoughts on Tariq's proposal. When he saw that Abdullah, for his part, remained silent and just kept smoking his cigarettes without giving anything away through his expression, Ibrahim asked him directly.

"And you, Abdullah? What do you think?"

As always, Abdullah hesitated a little before responding. He seemed either to be thinking it through or seeking the right way to frame his words. "I don't know," he replied in the end. "But personally, I always prefer to stay as far as possible from the head of the snake."

Tariq went on enthusiastically supporting his suggestion, telling stories he had heard about people who had obtained work in the palace guard, or tilling the President's fields, tending the gardens, shepherding the flocks, working in the kitchens or in construction, or as decorators, drivers, and so on. Tariq appeared to be absolutely delighted with his idea, and he kept trying to persuade them until he was persuaded himself. He finished by saying, "Let's get it all ready tomorrow. I'm taking a trip to Mosul the day after that. A good deed quickly done is doubly good."

That beautiful evening, as they conversed, reminisced, joked, laughed, and shared deeply around a teapot reheated many times over a bed of glowing embers kindled from the military chest, was the last time the three sons of the earth crack would gather together in this intimate way. Just as they had hoped, those embers made a truly special tea, and its flavour would remain in their memories a long time.

CHAPTER 16

The First of the Gardens

Less than a week went by before Tariq the Befuddled returned, truly flabbergasted. In a hurry, he drove his car into the courtyard of Ibrahim's house, never laying off the noisy – though occasionally melodic – car horn. Qisma hurried out to meet him as he got out, waving a paper in his hand and calling, "Is your father home?"

The question was barely out of his mouth before Ibrahim appeared in the door. Tariq rushed over and wrapped his arms around Ibrahim's waist, lifting him off the ground in his delight and twirling him in a circle as though he were a child or a doll. It was what they used to do as children when celebrating some victory. "Congratulations," Tariq kept saying. "Congratulations!"

He set Ibrahim back down and announced to those eagerly awaiting his news, "They've accepted you for the job in Baghdad! Next week, you'll be in the Palace of the Republic, you hero! This is it! All your problems are solved! Your entire life will change!"

Indeed, Ibrahim's life was utterly changed from that day. As for his problems – there is no such thing as a life completely free of those.

Tariq helped his friend with the move to Baghdad. He rented

a modest house for Ibrahim with two bedrooms, a sitting room, a kitchen and a small yard. The unusual thing for them was that the bathroom was inside the house, not outside, the way it is done in villages to banish bodily smells and the embarrassment of hearing people fart.

Qisma, who had become a beautiful young woman, was the most excited about the move to the city. It was something she had long been dreaming about. Once they arrived, she enrolled in the Teachers' Institute to continue her education. She had her own room in the house: she hung pictures on the wall of her favourite celebrities, she listened to the music she wanted, and she dreamed of freedom as she lay on the bed half-naked, something she could never do in the village amid a large family that did not allow space for any individuality, demanding everyone's participation in a collective unit that shared all things and resembled each other in every way, as dictated by the established traditions of the unbending social structure.

Tariq departed a full three days later, having arranged everything for them – the rent, the shopping, Qisma's enrolment in the institute, and a doctor for Umm Qisma's check-ups and ongoing treatment. He gave them the phone numbers of his acquaintances in Baghdad in case they needed anything, and now that they had a telephone, he promised he'd get in touch every time he went to Mosul or another city to make sure they were O.K.. They all thanked him deeply and sincerely. Qisma clung to him the hardest, expressing her gratitude with a hug and a kiss for this miracle she had longed for but never imagined would be realised so quickly or in this way.

The night before his appointment in the Palace of the Republic, Ibrahim was too anxious and excited to sleep. All through the night he kept reviewing the papers he would bring with him, checking again every ten minutes to make sure nothing was missing. On top of the stack, he put the most important one, the one on presidential stationery that stated he had been accepted for a job and detailed the time and place of his appointment. He kept staring at the eagle at the top – the sigil of the Republic – in terror.

He shaved and took out his one suit, which, ever since his wedding day, he had reserved for use on important occasions – he had only worn it two or three times. Qisma ironed the suit and sprayed it with cologne, she polished his shoes until they shone, she cleaned his prosthetic foot, and she made several adjustments to his outfit. As his wife watched, Ibrahim kept reviewing with Qisma the answers he would give to the different questions they were likely to ask.

He did not expect, however, that they would ask him nothing at all, and that he would begin his work the very first day. After passing through numerous military and civilian checkpoints and through various rooms to be searched, photographed, finger-printed and examined medically, he arrived in a spacious hall, fine in all its details, where he was made to sit with perhaps fifty others, men and women of different ages. A colonel entered the room, surrounded by a group of military men.

The colonel, with his thick moustache and stern features, addressed them: "We know all about each of you, maybe even more than you know about yourselves. That's why we chose you from the thousands of applicants who write to us every day. That means you are the elite, devoted to the leader, the party, the revolution and the country. Your records are clean and honourable, giving evidence of your loyalty, and most of you were heroes in the days of the war. Therefore, you are worthy of trust. What is expected of you is that you continue in this devotion, and that you assume a position of responsibility."

This laudatory tone of his voice changed abruptly to one more severe and threatening: "You will work in private places that demand absolute secrecy and discretion. So it is incumbent upon you that you follow this principle: 'See nothing, hear nothing, say nothing.' If anyone among you so much as breathes a word of his work outside this place, we will cut out his tongue. The cook who breaks a plate? We'll break his head. The gardener who cuts off a rose? We'll cut off his head. The cleaner who falls short in his cleaning? We'll make him fall short in his life."

It was a long address, bristling with commands, threats and promises. He kept telling them that they knew everything, that there were cameras everywhere, watching their every movement, catching even a black ant on a dark rock during an even darker night. Everyone had to stick to the job he was assigned and follow orders blindly, without poking his nose into what did not concern him. Things here ran more precisely than the most precise of clocks, and whoever disturbed this precision even in a small way: woe unto him!

Afterwards, they were transported in cars with windows so tinted it was impossible to see out, arriving at some place they estimated to be a little less than an hour away. Never in his life had Ibrahim ridden in a car – or any other vehicle – that was so clean, comfortable and fast, gliding along like a boat on a river. When they got out, they found themselves under large open roofs like those found in army training camps. But these were painted, cleaner, crowded with fancy cars and guarded by soldiers.

Nearby was a wall that stretched off to no apparent end and rose approximately thirty feet. They were led to a giant black gate in the wall. There was a small door set into the iron gate, also black, wide enough to admit one person at a time. Lining up behind a soldier, they went through the small door – the large gate remained closed – into a passage with several metal detectors that led to a large hall. On both sides of the hall were a vast number of doors, and there was a desk at one end, behind which sat a smartly dressed soldier. He asked each of them their name and then gave them their individual I.D. cards and badges, together with a key with a numbered keychain.

He said to them, "From this moment on, each one of you must remember his number."

Ibrahim looked at the key and read his number: 42. He repeated it over and over to himself until he had memorised it.

The soldier added, "You each have a room here, corresponding to your number. In that room, you'll find a uniform and the tools appropriate for your jobs. That's where you'll change clothes when you arrive and before you leave. Understood?"

They nodded their heads, and a few of them murmured, "Yes, sir."

Upon hearing that, the soldier said, "You address everyone here with 'comrade', not with 'sir'. Except the officers, and yes, you say 'sir' to them. Understood?"

This time, they all responded in a loud voice, "Yes, comrade!"

He said, "Now go. Find the number for your room, get ready, and wait until someone comes to show you your work. Understood?"

Ibrahim found room 42 on the right, nearly in the middle of the hall. He opened the door and went inside. He closed the door behind him and began looking around. It was a small room with a chair, a mirror, a clothes stand, and a wardrobe with two doors. Inside the wardrobe he found three blue work uniforms and three pairs of shoes, all the same size and style. There was a box of yellow latex gloves, a small trowel, a small scythe, several sickles (called *makzoom* in their dialect) of various sizes and shapes for cutting grass and plants, a box of bags, three hats, and other things he could not identify since he had never before seen their like.

He began taking off his clothes, which he hung on the hooks of the clothes stand. At that moment, he remembered what he heard about cameras watching everything, and that even if you did not see a camera in the room, it might be hidden behind a hole the size of an ant's arse, as someone had put it. So he tried to preserve his modesty and resolved never to forget the cameras even for a moment, and to act cautiously, with the knowledge that someone was watching him at all times.

He put on one of the uniforms and saw it was exactly his size. The shoes and the hat too. He looked in the mirror and saw that he looked very sharp. Then he sat down and waited, listening to the nervous beating of his heart.

After a while, someone knocked on the door and pushed it open before Ibrahim even had a chance to say anything. Ibrahim found himself standing before a young man who filled the entire door frame. He was extremely handsome and wore an impeccable olive-coloured military uniform without any rank indicated on the shoulder or arm. Ibrahim blinked his eyes rapidly as his whole body tensed up. The young man said, "Finished? Are you ready?"

Ibrahim had indeed finished adjusting his uniform, but before he could reply, the young man entered and pulled out a basket from under the chair. He began rummaging in the drawer as he went on talking: "Your job is to be a gardener, and more precisely, to take care of a rose garden. Each day, get your basket ready with a pair of gloves, a scythe, shears, a rubbish bag . . ." He went on naming the things as he took them out and tossed them into the basket. When he had finished, he stood up and said, "At six in the evening, when the day is done, put everything back where you found it, change your clothes and leave. You'll find the car that takes you back to the Alawite Garage in the centre of Baghdad. *Ookey*? You get me? Now come on."

Ibrahim followed him, carrying the basket, and they left the hall through a different side door. When he got outside, what Ibrahim saw would never have occurred to him as possible except as a vision of heaven.

It was a dream made real. Or else it actually was a dream. A wide-open space with no boundaries in sight, covered with gardens, fountains, palaces and statues. Everything was arranged with precise care: the paths among the greenery, the avenues of trees, the hills, the ponds, the arrangement of the buildings, the colours. Even the light and the air seemed complicit in this stunning feat of landscaping.

The young man's voice startled him from his dumbstruck reverie, calling, "Hey, come on, Uncle Ibrahim! Come and take a ride with me!"

There was a small open cart nearby with two seats and a cargo bed in the back. The young man took the basket from Ibrahim and pointed at the seat next to him. Then he began driving the vehicle, which glided away as though skating on ice, making no sound at all as it carried them along the clean paved paths laid out around the flower beds and the ponds.

Every time they went past a fountain, Ibrahim smelled a different perfume in the air. When the young man saw Ibrahim's wide eyes and heard him sniffing at the air breathlessly in an attempt to determine what was going on, he explained, "The water in these fountains is mixed with perfume, half and half. Each fountain has its own perfume, mostly French. Sorry, what do people call you – Father of . . . ?"

"Qisma."

"In that case, welcome, Abu Qisma! Welcome, uncle, to the President's gardens! Listen. Every day I'll bring you to your job. It's my responsibility to supervise you, and God willing, everything will be perfect. You get me? It's obvious you're a good man. I had a good feeling about you the moment I saw you. My name is Sa'ad."

Sa'ad brought him to what would be his place of work. It was a small, round house with mud walls, architecturally striking and beautifully made. The house stood on a circular platform in the middle of a lake and was connected to the shore by a narrow bridge about two hundred feet long. The balconies, doors and shutters of the house were all made of wood and decorated with intricate carvings. A garden ten feet wide encircled the house, filled only with roses. Every type of rose you could imagine, precisely arranged, and absolutely stunning in their colours and size. There were white chairs, and a white metal fence separated the garden from the water, about three feet below. The water was so clear and blue that it seemed to glow. Plants, moss, fish, turtles, crocodiles and hundreds of other creatures were easily visible in its depths. There were also various kinds of ducks, swimming calmly in groups around wooden houses built especially for them in the middle of the water, not far from the house on the island. On the far side of the lake were towering trees planted close together.

Ibrahim's main task was to care for these roses. He had to water them, keep them clean and orderly, watch for any that fell over or were broken by the wind, and keep an eye out for dust and any leaves that fell off. "You also have to keep turning the house to follow the sun, so that it's always shining down on the main entrance. You get me?"

Ibrahim stood there at a loss, staring blankly into the face of young Sa'ad. How could he possibly do that? "Excuse me – what? How?"

Sa'ad laughed. "Oh, don't worry! Listen. You seem to think you have to move the house around with your bare hands. Not at all! Come with me."

Sa'ad, still laughing, led him to a panel of buttons in a corner of the house and explained how to use it. "Listen. You just push this one, or this one, or this one, and the house turns automatically. Look."

The house started to turn, with the two of them standing on the edge of its marble floor. The rose garden and the chairs turned with them. Sa'ad added, "It's mounted on a circular iron base, which is the thing that moves. Look over there at the fence on the edge of the island."

And indeed, Ibrahim noticed that the entire circle was moving, with only the fence staying fixed in place.

"It's possible to move just the rose garden or just the house in the middle. There are circles inside the circle – you get me? His Excellency the President sits here, for example, and they move the garden in front of him however he likes. Your job includes cleaning the outside of the house, the chairs and the rails of the fence. Everything here you can see and touch – it's your job to look after it, keep it clean, keep it all in order. As for inside the house, that's not your concern. That's someone else's job. And I, of course, will come by every hour and a half or so. *Ookey?*"

When the young man left, Ibrahim stood there a long time, motionless, dumbstruck. It was enough just to take in the details of this place where he found himself, the breathtaking gardens spreading around him on the far shore: gardens and palaces and boats anchored across the lake; the chirping and warbling of birds, birds as diverse and magical as the flowers. He walked around the island looking for something to do, such as cleaning the rails of the fence. But everything was already clean and orderly, and there was nothing left to be done. Little by little, he began to notice some bits of straw or some dirt, trifling things like that. Later on, he realised that noticing such things was the key to keeping this place immaculate.

When that day came to an end, Ibrahim felt as though he had lived an entire lifetime, one completely different from his own. The day had seemed very long, longer even than those fear-laden days during the war when they would lie in wait to make an ambush. Unending surprise at what he saw, heard and smelled was his predominant impression from this life in a day. When he returned to the din of the city, and from the city to his house, he remained silent. The wonder and strangeness of it all, his inability to comprehend it or articulate the experience, weighed heavily upon him and made him feel that he had stepped out of time and space and existed as a creature from somewhere else, untethered from the reality of this world and even from his own body. But once more, Ibrahim's habit of submission and fateful acceptance, so deeply rooted in his soul, carried him through.

As the days passed, he recovered his sense of reality, and little by little he was able to work things out and bring some sort of mental order to the circumstances he suddenly found himself in. He was able to adapt to this system and his new way of life. What was particularly helpful in that process was the ease that young Sa'ad felt with him, and how Sa'ad came to spend most of his day chatting with Ibrahim, punctuating every other sentence with one of his phrases: "Listen!" or "You get me?" or an "*Ookey?*" spoken in English.

Sa'ad had found in Ibrahim a good, simple, trustworthy person to whom he could confide all the ideas and stories that crowded his mind. So he talked to Ibrahim about his humble family, which consisted of him, one sister and his widowed mother. He told Ibrahim about how he had had to leave school and work in clubs and dance halls as a lowly waiter, rising by degrees to become the most competent expert, able to taste, distinguish and serve various kinds of beverages, no matter what the setting or where the drink was from. After developing his knowledge through so much study and practice that he almost drove himself crazy, he became so good that he only needed to smell any open bottle to determine the type of drink it was, its provenance, the alcohol content and what it was made of. Indeed, most of the time he was even able to specify the exact year of the vintage.

Baghdad's most famous nightclubs and luxury hotels began competing to employ him. His reputation spread until the most prominent businessmen, the elites, and government officials all knew him. In the end, they brought him in to assume responsibility for the drinks of the President himself. The government sent him to London to take a month-long intensive course. He studied under eminent waiters, some of whom had worked in the palaces of the Queen of Britain and the Kings and Queens of Sweden and Spain. Sa'ad's expertise grew all the more, and he performed better than even the best-known experts due to his specialised knowledge of drinks native to the Orient.

Sa'ad would sometimes tell Ibrahim about that month when he had lived like a king in London, but most of the time he would talk about his experiences in Iraq, moving between the President's palaces, working at the bars and serving the President's guests, choosing which special drinks to import for the President, as well as which occasions were most appropriate for each, depending on the season, the meal, the mood, and various other factors.

What prompted Sa'ad to speak was bitterness. They had replaced him with someone else, a Russian with many degrees and certificates, even one in medicine, who also had a team of assistants. Whereas formerly Sa'ad was always travelling with the President in his planes and his boats, always receiving presents and money, and constantly enjoying surprises that filled his youthful soul with delight, he was now demoted to a supporting role and set to work supervising the gardens. His new job brought virtually no surprises. So he filled his time by reliving memories of his former life, what he had known and still knew, and found compensation for his loss in the wide eyes and baffled expressions of this simple peasant, Ibrahim. So Sa'ad spent most of his time each day with Ibrahim, talking about things he had seen or heard about. He sometimes took Ibrahim on his rounds through the gardens, far beyond his station at the house with mud walls. As Ibrahim's surprise and wonder increased with everything he saw and heard, so grew Sa'ad's eagerness to tell him more.

CHAPTER 17

Stories of the People's Palaces

Sa'ad's eyes blinked rapidly, and his whole body bristled with excitement. "Listen, brother!" he said. "I even worked in the *yakht.*"

When he saw Ibrahim's confused and enquiring look, he realised that Ibrahim did not know the meaning of the word *yakht.* "Look – it means a boat for the sea, big as an oil tanker. It's in the port of Umm Qasr, and it's called the *Victor.* Yes, even the yacht has a name. It's more than three hundred feet long, and I've heard that it cost fifty million dollars. Every window is bullet-proof glass. It has a helicopter pad, a swimming pool, a theatre, a bar, a garden, a doctor's clinic, and the best electronic equipment in the world. Hundreds of specially trained soldiers from the Republican Guard protect it. It was made in Finland to match the tastes of His Excellency the President. The wood is of the highest quality, the furniture is inlaid with gold and silver, and the hall in the centre can hold more than two hundred people.

"When the President goes down there in a small plane, or one of his sons or his guests, the entire harbour, both water and sky, is transformed into a hive of activity, and you see intensive patrols by security forces in every direction. Speedboats criss-crossing the water as though stung by a bee! You get me?

"Well, as for the rooms, there are five magnificent bedrooms reserved for the President and his family. And the restaurant on this yacht is kept stocked with the very best in food and beverages. I was the one who picked out the beverages. There's a gymnasium too, you know. Even the corridors – leading to all those rooms, halls, upper decks and the balconies overlooking the water and the horizon – are beautiful. They have carpets spread everywhere, delicately woven by hand, thread by thread, and the walls are covered with paintings and other decorations. Precious objects hang from the ceilings, each one a masterpiece in its own right. I remember a gold one made to look like the World Cup trophy.

"Listen! You know what? In Baghdad's Mansour district, there's an incredible secret palace that is very, very private, reserved for His Excellency the President's very, very private things. He goes there some nights when he wants to relax and get a little break – you get me? You know, when he wants some entertainment … you get me? There are two buildings that open towards each other. Some of the bedrooms are covered with mirrors, even on the ceiling – don't ask me why! Whenever I went into one, I felt strong, as though I were an entire army. The lamps there are various colours, and some of them are shaped like naked girls – the lamps! Yes, and I saw two big paintings with positions. Positions . . . you get me? Many walls near the beds were covered with imaginative drawings of women … in various … positions.

"In the corridors they have paintings in the style of the Renaissance in Italy. That might be what it's called – I asked my sister one time the name of paintings like these, which I had also seen in a magazine. She was in college and loved painting, and that's what she told me. In the paintings there are powerful men fighting lions and tigers, or killing crocodiles or dragons or enormous, many-headed serpents with swords. I saw a bronze statue of a man with bulging muscles and a thick moustache struggling against a fire-breathing dragon.

"There are a few big photographs, up on the third floor, of the Leader embracing bare-chested women who are stunningly beautiful, including one where he's hugging some woman in a magnificent bed and laughing. The rooms are big, each one the size of my house. Ah, how I dream of owning a house designed just how I want it! In those rooms, I saw more than one big bed with golden statues of mermaids rising up as bedposts. Of course, there's a T.V. in each room, and each one has a big bathroom with taps shaped like roses and golden daggers, matching the colour of the bath sandals. The waste baskets are shaped like hearts. In the closets are pyjamas and video cassettes. The beds are what they call *keeng seyz*, which means they're wider than a normal bed for two people. They're attached to the walls, with mirrors on both sides and above them. When I went in once to check the drinks in the refrigerator, some of the cupboards and drawers were open. There were silk pyjamas and nightshirts, underwear, shorts, T-shirts, bathrobes and other clothes I didn't recognise, all brand-new and wrapped in plastic.

"The curtains are made of pink chiffon. The pillows are shaped like hearts in red, blue, orange and pink. In one of the rooms I saw a painting covering the entire wall with a girl playing the oud, like the one in *A Thousand and One Nights*. There's a main bathroom with a *jaakuuzee* . . . Don't even ask me what a *jaakuuzee* is!

"One entire wing of this palace is a dance hall, a disco like the ones they had in the seventies. The carpet's brown and there are tinted mirrors and balls of coloured lights hanging from the ceiling. There are shelves of tapes and records of every song in the world, including *chobi* dance music from Iraq, Madonna, Michael Jackson and a band called the *Bee-Jeez*. These strange words you hear me saying are foreign words and names. I'm saying them just how I learned them, and I don't know how we say them in Arabic since I didn't finish school. Or maybe these words don't even have an equivalent in Arabic. Who knows? Moving on . . .

"The bars in this place have all different types of drinks. In the future, I dream of assembling a bar like that! Bottles of Johnny Walker whisky, Otard cognac, Rioja, gin – the list goes on and on. Some of the bottles themselves could be considered works of art, brother.

"One time, I saw glass bookcases filled with an astounding collection of pottery stamped with the princely seal of the Sabah family in Kuwait, no doubt from the days of the war there.

"In the other building are roses and various weapons, Kalashnikovs, Sig Sauer rifles, Russian, Spanish and Belgian pistols – including the 5.7 mm – Beretta and Smith & Wesson revolvers, and cases of ammunition. I mean, there's an entire arsenal from each of the main companies. In various rooms I saw a gold-plated automatic M.P.5 rifle with the President's name engraved, a Colt

38 Diamondback, a Magnam 357 and other weapons I didn't recognise, all of them with instruction manuals. In other rooms, the cases were stacked to the ceiling.

"But the thing that would astonish you, Uncle Abu Qisma, is the garden between the buildings. It has squares of flowers more beautiful than these, grilles made out of marble for cooking meat, and a bar with shelves crowded with bottles of Spanish, Italian, French and South African wine, some of them from the 1980s or older, as well as Russian vodka, Scottish whisky, French champagne, gin and Cuban rum. There were boxes of Marlboro and Kent cigarettes and Cuban cigars.

"The outdoor chairs are shaped like oyster shells, crowns and hearts, and there are chairs that are bags with grains sewn up inside and resembling hearts. Some of them have plastic flowers sewn on. On the ground floor is a kitchen that seems like a hospital since it's so clean and filled with fancy machines and work areas. There's a special cinema painted dark blue. It only has a few seats, which are very comfortable, with soft, pink cushions. As for the big swimming pool, its water circles around in a whirlpool, around and around."

Ibrahim wondered to himself what it all meant: the heart shapes and the weapons, the difference between water flowing from a golden tap and from a normal one, and the meaning of all these objects and colours that nearly made him dizzy just to hear them. Meanwhile Sa'ad kept rattling off his descriptions with delight.

"On the west bank of the Tigris River, you've got a district hidden away from the eyes of ordinary people by very tall fences.

Do you know it? It's a spot with a rustic atmosphere since His Excellency the President grew up in the countryside, and naturally he misses it. He's a genuine person who loves the simple things, just as we all know, right?

"I saw another palace there by the river consisting of seven large buildings. It has swimming pools, gardens, fountains, and various gyms for things like jumping, running and lifting weights. There are floors of gleaming granite, giant television screens and small boats, the fronts of which are carved like mermaids or leaping dolphins, used for gliding along waterways that pass in and out of the palace. The sides of that palace are decorated with marble reliefs and polished stones. I know one of the Greek women who work there, and she told me lots about it. Maybe they'll transfer you there some day.

"The garden out the back is a broad field stretching down to the river. There are statues of horses, falcons, half-naked women, and fierce lions covered with gold leaf. It's the absolute pinnacle of splendour and luxury, epitomised by a swimming pool so beautiful you wouldn't mind drowning in it! There's a huge garage with every kind of car, old and new, strange and rare: a bulletproof Mercedes, Chevrolet sports cars, cars with roofs that fold back, some that are overlaid with gold or silver. And gardens, gardens, yet more enormous gardens.

"On some of the walls of the buildings, looking down from above, there are pictures of the Leader in various outfits, doing various things: cantering on a horse, firing a rifle, eating watermelon, brandishing a sword, cutting birthday cake, riding in a tank, or drinking tea. There are statues of him, either full-length or just the top half of the body, some showing him with arms raised. The marble facade of one of the buildings has a big relief sculpture of His Excellency's face. Lower down, there are smaller sculptures of the heads of Nebuchadnezzar, Hammurabi and Saladin al-Ayyubi.

"Inside, hanging by a granite staircase with golden railings, there's a picture of His Excellency's family in formal dress. I think it's where the women and children stay since it has more closets than you can count, filled with thousands of articles of women's clothing, belts and shoes. There are enough shoes to wear five different pairs every day for a lifetime. There are children's toys everywhere, including cars, tanks, trains, aeroplanes, boats and little bicycles made of silver.

"That's what the Greek woman told me. We were speaking in English, you get me? I mean, I know a bit of English from my days in London. Ah, how nice it was there! Sometimes I hope to go back, but I can't leave my mother and sister here all alone. We can't bear to be separated. My sister would like to come to London with me, but my mother utterly refuses. She says, 'I'll never leave Baghdad! I'll never leave my home! Iraq is my country. I was born here, and here I'll die!'"

For a moment, Ibrahim thought that this young man must be dreaming: living in a dream and dreaming of another life, in which he dreamed yet more dreams. Ibrahim imagined the tangled mass of dreams wrapped within dreams.

"The furniture is of the most splendid kind ever made by the hands of man. The decor too. The doors, windows, balconies, stairways, ceilings and walls are decorated with the most magnificent ornamentation. The bathtubs and sinks have taps in different shapes, the door handles are made of gold and silver and the indoor swimming pools each have a unique design. There are inner tubes for lying on the surface of the water and *Kreesteeyan Deeyoor* towels. Don't ask me what *Kreesteeyan Deeyoor* means.

Of course, Ibrahim did not ask him. Regarding everything Sa'ad said, he just asked himself, why gold? What difference does it make for door handles to be gold?

"There's a wing for medical clinics, including a dentist's office, a clinic for eye examinations, and another for plastic surgery. Next to them is a luxurious hair salon, its shelves filled with fashion magazines. On the top floor there are T.V.s, recording equipment, a cinema and a stage. The roof has gardens. In the middle of one of them is a big bedroom in the shape of a dome. Its roof is transparent glass so you can see the rain and the stars at night when you are lying in bed.

"There are pens for lions, cheetahs, hyenas, monkeys, peacocks, gazelles, sheep and goats. One time, His Excellency's wife ordered us to throw a live goat to the hungry cheetahs, and they devoured it in the blink of an eye. Sometimes they make these wild animals hungry and throw in traitors or members of the opposition, recording it all on video in the presence of His Excellency or his sons, who watch on comfortable chairs near the fence beside tables covered with drinks. I would be the one pouring the drinks. I was working there less than two months ago.

"The palace is gigantic, with so many rooms. I counted one hundred and forty offices, sixty-five bathrooms, twenty meeting rooms, twenty-two kitchens, and too many other rooms to count.

There are five big halls for dancing, one of them as big as a sports field. To make one quick tour around those palaces would take hours – no, days, maybe – passing through the corridors, the lobbies, the grand halls, the mirrors, the gardens, the water canals and the tunnels.

"But the wing reserved for the Master is found on the other side. There are many books in his bedroom, all in Arabic. Books about history, tribal genealogy, Bedouin poetry and memoirs by people like Stalin, Mussolini, Castro. Most of the books are about him, though. I think he likes French suits, Russian hats and Italian jackets by Chanel and Lucca. His ties come in such a variety of colours and designs that it makes your head spin. His clothes are kept in private closets on the top floor in one of the buildings in the palace compound, which extends for miles along the banks of the river. There are dozens of military and civilian uniforms, Iraqi and foreign, white and black, light blue and dark blue, every colour. Row upon row of elegant shirts with gold and silver buttons filling big closets I couldn't say how many yards long.

"One time, I started putting drinks on the coffee table in the middle of one of the rooms when I saw a family photograph album. There were wedding pictures, pictures of His Excellency cutting a cake with a gilded sword, pictures of his children – just the boys.

"I also saw a hat like the one he was wearing when he fired his rifle in front of the crowds in Celebrations Square. That's the scene we always see on T.V. – do you remember it? Some of the rooms have albums with thousands of photographs of the Leader in various costumes and poses. He appears as an Arab knight, a noble Bedouin, a Kurdish *aga*, a diplomat, a construction worker, a peasant, an army general wearing a uniform covered in medals, a tribal sheikh, a Russian oligarch, a mountain climber, a swimmer, a hunter and a pilot. There are pictures with presidents, kings, emirs and celebrities, and many others with army brigades on the front lines or at military parades, meetings with generals and officers, giving speeches, comforting widows, receiving tribal sheikhs, kissing babies, praying, or greeting bearded men. There are albums with old pictures from when he was a child and as a young man some three decades ago, leading gradually to the newer pictures. I too have some pictures taken with him that I've had enlarged and are now hanging in the sitting room of our house.

"Anyway, His Excellency's palaces, like His Excellency's family, number in the hundreds and are found in every corner of the country. In the region of his birthplace alone there are more than one hundred and fifty palaces. His Excellency says they are the people's palaces, for he loves the people and the people love him. At the same time, they make us look good by making it clear to foreign guests who visit our country the vast splendour in which the Iraqi people live . . . Yes, it has to be like that, for God delights to see the effect of the blessings He has showered on His servant. Right, uncle? What do you think?"

"Yes."

"It's true, right?"

"Yes, yes, comrade. Your words are golden."

"You get me."

CHAPTER 18

The President Slays the Musician

Ibrahim realised that Sa'ad had begun to trust him. No, it went beyond trust. He might have felt an affection that rose to the level of love. It could have been that he found in Ibrahim something of what he imagined about his father, or just that Ibrahim always listened to him and showed understanding. When speaking, Sa'ad had two phrases that he repeated nearly every sentence: "Listen!" and "You get me?" Even though Ibrahim would not respond with "Yes, I hear you," or "Yes, I've got you," his features and his eyes said precisely that, something that put Sa'ad at greater ease than if Ibrahim actually used those words. Indeed, if he had said "I hear you" or "I get you" each time, perhaps he would have embarrassed or annoyed Sa'ad by pointing out how often he repeated those phrases.

One of the results of this trust was that Sa'ad began taking Ibrahim to work in different places, sometimes for hours and sometimes for days, to fill in for other people who were on holiday or had been transferred. During one of these assignments, Ibrahim saw the President for the first time. It happened on the far side of the small man-made lake, in the forest that faced the house with mud walls where Ibrahim worked. Sa'ad ushered Ibrahim in among the trunks of the enormous, terrifying trees and said, "Listen. Clean the ground and put everything in order. You get me?" Then he left.

As usual, there was no real work to do. A few leaves and twigs had fallen here and there; some bird droppings; dried grass crossing over the lines prescribed by the circles, triangles and eight-pointed stars built around the tree trunks. He saw trees unlike any he had seen before. They did not resemble each other, and some of them had fruits of unusual shape, size and colour. With their ancient and enormous trunks, reaching up into the sky, some of the trees looked a thousand years old. When had they been planted!? The sky was entirely blocked out, with just a few splinters of blue breaking through high above when the wind moved the leaves.

Ibrahim thought they must have made a mistake in putting him to work here, especially if they had done it because he was once a farmer. Even though he had been born in the countryside and grown up in the fields like any other plant, not a single farmer in this country planted flowers or spent their life caring for strange trees like these. Trees just took up land, drank water and prevented you from seeing the sky. Most of them did not bear fruit, and even if they did, the people did not know what to do with it.

In this sweet shade and silence, broken only by birds hidden in the treetops above, in this leisurely seclusion, Ibrahim felt a rare ease, a tranquillity unlike any he had experienced. Or at least, not since childhood. He somehow got to thinking about his life, and for a moment he realised how far he had lost touch with who he was and how much time had passed since he had taken himself away to reflect in silence like this. He wished there was some way to tenderly embrace one's own soul as though it were another human being. That longing in his spirit was so powerful that it brought tears to his eyes.

There was no sky and no horizon to look out upon, the kind of view that helps one gaze deeper within. Without coming out from among the trees to the open shore, Ibrahim approached the lake. He sat on the ground some yards from the water, so that he could see it but would not be visible to anyone else. He leaned back against one of those wide tree trunks and stretched his legs out, crossing one foot over the other. He felt a cool pleasure steal into his skin from the damp grass below. Tree trunks closed in on all sides, though there was a narrow silver gap between the trees ahead of him, allowing him to see the shore, the surface of the water, the other side and a bit of the sky. He sighed and took a deep breath as though to swallow up the gentle breeze gliding off the lake. He wished he could just stay there and keep things exactly as they were until he had quenched his need for rest, for the air, for stillness. If only he were cut off from everything and forgotten by the world! Let everyone forget him so he might commune in freedom with his authentic self! Or at least be free to forget himself.

Ibrahim's thoughts soon returned to his life, and from his very depths, he murmured in an audible whisper, "O Lord, my God, all praise and thanks be thine!" He was thinking of Qisma, this girl who had grown up so fast, already a woman, who dressed well and put on perfume every morning to attend the Teachers' Institute so gladly. He watched her as she blossomed and grew happier every day. His material situation had improved, for in addition to a good salary, they provided him with what was called "the national gifts", a certain amount of cash arriving in an envelope on every national holiday – of which Iraq had very many, indeed! He spent it all on his wife's treatment and to provide for Qisma's every need. Unfortunately, his wife's health was getting worse, while Qisma was spending more on herself, her clothes, her friends and her car, which he had bought for her so she could drop him off every morning at the Alawite Garage before going to her classes. (From there, he took a bus to the presidential palace along with the others.) Two evenings a week, Qisma would take her mother to the doctor, until the doctors had insisted two weeks earlier that she remain in the hospital for intensive care.

He felt the special card in his pocket and remembered what Sa'ad had once told him: "This card is very important. It has true power. With it, all doors will open to you, and no-one will get in your way. With it, you can go anywhere you want in this country. It makes everything easy. You don't need to wait in line, and the military checkpoints won't search you. Indeed, soldiers and officers will even beg your pardon when they see this card, which comes straight from the Palace of the Republic. Don't you see this symbol and this stamp, man? Don't you see what's written at the top? With it, you can do anything – and terrify anyone – you want. You get me?"

But Ibrahim had never thought of using it. He wished his wife's health would improve so she might enjoy the way things were for them now. It would be a compensation for her anxiety over his long absence during the wars – and his compensation for that deprivation too. But unfortunately, she just got worse. Nevertheless, "Praise be to God!" he said. "Everything is fate and decree."

He began thinking of the forthcoming holiday and of the gifts he would bring to his family in the village, his friends Abdullah Kafka and Tariq the Befuddled, and all his cousins. Qisma would certainly help him pick them out. He would visit the river there. He would sit with his family for as much time as he had. He would—

A sudden commotion interrupted Ibrahim's reflections, jolting him out of his pleasant and contemplative solitude. He could see a group of soldiers blocking his view of the lake and the shore through the gap in the trees. They were throwing various kinds of fish, all different sizes, into the water. Then they left. Other people immediately took their place and planted a large umbrella in the ground, under which they placed a wooden chair with cushions, facing the water. A short distance behind it, facing the same direction, they put a second chair – a normal one, far less costly than the first.

Ibrahim's heart was pounding, but he did not move. He had no idea what he ought to do in a situation like this. He also did not know how long he'd been there. It was late afternoon and the working day had certainly finished, but neither Sa'ad nor anyone else had arrived to pick him up.

Then . . . was it him? Yes, it was! The President! He approached slowly and sat on the wooden chair by the water. Two smartly dressed soldiers set up a small table with gilded edges beside him. They were followed by a civilian, a foreigner with blond hair, who approached and laid the table with a bottle, a glass, a plate and some other things that Ibrahim could not see clearly. Another man came with a thick Cuban cigar that he lit for the President, followed by another who brought a long fishing rod. The President took the rod and cast the line in the water. Then he sat quietly, smoking and drinking, all alone. Or at least, Ibrahim could not see if there was anyone with him because of all the tree trunks. It was utterly silent.

The President was wearing a foreign hat and a loose-fitting shirt with a flower pattern. He smoked and drank calmly from his glass, his face towards the water and his back to Ibrahim, who felt so violently disturbed that he was sure it was all a dream. Ibrahim endeavoured not to make the slightest movement. He started breathing as shallowly as he could, and he rested his arm over the stump of his left leg and grabbed his artificial foot to prevent any involuntary motion that would rustle or knock into something.

Ibrahim could not see the President's face clearly except when he turned to one side or the other. He found him to be a normal man with a normal moustache. But he had an authority that was not normal, something obscure and indefinable. In the flesh, the President appeared more normal than he did in pictures, where he seemed to be encircled by a magic halo. But on the other hand, his actual presence was more terrifying than the adoring popular pictures would have you believe.

The President began reeling in the line vigorously. He had caught a big fish, one that the soldiers had thrown in only a little while before. He reeled it in, closer and closer, until he pulled it out of the water and held it in front of his face. He looked at the fish, smiled into its eyes, and turned. A general from his bodyguard hurried forward, took the fish off the hook, and threw it back in the water. That pattern repeated itself several times over a period of time that Ibrahim could not quantify.

Then the President turned and made a motion with his head. A man was brought over, a civilian in his seventies or eighties, carrying an oud. They sat him on the second chair, and trembling, the man started playing.

It was the famous musician Nabil. Everyone knew him from seeing him playing on television, accompanying singers of every generation going back to the days when Iraq still had a king. He was called "the professor", and it was said that he taught other oud players. He looked older than he did on television. This was the first celebrity Ibrahim had seen in person. He thought that if he escaped, he would tell Qisma about it since she loved celebrities. This incident would become one of the memorable events of his life. Then he remembered that he was forbidden to speak about anyone or anything he saw or heard here.

The musician was dripping with sweat, dressed in a suit and tie. He was trembling, yet he played gentle melodies, mostly traditional folk songs. But he would immediately break off in the middle of a song whenever he saw the President's finger trace a circle in the air with the clear meaning of "another". It went on like that until the tenth fish or so. Then the President turned to face the musician. Someone hastened to turn his chair for him and disappeared in the blink of an eye. The President was face to face with Professor Nabil, who attempted to rise. The President motioned for him to stay seated, and he slumped back down. The President put his foot on one of the musician's knees – the oud was resting on the other – and he motioned for the musician to continue playing. Then he began wiping the bottom of his sandal on Nabil's shirt, calmly rubbing the musician's belly.

A moment later, the President gave the oud a kick and it fell to the ground. He pulled the musician's tie forward until Nabil was bent double and said in a soft, though terrifying, voice, "Heeey...How's it going, Nabil?" Without waiting for an answer, he went on: "And how are your daughters doing? How about your lofty position, your great fame, and the big house that our revolutionary government has given you?"

The musician stammered, "Everything is perfect. Everything is going as well as can be, sir, thanks to your generous care for me. May our Lord preserve you, may our Lord preserve you!"

"No. No, it appears that you are not content. I hear you speak of freedom and democracy when you get drunk at your private parties."

"No! No, sir, never! You are freedom. You are democracy. You—"

The President interrupted him, bringing forward a glass with his free hand while still pulling at the musician's tie and digging his sandal even harder into the musician's chest.

"Something to drink?" he asked evenly. Then he yelled, "Drink!"

As soon as the musician began to reach out his trembling hand, the President threw the contents of the glass in his face.

Then he threw the empty glass over his shoulder into the water. He took the bottle from the table and offered it to the musician. "This is the best and most expensive drink in the world. Drink it, all of it, and you'll be richer than all of us."

The musician took the bottle, while the blond servant brought another of a different colour and shape. He set it on the table and disappeared.

The President turned and called, "Faisal!"

A man wearing pyjamas came up and gave the President a pistol. It was the minister of defence. Ibrahim could hardly believe his eyes. This august military man, the mere mention of whose name caused a shiver in one's veins; this man, who never appeared in the media except in full uniform decorated with stars, swords, insignia and medals, with a severe expression on his face: Ibrahim would never have imagined that he slept like every other human, and even if he slept, surely it would be standing up, in full military regalia and a state of perpetual readiness. When the President mentioned him on television, he went through all his titles and his ranks before mentioning his name. Now he just called him "Faisal", nothing more, and Faisal appeared in his pyjamas, handed the President a gold pistol, and withdrew with a bow and deliberate steps.

The President half turned to face the lake without letting go of the musician's tie. He began shooting at the ducks swimming there as he laughed hysterically until the pistol ran out of bullets and he threw it aside. The minister of defence hurried up with a hand grenade. The President held down the lever on the side and looked at the minister, who hurriedly pulled out the safety pin.

The President looked at the grenade in his hand, then he stared at the musician and smiled. He rubbed the grenade on the nose of the musician, who was trembling and swimming in sweat, hunched over like a broken finger. Then, without turning around, the President threw the grenade behind him into the lake. It exploded, sending high in the air a fountain of water that blended fragments of ducks and fish with the mud and algae. The President let go of the musician's tie and turned to survey the surface of the lake, which was covered with flashes of white, the bellies of fish flipped over on their backs, twisting in the last throes of death amid a crimson surge of mud, grass, duck feathers and blood.

For a few moments all was silent. The President took a gulp from his cup. The minister offered him another pistol, and from the other side, someone set a pigeon free into the air. It went flying past the President, and he fired at it. Another went by, which he shot at, and another and another. He would hit some and miss others. It went on until he emptied the pistol and threw it aside. The minister immediately offered him an A.K.-47, and the person on the far side began releasing the pigeons in a flock, and the President fired a shower of bullets at them. Most of them fell dead, careening out of the sky into the water, while a few lucky survivors flew away to safety.

The President stopped and gestured with his hand. Two men came forward and lifted the musician by his armpits since he was no longer able to stand on his own. They stood him up on the wooden embankment with his back to the lake. He fell to his knees, crying and pleading with words that did not form sentences.

The President said to him, "You talk about freedom and democracy, eh, Nabil? You, to whom we have given more than you could have even dreamed? You, who did nothing more than chase after whores in the clubs and sing for the entertainment of drunks until we raised you up. You fool! You good-for-nothing! You've spent your life buzzing on this clumsy board of yours. You've done nothing useful in your entire life except buzz around like a fly on manure. Get up."

The musician tried to rise, but his strength failed him. The two soldiers helped him up and then stepped away.

The President said to him, "Sing 'Ducky, Ducky'."

The old musician began singing the well-known children's song:

> Ducky, ducky, swim in the sea
> Tell the fish the net you see
> Swim, swim away, and keep yourself free!

The President demanded another children's song:

> Yes, nightingale? Yes!
> Have you seen a sparrow? Yes!
> He pecks at the bowl? Yes!
> The milk and the seeds? Yes!

Wrapped in his tears, his sweat, his snot and his fear, the musician sang in a hoarse, choked voice while the President laughed loudly. Then he turned, and they released a pigeon for him behind the musician's head. The President shot at it, and at another and another. He shot again and again as the bullets whizzed past the ears of the musician, who started and jumped. The President laughed at him and ordered him to sing "Ducky, Ducky" again. It went on like this until he turned and his men released another flock of pigeons. The President hosed them with such a spray of bullets that the air shattered with the noise. Then he lowered the rifle until it was aimed straight at the musician, and unleashed a hail of bullets at point-blank range, driving him back and down into the water.

The President approached the shore, looked down, and spat. He turned around as though to leave but paused when his foot hit the oud. He looked at it, and someone picked it up for him. He took it between his hands, kissed it, and examined it like a child receiving a long-awaited toy. It was as though he were touching a musical instrument for the first time. He raised it to his chest and began strumming the strings, trying to play, as if he were the only person there. He tried again but failed to produce even two notes that went together. Scowling, he threw the oud into the water and continued on his way.

CHAPTER 19

Both Sides of the Television Screen

Ibrahim did not know how long he remained frozen there afterwards. Long enough for his legs to fall asleep. There was a commotion followed by a prolonged silence, which made him think they had left. The first move he attempted was to swallow. The effort hurt because his throat was so dry. He touched his shirt and found it sticking to him due to the sweat, and he feared he had wet his pants because it was damp down there too. He felt he had never experienced anything as terrifying as that, despite the wars and the blood, the dead men, the severed body parts, the executions and the bombardments he had seen: everything connected to living hand in hand with death – or rather, with murder.

But the way this incident struck him was entirely different. Perhaps because it had been unexpected, outside the framework of battles and fighting. Perhaps because he had never imagined that the President would be a normal man like this. And that he killed with his own hands. Or perhaps because he could not discern his own attitude towards all of it, and what he had to do, or how he ought to feel. He felt superfluous; he was an unwanted parasite, an unseen ghost. What if someone had noticed his presence? What would they have done to him? What ought he to have done? Perhaps they had done it on purpose, with some plan in mind, knowing that he was there. No, impossible! For a moment, he wished that one of the bullets the President had fired in various directions had come his way and killed him silently in his hiding-place: a solution to the crisis in which he found himself, a release from the ordeal and the terror that had befallen him.

In the midst of the silence, he heard a gurgling and something splashing in the water, coming from the direction where the body of the musician had fallen. Most likely Nabil was still alive, Ibrahim thought, the remnants of his soul struggling against death. He trembled because he did not know what he ought to do. What could he do now?

Then he heard the rustling of footsteps in the forest behind him. Footsteps coming ever closer. He froze in place and found himself turning involuntarily. He saw nothing among the tree trunks, but the footsteps were getting closer. Then he heard Sa'ad's voice calling him. "Uncle Ibrahim!" The voice was not loud, but just the normal tone of Sa'ad's call when he came looking for him: "Uncle Ibrahim! You hear me? Abu Qisma!"

He was certain it was Sa'ad, and he put out a sound that resembled, "Yes." Then he was able to speak more clearly: "Yes. Yes, I'm over here, comrade." He got up, supporting himself with the tree trunk and whatever determination remained within him.

Sa'ad apologised for being late, and said that things were just like that sometimes. "You get me? The President goes around without any fixed appointments, and he does whatever he wants whenever he wants without any advance warning or notice. Of course, you can't approach him without permission. Naturally, everything is subject to his orders, his desires, his mood – you get me? Did anyone see you?"

Even in normal circumstances, Ibrahim was a man of few words, but it went far beyond that now and he was scarcely able to speak. He shook his head. Sa'ad sighed with relief. "Praise God!" Then he asked, "And did you see him?" Ibrahim only had to hint at shaking his head again for Sa'ad to go on speaking. "If you had seen him, I would have asked who brought his drinks. Was he blond? The Russian? Do you know that I was the one who used to do that, and more than once in this exact place? I would bring the drinks, and he would fish and shoot ducks and pigeons."

By way of an apology, Sa'ad decided to drive Ibrahim home in his own car. He took him to the door of his house without enquiring about the address, but Ibrahim did not ask how he knew it. No doubt Sa'ad knew everything. Was he not one of them, the government? That is how Ibrahim explained the matter to himself, and he did not insist on Sa'ad coming in. Sa'ad left, singing to himself, as darkness fell.

On the way there, Sa'ad had not stopped at any red lights or observed any traffic signs. It seemed that the police knew him, and for that reason, no-one interfered. Some even gave him a military salute from a distance. Sa'ad informed Ibrahim that a magnificent dinner party would be given three days later in the gardens of one of these palaces to commemorate the President achieving some position decades earlier.

"Listen – there's going to be an amazing party. Fewer than two hundred people have been invited, primarily the most beautiful women from Iraq and abroad. You'll see a long table covered with food and drink, the quantity and variety of which cannot even be imagined. It will be more than they need, of course, and afterwards the workers can eat or take home whatever they want. Do you want me to put your name on the team of servants? You'd be able to bring along just one person – a woman, on the condition that she is beautiful and dressed as finely as she can be!" He laughed and went on. "They also give us substantial cash gifts. I'll be there on the team serving drinks, and you'll get to see my skills. Do you want to?"

Ibrahim shook his head, no. Sa'ad was silent for a while. Then he said, "Yes, you're tired. As a compensation for having kept you waiting today, I'll give you a two-day holiday. On top of that, just come the day before the party and the day after in order to put the garden back in order and take care of the flowers." Sa'ad began singing, "*Hey, uncle, you sell the roses. Tell me how much they are, tell me, tell me . . .*" and so on, until they arrived. Under the intoxicating influence of that song, he said, "And here you are, honoured rose uncle, Abu Qisma. By your leave, my good sir!"

That was the last time Ibrahim saw this good young man alive.

When Ibrahim went inside the house, he found his daughter in the living room, lying on the couch in front of the television with her nightshirt riding up so it barely covered her legs. She was talking on the phone in a whisper, and as usual, her perfume filled the room. As soon as she saw him, she hung up and lazily adjusted her position. She asked him why he was so late, and he responded with a single word after sitting on the other end of the couch, placing his head between his hands: "Work." She asked him if he had eaten dinner or wanted anything, and he replied, "Water." Then he quickly followed that up by insisting, "No, not water. Anything else. Tea, I want tea." Qisma got up and went into the kitchen.

Ibrahim breathed deeply. He took off his artificial foot and the shoe on his other foot and lay back to relax. But he suddenly sat straight up when he noticed the musician Nabil on the television. He came closer to the screen and took a good look. It was him. The musician Nabil, wearing the same suit, the same tie that Ibrahim had seen pulled forward today in the fist of the President, and the same shirt on which the President wiped the sole of his shoe before peppering it with bullets. But as usual, Nabil looked younger on the screen, more glamorous under the lights. He was playing his oud and sitting at the front of a troupe of musicians lined up behind a singer celebrating a national festival. At least, that is what it said at the bottom of the screen. All the songs were extolling the President; however, those too were considered patriotic songs of the nation. That is, if they even deserved to be called songs. Up in the top corner of the screen, he read the word "LIVE". Ibrahim came closer still until his eyes were almost touching the screen in order to confirm the word "LIVE". Then he withdrew and remained on the edge of the couch, astonished by what he saw.

He could not help noticing that the cameras seemed particularly drawn to Professor Nabil, focusing on his face, serious, smiling, swaying as he played, gazing off in the distance. And there were other shots of his fingers as they strummed the strings.

He appeared more frequently than the other musicians and the audience, only a little less than the famous singer – at least, that is how it seemed to Ibrahim, as though they wanted him to be sure that it actually was Nabil. It was as though Ibrahim had gone mad and was conjuring up the image of this musician whose murder he witnessed just a few hours before.

When Qisma entered with his tea, he immediately asked her, "Does it say 'LIVE' at the top?"

"Yes."

"And this man playing the oud – is it the famous musician Nabil?"

"Yes."

After he was silent for a moment, he took the tea from her hands and asked, "Do you think the broadcast really is coming to us live or was it recorded earlier?"

"What does it matter if it's live or not! The important thing is that these guys know how to take life by the teeth!"

When she saw he made no response, she thought he might not have understood her expression "to take life by the teeth", so she sat on the edge of the couch and went on talking fervently. "There are people who really know how to make it in this world, how to rake in the money and glory, and how to enjoy life."

"Life! Do you think that they are really alive?"

"Of course they're alive! Indeed, more than alive, not like all the rest of us, the living dead."

Based on his intuition and how well he knew his daughter, he could tell she was drawing him in another direction, the way she usually did when provoking him and making him feel somehow at fault. He did not know quite why she was so hard like this, so cold, as though she'd felt an aversion towards him since she was young. He remembered those moments in which he sensed the transformation in her attitude, her disengagement, such as the first time she saw him with one foot and knew he was impaired. He sometimes used to justify it by telling himself that he had never been with her for very long, and he used to think that, as she got older, with the passage of time, she would forgive him when she understood that his absence had never been something he wanted. But although she was grown up now, still she mistreated him even when he remained silent before her and avoided confrontation, aware that he would always lose because he could not speak as well as she did.

"Everything is fate and decree, my daughter."

"No fate, no decree and no watermelons! It comes down to will and intelligence. Every person can achieve what he wants and live the life he wants. You just have to know what you want and devote your mind and energy to getting it!"

"There are some people like that, born big in the world, with power or money or a high position. Every person has his fate. As they say, 'Everyone is guided to that which is created for him.' Everything is preordained. Every person has his fate. Not everyone is equal."

"Indeed, not everyone is equal because some people don't want that equality – they don't seek it. But those who do want it will get what they aim for. And those who are inclined to submission and obedience, who are content with a marginalised life in the shadows – they'll be exploited by others and will remain in the shadows, marginalised for ever. That's if those who are stronger, richer and bolder don't crush them."

Ibrahim realised that he would never succeed in persuading her of any of his convictions. He actually believed what he said, and he did not suffer from jealousy or hatred or pursue ambitions that did not correspond to his lot in life. He had grown accustomed to contentment in and of itself. But it was no use trying yet again to make her see his point of view, so he just repeated the expression quietly: "Everything is fate and decree."

Qisma jumped to her feet, enraged. "Aiii! Once again with fate and decree?! Don't you have anything else? Don't you get bored repeating that? Haven't you put that to the test throughout your whole life? You can see for yourself where it's got you. You've spent your life as a soldier under the command of officers half your age, who became officers in just two years and with half the effort. You lost your foot, while they got the stars and the medals. Now here you are spending the rest of your life as a servant in the gardens, and no doubt there's another even younger officer who humiliates you and drags you around like a sheep wherever he wants. So don't tell me that! There's no fate, no decree. And no asphalt!"

She stormed off to her room and slammed the door behind her. Ibrahim remained where he was sitting, head bowed, alone. But Qisma opened the door again and stuck her head out to yell, "Even if you are satisfied with your life, I'm not satisfied with mine, and I'm going to work out how to change it!"

Then she banged the door shut. Just as quickly she opened it again and stuck her head out once more to follow up: "And just for your information, I hate being called Qisma! Why did you name me after this fate of yours?" She slammed the door even harder.

Ibrahim wished his wife were there at that moment. He wished he could fall on her shoulder and weep. Her gentle fingers would stroke his head, and her low voice, like the whisper of trees or a murmuring river, would calm him. He wanted to tell her everything he had seen that day. He wished his daughter were like her mother, or at least that she had half her mother's good nature, half her calm. But fate had decreed that his Qisma should be the opposite of them both since his wife resembled him in nearly everything, not least his contentment with his lot in life. How he needed her at that moment! How he needed a majestic moment of solitude and comfort like the one he had experienced among the strange trees before what happened had happened, before he saw what he saw.

How he longed for Umm Qisma! Ibrahim thought he would go to the hospital that moment, go to her, embrace her, care for her, complain about Qisma's violence towards him, and ask Umm Qisma's pardon for every way he had failed her during their married lives. He would make her understand. Or help her come to see that the course of his entire life had not been determined by his own choices, and that he had not been given any opportunity to change it. Every aspect of his life had been imposed by circumstances and decided by others. Even his marriage to her, for as she knew, his father had proposed it and hers had agreed to it. It might have been the only choice to have worked out well, the one most suited to him. He would tell her everything. Only she could understand what he wanted to say, even if he did not say a word.

Ibrahim stood up on his one leg. Then he sat back down, remembering that he had a two-day holiday and that the hour was late. She might be sleeping, or they might not let him in.

He sipped his tea as the national festival went on. Nabil was playing behind a young singer the same age as the musician's daughters. Ibrahim stared at Nabil once last time on the screen, which was actually the last time they showed him. He turned off the television and hobbled towards the bathroom. On the way, he stopped at the door to Qisma's room and bent his head to listen. He could not hear anything. Then he gave two light knocks and said, "Take me to the hospital tomorrow before you go to the institute. I have the day off."

He took a step towards the bathroom but came back to stand once more in front of her door and call, "Sleep well!" He walked further down the hall and finished the sentence quietly to himself, "my daughter."

CHAPTER 20

A Bouquet of Flowers and an Orange

As usual, Ibrahim woke up early. By the time Qisma was up, he had shaved, showered, put on cologne and polished his shoes. He dressed in the suit he kept for special occasions. Then he set out breakfast in the living room while Qisma finished washing and getting dressed before coming to eat with him. They exchanged no words apart from a "good morning" and a "thank you", and a "goodbye" when she dropped him off at the hospital. He told her there was no need for her to come and get him; he would return home by himself in a taxi.

As soon as his wife saw him, her pale face lit up. Ibrahim's heart flashed with joy like a long vacant house when the lights first come on. She had been lying back on the hospital bed, but sat up and reached out both arms to receive him, even though one was connected to an I.V. drip. She smiled with a sweetness that enchanted Ibrahim. It made her so happy to see him walking towards her in the suit he wore on their wedding day. Throughout the years of their marriage, their entire relationship had been an endless cycle of absences and reunions, and beyond the confines of their bedroom, they had never been alone like this, just the two of them, without relatives close by. It was as though they were meeting for the first time, and there was something of that sense of mutual annihilation that is felt with love at first sight. Ibrahim bent over and held her in a long embrace. They nuzzled one another's neck. Ibrahim ran his hands along her back and up to both sides of her head, his eyes shining with tears that did not fall.

He sat before her on the edge of the bed. In the morning light pouring through the window, she appeared the most beautiful woman in the world, even though she had become thinner than anyone he had ever seen. Despite that, he found her in a better mood than the previous times he had visited: more radiant, affectionate and vigorous.

A nurse came with the breakfast trolley. Ibrahim insisted on feeding his wife with his own hand. Every time she indicated she had had enough, he insisted she sip another spoonful of soup, and joked with her until she complied. It went on like that until he had helped her eat an entire breakfast.

She told him she was better, but that she longed for home, for their village. She longed for her normal daily life with him and with Qisma. She thanked him for his patience and for taking care of her, and she asked his pardon for all her shortcomings. He repeated the very same words of gratitude and apology. After the doctor came and she took her medicine, Ibrahim asked the doctor whether it was possible for her to walk around a little. The doctor said it all depended on her own wishes and ability.

Ibrahim helped her stand, and she leaned her arm across his shoulders. His arm was around her waist, while in his other hand he carried the I.V. bag. They started slowly down the white hallway, taking as much pleasure from their walk as they would strolling along the banks of a river, with the close-set windows standing in for the flowing water. They went outside to the garden and chose for themselves a secluded stone bench in the shade of a fig tree. As soon as they sat down, she said she wanted to touch the grass. Ibrahim wanted to pluck out a handful for her, but she stopped him, saying that she wanted to feel it where it was. He helped her down to the ground, and they sat there together. She began running her fingers through the grass, touching it with a deep tenderness, as though playing with the hair of a sleeping baby.

Ibrahim was delighted and felt optimistic to find her this way. He did not talk about anything that could distract from these moments he was sharing with his wife. He forgot – or ignored – everything he was going to tell her. They recalled memories from the village – funny childhood stories, their neighbours and friends – and more than once they laughed. He reassured her that he was doing well, and that he lacked for nothing apart from her health and her presence at home. Without her, he said, life had no flavour and no meaning. He needed her in everything, and her presence was necessary for him to feel his own existence. He hinted at what he had learned about his relationship with Qisma – he was no good at reaching an understanding with her and did not know how to get close to her.

Ibrahim's wife comforted him with the same words she always used, saying that Qisma was a good-hearted girl, even if she was somewhat irritable, difficult and stubborn. She asked him to be as patient with her as possible, and to take care of her, in case her own absence was prolonged. Her tone shifted as she said, "My last wish is that you be patient and forbearing with Qisma, no matter what, and with yourself, too."

When Ibrahim tried to stop her from using this valedictory tone, she cut him off to say, "I forgive you everything, Ibrahim. You are a very good man, and I am content with you."

Tears choked them both, and they fell silent together. Then he repeated the same words to her. "I forgive you everything, Umm Qisma. You are a very good woman, and I am content with you."

They embraced, and for the first time in their entire lives, she whispered in his ear, "I love you." He squeezed her tight, forgetting the frailty of her body, and replied in her ear, through his tears, "I love you."

They remained like this a long time. After a while, they changed the direction of the conversation entirely and began talking about daily things and what they would bring as gifts during their next trip to the village.

The day passed quickly, as the days of lovers do; and slowly, as the days of lovers also do. They ended the visit sitting in the same way, with him on the edge of the bed in front of her, and her lying back. Meanwhile, the window gradually grew darker, and city lights shone through it, decorating the night sky. Sitting there under those lights, Ibrahim thought she looked like a royal doll.

He had spent the entire day with her and did not leave until she fell asleep with her hand in his. He kissed her forehead and walked home, enjoying night-time in Baghdad for the very first time. He passed through old streets and the working-class markets where the fragrance of tea and smoke from water pipes emanated from the cafés, mixing with the pungent aromas coming from restaurants and the carts of street vendors. He crossed the bridge, stopping in the middle to look down at the waters of the Tigris. It reflected the lights from the banks and from the sky, and Ibrahim inhaled a clean breeze that refreshed his spirit.

He looked back at the hospital building and tried to guess which of the many windows was his wife's. He thought he had picked it out and focused his gaze upon it as though staring into her eyes. He pictured her lying behind it comfortably, her pallor enhancing her beauty, her contentment making her resemble the angels of his imagination. He recalled how the last word of their conversation was also the name of their daughter, Qisma. It was the last thing she had said to him, which he repeated. They had smiled together, and then she had nodded off.

"That's life," she had said. "Everything is decree and fate."

"That's life. Everything is decree and fate." Their smiles almost dissolved into laughter, as though they were co-conspirators.

Ibrahim now smiled at her from the bridge and sent her a heartfelt kiss through the night air. Then he continued his journey with a feeling of contentment. Indeed, he felt true love and was certain that no-one in this universe could understand him or feel the same thing apart from her.

He filled himself up with an excellent meal of kebabs and left a good tip for the waiter. When he bought a glass of tea from a boy in the street, he paid double, and the boy thanked him and invoked God's blessing of health and prosperity for Ibrahim and his family. Ibrahim began giving generously to every homeless person and street vendor he passed because the idea of them praying for him and his family appealed to him greatly. He thought that the prayers of one of them just might be answered. That night just might be a blessed night.

In the side street leading to his house, he was whistling some tune or melody. But he stopped with a shudder when he recalled what had happened to the musician the day before. He struggled to drive the memory from his mind, recalling the hope which that day's meeting with his wife had given him, and how she might be better tomorrow. He would bring her a bag of oranges because she loved oranges: their colour, their taste and their smell. He would even bring her a bouquet of flowers. That would certainly make her smile, even as she chided him because it was something only city-dwellers did.

He would confess to her that this late-night walk of his had made him feel a certain affection for cities. It was as though he were discovering them anew, feeling out the pleasures of wandering through the markets and along the pavements at night, among the columns of street lamps, the close-set buildings, the noisy crowds, and the quiet alleys. He even liked the rumble of the cars driving by. Until now he had only passed through cities, when moving from one army unit to another. It was just a matter of being transferred from one truck to the next. He might buy sandwiches or whatever was available from street carts selling food at the bus depot. If the trucks were late, he would spend the night in a cheap, dirty hotel, in a shared room with other soldiers or travellers passing through: immigrants from Egypt, Sudan, or India. Or he would sleep out on the grass of the city squares, fully clothed in his uniform, using his bag as a pillow.

Ibrahim felt he was better, stronger. A spontaneous desire welled up inside him, and he thought that as soon as he entered the house, he would try to act differently with Qisma and be more open and trusting. He would say to her, "You are my daughter, and I love you. Come, let me hug you. Tell me whatever you want to say without holding anything back. Everything, whatever it might be. This time, I wish for your wishes to triumph over mine." He would explain that her mother was a wonderful woman, whom he loved, and that she was getting better. He would tell Qisma he was happy with both of them in his life, and that his life would be dedicated to them both. He would joke with her, and he would act towards her the way he had behaved with her mother today. He had seen its remarkable results, even though he had not consciously planned to act in a certain way – it just happened. Nevertheless, he had learned from it, and he realised that expressing what was in his soul was a magical thing. He would ask Qisma to go with him the next day to the hospital to see Umm Qisma for herself. On the way, she would help him choose a bunch of flowers fit for lovers, not for the sick. Yes, he would say that to her, and they would buy the oranges for Umm Qisma together.

He entered the house in a rush, eager to embrace Qisma, but he found her asleep. He looked at the clock on the wall and saw that it was past three in the morning. So he moved quietly around the house and put off till the morning all the cleaning he wanted to do. It was enough just to take off his clothes and throw himself on the bed, where he immediately plunged into a deep sleep. He slept ravenously, deeper than he usually did, and as a result he woke up late but completely refreshed.

Qisma had already left the house, and the clock pointed at noon. He did not regret the late hour. It was probably for the best: if he needed all that sleep, his wife would certainly need it too, especially since he had tired her out with his company for the entire day and prevented her from taking her usual nap. Ibrahim turned on the television as he began preparing his breakfast, but he quickly turned it off when he saw they were broadcasting yet another national festival.

He slipped into Qisma's room, which in its chaos resembled a cosy nest, crammed with perfume bottles and with big posters of celebrities covering the walls. He thought about making her bed for her, but he preferred to leave it as it was. It made him happy to see all the books on the bedside table, though he did not have much sympathy for the piles of colourful gossip magazines. He passed them all by and looked at the music tapes piled near the tape player. He shuffled through them, avoiding all the sad Iraqi music he recognised. He wanted something entirely different. He picked an English recording and put it in the player. Of course, he did not understand a word of the lyrics, but he liked the noise and the rhythms of the music, which were different from what he was used to in Arabic music. This is what he wanted, something different: different voices and words he did not understand. He turned up the stereo volume and went out of Qisma's bedroom, leaving the door open. The strange music shook the air inside the house and inspired Ibrahim with an unusual vitality, such that he sometimes bobbed his head and shoulders to the beat. He even shook his hips as he made tea. He turned to look around, smiling to himself – or at himself. Then he continued his spontaneous movements as though he were a teenager.

Ibrahim ate breakfast, showered, put on cologne and dressed himself in the same suit as the day before. He bought ten oranges from the local shop, picking them out himself one at a time. He took the ripest he could find and polished them with his handkerchief to shine them up. When he got out of the taxi in front of the hospital, he went over to the kiosk selling flowers. He asked the old crippled woman working there to put together the most beautiful bouquet for him. She began rolling back and forth on her wheelchair, picking out the flowers he liked. He tipped her generously and entered the hospital, pleased to have arrived by chance at lunchtime – another opportunity for him to feed his wife by hand and insist on her getting more nutrition.

But when Ibrahim arrived at her bed, he found it empty, though her things were still there. She must be in the bathroom, or perhaps they had taken her for some kind of test. He wanted the surprise to be even greater and her smile to be even more beautiful, so he set the bouquet of flowers in the middle of her pillow like a head. He emptied the bag of oranges onto the bed, spreading them out like a body. He covered the oranges and flowers with the diaphanous white sheet and sat facing the door, waiting for Umm Qisma to return.

CHAPTER 21

The Funeral Leave

Ibrahim knew he and his wife were fortunate. His new job had come through for him, and things had fallen into place for her to be treated at this private government hospital. He wished his father were still alive to be treated here too, for this hospital was one of the few good ones in the country; no-one came here except celebrities and high-ranking government employees and their family members. Even the doctors and nurses addressed him with a respect he was unaccustomed to, calling him "comrade" and "sir". But the doctor who treated his wife was even more polite than usual today, going even further in his words of affection and respect. He led Ibrahim into his office and began explaining his wife's illness on a scientific level, using terms Ibrahim did not understand. Indeed, he did not understand the majority of the doctor's words. So he contented himself with bowing his head in silence, since the long and the short of what the doctor wanted to convey in this discourse was that his wife had died.

Ibrahim did not open his mouth once. The whole conversation was carried by the doctor, who appeared not to expect Ibrahim to say anything and was trying to fill the silence. The doctor got up to bring him a glass of water. Ibrahim drank the whole thing. Then the doctor pointed at the telephone on the table. He hurriedly pushed it towards Ibrahim and left the office. Ibrahim called the central office for his work, and they informed him that it was necessary to come in person with the hospital death certificate in hand. Then they would give him ten days' leave.

Ibrahim went to the information office at the Palace of the Republic with one piece of paper, and he returned with another. He had not expected the transaction to be this quick and easy since the usual way of things was exhausting and involved boring queues, bribes to be paid, humiliations endured and thick files full of ink-stained papers that had already been stamped dozens of times. For a moment he hoped he would see Sa'ad there, even though he knew the young man did not work in this office. He felt a desire to tell someone about his great loss, if only to receive the traditional words of consolation.

He went back to sit alone in the house until Qisma came home late. She did not appear to be affected too much, and immediately started discussing the details of transporting her mother's body back to the village. She said she would go to the institute in the morning to ask for time off. He would go with her so that they might head straight to the hospital afterwards in order to load the coffin onto the roof of the car and set off on the journey.

During the hours of the trip from Baghdad to the village and during their stops, they hardly exchanged a word. Qisma just drove the car, swearing at the other drivers and expressing her frustration with the farmers' tractors and their herds, which wandered across the streets without any sense of order. As for Ibrahim, he felt his wife's body, tied to the roof of the car, as though it were a bird's soft wing caressing his head. He wished she were sitting with them now. He would be beside her in the back seat, squeezing her hand, or leaning her against his shoulder. He would look at her peaceful face and speak to her the last words that remained stored up from the passage of decades.

Ibrahim was tempted to tell Qisma about this desire of his – perhaps they would take Umm Qisma out of the coffin and sit her in the car with them. But he feared that Qisma would be horrified at his suggestion and he would have further marred her opinion of him. She would think he was crazy as well as a weakling and a good-for-nothing failure. He feared her reaction, whatever it might be. So he slumped further in his seat, retreating into himself and his silence. He fell back into his habit of submitting to fate, which had struck him yet another blow. Every time he thought things were easing up, it knocked him back down, dragging him by the ears from a bad situation to one that was worse. It had been that way his whole life. It was his destiny. Everything was fate and decree.

In the village, the funeral ceremonies lasted three days. It was a simple affair, just for relatives. Tariq played a major part in them, preparing the burial, performing the funeral prayer, reciting the Qur'an, proclaiming Islam's tenets about death and the life to come, welcoming the mourners, and seeing them off. Nor did Tariq neglect to attempt to persuade Ibrahim to remarry: "You are still young, brother! Your daughter has become a woman who will soon get married and leave you by yourself."

Ibrahim, of course, did not reveal to him the secret reason for his refusal. He had no desire for it, nor did he truly understand what marriage was about, But more than that, his condition rendered him unfit for remarriage.

As for Abdullah, he was content to visit the cemetery in the days following the ceremonies. He knew Ibrahim would be beside his wife's grave. He found Ibrahim there with his head bowed and came up behind him, placing his hand on his shoulder and kissing his head. He sat beside Ibrahim on the ground, smoking. Umm Qisma's grave was in front of them, and Zaynab's was not far away, along with the seven others that formed the core of the new cemetery.

Abdullah offered Ibrahim a cigarette, but he refused until Abdullah insisted he take one. Abdullah said to him, "Is it any surprise, Ibrahim? Aren't our lives – everyone's, but especially yours and mine – always tied to death and the dying? We have lived with death and got to know it better even than life. Personally, even now I still haven't deciphered the exact meaning of life. I just don't understand it. I can't see anything of value in this gelatinous mass of humanity that fills its time by fighting itself, knowing that the end result is extinction. Have you understood anything about life? About its meaning? If so, fill me in, even if it's just a guess. Personally, I suspect that I know death better, and I imagine that it is preferable, more peaceful . . .

"There's no way death could be worse than life. Even if it's just unending non-existence. I don't have the sense that death will be another life, like this one, for instance, or somehow different, with new conditions and circumstances. If I'm wrong about that, then all of this is a meaningless joke on an even bigger scale. Personally, I have felt so much pain that pain no longer hurts me. And I decided long ago not to feel regret, not to feel sorrow, and not to suffer. Every outcome would be equal as far as I was concerned. I decided not to tire myself out and work myself up over things I couldn't do anything about. I have nearly envied the dead sometimes for having dispensed with all this mess, turning their backs on it all. Or rather, I no longer envied anyone, neither the living nor the dead. Listen, my friend . . ."

Abdullah fell silent, unable to find the words to express this great thing at work inside him. Struggling to get hold of the idea and the precise words, he said again, "Listen carefully, my friend . . ." And when he could go no further, he finished the sentence by saying, "Take another cigarette."

They looked at each other and burst out laughing together, laughing so hard they were still shaking several minutes later. Then they embraced. "Shit," Abdullah said. "God damn it all. Let's go to the river."

On the way, Ibrahim tried to tell Abdullah about what he had seen in his work in the gardens of the presidential palaces, since Abdullah was the only one who would understand him and would keep the secret. But Abdullah cut off Ibrahim's attempts before he went too far by saying, "I know what you will say. Or else I don't want to know anything about any of that – neither about the palaces, nor the types of people, and not about the things you saw or the gardens. For in the end, what are they apart from communal graveyards by another name? The whole country, the earth, nay, the entire universe itself – isn't it all just a communal graveyard, crumbling sooner or later into oblivion? And even if the universe were to go on, when all is said and done, what is it apart from a meaningless eternal expanse? Let's just swim and play a little in the river."

Ibrahim spent the rest of those days beside his blind mother, who had grown very senile and was now hunched over like a question mark. Most of the time, he would sit on the floor leaning against her, and he felt her tenderness seep into him. Sometimes she would touch his face and his hands, his back and his feet. She would massage his head. He sensed she was the one who understood him best, even though her speech would jump at random between memories, topics and names. She talked about common everyday things and about childhood. She talked about events from a time no-one remembered or cared about any longer; about people who were forgotten even by their grandchildren; about the harvest and those who got rich off of it; about the floods; about people getting married and fighting and talking and dying. She talked about customs that had been lost, marriage and funeral customs, recipes and mediations, about how to make yogurt and butter. Her speech – which made no distinction between the living and the dead, animate beings and inanimate objects – cut through his mind like a knife and made him feel that his entire life were just another ordinary drop amid a vast, enormous ocean of innumerable drops that comprised everything around him: people and their stories, being and possessions. Umm Ibrahim was entirely neutral, and times, places, people, circumstances and everything else were all the same in her eyes.

As for Qisma, she kept urging that they return to Baghdad because she was bored in the village, pleading the urgency of her exam schedule and the need to study. So after spending a week there, they went back, driving once again in silence.

Ibrahim spent the three remaining days of his holiday gathering all his wife's things – clothes, bags, shoes, and so on – to give to the neighbouring church. He only kept her wedding ring and the shawl she wore around her neck most often; he could still smell her scent on it whenever he missed her. He also kept a half-empty bottle of her perfume. Meanwhile, he gave all her gold earrings, her necklaces, her rings and her simple silver bracelets to Qisma.

He spent entire days and nights wandering around the city on foot, slowly discovering it. The din of the streets and cafés distracted him from his thoughts, and walking wore him out so much that he fell into a dreamless sleep without any restless thoughts in bed beforehand. During one trip, the beautiful facade of a bookshop in the middle of the capital stopped him, and the display of books inspired him with a feeling of peace and a sense of the world's deep roots. As he regarded numerous covers and titles, he found they made him imagine other worlds, different from his own. He went inside, and spent long, relaxing hours looking at books and flipping through some of them. He ended up buying two translated novels, a volume of poetry, a religious book and a small edition of the Qur'an.

And when Ibrahim came to the shelves of pens and notebooks in their alluring colours, sizes and shapes, he purchased a black pen and a large notebook with a light-blue cover, the colour of a summer evening. He told himself that maybe he would write down in this notebook what was going on in his mind. He would open himself up here, if that was what he needed, since he had no-one close with whom he could talk about himself. He would also use it to write letters to his wife.

Ibrahim left the shop, satisfied, pleased with himself for having arrived at this idea.

CHAPTER 22

Notebooks and Corpses

On the morning Ibrahim returned to his work, they immediately informed him that his job had changed. He was driven for half an hour in a private car to a different gate that resembled the one from his old job. On the other side, an officer came to talk to him who looked just like the previous one. Indeed, he looked like every officer here – they all seemed to resemble the President, with their moustaches, their tailored and carefully ironed olive suits, pistols at the hip, polished burgundy shoes and imperious tones of voice.

In an impressive office, where a photograph of the President filled the entire back wall, the officer told Ibrahim exactly what the first officer had told him, almost as though they were airline stewards explaining emergency exit procedures to the passengers: you are forbidden to speak to anyone about what you see and hear in this place, you must be exact in observing deadlines and obeying orders, and so on. Then he added in a gentler tone, "It seems that your superiors were pleased with you and put great trust in you. They wrote excellent references, which is why you have been transferred to this sensitive place. This trust is not granted to just anyone. Your hours will be reduced, and your salary will be higher. You will work from one at night until five-thirty or six in the morning. A private car will come every day to your house to bring you here and then take you home after your shift. Please, come this way."

He led Ibrahim through the building, which resembled the previous one in its design. Coming out the other side, they entered spacious gardens and vast open spaces. There was a cart like the one in which Sa'ad used to drive him around.

"I'll teach you how to drive it yourself. It's very easy."

They got in, and the officer began explaining how it worked: "You press this button to turn it on, then you press this pedal with your foot, and it goes automatically. There's nothing for you to do besides guide it with the steering wheel. Here, you try it. Now I'll show you the way. That's easy too. Do you see that hill? That mountain, I mean? Just go towards it, following any of the paths you like."

There were countless intersecting paths winding among fountains, gardens, towering trees, canals, small lakes, and arched bridges. The closer one came to the high hill, the taller the trees became. The top of the hill – or "the mountain" – was covered with trees, and he saw small, man-made waterfalls tumbling down it. At the very top was a small palace with wide balconies looking out in every direction, projecting its power to each horizon. Between the forests surrounding the hill were wide-open spaces where nothing had been planted. In some of them, Ibrahim saw groups of donkeys, camels and dogs wandering around. Two people had brought them straw from somewhere on a cart that resembled his own.

The officer guided Ibrahim to a building with two rooms, a

small guardhouse, and told him, "There's no key. You just press here and the door opens for you."

Ibrahim found himself in a narrow chamber with a chair and a rug. There was a refrigerator and a large wardrobe against one wall and shelves with torches and toolboxes on the other. As for the back wall facing the door, it was empty apart from a large photograph of the President laughing. There was one additional door that led to the bathroom.

"This is where you'll be working. Here you'll find the clothes you need, and here in these boxes are your tools. If you need anything else, just let us know."

Ibrahim noticed that his work equipment was somewhat different from what he had had before. They appeared to be the tools of a real farmer and not a gardener. He found two large shiny shovels with sharp edges, a box filled with new pairs of gloves still in their bags, a heavy ploughing hoe, a pickaxe and other tools for excavating. There was also a standard wheel-barrow in the corner.

The officer said to him, "Good. You'll come here every day, put on the work clothes, and wait. If someone comes, he'll tell you what you have to do, and if no-one comes, you stay here until the end of your shift and then you leave. Understood?"

"Yes, sir."

When Ibrahim got back home, he reviewed everything the officer had told him and taught him. He went over it all several times and tested himself on how to drive the cart, the paths he had taken, where the small house was, the button that opened the door. He also tried to guess the nature of his new work. Without a doubt, it was Sa'ad who had recommended him to his superiors. Did they now intend to treat him like a real farmer with a real shovel and not just a gardener who spent his day brushing dirt off flowers he did not even know the names of? Would caring for those donkeys, camels and dogs be part of his work, like the two men he had seen? In a way, he felt that his new job might suit him better, for it seemed solitary and free from any concrete responsibilities. On top of that, the fact that it took place late at night meant he was a peripheral figure, one who would be kept away from the eyes of direct supervisors, with no expectation that the President or anyone else might visit.

For all he reassured himself, Ibrahim's heart did not cease to contract whenever he left for work. The feeling got worse with each passing day. Indeed, his breath nearly failed him when he first realised – and then felt with his hands – the true purpose of his new job.

On the first night, around three in the morning, a military ambulance stopped in front of the door of his guardhouse. Two soldiers got out and greeted him. Then they dragged two corpses out of the back door of the ambulance and threw them on the ground.

They said to him, "You're new? Fine. It's up to you to bury these bodies in any spot among the open spaces found here, in the areas between the trees. It's not important how you bury them – vertically, horizontally, standing up, or at any depth whatsoever. The important thing is that you bury them without leaving any visible trace on the ground. Meaning you smooth out the surface however it was, or you make it like it is here, as you see it now – there are bodies buried right here. Understood?"

"Yes, sir."

"Say 'comrade'. You only say 'sir' to the officers."

"Yes, comrade."

Then they left.

Ibrahim's life was changed utterly. His new existence was heavier, sadder and darker, and not just because the night became his work day and the daytime was his night to sleep. If Ibrahim had originally been a man of few words, he was now entirely mute for fear that uttering even a single word might hint in some small way at the nature of his work and what he saw, heard and thought there. He began avoiding people's gazes so that no-one could read anything in his eyes or see this shame he felt.

Ibrahim rarely saw Qisma now, due to the difference in their working hours. He avoided getting to know anyone new and sought to evade every encounter. If by chance he ran into a neighbour in the street, or had no choice but to talk with a shopkeeper, he rarely uttered a full greeting or responded clearly. His words were obscure mutterings that hinted at – rather than expressed – a meaning. Ibrahim became more isolated, more introspective, and more solitary. By not seeing others, even as hardly anyone ever saw him, he sank further inside himself with each new corpse he put in the ground. It was as if he were digging his own grave, a grave without any relief or respite, where he saw nothing besides darkness and confusion.

In the first few days of his work – or rather, the first nights – the horror of being alone with these bloody corpses in the shadows of thick, towering forests made him shiver. But with the passage of time, he got used to it. His heart resumed its regular rhythm, the trembling of his arms and his legs faded, and he started carrying the corpses like any other sack. He would put them in the wheelbarrow and push them around, looking for a place to bury them. He no longer feared to look in the faces of the slain, no matter how disfigured, and by reading those faces, to learn how they were killed. In his world, these night-time bodies regained their dominant essence of humanity, and he sometimes felt he was one of them.

Even the driver who picked him up at his house was silent like him, and they exchanged no words beyond a greeting. They were usually content with a nod of the head, a glance, or nothing at all. It seemed that this man, too, had seen or lived through things he did not want to talk about. Like an old married couple, old friends, or prisoners sharing a cell who had exhausted their supply of words, they were equally content not to trouble one another. They did not even ask each other's names. It was a rare and harmonious relationship.

It was extremely uncommon that a night would pass without a corpse. The number would range from one a night to up to ten on occasion. He learned that the corpses killed by bullets belonged to soldiers, while the ones that were hanged were civilians. This was the general rule, though exceptions to it became the more fundamental rule. The one thing the corpses all shared was evidence of torture before the spirit left the body. All of them had been subjected to cruel – sometimes inventive – methods of torture. He forced himself to guess these more innovative methods once he had become familiar with the standard repertoire, which included whipping, beating, piercing, electric shocks, cigarette burns, and so on.

As far as was possible, Ibrahim would try to restore dignity to the torn disarray of the bodies and close their open eyes. How often he read expressions in those eyes! It was almost as though he could hear them speak. Some were frozen in the last moment of confusion, watching in terror as the killer approached for the final blow. Some seemed to be holding back words, while the longing of others burst forth: desire for parents, for children, or even for an opportunity to speak, for a mouthful of water or a breath of air. Some of the faces seemed happy, betraying a remarkable calm that Ibrahim seldom found in the faces of the living. Perhaps because their final thoughts were that at last the torture had come to an end.

He saw corpses with slit throats and others pierced with bullets like a sieve. Their oozing blood would soak him when he picked them up. He found no more than one bullethole in the head or heart of some corpses. The holes in others were made by an electric drill, nails, or by the point of a sword. He saw all manner of burns, from cigarettes or electrical shocks, and bodies that had been impaled on a stake. Some of them had genitals cut off, fingernails pulled out, tongues removed, ears clipped, noses mutilated, fingers broken, scalps swollen where tufts of hair had been ripped out, eyes gouged out, skin flayed in strips, or lines scored with razor blades. Others had been skinned alive.

Ibrahim began trying to guess the pretext for each execution, based on the method of torture employed. Whoever's tongue was cut out must have uttered something the government did not like. Whoever's ears were cut off may have heard something against the government without making a denunciation. Whoever's genitals were removed . . . maybe it was something to do with honour or a breach of it, either in word or deed, or in revenge for an insult, or a criticism of someone's courage or manliness, or perhaps in the course of an interrogation. Whoever's fingers were broken or whose hand was missing may have stolen something or written something. But why had some of them died under the rending teeth of beasts of prey – lions, tigers, crocodiles, or even dogs? The faces of these corpses preserved a terror that was impossible to describe.

Ibrahim's life went on like this, as though he lived in a different world, or even on a different planet altogether: isolated and savage, nothing to see besides darkness and death, human flesh and blood. He no longer counted the days as they went by, nor did he calculate when his holidays would arrive or how his savings were piling up. One night, he thought he would leave this work. Anything would be better than this, even begging on the streets of the capital, pleading for the charity of others. But they would not let him leave this job of his own volition. They would surely kill him to cover their tracks and to erase the memory of these corpses by eliminating any witnesses.

Ibrahim could not even find within himself the courage to express this desire to them, they who measured everything with grandiose words he did not understand. Words like treachery, honour, dissent, nobility, loyalty, weakness, courage, power, fealty, transgression, and so on: big words connected to a homeland that was defined by the President. The definitions and connotations of these words, at least as they understood them, escaped Ibrahim. Ibrahim's problem was that he was never sick, so it was impossible to fake an illness because they would investigate and find him out, prosecuting him for dissent or treachery or conspiring against the homeland.

But he began to find a certain equilibrium in the idea that he was performing an important role, indeed a humanitarian one. It might not be directed towards the living, but it was nevertheless a service to the dead. To the greatest extent possible, he conducted burials that befitted these corpses. He organised their remains and laid them out with the dignity owed to a deceased human being. In his heart, he recited the Qur'an over them, along with simpler words of his own; the final recompense that must be offered to a human being, regardless of how he had lived his life, or the reason and manner of his death.

When he had been thrown into the wars, it had hurt him badly to see bodies – even those of enemies – abandoned on the battlefields, bloated, disintegrating out in the open at the mercy of the elements. He used to think of them, and also of their families, who waited and received no answer beyond the word "lost", and suffered agonies of hope as everything connected to "the lost" was put on hold. It pained him to see human corpses mangled by the teeth of wolves, dogs, fish, vultures, and other beasts of the field, the sky and the deep.

In this land too, in these broad yet secret expanses within the city, he would sometimes discover earlier corpses thrown in however which way by those who had buried them – head down, lying on their stomachs, sitting or rolled up, their limbs wrapped around them or splayed out. Whoever held this position before him must have dug any kind of hole and not cared how he threw in the bodies before piling some earth on top of them. Ibrahim would rebury these corpses, even if was just their bones, in a proper manner, laying them out on their backs or their sides, straightened out, with their heads on a pile of earth for a pillow. He felt as though they sighed with relief, and he would hear them thank him. Then Ibrahim would feel a gentle sense of relief himself.

Ibrahim was still consumed by guilt over his inability to do anything for the body of his friend Ahmad al-Najafi. This was therefore an opportunity to ease the pangs of a conscience that still haunted him. Faced by all this suffering and wanting another taste of that blessed sense of relief, Ibrahim came up with the idea of making a record of all the unknown corpses. He would name them, provide a description and specify their resting place so they would not remain simply "lost" or "missing", like the hundreds he had seen and the thousands he had heard about in the wars and the mass graves.

He remembered the big blue notebook he had bought to write letters to his wife. As soon as he got home, he took it out and shut himself up in his room, sprawled out on the bed. He began recalling all the corpses he had buried since the beginning, trying to specify the places and dates of their burial. He ran through his memory of the days, trying to place each corpse in its own time. He was content to record the most salient feature of the body: an approximate age, for example, or certain distinguishing marks, like a mole on the cheek, the size of the nose, the shape of the ears, a tattoo on the arm, whether they were bald or going grey, how many feet tall they were, how big were the feet themselves, whether the toes were crooked and twisted. And if he did not find anything in particular, he described their clothing, for most of the slain came to him in their own clothes.

He drew maps of those open spaces, specifying locations by how far away they were, and in which direction, from that man-made presidential hill. He indicated the exact burial site of each corpse. Many had names he recognised, for they included ministers, officials, soldiers and celebrities he knew from television. He had hoped to find the body of the musician Nabil among them, but he never saw it. Perhaps they took it somewhere else, or maybe they left it as food for the crocodiles brought from Africa, and for the fish and the fat water vipers.

The notebook was so secret that Ibrahim would hide it inside the house, leaving clues to remind himself where it was. He bought more notebooks, and over time, he was forced to buy many of them. Their covers were of different colours, and he numbered those of the same colour in a series. He created a complete world for himself, set apart from the outside world, and abandoned himself within it. The more he was engaged in it, the less time he had for thinking, reflecting and remembering, which he found even more exhausting.

Later on, as a way to deal with corpses that were so disfigured that there was no particular distinguishing mark to be found, he began taking something small from each, such as a shirt button, a watch, a ring, or a scrap of fabric from their trousers or shirt. Sometimes even a piece of the body itself: a dangling fingernail or a lock of hair plucked out along with a bit of the scalp. He put these things into small bags with numbered slips that corresponded to numbers in the notebooks, where he recorded the usual details – the date and place of burial, a description of the corpse, its clothes and what torture it had been subjected to. Then he organised these bits and pieces into shoeboxes or any other cardboard boxes that came with the things he bought. Most helpful of all were the documents he occasionally found in their pockets – some kind of I.D. card or a doctor's prescription, a tax receipt, or a water or electricity bill – for these provided him with all the necessary information apart from the date and place of burial.

CHAPTER 23

Nisma's Wedding

Ibrahim's absorption in this self-created world, on the margins of the world of the living and amid the debris of human cruelty, gradually took him away from the things that occupied the living. He began to feel that he had more in common with the dead than with those still alive: he belonged more to their world. The dead did not cheat you, they did not lie to you, and they did not hide things from you. They did not try to extract anything from you, had no hidden agenda, and played no games. They made no demands, nor did they impose anything. They were the mild-tempered. If you showed them respect, they thanked you, and if you neglected them, they did not blame you.

A habitual silence became firmly rooted as his primary mode of communication, including with his daughter Qisma. The few times they met – in the living room or kitchen before she left in the mornings or in the evenings before he did – they hardly exchanged a word. Each could tell from the other's footsteps where they were going, be it the kitchen, the bathroom, the living room, or outside. They each created a private world, set apart in their rooms, which the other did not enter because it would not have crossed their mind to do so and because there was no need.

This difference in their schedules cemented their isolation to the point where Ibrahim was only just able to hang on to the fact that she was his daughter, his child, not just some strange woman existing in the flesh before him. That is how he saw her: as a stranger living in the next room. The most he could say about her was that her features resembled those of his wife. She was a living memorial to the face and bearing of her mother. And that, in any case, was better than just having photographs hung on the wall.

The silence, isolation and independence combined to form a more peaceful type of coexistence. It was what each of them needed in order to root themselves more firmly in the different worlds they had brought into existence. It carried over even to money, which he would leave for her every month in an envelope on the television stand. In turn, she knew what he wanted when she went shopping. His needs were simple and did not change, never going beyond the food and drink she would have bought anyway, for he seldom bought clothes or any of the things that other people seemed to need.

Qisma formed her world just as she wished, without any interference, impediments or criticism. She arranged it according to her fancy – or at least, that is what she believed. She became acquainted with an officer, the brother of one of her friends in the institute, and she would go out with him wherever he liked, or wherever she did. She was like all the other young women of her age and circle. A romantic relationship, dates, drinking juice in the corners of cafés, love songs and views on love to exchange, holding hands, sweet nothings repeated, passion stirred up by provocative looks, waves of frustration and satisfaction, and something to show off in front of her female colleagues. Dreams, more dreams, and lots of talking. Lots of talking, just as there is when any man and woman agree that they love each other.

Like Qisma, the officer was ambitious, only more so, and Qisma reinforced these ambitions within him. He loved keeping up appearances, or "fulfilling the duties of their station", as they preferred to call it. He dressed in an olive-coloured uniform, with a pistol at his hip and stars on his shoulder. He had a car in the latest model and a swagger in his step. He wore cologne – lots of it – the most famous and expensive brands, as well as gold watches or gold chains around his neck. He was graceful. He always paid the closest attention to shaving, trimming his moustache, and polishing his shoes. He observed his appointments with exactitude and showed deep concern for scheduling the hours of each day. He dreamed of more money, more status and more power. He had great confidence in himself, in his masculinity, and in the firmness of his reality. His friends flattered him.

He was an officer in the Republican Guard, enrolled among the bodyguard. He told Qisma that he defended His Excellency the President. She told him that her father also worked close to His Excellency the President. Of course, he did not inform her within which rank or degree of the bodyguard he served – there were said to be seven circles, or sometimes more, according to people who knew the leadership structure. But this did not matter much to Qisma. What mattered far more was that they agreed that they would join the highest echelon of society in terms of money and status, and they would be able to buy whatever they wished. For that reason, she too did not inform him of her father's actual work as a gardener in the presidential palaces. When it came down to it, she did not want to know about it either. She realised that, no matter what happened, her father would never rise above the rank of subordinate, a marginal man under the orders of others.

Her officer often spoke to her about his admiration for the person of His Excellency the President: his manliness, his strength, his firmness, his wisdom and his intelligence in exploiting situations and the entire country – its people, animals, plants, lands, natural resources, water, air, everything – for his benefit. For that reason, he emulated the President and imitated him in everything: his appearance and his voice, the way he moved or held still, what he supported and opposed, and his style of thinking and speaking. He became a carbon copy of the President, lacking nothing but the President's power. However, the officer's competitors were legion, for people like him multiplied boundlessly in that period. Meanwhile, the government presented that model in every form of media, as though it wanted everyone to be yet another image of the singular Leader, the Commander of Necessity, the exemplar in everything.

For a period of months, apart from detached, formulaic salvos – words limited to greetings and questions about where to find salt, spices, or sugar in the kitchen, or to say they were out of something, or that something was broken, or that an electrical switch or a doorknob had been fixed – Ibrahim and Qisma only exchanged words approximately twice. To be more exact, it was she who spoke and he who listened.

The first time, Qisma complained about a rotting odour coming from Ibrahim's room, saying that he could not go on neglecting to clean it. She left the house, muttering. It was then that Ibrahim noticed this smell for the first time, perhaps because he was used to the putrid smell of corpses, their blood mixed with urine and faeces, the flesh already rotting from long periods of imprisonment and torture. On top of that, Ibrahim had been ordered not to clean the manure off the ground where he buried the bodies.

Ibrahim left the house and came back inside several times, sniffing with the earnestness of a police dog. He walked from the front door to his room more than once in order to locate the smell. The remains of very small bits of flesh attached to fingernails, scraps of skin, and pieces of clothing had begun to rot. Looking through his archives, his record of the identities of the dead, Ibrahim hastened to clean where he thought that would be sufficient and to bury in the yard whatever was impossible to clean, keeping only what was dry and not liable to rot. When he was done, he cleaned and organised his room a second time. He even went so far as to leave the window and door open for an entire day. Then he sprayed it every day with the last bottle of his wife's perfume.

The second time was when Qisma informed him that she had got to know a man, the brother of a friend of hers in the institute. She had fallen in love with him, and he would be coming to get engaged to her next Friday evening. Her father had to be there, and he must not object. She dropped this news just like that, all at once. Qisma stressed that Ibrahim must dress up, look his polished best, and be welcoming and agreeable. If not, she would proceed to do as she pleased and get married to this man with or without her father's permission.

Ibrahim said nothing except to ask her age. Qisma told him

that she had passed twenty years. They smiled at each other, though each held a different thought behind the smile.

The following day, Qisma bought Ibrahim a shirt and tie, shoes and a new suit because she knew he would wear the one suit he had, the cut of which no longer matched the current style, just as its fabric had become threadbare. They spent all of Thursday together cleaning the house, rearranging the simple furniture, and shopping. Ibrahim went to the barber for a haircut for the first time in his life, for he would always just cut his own hair. When Friday morning came, they spent it preparing a special meal of various grilled meats, juices, fruits and desserts. After that it was time to try on the new clothes. Each of them asked the other for their opinion and comments. Those few hours were the most pleasant Ibrahim had ever spent with his Qisma, the time he was closest to her. He felt as though he were a child and she his mother, arranging his clothes, combing his hair, adjusting his tie, telling him how to sit on the couch when the special guests arrived. He felt as elated as a young boy, delighting in his mother's care and satisfied in his sense that she was satisfied with him, or an obedient child, happy that his obedience pleased her. At each touch from his daughter, Ibrahim felt a downpour of tenderness.

Qisma informed Ibrahim what she had told the man who would become her husband about her father, that he held an important position and a critical role within the presidential palaces, overseeing the administration of the President's gardens. As they were getting ready, Qisma also chose a moment to inform her father, so he would not be surprised, that she had chosen a name for herself, Nisma, not Qisma, and that is what everyone had known her by ever since they had come to Baghdad.

Qisma asked her father to behave according to what she had told her future husband about him. Ibrahim had to convince him "that this is actually who you are, but that you treat the matter lightly, and that you don't know how to exploit the situation and show it off like others would". She told Ibrahim that this point was important to her and to her future with the man who would become her husband because it would make him treat her with greater respect and maybe even with a kind of fear. Or at least as an equal, and not just as the daughter of a farmer and former soldier who had come to the capital from a remote village. Ignoring the real nature of her father's work, she wanted to give a certain obscure majesty to his position, just as the social game had taught her to do and just as her officer did. For ever since she had first become aware of things, Qisma had recognised that her father was bound by silence and submission, incapable of expressing anything. She was so used to it that she despaired of Ibrahim being able to talk about anything at all.

Ibrahim worked hard to remember everything Qisma charged him with, and he focused his attention on carrying it out exactly as she wanted. The young man came in his olive uniform with its two stars denoting the rank of first lieutenant. His parents came with him in their elegant clothes of the popular Baghdad style. Ibrahim received them at the door and welcomed them, leading them into the living room. They all repeated the traditional words that are exchanged on occasions like this as though they were performing memorised roles in a dramatic reading. Words like honour, dignity, protection, blessing and happiness: "It's an honour for us to request the hand of your daughter," "We swear she will find dignity and happiness in her life with us," "She will be in safe hands," and so on. The young man kept referring to the fact that he was in the President's bodyguard, without specifying, of course, to which of the seven – or seventy – circles he belonged.

Ibrahim was used to this kind of officer, both minor and major. Looking alike and always aiming to resemble each other, they spoke rigid, traditional words with a flourish as though they were the ones who chose the words and fashioned these phrases. Ibrahim could not see what set this officer apart from all the others, and by force of habit, he nearly addressed him as "sir" at times before regaining his focus and recalling what Qisma had set out for him. The officer said, with that same air, that he wanted to hold the wedding the following Friday, for he was a practical man, everything was ready, and there was really no point in wasting time on a long engagement. His parents nodded their heads in support.

Between the time they left and the wedding night – which was celebrated in the Sheraton Hotel in the middle of Baghdad – Ibrahim scarcely saw Qisma. Even on the night of the wedding, which baffled him with its noisy spectacle of drinks, food, guests wearing shining clothes and perfume, music and dancing. He did not have time to admire Qisma in her wedding dress. Everyone was greeting everyone else. Everyone was laughing, eating, drinking, dancing, moving here and there. It was a great mass of people dressed up like dolls, a different world that had no relation to his private world of the dead, and no relation either to the world of normal living people, the people in the streets with their despair and poverty. It was like a dream, or like a game, a whirl of overpowering perfume, feasting and flattering small talk. As though there were no such thing as death. As though there were no such thing as other people, no other world beyond this hall.

Ibrahim felt entirely out of place here, as he watched the scene unfold from a chair in the corner, stealing glances between the gaps in the people standing about to catch a glimpse of his Qisma, who had now become someone else's Qisma. She appeared to be a different woman, someone he did not know, with her face made up and her arms covered in henna tattoos, glittering in a white dress and a golden tiara. So much white, like a burial shroud. She was smiling, happy, and in harmony with everything around her, and Ibrahim could not connect her with that child he had fathered in a mud house and carried on his shoulders or on the back of a donkey to the nearby fields where she played in the mud of the irrigation ditches.

This was the first and last time Ibrahim ever entered a grand hotel like that. All the times he had heard about it in advertisements or seen its towering edifice from afar, or all those nights he spent as a soldier sleeping in the public squares imagining who stayed there, it had not seemed relevant to him; it was reserved for others, people higher than himself. Likewise, he had never in his life attended a party like this, which existed on a different plane altogether. So as soon as he returned home at the end of the night, he hastened to fold it up in his memory because it did not correspond to any of the other pages of his life. It was something foreign, something that passed through him but had no connection. He contented himself with remembering the last thing Qisma – or Nisma – said to him before the cavalcade of cars took her away into the night.

"Take care," she had said. "If you need anything, let me know."

It seemed that she said it in the same way everyone said it, a polite formality, without meaning or intending anything by it, and without her telling him how to do it: she did not give him an address or a telephone number. He justified this by telling himself that she must simply have forgotten, overwhelmed with the details of her wedding. But she did not do it in the following days either.

He wished he had embraced her, held her to his chest, kissed her forehead or her hand, or that she had done something of this sort. He kept exonerating her: perhaps she had forgotten in all the excitement, or she was worried about messing up the arrangement of her clothes, her make-up, or her hair. He excused her, and he buried that wish of his in some grave. There was no limit to the dead wishes he had been forced to bury in his depths, one after the other.

She disappeared from his life and did not come to visit. She was content to call on the phone after a month, exchange the usual greetings with him, and disappear again. And Ibrahim returned to his solitude, to his world of the dead and their records. He even felt a kind of liberation, a sense of leisure and a greater absorption in his solitary world, which existed by itself and for itself in his bedroom, and from there spread all over the house, taking over new corners for its archives and tokens.

CHAPTER 24

The Flower-Eaters

A creature from the North Pole will die if transferred to the desert, and vice versa. Man may be the only creature able to adapt to life in any place and circumstance. Ibrahim had lived in deserts and mountains, in hot and cold climates, in sadness and fear and joy. He had lived through conditions as diverse as could be imagined. All of that had been demanded of him. He did not remember ever having made a decision that was his own choice, taken by his own desire or volition, the kind of decision that Qisma used to demand of him.

They had never given him the opportunity to choose or to want, so he got used to adapting himself, and now here he was, adapting himself to his role as a gravedigger. Indeed, he became a professional at it, and the trust of his superiors firmly settled upon him. For his own part, Ibrahim no longer had any other activity in life, and he was unable to detach himself from this work. The secret records of the buried were Ibrahim's sole independent undertaking, the one thing he did purely from his own desire – and against the wishes of his superiors, no doubt, though he was not able to reveal it to anyone. On the contrary, keeping his archive a secret demanded all the more effort and caution. Therefore, this desire of his, which Qisma, ironically, was utterly blind to, was of no use to him. But in any case, it was his own desire, his own world. He was undertaking something that would have a use, and through this act, the enduring pain in his conscience was relieved. He began developing the archives further, taking advantage of his solitude in the house and his near complete freedom from any obligation to anyone.

Later on, he set about inventing symbols and new shapes for writing. He arrayed all the letters of the alphabet on one side of a page, and across from each of them he made up a different shape, devising a new form of writing with an invented alphabet even though it spoke the same language. Then he carried out a series of exercises until he had memorised them backwards and forwards. His motivation was twofold: he wanted more secrecy and also to elaborate on additional details without relying on abbreviated hints and non-linguistic symbols, which he might forget with the passage of time, and which he sometimes found incapable of capturing what he had witnessed and wanted to record. For whenever he thought that he had come to know every possible style of torture and killing, a corpse would surprise him by what it had been subjected to. When it came to torture, they were inventive and artistic to a degree that could scarcely be imagined. He started wondering about the secret behind that and what it all meant, remembering and now understanding more of Abdullah Kafka's wonderings. Were there people who enjoyed torture? Why did they invest so much time, money and effort creating all these torments, given that the goal and the end result were to be rid of someone, make him disappear and murder him? Why didn't they just kill him and be done with it? He was unable to find a logical answer to that, and, according to his habit, he would explain things as he always did, that every person has their own business, and certainly there were many things – both in people and in the world – that he did not and would never understand.

When Ibrahim rewrote in his new code all the records he had previously made, it consumed a full month and required the purchase of multiple notebooks. He discovered he had recorded information for more than two thousand corpses, among whom the number of women did not exceed 10 per cent. They were of different ages, from children ten years old to men older than eighty. Some of the people he buried were famous, though he did not know any of them personally apart from young Sa'ad, his first supervisor in these gardens, who had recommended him for this very position. Recognising his body had been easy because they had not tortured him much, nor the corpses that accompanied him, three other men the same age, wearing the same olive suits. Even though they were new corpses, they were already somewhat bloated. The smell of alcohol emanating from them overwhelmed any other smell. Apparently, they had been forced to drink an enormous amount of it since their swollen stomachs would gurgle with liquid whenever he moved them. Then they were hanged with regular ropes, the fibres of which still stuck to their necks.

Ibrahim dug a separate grave for them since they were the only corpses that had arrived, as it were, in one piece. He recited the opening sura of the Qur'an for their souls without stopping to think long whether that was allowed from a religious standpoint or not, given that they went to the afterlife with their bellies and veins full of liquor. But he did wonder to himself whether this news would somehow reach Sa'ad's mother and sister so they would not keep wondering, being miserable and humbling themselves with questions and bribes in a quest to seek him out, a quest that would not get them anywhere. He could not come to any conclusions, and he satisfied himself by thinking that it was perhaps his good fortune that Sa'ad had not told him his home address or any other information that would lead Ibrahim to his family. There was nothing he could do and nothing to torment his conscience.

One rainy night, they dumped seventeen corpses at his feet, and two hours later brought nine more. He stood in front of them, every fibre of his being uttering a protest. The bodies were covered in mud, manure, blood and rain. One of Ibrahim's hands held a torch, and the other his artificial foot, which had been transformed into a swollen lump by the mud and grass that stuck to it. He had pulled it off because it kept sinking in the ground every time he put his weight on it. Ibrahim appeared old, contemptible and despairing to a degree that would inspire the compassion even of the trees, the stones and the rain. After watching him for a while, they said in a supportive tone, "It's O.K. Manage as best you can right now, and we'll inform your superiors so they can send someone to help as soon as possible."

Ibrahim did not finish until dawn, when he returned to the guardhouse tool shed. It was a long walk back since he had been forced to dig graves in different clearings in the forest of tall, rough, fruit-barren trees that circled the man-made hill with its delicate waterfalls and its shining palace wearing balconies on its head like a crown. As soon as he sank onto the chair to catch his breath, worn out and not yet washed, he plunged immediately into a deep sleep.

It was already noon when Ibrahim awoke. He looked around. The picture of the President stared back in his face. He immediately got up and went to the bathroom. He showered and stood for a long time under the water, clearing his mind of everything. It was equally cleansing in body and mind. He felt relaxed, and even thought about sleeping some more. When he had dressed in his usual clothes, he sat back on the chair and decided that he had no choice but to remain there until the coming dawn. But he felt a sharp hunger and he only had a bottle of water, so he got up and opened the door. The sky was perfectly clear.

Ibrahim saw herds of donkeys and camels occupying the clearings, feeling assured in the warm sunshine. The two shepherds were sitting near them. Each of them had a staff in his hand, and they were talking. Meanwhile, the dogs gathered a little further on under the shade of the nearby trees. Ibrahim walked towards the shepherds, who had turbans wrapped around their heads and were wearing the kind of long, close-fitting robes that were pulled on over one's head like a shirt. They got up when they saw Ibrahim approaching. Ibrahim greeted them and asked them to sit back down, which they did. He sat with them on a large tree trunk lying nearby, one that Ibrahim knew well from the many times he had rested on it while he worked. When Ibrahim told them he was famished and did not have any food, they instantly relaxed. They became more natural and visibly more comfortable, their faces free from confusion or tension. One of them took out a piece of bread, some cheese, an onion, cucumbers and a few tomatoes from the cloth bag beside him, while the other set off with a bowl to bring back milk from the nearest camel.

Ibrahim found them to be simple, good-hearted and spontaneous. They had a powerful connection with the land, even more so than he, for the upheavals of his life and all the times he had been pulled far from his village and the fields had weakened his identity as a farmer. It quickly became apparent that they were Bedouin. Their movements, their faces and their accents made that clear. Ibrahim felt an almost immediate familiarity with them, an intimacy he had not enjoyed for months, since he no longer sat or spoke with anyone. Their spontaneity awoke in him a need to be spontaneous too, if only for a few moments. He wanted it badly, and he gave in to that wish, especially when he saw one of them smash the onion on his knee with a single blow of his fist and offer it to him.

They told Ibrahim they were brothers – twins – and that they had come from the desert. They had been caring for "the Pres'dent's own", that is, the President's animals, for years and in various places. Their father had been doing this work since he was their age, and he now tended larger flocks near Lake Habbaniyah – he had arranged for them to be appointed to this role. They had another brother and also cousins who were shepherds in other cities, palaces, gardens and deserts, looking after sheep, goats, cows and gazelles. They told him that this work saved their families from having to travel in search of pasturage, as they used to. As a result, they now had houses – palaces actually – on the outskirts of Hadar.

"This is my brother. His name is Fahd, and my name is Jad'an. As for our older brother, his name is Tariq."

Ibrahim recalled the Bedouin Jad'an, who had spent a month in the village after the harvest season every year, together with his daughter Fahda, with whom Tariq had conducted a risky love affair. Could they be related? He gave them all the details he remembered, and they told him that this was their grandfather, they were the sons of his daughter Fahda. "She is the one that gave us these names." As for their grandfather, he had died years ago.

They told Ibrahim that they had never been to the city. The President loved their father and them too, and they loved him very much. They saw the President as the very embodiment of manhood. "He's like us, cousin, from the countryside, from the desert. And like us, he loves animals more than he loves people. He's not some fancypants like other fake city-dwellers. Do you see his house? That one, up on top of the hill? He often goes there to leave his cares behind and sits for hours watching over his flocks. Sometimes he comes down to ride the camels with us, or he milks them, or we ride donkeys, and we race and laugh. And he doesn't get angry with us when we beat him. He loves to drink camel milk and eat gazelle meat."

They addressed Ibrahim as "cousin", and when they talked about the President, it came out in their dialect as "Mr Pres'dent" or "the Exalted Reader". Each time, they added phrases such as "God preserve him", or "May God grant him long life". They were so open and spontaneous that it was impossible to doubt their sincerity or their belief that what they said was true. Ibrahim thought they alone would be able to say and do what they wanted in complete freedom when they were with the President. As for the rest of the millions in this country laced with fear and doubt, their hearts pumped caution through their veins that chilled any sense of security.

Regarding the pleasure the President took in watching his donkeys, camels and dogs roaming here above the bodies of his victims, it did not occur to Ibrahim that this behaviour was a careful study in the humiliation of his adversaries, even after they were dead. The President took delight that they ended like this, their fates unknown to their loved ones, buried haphazardly with no gravestones, no witnesses, as though they themselves were nothing, and would forever be nothing. It was as though they had never existed, down there under the manure of donkeys and camels and the urine of dogs. Abdullah Kafka explained all that later when Ibrahim returned to the village and told him about what he had seen and lived through.

The Bedouin asked Ibrahim about his work, and he did not tell them he buried corpses here under their feet, but instead described his first job, caring for the flowers. They remarked in all seriousness, "Oh-ho! You know what, cousin? We consider your work to be much harder than ours."

When Ibrahim asked them why, they said, "The flowers and the trees are incredibly varied. There are many strange kinds, and we've never seen anything like them in all the regions we've come to know. It would be hard to tell this one from that, or the name of one from another, or how to treat each one. As for these animals, we know them individually, as well as we know ourselves. Do you know all these flowers of yours so well?"

Ibrahim replied honestly. "Not at all! I'm like you, a simple farmer and villager, and I've never seen things like this in my life. But I do what I can."

"Do you know, cousin," Jad'an said to him, "if they put us in charge of them, by God, we'd eat them!"

At this, the three of them burst out laughing together, startling the nearby donkeys. "Yes! By God, cousin," Fahd said, "back home, we know all the plants, and we know which can be eaten and which can't. But here! I swear to you, every time we pass near them and see all this sweetness and how big they are – juicy like the cheeks of young girls – our mouths begin to water! But our problem is that we don't know which ones can be eaten and which can't."

Then the two of them began reciting Bedouin poetry about flowers, women and love. They also broke into a few songs.

Ibrahim asked them about the dogs gathered here, and they raised their hands dismissively, saying, "As for those dogs, a dog like them looks after them."

When they saw that he did not understand, they pointed out an individual he had not seen before. He was crawling around on all fours, living among the dogs as though he were one of them. The Bedouin told Ibrahim they had known him since he first came here, and that he never spoke, just howled and barked. "He truly deserves his punishment. When he caused the death of a dog belonging to the little mistress, she was very sad and gave her judgement that he live the rest of his life as a dog among the dogs." By little mistress, they meant the President's youngest daughter.

The Bedouin told Ibrahim they were both getting married at the same time during the coming festival of Ramadan to two sisters, cousins of theirs, and that "the Reader" had promised to give them a thousand camels at the wedding.

Ibrahim did not know how long he had spent with these two young Bedouin when he returned at last to the guardhouse. Before he left, they gave him more of the bread and onion, along with some pickles, cheese and camel milk. They also invited him to attend their weddings, embraced him, and said they hoped to see him again, listing all the places where they might be found and the many pens, passages and tunnels that the herds passed through.

"God willing!" Ibrahim replied. He did not tell them that his shifts began at midnight, and that he had not understood most of what they explained to him to prove they knew all the gardens' secrets. But he did grasp that there was a whole other world beneath his feet, an unending network of tunnels.

Ibrahim sat on the single chair in the guardhouse and went through the details of his meeting with the two Bedouin men, whom he had started calling "the flower-eaters". He could not keep from smiling every time he thought of how they had burst out laughing when they said they would eat all the flowers if they only knew what they were.

That meeting broke something frozen inside him. The company of those two men from the desert was a balm that revived a soul he thought had dried out and withered, never again to feel anything. That meeting was the pumping on the chest of a drowned man to force out the water and bring back breath and life. Suddenly, Ibrahim decided he would try to get close to people again, that he would start going to coffee houses, playing dominoes, buying books, stopping at the fruit and nut stands, sitting with shopkeepers, bakers, barbers and the man selling propane canisters in his neighbourhood. He thought he would try to arrange to see Qisma. Things like that. He would not have to tell anyone about the nature of his work. He had to draw a line between his work and his private world where he archived the dead, on the one hand, and the relationships he was going to pursue, on the other. He felt renewed, excitement twitching restlessly inside him. He longed to respond to that desire.

Ibrahim took pleasure in thinking like that – dreaming, really – until the military ambulance pulled up at midnight. Four people got out this time and proceeded to unload six corpses. Pointing at the two new assistants, the driver said, "These guys are under your orders. Teach them the job."

The driver took off with the other man, leaving Ibrahim with the corpses and the two young men he had pointed at. They were in the prime of their youth, taking pride in their health and their bulging muscles. Ibrahim began to explain the nature of the work. He took them into the guardhouse and acquainted them with its features. Then he told them how to move the bodies, bury them, and leave the surface of the ground level like it was before. He found the young men to be vigorous, exuberant even. It did not cost them any effort to dig the graves and carry the bodies, the way it did for him. It was as though they were playing some kind of game as they tossed the corpses into the graves like bags of rubbish. No different!

That upset Ibrahim, and it was then that he decided to take at face value what the driver had said: "These guys are under your orders." At first, he had thought it was just something that was said and had not treated them that way. So now he tried it out. He stopped them and said in a harsh voice, "Human beings are not buried like that. No matter the reason for their death, there must still be respect for the dead."

They immediately complied and stopped playing around. Ibrahim began explaining to them how to gather the limbs of the corpses, no matter how torn up they were, and to arrange them in their proper places as best they could. Then they must lower them into the grave gently, as though still alive, and turn their face toward the Ka'aba, and so on. In this way, over time, the young men became his obedient subordinates, and Ibrahim only needed to direct them, without being forced to do anything himself

The young men were transformed into consummate professionals. As a result, Ibrahim's supervisors began transferring him by helicopter from time to time to other cities and different gardens and palaces belonging to the President. He saw that most of them were located on elevated places or beside rivers and lakes. Each one was a different world, astonishing in its design and atmosphere. They would leave Ibrahim there for a day or two so he could train other young men to the same professional standards he had established. Through it all, Ibrahim never stopped recording the descriptions and the locations of the corpses he saw being buried, no matter what city they were in. Every time he returned home, he would dedicate a new notebook to the city he had just visited.

Just as before, whenever Ibrahim thought that he had seen everything, the corpses would continue to surprise him with the new ways they had been tortured and killed. Among them was the one that took more than two pages to describe, more than he had previously written for any corpse. It was delivered one night when he was with his first students in the gardens on the outskirts of Baghdad. They received nearly forty corpses, all at once, all subjected to unimaginable torments. The two boys turned pale at the horror of it. But the corpse that caught Ibrahim's eye was one that had had every single bone crushed and its skin slowly stripped away, piece by piece. The skin of the feet had been peeled off like socks. The skin of the head and face removed like a hat and a mask. The skin of the chest like a shirt coming off. Skilfully stripped and flayed, limb by limb, piece by piece. It was hard for Ibrahim to close its eyes due to the extreme terror found in them – every time he tried, they burst wide open again as though they were prisoners shrieking out. But the thing that most captured his attention and formed the essential basis for identifying the corpse – and without which it would have been impossible to record anything useful – was the right arm. It was entirely untouched. And when Ibrahim examined it in the light of his torch, he found that the arm bore a tattoo in the shape of a heart, and in the middle was the name of the President.

CHAPTER 25

The Fall of the Capital and the Return

Ibrahim was now teaching gravediggers rather than digging directly with his own hands. He started to find more time for himself, since they granted him a day's leave after he returned from each trip to the palace gardens in another city. Having travelled between military camps, trenches and different fronts during the wars, he crossed the country moving between the palaces. Once again he had no choice in the matter.

With the extra time he had, and given that he was less tired than he used to be upon arriving home, Ibrahim began going out to walk at night, traversing Baghdad's alleys, bridges and markets. He had exchanged his artificial foot for a new one, better designed and made for him by the private hospital in which his wife had died. He was thinking more and more about Qisma. He did not want to bother her, nor would he demand anything of her or meddle in her life. All he wanted was to see her and reassure himself that she was O.K. He also wanted to give her some of the money that was piling up for him, however much she wanted, seeing as he had no expenses.

But this sense of relaxation was short-lived. By early 2003, it became clear that Iraq was under serious threat of invasion, and with each day that passed, the international community became increasingly committed to the catastrophe they were poised to unleash. The number of bodies delivered for burial each night mounted, forcing Ibrahim to pitch in to help the two young men. Sometimes, they did not finish until morning. Things got even worse – groups of soldiers came with other groups of soldiers, blindfolded and hands bound. They would dig a long trench, or they would bring a bulldozer to make a pit without measuring it out. They would line up the blindfolded men at the edge of the pit and open fire. The dead would fall like autumn leaves, even though it was spring. Then they would order the bulldozer to cover them in soil, and they went off to repeat it all somewhere else, without stopping to confirm that these men were actually dead. They brought another round . . . and another. The majority of the dead at that time were soldiers and high-ranking officers. The soldiers who served as executioners would yell various insults before opening fire; dirty, angry, hysterical words, the least of which were: "Traitors! Cowards! Weaklings! Dogs!"

As soon as the first American air raids began over Baghdad, specifically around the presidential palaces, everything was thrown into disorder. The work there was neglected, and most of the gardens were turned into military camps. On the hills and in the middle of the forests, they set up artillery, anti-aircraft guns and small rocket platforms. Earthworks were constructed and sandbags piled up. It was all turned into a garden for weapons of every size and type. As Sa'ad had once told him, all the palaces and splendid buildings were constructed over bomb shelters. In some corners of the gardens, trenches had been dug out beforehand, hidden among the plants, flowers and henna hedges. On both sides of the paths inside the palace grounds and along the roads leading there from the city, they quickly reinforced the military checkpoints with sandbags stacked high to meet the foreign invader. The palaces were transformed into barracks teeming with soldiers and munitions. The air was filled with tension, alarms and the smell of gunpowder, blood and smoke.

The civilians working there were given envelopes of money and A.K.-47s and pistols. They were told, "Take an extended holiday until we send you further orders over the radio. Use these weapons to defend your homes and the government institutions in your neighbourhoods. Kill the invaders and the traitors. You are allowed to kill anybody whose devotion to the country you doubt, anyone in whom you sense treachery or reluctance to defend the country."

Ibrahim returned home. Like everyone else, he bought all the tinned food and beverages he could, and then he locked the doors. Alone in his living room, kitchen, bathroom and bedroom, alone with his television and radio, Ibrahim would occasionally look out the window or go up on the roof to see the smoke rising from all sides of Baghdad. The explosions from missiles and air bombardments, especially in the vicinity of the presidential gardens, never ceased. Day blended into night. The city was transformed into a living hell for days and weeks that seemed to last for ever. Finally, in April, he saw American tanks passing through the streets of his neighbourhood, in front of his house. He remained secluded, coping day to day with as little cold food, drinks and candles as possible because the electricity had been cut off. Telephone lines had also been cut, as had the roads in and out of the city. Nothing reached him from the outside world except a radio broadcast with a broken signal and that which he saw with his own eyes from the windows, the roof and the keyhole in his front door, which he had not opened since hiding himself away.

It continued like this until, one afternoon, he heard the sound of people calling out, including the voices of women and the cries of children. He opened the door and saw several individuals and families carrying suitcases and bags, in cars or in carts pulled by horses or donkeys, the kind of cart used to distribute propane tanks. A man carrying a big suitcase on one shoulder passed by, his other hand pulling along a child. His wife was beside him doing the same thing in her full black robe – carrying a suit-case on her head while leading a dishevelled girl by the hand. They were hurrying along, panting, and Ibrahim found himself calling to them, "Where are you going?"

The man breathlessly informed Ibrahim that now was his chance to escape: everyone was leaving the capital. "The world is turned upside down, brother! If you have relatives or acquain-tances outside the capital, in the villages, seek refuge with them. And if you can, leave one of your sons in the house to guard it – there are thieves everywhere. Chaos and plunder! Everything is a shambles! The world is turned upside down, brother. Upside down, upside down! Come on! Come on! Trust in God and save yourself." The man went on in this way without turning to face Ibrahim, as though talking aloud to himself, until he disappeared around the corner.

Ibrahim went back inside and filled his pockets with stacks of cash. He made sure the windows and doors were locked, and then he left, taking nothing more than a bottle of water. He headed toward the Alawite Garage, walking for a while and riding for a while with a crowd of people in the back of a pickup truck. At the station, he found a car to give him a lift to Samarra, and from there, another car to Balad and another to Baiji. It went on like that until he reached his village at sundown.

From the time Ibrahim left his house in Baghdad until he reached his house in the village, he had seen dozens, if not hundreds, of corpses lying along the streets and roads. For a moment, he thought he might have an opportunity to bury some of them, but it was not a question of his wishes and his abilities. Everything was left to chance and luck – or rather, to fate and decree. And Ibrahim's *qisma* was to arrive at last at his home in the countryside. He had saved himself, but he had returned without his Qisma, and had no knowledge of her whereabouts or what she was going through. That was what concerned him the most, and he thought about her all the more when he found himself alone once again in the house where he and his daughter had both been born. Alone, since his mother had died while he was away, and his sisters and his younger brother had set themselves up in their own houses long ago, accepting that the family home would pass to the eldest son.

Ibrahim spent the days slowly refurbishing everything, starting with the garden. He repaired the corners of the house, the door handles, window latches and the empty livestock pen, which had all become dilapidated during his absence. Fortunately, his family had continued caring for the fields, so there was not much for him to do there. So Ibrahim contented himself with visits to his siblings, visits to the graves of his parents and his wife, and meetings with Abdullah, usually in their old place on the banks of the river.

On rare occasions, Tariq would join them. Tariq was resentful and angry about what had happened. He would launch into tirades, his blood boiling, cursing "the invasion, the occupation, and this new imperialism that has devastated the country and turned its borders into a drinking hole for everyone and his brother from the neighbouring countries, for intelligence services, death squads, terrorists, suicide bombers, spies, and all the various merchants of war." He would go on in this way, furious, with spittle spraying onto his beard: "They've come from every direction, assembling here to settle their filthy accounts on our soil, above our heads. Times past were better than what these people have brought, for at least then there was one enemy we knew to keep at a distance. But now there are a thousand enemies from a thousand factions. We no longer even know who's an enemy and who's a friend."

Abdullah would interrupt from time to time, exasperated by Tariq's fiery sermon, saying, "All epochs have been shit. That which went before was no better than what's happening now, and what is to come won't be any better either. All of it is shit piled on shit. Since the day this country was established on this soil, it has never seen ten continuous years of peace, and it appears it never will."

They watched the sun slowly set behind the mountain across

the way, as the magic of the twilight reflected off the surface of the water, and returned to the village before the gnats intensified their attacks, passing along narrow dirt tracks between the fields, the same tracks they had followed as children. They felt an assurance, a sense that nothing had changed and that all that had happened was merely a transitory external disturbance, something outside them, not internal. They recalled the same memories, anecdotes and tales they had been repeating since childhood, laughing as they traded the same jokes and jibes.

Some evenings, Abdullah would pass by the cemetery because he would find Ibrahim there. Other evenings, Ibrahim would go to Abdullah's house to drink tea and then they would go together to the riverbank and sit in silence. Abdullah was content to smoke and stare at the water, and Ibrahim would wash the stones in front of him before throwing them – burying them – in the water. If they spoke, their conversations consisted of Ibrahim sharing his questions and Abdullah providing answers that wove their way towards the conclusion that there was no meaning to anything, and that the best available solution lay in letting go of illusions, abandoning all ambitions along with greed, desire and the urge to possess.

"So don't desire anything, brother Ibrahim. Don't expect anything. Then you'll feel at peace and nothing will make you anxious. Everything will be alright, no matter what happens, because you didn't want anything different."

Ibrahim told Abdullah that the only thing he wanted now was to be sure that Qisma was safe; there was nothing, nothing at all beyond that. He was tortured by how helpless he was – where could he begin his search? He did not know her address – he did not even know the name of her husband or his family, just as he was at a loss as to what name he would ask for, Qisma or Nisma. It was something he mulled over in his head a hundred times every day, and each time he would arrive at the same defeated conclusion.

Abdullah Kafka explained to Ibrahim the meaning of tending herds of donkeys over the bodies of the dead, and it was Abdullah who provided Ibrahim with some semblance of peace, comfort, freedom and security. Tariq would not always join them since he was off putting his affairs in order and rearranging his relationships with all the opposing factions, just as he was wont to do – a practice he had inherited from his father. He sought to establish connections with the occupiers and with those fighting against the occupation, with the thieves and the police, with the remnants of the former regime and the vanguard of the new regime, with Sunnis and Shiites, Arabs and Kurds, Muslims and Christians and foreigners and Iraqis. He sought to find a profitable balance that would allow him to keep living the life he had grown accustomed to.

If Tariq did join them, he would argue with Abdullah. Meanwhile, as usual, Ibrahim would stay silent. But their affection for each other did not change. Each of them knew the others like the lines on his hand, and each of their meetings, no matter how much they yelled and contradicted each other, would end with a sense of catharsis, the feeling of a man meeting himself. Each of them took an interest in the details of the others' lives as much as in the details of his own. Each would help the others organise their thoughts and the affairs of daily life. And the one thing they shared above all was Ibrahim's sorrow and anxiety over Qisma.

Until the day she came back, carrying in her arms a baby she said was her son.

CHAPTER 26

Where the Living Meet the Dead

Qisma appeared to have grown a great deal older, old beyond her years. Her features had matured: they were those of a woman who was a mother, not a woman who was a daughter. In addition to patience and endurance, it was clear that motherhood had taught her to be more understanding and accepting of those around her, and to leave behind – if only a little – the veneration of the self at the expense of others. She had grown calmer.

Meanwhile, Ibrahim remained as he ever was, eager not to do anything that might provoke her. What mattered to him was that his daughter now lived under his roof, in the same mud house in which they had both been born. In addition, there was this new blessing that filled their home with life and broke the usual silence between them. Ibrahim displayed a devotion to the infant that rivalled even a mother's love. He did not neglect the baby for an instant, attended to all his needs and brought him along with him wherever he went. He would carry him on his shoulders, feeling that the head of his grandson ennobled his own, as though the child were an emperor's crown. He granted him all the time and attention he had been prevented from showing his daughter, and he would sometimes take him to visit the grave of Umm Qisma, telling the infant all about his grandmother.

The only thing Ibrahim did not like about this child was his name, since his father had chosen to name him after the President. Everyone, including Qisma, was aware of Ibrahim's distaste, even though he never referred or alluded to it. But Qisma and the others did notice that Ibrahim did not call the child by his name even once, but rather would say, "Come along, my son!" or "Take this, my dear!" And if he presented the boy to someone, he would say, "This is my grandson, the son of my daughter, Qisma."

And even though Ibrahim did get used to the name and was resolved not to ask Qisma about anything, over time she began to tell him of her own accord the reason she was so late in returning to the village. Ever since the Americans entered Baghdad and the regime fell, she had occupied herself with two main tasks. The first was to remain at her magnificent home in order to guard it against looters. The second was to search for any information that would shed light on what had happened to her husband. Qisma's sister-in-law had joined her in this search, together with other relatives of missing persons she had got to know during the process. She said her husband suddenly went missing shortly before the fall of the regime. Neither she, nor his family, nor any acquaintance or friend had been able to discover anything about him, even though they knocked on every door and followed up on every lead. Qisma had hoped, for instance, that he might have been put in jail and would return after the collapse of the prison system. Or maybe he had fled the country and would now return, or that she would come across his grave if he had been killed. But none of these things had happened, and from the day of her husband's disappearance until then, she had learned nothing of his fate.

She told Ibrahim how, before the fall, she had gone to all the hospitals and police stations, asking them to inform her of any news that reached them about her husband. She gave them her telephone number and home address in case they came across an unidentified corpse or even a lost madman. But now thousands of unidentified corpses littered Iraq from one corner to the other, and great hordes of the insane had been released when the doors of all the hospitals for those with nervous disorders and psychological illnesses were opened after the invasion. The former patients now roamed the streets and back alleys as easy targets for murder, rape and enslavement, if they did not first fall prey to illness or injury.

Little by little, Qisma told her father the story of her sufferings, a bit more each day. But just as Ibrahim kept the secret of his sterility hidden from her and everyone else, Qisma was also holding something back. She had decided to cover it up, even within herself, for she had no other solution. It was a way of protecting herself from being destroyed by memories and doubts, for it was not long after that accursed night that she discovered she was pregnant, and she did not want to plunge into the whirlpool of unanswerable questions about who her baby's father was. Fortunately for her, when the baby was born it resembled her alone. "He's my child, mine," she said to herself. "That's the important thing."

Qisma's husband had been elated and proud to the point of giddiness when they were invited to a private party in one of the presidential palaces. She adorned herself as beautifully as she could, and she felt, just a short time into her marriage, that she had climbed the social ladder quickly. Indeed, that she had jumped to the rung that led to the throne.

At the palace, it was necessary for women to enter through one door and men through another before arriving at the magnificent party chamber, which opened on one side to long tables loaded with food and drink under the festive lights of the gardens and fountains. Qisma entered through the women's door, then passed through another door, then another and another, until she found herself alone in a lavish bedroom. She was confused, and then shocked when the President came in to meet her. Without any preliminaries, he ordered her to do what he wanted. So she did what he wanted, and he did what he wanted with her. Afterwards, Qisma spent the rest of the party sitting beside her husband, deaf and mute. She was not conscious of the crowds of revellers, the voices of the musicians, the food, or anything beyond a foggy mix of vibrating, intermingling colours. She certainly could not eat anything, telling her husband that she felt sick and had a pain in her stomach. When they got home, she did not ask him about who or what he had seen at the party, nor about what he had eaten. Indeed, she was unable to mention it in front of him, or even to recall it on her own, ever. She decided to doubt that it had actually happened. She decided to forget it.

She told her father about her journey in search of her husband after the fall of the regime, saying she had discovered a different Iraq, one that did not tally with what she had known before, and that once would have been unimaginable. Together with hundreds of others who had also lost relatives, she went to dozens of community centres that had recently opened – most of them staffed by volunteers – to help people find information in archives taken from the offices of the security apparatus and the old intelligence service. She said those archives listed about half a million Iraqis who had gone missing over the last two decades, not counting those who had been lost in the wars or those who had been executed but whose bodies had been turned over to their families.

Qisma went around to many communal graves that had recently been discovered in various parts of the country, including some that contained thousands of skeletons. Some people had information, death certificates, or identification numbers for their missing relatives. They exhumed one grave after another until they found them. But Qisma did not have any official information or certificate. All she had were stories and clues she had gathered from people who had known either her husband or those who had disappeared with him. She followed the threads of every rumour or story that reached her, including what she heard from astrologers, palm-readers and diviners, as well as other old women who performed magic. She resorted to them in desperation, willing to pursue any glimmer of hope, even if it was just the kind of nonsense that she would never have believed before. She was told many things. That her husband had loved another woman; they had married secretly because her family had resisted the relationship, seeing as he had joined opposition parties working outside the country, to which he ended up fleeing. She also heard that he had been assigned a secret assassination mission and was killed in the line of duty. That he had taken part in an attempted coup with forty members from the special unit of guards he belonged to: the plot had been uncovered and they had all been executed.

Qisma said it was this last possibility that seemed most plausible to her because she had met with the families of her husband's companions in that special unit, and they talked to her about the same thing. Their brother or their husband had been imprisoned for attempting to overthrow the government, and they had all disappeared at the same time. They were going through the exact same thing as her and like her they had still learned nothing about their relatives.

She also believed the story about the coup because her husband actually had wanted to become president. He admired the President greatly and modelled himself on him, though at the same time he hated him and felt him to be a personal adversary. Her husband believed himself to be more worthy of the presidency: he at least had obtained his diploma, while the President had not; he was in the military and a real officer, while the President had weaselled out of the mandatory military service; he was a native of the capital, Baghdad, while the President was from an obscure village; he was from a well-known and deeply rooted Baghdad family, while the President did not know his own father. For all these reasons, he considered himself to be more worthy and more deserving than the President, ready to take his place.

"On the other hand, my husband admired the President for having achieved what he had and for ruling the country and mastering its people despite having been a nobody and an orphan, with no qualifications to speak of. My husband hated the President, but he also admired him, to the point of loving him. After all, he did insist on naming our son after him. And when he first entered the military college, before I knew him, he tattooed the name of the President on his arm, encircling it with a heart, just like lovers do."

At that moment, Ibrahim started asking his first questions in rapid succession: "On which arm?"

"The right."

"Was it in exactly this area?"

"Yes."

"This big?"

"Yes."

"And what was the precise date he went missing?"

She told him the date. It was just before the night he had buried the body with the shattered bones and all the skin peeled off except for the tattooed forearm which had not been hurt at all. For the first time, Ibrahim told Qisma in general terms about his work. He went into more detail about his archive of information about the missing. He told Qisma that he had buried a body with the tattoo she had described to him, without saying anything about how the body had been skinned like a sheep that had been slaughtered.

They set off in Qisma's car for Baghdad. On the way, Ibrahim told her some more of what he had been through. But he hesitated and held back many of the details in the fear that he would cause further damage to the image she had of him and perhaps lose her all over again. He was surprised to find that her reaction was the exact opposite of what he had expected. Qisma praised him for keeping records about those corpses, describing what he had done as important and heroic work, an unparalleled act of nobility and humanity.

Ibrahim experienced a release within his soul. It had torn his heart that she had considered him worthless and rejected him. The words of praise he had just received produced elation beyond any other words he had heard in his life because they came from his daughter. Greedy for her approval, Ibrahim began telling Qisma more, hoping to win more of her approval. He brought up the time she had called his attention to the offensive odour emanating from his room, and he explained what had caused it. "That was the very beginning, and since then, I have been keeping records of thousands of bodies in Baghdad and in other cities where I've overseen burial sites."

When they arrived at his house in Baghdad, Ibrahim watched as Qisma laid her child on the couch in the living room and pressed on ahead of him into his bedroom. He followed her inside and began taking the records out of their hiding-places, and he showed her the shoeboxes filled with bags of identity cards, hair clippings and small items he had taken from the dead. Qisma began leafing through the notebooks he threw on the bed. She was struck to find them written in a strange language she had never seen before. He explained that it was a script that he had invented himself, and no living soul in the world but him knew how to read it. At that, Ibrahim read in Qisma's eyes a wondrous look of surprise and admiration that renewed his pride and elation. He pulled out the notebook he expected would contain the date of her husband's disappearance, and he began to read out the gist of what he had written, skipping over many of the unpleasant details. But Qisma insisted, so he started again as she broke into sobs that shook her whole body.

At night, after they had eaten dinner and put the child to bed, she took a small notebook of phone numbers out of her bag. She pulled over the telephone, setting it in front of her on the couch. She noticed that the telephone indicated "SAVED MESSAGES". She listened to them and discovered they were from her, the only two calls she had made to him while he was gone. She had said nothing in messages beyond greeting him and letting him know that she was fine. She asked Ibrahim if he had listened to them, and he replied that he did not know how to use the answering machine. Indeed, he could not recall ever having used the telephone; it happened so seldom he had forgotten. He asked her if she had left her telephone number or address in those two messages. With a painful stab of shame and regret, she told him she had not.

Qisma began making dozens of calls, one after another, to her husband's family and acquaintances, as well as to the families of his companions who had disappeared with him. She also called the families of other missing persons, the people she had got to know during her search, sharing what she had discovered with them and telling them all to come in the morning. Ibrahim sat next to her, watching the way she spoke and remembering those nights when she would isolate herself with the phone, lying on the couch, half naked, no doubt talking to him, her poor officer.

Neither Qisma nor her father slept that night. They kept preparing maps and organising the specific details of the corpses connected to the families Qisma had called. And so they all went together in a caravan of cars: more than a hundred people from sixty families. They all took part in the digging and brought away with them the remains of their dead, their grief mixed with the relief that came from knowing their final fate. Then they headed off to their own cemeteries to rebury their loved ones in a fitting manner, in clear and well-marked graves.

Soon, the news spread through the city, and people flocked to Ibrahim's house. With Qisma's help, he provided them with the relevant information. It went on like that for just under a month, a long, exhausting month during which he gave out most of the information he had about those who were buried in Baghdad and its suburbs. Only a very little remained, apart from the notebooks relating to the other cities. Ibrahim and Qisma were overwhelmed by fatigue after receiving so many people at all hours of the day and night, so Qisma took Ibrahim to her house so they might rest a little. He found it to be magnificent, with impressive furniture and balconies overlooking the river. They slept there and sat on the balcony, sipping tea and staring at the water for a long time until they felt refreshed. After two days, they locked up the house and went back to the village. But families of the missing from various cities around the country began following them, enquiring after Ibrahim and turning up at his house in the village. Qisma agreed to organise things for them, and because the rest of the archive remained in Baghdad, she set a precise time and place when her father would undertake a visit to each city, carrying his records, ready to hand over whatever information he had.

More than once, Tariq came to Ibrahim at night, trembling, sweating and confused – afraid for him. In private, he warned Ibrahim, advising him to stop what he was doing, and indeed, to deny it. Tariq explained that it had reached his ears from contacts among the resistance and elements of the former regime that people intended to kill Ibrahim because they considered him to be slandering the image of the former President and the period of his rule. They said that Ibrahim was in league with traitors and that the claims he was making were based on lies he had invented. Moreover, even if it were true, and he was leading the people to actual graves, they would still kill him because, in their view, that was a betrayal of the trust and confidence the former regime had bestowed upon him.

The next night, Tariq came in the same state of agitation to inform Ibrahim that it had reached his ears from his connections in the new government that they or their supporters intended to kill Ibrahim in order to purify the country of all adherents of the former regime, anyone who was a sympathiser and participated in its crimes in any form whatsoever. What Ibrahim had done provided decisive proof that "You were in the inner circle and deeply trusted by them, counted among the leadership of the dying dictatorial regime."

Tariq pleaded with him, "Stop what you're doing, Ibrahim! Indeed, deny it, deny all knowledge of it! You have to flee to some secret place, somewhere safe, until this storm passes. If you want, I'll arrange that for you. They'll kill you, Ibrahim! They'll kill you, brother. If one side doesn't kill you, the other side will. Your blood will be shed in vain by the death squads, just as is happening all over this country every day."

But even though he believed him, Ibrahim did not follow Tariq's advice. He could not stop himself from going down this path, not after everything he had gone through and everything he had done in preparation for a moment like this, a moment he had never expected to arrive. He felt it was all a gift God had given for his benefit. He had never thought he would be so useful to people, and as a result, he felt an even deeper sense of peace when he saw their faces light up with immense gratitude, indebtedness and tears of relief when the hard search for lost loved ones came to an end. For that reason, he refused to take any gifts or the large sums of money they offered him. His conscience was finally clear. His self-recriminations for having left the body of his friend Ahmad al-Najafi in the desert could be laid to rest. The most important aspect of it all was the respect and esteem he was surprised to receive from the person who meant the most to him, his daughter Qisma. That was something he had never expected. So he decided to keep going until he had delivered the last bit of information he possessed to its rightful owners, even if he had to search them out himself.

On the second day of Ramadan, in the year 2006, he agreed with eight other villagers to rent a van to go to Baghdad. They planned to meet in the main street in front of the village café, and each of them had his own reasons for visiting the capital. Some of them were young men seeking opportunities for work or wanting to register in the security forces, who were the only ones hiring at that time. Older men were making the trip to arrange their pensions, and others were seeking lost loved ones, new and old, in the city.

They set off an hour after midnight, just as they had agreed, so that they would arrive at dawn and could take care of their affairs early in the day, before the heat became too intense, since they were fasting. But before the sun came up, their severed heads were returned in banana crates to the same place they had set out from.

CHAPTER 27

Remarriage

In this country where no bananas were grown, the village awoke to the heads of nine of its sons in banana crates. Along with each head was an I.D. card to identify the person since some of their faces were completely disfigured, either by torture preceding the beheading or something similar after the slaughter. Their characteristic features were no longer sufficient to distinguish them. One of these cards bore the name Ibrahim Suhayl.

The first person to notice the crates was the herdsman, Isma'il. All traces of sleep fled his eyes, and he began screaming at the top of his lungs. His donkey jumped, his flock of sheep froze, and the pigeons and sparrows launched from treetops and rooftops. The last silver light of dawn had filled the street, and the sleeping village was calm and still, apart from the crowing of a rooster and the barking of a distant dog, responding to another dog in some yet more distant corner. Some people rushed towards him from some of the village houses – then all the people from all the houses, after someone raised the alarm over the mosque loudspeakers.

It was on the third day of the month of Ramadan, 2006. According to history, that was when something called America had occupied a country named Iraq.

When they informed Abdullah Kafka that the head of Ibrahim was among the nine, he replied, "It is finished! He has attained his rest. For this time he has truly died, leaving us to the chaos of fate and the futility of waiting for our own deaths, we the living dead."

Abdullah fell silent, frozen as a stone. Then he began to smoke and smoke and smoke. And for the first time, the people saw tears stream from his unblinking eyes. He did not wipe them away, and he did not stop smoking.

And when the news reached their third, Sheikh Tariq, he felt faint and nearly collapsed. He sat down quickly, propping up his spirit – so as not to kill himself – by reciting the many religious sayings he had learned by heart. He wept and asked God's forgiveness; he wept and cursed the devil so as not to be driven to despair; he wept and wept until his tears wet the edges of his red, henna-dyed beard.

Questions from the onlookers saved Tariq from succumbing to an even longer bout of sobbing. "What do we do, O sheikh? Do we bury the heads on their own, or do we wait until we come across their bodies and bury them together? They were killed in Baghdad, or on the road to Baghdad, and now Baghdad is a chaos choking on anonymous corpses, buried explosives, car bombs, foreigners and deceit. It might be impossible to find their bodies."

Tariq said, "It's best to bury the heads, and if it happens that their bodies are discovered, they can be buried too, either with the heads, or separately, or in the place where they are found. Our sons and brothers are not better or more venerable than the prince of martyrs, Hussein, grandson of the Prophet, whose head they buried in Egypt or Syria while his body stayed in Iraq. Make haste to bury the heads, for the way to honour the dead is to bury them."

Only Qisma, the widow who became an orphan that early morning, opposed them and wanted the head of her father, Ibrahim, to be kept unburied until his body was found. But her resistance was in vain when the men refused and rebuked her, saying, "Hold your tongue, woman, and cease this madness! What do you know about such things?"

They pushed her away to where the women were gathered. Only her neighbour, fat Amira, supported her, screaming that she wanted to preserve her husband's head in the freezer until they located his body.

Qisma wavered a long time: she would take one step forward and fall two steps back. But in the end she resolved the matter and decided to go to the house of Abdullah Kafka. Her relationship with Ibrahim's brother had been nearly severed when she got married. Besides, he had the burden of a large family on his shoulders, and a herd of sheep and goats. Abdullah would be the most appropriate person to help her in the search for her father's body. He was her father's closest friend, and he was the only one to whom her father had revealed his secret at a time when the mere knowledge of it would lead to execution. She remembered what her father once said to her: "Tariq and Abdullah are my closest friends, but I love Abdullah more." And Abdullah also had no family or work to hold him back, and he was not afraid of anything, not even of death itself.

In these ways, Qisma shored up her conviction that the decision to approach him was sound, despite the doubts and rumours, followed by scandal, that would result if a young widow were seen entering the house of an unmarried man at the far edge of the village. But she had not wanted to broach the issue with him in front of the villagers, the very people who had dragged her away on the burial day and rebuked her, together with fat Amira. And given that Abdullah Kafka spent most of the time at the café, often from when it first opened at sunrise, and he did not leave until the door was locked after midnight, the only choice was to seek him out at dawn. It was not easy for her to take such a risky decision. But it was not the first of its kind in her life.

She passed bitter nights of broken sleep, when hot tears of sorrow for her father alternated with racing thoughts of what she wanted to do. Then she made up her mind to proceed. She was not sure why she carried her baby with her, even though he was fast asleep. He stirred uneasily but kept sleeping as she lay his head on her shoulder as though tucking in a corner of her shawl. Perhaps it occurred to her that bringing him would dispel doubts should someone happen to see her, or that she could somehow protect herself with him. Or maybe she thought that when Abdullah saw the baby, he would be more sympathetic towards her, even though she was aware of his wrath at the baby's name, given that the baby's father, a native of Baghdad, had wanted his son to bear the name of the President.

Would he possibly agree to accompany her to the burning city of Baghdad to search for one corpse amid the thousands, when he was the one who had not stirred from his seat in the café to attend the burial? Would he tell her what she wanted to know, more about her father, when he was the one who remained silent nearly all the time? She had turned these two questions over in her mind as she tossed in bed, recalling everything she could about her father and feeling guilty for having fought with him and gone away for years despite being his only daughter.

At the same time, she was impelled by the challenge to prove to everyone that a daughter, too, is worthy of carrying her father's name and can defend it, along with his memory; that it is not only the male child who carries the father's name and continues his line, as was said. She realised now, more than ever before, the extent to which her father Ibrahim had suffered on behalf of his parents and his siblings. And also for her and because of her. She felt that more now that she had become a mother and a widow, like him, who, as a father and a widower, had refused to get re-married after the passing of her mother, both to spare her a step-mother who would harass her and for the sake of the secret.

Her young suitor had swept her away. And her desire for a different life, to be like the others, and her egotistical preoccupa-tion with herself and nothing more, had prevented anything that Ibrahim told her from being preserved in memory. She had not wanted her memory to become a storehouse for the remains of his memory, especially during the years of living, studying and getting married in Baghdad. She had wanted to expunge her childhood in this village and bury the truth that her parents were poor, simple villagers.

Meanwhile, Ibrahim's sole consolation existed in the wish to tell her things; she was his only daughter. And if she were not an extension of his own memories and the memory of him, all that he represented would dissolve and vanish, and nothing frightens a man more than that. He had wanted to seize every opportunity to tell her stories. Sometimes he would repeat the same stories and go into detail. Indeed, sometimes he would cry or laugh as though he were reliving that which he related.

This cautious, earnest desire, visible in his eyes, had forcibly left a part of his memory within hers, even though it was in the form of scattered pieces. Anointed by a feeling of regret, she began trying, after his death, to gather these stories, to recall them, to tell them to herself and to hear them in her own memory this time. She realised there were many holes in her father's biography, many gaps in her knowledge of him, which she needed to fill with the help of others if it were to be complete.

And deep down, she decided to tell her son, too, when he got older, about his grandfather. She now saw him as a hero, even if heroism was no longer esteemed in this country where heroes and traitors, humanity and savagery, sacrifice and exploitation were intertwined, and everything mixed together amid battle smoke, chaos, blood and destruction. True heroism lay hidden in self-denial, and that is primarily what her father Ibrahim had practised throughout his life with a remarkable patience and submission. She had found those qualities so detestable that she searched for the exact opposite in her husband. But now, having grown up and returned to the village as a widowed mother, she began to see things in a different light. "With all its blows," she said to her neighbour Amira, "life teaches a person to understand better the meaning of life."

She knocked on the door quietly at dawn. She had not expected that he would hear her first attempt, but it opened at once.
She did not see any sign of surprise on his face or anything that
suggested he had been asleep, but he assured her he had been
sleeping, and it was just that it was now in his nature to wake
up in an instant. He only had to open his eyes to be fully awake –
it was something he had got used to during his captivity.

Abdullah closed the door. She sat in the living room with the
baby sleeping in her lap. He asked if she wanted him to make
her tea or breakfast. "No," she said. "Please, sit."

He sat in front of her, smoking. Then he moved further away .
when he saw his smoke wafting close to the baby's nose. She
began with a long introduction, starting off with an apology for
coming in this way, at such an hour and without any prior notice.
But she insisted on searching for her father's body no matter
what it cost her. She was of the opinion that Abdullah was the
best person to accompany her in this mission and that her father
had trusted and loved him more than any other person. But
Abdullah mumbled a few words and shook his head in refusal.

"I beg you."

He thought for a moment, and then shook his head without
a sound.

"Why?"

He said that he was not interested. It was not important to
him, nor was anything else, so he would not be of any use to
her. Once more she insisted, and he repeated that he could not
help her in this mission because he had not seen Baghdad for
many long years, and things there had no doubt changed. Or

rather, everything. There was nothing there he knew, and he did not even know how to interact with people when it came to such matters.

She told him she knew Baghdad well and would take care of everything – all she was asking was that he be her travel companion so that there would be a trustworthy man at her side through the chaos. He was the most suitable person because he had no obligations and could stay with her however long the search took. He told her any other man would be more useful and a greater help to her in this matter. But she came back to her insistence that he was the best man for the job, for besides the fact that he was free from any obligations, everyone in the village respected him and knew how close he had been to her father. Therefore, no-one would make any indecent comments about them, but rather they would see the matter as entirely proper and would esteem his stance.

The room was beginning to fill with Abdullah's cigarette smoke, so he opened the door. Qisma kept insisting, and he kept refusing. Indeed, he tried to dissuade her from her decision to travel, saying that what she intended to do had no meaning, and that it would not change anything now that Ibrahim had met his end and died.

Qisma asserted that this matter meant very much to her, just as it had to her father. He deserved this simple, final honour at least, when he himself had spent years striving to gather together the limbs of corpses and arrange them for burial as befits a human being. He had risked his life and endured a gnawing terror for the sake of guiding people to the bodily remains of their loved ones.

For that reason, his body deserved to be treated in the same way he had treated the bodies of thousands of people.

"There's no use in any of that," Abdullah told her. "No meaning. Everything has come to an end. Ibrahim has come to an end."

Qisma rose in anger and yelled at him: "Ibrahim has not come to an end and he never will! Ibrahim is present and will remain present in me. I am Ibrahim. This son of mine is Ibrahim. Iraq is Ibrahim, and Ibrahim will remain in the memory of the people who knew him, to whom he always extended a helping hand!"

Abdullah stood up in front of her, confused. Her anger and harsh tone had surprised him, and he seemed to wake up only in that moment. He was shaken by her vitality, and he submitted in some way to this explosion of hers.

Qisma let herself go as the words kept pouring out. "If you have come to an end, or if that's what you claim, that's your business, so do what you want. As for Ibrahim, he won't come to an end. Ibrahim is in all of us. He's in you too, even though you spout denial and meaninglessness on account of laziness, fear and despair. You were always on Ibrahim's mind, whether you were present or absent. But you're an egoist who thinks of nothing but himself, and that's why you don't see a meaning in anything or anybody. If things have no meaning, then it's up to us to create meaning for them. Take gold, for example. If life has no meaning, then it's up to us to produce some meaning for it, even if it's only an illusion. Isn't nihilism another illusion?

"I know you through my father. I even know your favourite word and how you always respond, that everything is 'shit'. This word, by the way, is frequently on the lips of those proud, vain people who are the exact opposite of you, the rich, stupid ones with power in their hands, the people who brought you where you stand today. Ibrahim always strove to be useful in some way wherever he was, in everything he thought and said and did. That's what he had to be, for every living creature – indeed, every single thing – has a role and a particular use in this universe. Even shit, by the way, has its uses. Do you hear me . . . Kafka?"

She fell silent, catching her breath and looking sharply in his eyes as he looked back. It lasted a moment, and then they started laughing together. She sighed, calmed down and said, "Well, and now?"

When Abdullah shook his head, Qisma stormed out, slamming the door behind her. He called to her through the window, and she stopped without turning to face him. "Talk to Tariq," he said. "He's better at this sort of thing. If he says no, tell me. I'll know how to convince him."

She did not reply, nor did she turn around. As she receded into the distance, pressing her child to her chest, Abdullah kept watching until she disappeared. He felt something new stirring in his depths. This woman had shaken him. She had awoken within him feelings that he had considered to have died. It was as though she had placed before his eyes glasses that restored his ability to see things in a different way – a better way. It was not because of her logic, of course, but rather her trusting tone, which had truly pleased him.

He remained standing at the window for a long time, smoking and giving in to the imaginative possibilities that bubbled up inside him. Maybe if he lived with this woman, his life would change. Maybe he would find the illusion of some meaning for life, or else something that would divert him from feeling its lack of meaning until it was all over. It was as though he felt eager, or compelled, to be useful. He allowed himself to think that if he married her, perhaps, he would try to get his Uncle Isma'il married too, and Isma'il would come and live the rest of his life with him as a compensation for the injustice that they had laid upon him. And if she married him, perhaps, then . . .

But then he said to himself, "This is useless prattle. It's impossible." He closed the window and went back to bed.

A little before noon, Qisma went to Tariq's house. She found him in the living room, playing with two of his young daughters. He was delighted to see her and welcomed her warmly, taking the baby out of her arms and hugging it to his chest. He kissed the baby, and it reached its hand out to Tariq's beard, which Tariq bent down to him. As soon as they were seated and Tariq learned that she had come to him with something important, he sent his daughters out of the room, saying, "Go and play in the garden!" They left, and Qisma told Tariq why she had come.

Tariq remained silent for several moments, watching her and thinking as he combed the edges of his beard with his fingertips. This was an opportunity that had never occurred to him. Indeed, she was a miracle that God was secretly sharing with him, a gift from the heavenly Lord. For since she had arrived as a widow in the village, he had privately been thinking that this woman would be a treasure to marry. If his two oldest sons, Ibrahim and Abdullah, had not already been married, he would have persuaded one of them to marry her. Indeed, he thought about trying to convince either of them to take her as a second wife, but he gave up that thought because he knew his children too well. They were different from him and from his father: obedient and submissive to their wives, loving them and fearing their anger. As for the other son, he was still young.

And so he had turned his thoughts to himself. If she would be content to marry him, things would turn out as well as could be. For she, like him, knew life in the village and in the city. She was connected with important people in the capital, and he heard earlier that she had married an important man, someone from a rich and well-known family, and that she had an impressive house in the centre of Baghdad. But he had put aside all these thoughts. He realised it would be impossible to bring that about. She would never be content with him as a husband – he was her father's age and her father's friend. Indeed, he was almost a father to her. What would people say?!

"But God's compassion is bountiful, and he grants you blessings where you don't expect them." Thus Tariq thought with a rush as he focused his thoughts on how he could take advantage of this opportunity. Merely the attempt was a chance to take delight in his gift with words. Going out of his way to repeat the word "you" (stressing the feminine form of the pronoun) so that he would know its impact on her soul, he said, "You and your father are part of me, and I am part of you, as you well know. For that reason, you are always welcome here. You do not ask – rather you command, and I am prepared to do everything you request of me, no matter what the cost. Be assured that I am ready to sacrifice anything to please you and help you."

He observed how his positive words fell on her. As he saw it, expressions of this kind, no matter how generic, oft-repeated and traditional, had an effect on women as though they were new words, and the words themselves brought joy regardless of whether it was actually possible to put them into effect. Women felt words more deeply than men did, and they valued them more. Rather, they found different interpretations for them than men did. Women savoured words as though they were pieces of candy.

"In order to undertake this mission – and I salute you for considering it, just as I am honoured that you have chosen me to share in it with you – it is necessary for us to think how to go about it in such a way that the problems it brings do not exceed the relief it grants our hearts."

She asked what he meant, and he launched into a long explanation, marshalling his entire linguistic ability and his experience to select the words that would persuade her it was necessary to find a social description for their companionship, a description that would not leave any space for doubt or gossip, especially since he was a teacher and a mosque imam. He was an honourable man and the son of an honourable man, and his reputation was the most valuable thing he possessed. Given that the mission might last a long time, they would be forced to spend numerous nights far from their homes, staying at her house in Baghdad. Certainly the people would start winking at each other and dropping certain remarks, and he was concerned for her reputation as much as for his own. He was a transparent man who preferred to conduct all his actions under the bright light of day.

She realised what he was getting at, even though it had never previously crossed her mind. But she did not feel any shock, nor did she reject either his logic or him as a person. His experience allowed him to sense the opening, and he sought to take advantage of her encouraging reaction. He began by repeating how highly he valued her idea of searching for the body of her father, imbuing the matter with a certain sacredness and expressing his sense of delight and honour that she would choose precisely him to share in this mission with her, saying that he wanted to do that with his entire heart and soul. After that, he went deeper into the subject, assuring her that if he obtained this good fortune, he would make her the apple of his eye, he would care for her and he would allow her the freedom to live either in the village or in her house in Baghdad, or else to go back and forth and live in them both. She would be able to work with him, teaching in the village school or in Baghdad, or she could choose not to work, for prosperity was assured. ("Thanks be to God!") He would be the best father to her child, and so on. "We have to do this, even if only on paper, orally and legally in front of the people."

"Let me think about it," she replied as she got up.

Tariq tried to make her stay for lunch, but Qisma made her excuses, thanked him and left. Meanwhile, he remained in the living room alone, stroking his beard, rubbing his hands together and smiling with a dancing heart.

CHAPTER 28

The Sons of the Earth Crack

That night, the three of them scarcely slept. Abdullah Kafka, Tariq the Befuddled and Qisma Ibrahim – each of them, isolated in their houses, was thinking, both of themselves and the others at the same time. Not one of them had anyone nearby, the closest kind of friend who knew them and understood what was going on inside their heads, someone they could ask for advice. In any case, each of the three had become accustomed to trusting their own way of thinking and their independent convictions.

Upon reflection, Qisma found that the justifications for accepting were greater than the reasons to refuse. She had not thought before about whether she would remarry or not, much less when or where or how. Nevertheless, resolving this question early and under these conditions would be better than making up her mind to wait for an ideal person she might never find, someone who suited her situation as a widow and a mother, half of her in the village and the other half in the city, and with her former husband half a hero and half a traitor, according to how different people saw him. Tariq knew her, and she knew him. There were bonds of trust between them that were almost familial. She felt no desire to waste time introducing herself to someone else and getting to know him with all the details of his life and his memories and all that.

Tariq and she were similar in many ways. Apart from their age, there were no significant differences. Like her, he was a native of this village who loved the city and was drawn to fine appearances, numerous social relationships, the enjoyment of life and the seizing of opportunities. His level of education matched hers. Through him, she would find the security and the father figure she had denied herself by causing a rift with Ibrahim early on, not realising how important was the bond between father and daughter until she became a mother. Through Tariq, she would learn more about Ibrahim. She would restore him in her memory and in her spirit. She would find a concrete way to work through the regret she felt for her cruelty towards him, a regret she had only come to know when it was too late. Despite the house, the fields and the memories her father had left her, Qisma imagined that his spirit would feel more at ease about her future were she in Tariq's hands. And she did not doubt that Tariq would respect her and would share her desire to preserve the memory of her father.

As for what might be considered reasons for refusing – namely, the difference in their age and the fact that he was already married – they did not appear as such in that society in general, particularly in a village. On the contrary, in her relationship with him, these differences would be points of strength, working in her favour, and points of relative weakness for him.

Qisma kept going back and forth in this way. She recalled that distant memory from her childhood of when she had seen

Tariq's son, who was her age at the time, sitting in his father's lap as Tariq played with him tenderly. She remembered Tariq's laughter, his witticisms and that piercing cologne of his which never varied; she had smelled it again that morning when he received her. The memory was one she had recalled many times given that it formed a turning point in her life, when she began comparing him with her father, and she wished – or even longed – for Tariq to be her father. It was from that moment, too, that she began to feel her femininity and her independence.

She decided, therefore, to agree, and she began to imagine herself as Tariq's wife. She smiled as she connected this decision to that childhood memory. After all these years, she deserved to realise her old childhood desire of sitting in his lap. "Glory to God in the highest!" she said to herself.

And with the first light of dawn, Qisma approached her fat neighbour Amira, who was baking bread in her oven, which abutted the low mud wall that ran between their houses. Amira was the person in the village who Qisma had the most to do with. She was the one who retaught Qisma how to care for and milk the two cows, how to bake in the red mud oven, and it was from Amira that Qisma drew all the news of the village. She considered Amira to be a friend, to a certain degree, and Amira had shared with her in the tragedy that had befallen their loved ones. Amira was the only one who agreed with her regarding the necessity of searching for the bodies. Indeed, Amira had gone even further in that she wanted to preserve her husband's head in the freezer or else have it salted, but the men of the village had forcibly prevented her from doing so.

Qisma asked Amira to send one of her young sons to the house of Sheikh Tariq to tell him to come to Qisma's house because she wanted to talk with him about an important matter. Within an hour, Tariq arrived in all his finery, his fragrant cologne leading the way. Qisma led him into the living room and prepared tea for him, trying hard to behave like any village woman – good, hospitable, welcoming, refined and submissive. She appeared exceedingly, and uncharacteristically, pliant.

They discussed the matter from just about every angle, and each of them agreed graciously to the requests and the conditions of the other. Together they decided to announce their engagement that evening in the presence of the most prominent relatives of both parties. But they would not get married until three or four months had passed – or else they would choose the date at a later time – on the condition that they would not put on a large reception but would be content with a dinner banquet with glasses of juice and tea for a small group of the people closest to them.

Afterwards, they agreed to start their search for Ibrahim's body the following day, saying that this journey would also be an occasion for getting to know each other better and discussing their forthcoming wedding.

Tariq was delighted when he left her, elated, feeling years younger than he had when he left his home. He bid her farewell with the sweetest smile he could muster, and when it was time to shake hands, he squeezed hers in an intimate way. As soon as he was gone, Amira came in to see her neighbour, and Qisma told her everything. It was natural that the news should spread in the village from one end to the other before the sun went down, and even people who were not invited came to the engagement dinner. In that village, just as in every other, people would invite themselves anywhere they wished and the owner of the house had no choice but to welcome them.

The next morning, Tariq parked his car in the courtyard of her house. He was an elegant traveller with his beard trimmed, dressed in his finest clothes and wearing his cologne. He had told his younger children to clean the car and stock it with everything they would need. Then he sprayed the interior with cologne. (He had bottles of it stashed all over the place: the bedroom, the living room, his office at the school, his prayer niche at the mosque and the glove compartment of his car.)

Qisma and her son were in the back seat, and Tariq studied her face in the rear-view mirror. No sooner had he turned the car around and guided it from her house into the first side alley, than fat Amira stopped him, standing in front of the gate to her courtyard with a big suitcase in one hand and a thick book in the other. She told them she too wanted to go with them to search for the body of her husband. After Tariq absorbed this surprise and thought it through, he told her that the journey might last days or even weeks, and that it would be arduous, requiring them to go back and forth between hospitals, police departments, volunteer organisations, government agencies and even the new cemeteries. Amira had a house and a flock of dependants who needed her care. Since her husband had been killed with Ibrahim in the same incident on the same day, they would undertake to ask about him and the other murdered sons of the village. Certainly, coming across one of them would mean locating them all.

Amira reflected a little and then stepped away from the car, either satisfied or still thinking, and Tariq pulled away without waiting for her answer. There was nothing for her to do but bid them farewell with invocations for God's blessing. When the car had turned from the alley and begun its course through the main street and arrived in front of the café in the middle of the village, Tariq and Qisma saw Abdullah Kafka stretch out his arm in front of them, motioning for them to stop, which they did. He peered in through Tariq's window and said, "I want to go with you."

Qisma and Tariq looked at each other in surprise; then Qisma looked at Abdullah in even greater surprise. He said to her, "I want to be helpful in some way, even if only to watch over the child."

Qisma smiled at him, realising that he was referring to what she had said during that angry exchange in his house. Meanwhile, Tariq replied by saying, "But you would be harmful, not helpful."

"Why?"

"We have a child with us, and you're a smoker. You can't drop the cigarettes from your hand even for a minute."

"Ah, true. But I won't smoke in the car. Stop two minutes for me every hour, or every half-hour, say, so I can smoke outside."

Tariq was silent for a moment. Then he glanced at the child and saw an indication on Qisma's face that he should agree, so he said, "Come on. Trust in the Lord."

So Abdullah threw away the cigarette from between his fingers and got in, sitting beside Tariq at the front.

The three of them together experienced a feeling of the union that the two men had felt together at other times. Due to the intensity of the emotion, Qisma cried silently. Seeing her tears in the mirror, Tariq asked what was wrong, and she said, "If only my father were here with you two now so that your eternal trinity, the sons of the earth crack, would be just like it always was, like people knew it." She sobbed as she said, "I will take the place of my father. Consider me to be him. I don't like to see your triad lacking. I want you to speak to me like you spoke to him. And I want you to tell me everything about him. Everything."

At this, they found themselves speaking words imbued with wisdom, revealing the maturity they had gained from each new stage of life. They recited such axioms as: it is better to be joined together than to be apart; a single hand cannot clap; four eyes see better than two; an illness in one part of the body will hurt and disable the whole.

Abdullah indicated to Tariq that he should stop the car, even though they had not even left the village. He quickly got out and lit a cigarette while Tariq scolded him jokingly, "You said every hour or half-hour, man!"

Abdullah muttered as he sucked greedily at his cigarette. "It's O.K., it's O.K.! Bear with me just this little bit, man."

He quickly gulped down what he could of the smoke. Then he threw aside the cigarette, only half consumed, and got back in the car.

They travelled a few more minutes, passing out of the village and into the outskirts. Tariq said, "I'm convinced our mission will be a success." When he did not hear a response, he added, "I have a surprise for you both there in Baghdad."

He gazed at Qisma's face in the mirror to read the effect of his words; then he turned to Abdullah beside him. When he saw that they were looking at him and waiting for him to finish, he went on: "I know an important person in the new government."

Tariq kept pausing his narrative in this way, taking pleasure in the sense that he was stoking their curiosity. He enjoyed how their glances were directed towards him in anticipation.

"He's an agent in the ministry of national security, responsible for the security side of the purification commission."

Qisma said, "Yes, someone like that would be able to save us a lot of hardship in our search. That is, if he really agrees to help us."

Tariq was quick to reply in a loud and vaunting voice, "He most certainly will help us! He is not just a superficial acquaintance but rather a son of our village, and this is the surprise I have for you."

"Who is he?"

"He's Jalal, the son of the mayor, may he rest in peace. Our families told us stories about Jalal and his journey abroad before we were born, before all news of him was cut off."

Abdullah felt a thunderbolt pass through his body and spirit. In a single moment he felt himself contracting to the size of a pebble. His heart nearly stopped beating, and his throat constricted to the point of choking.

Meanwhile, Tariq continued his discourse with enthusiasm:

"He had changed his name to Jalal al-Din, Sayyid Jalal al-Din. But with my skills and special connections, I was able to identify him. Indeed, I've met with him, and we agreed to keep in touch and revive the intimate ties of friendship that had existed between our fathers."

They had come alongside the cemetery, and Abdullah said, "Stop, stop! I want to smoke. You were right – I will be more trouble than I'm worth. If we keep stopping like this, it will be like we're travelling to China and not to Baghdad."

They laughed.

"I can't. I can't!" He got out, adding with more seriousness and a sad, gentle tone, "I'll stay here, with Ibrahim's head. You two take charge of the search for the rest of him." Then he closed the door, lit a cigarette, and set off, going up the side of the cemetery hill without looking back.

Shock, apprehension, words and questions began boiling inside him, mixing together and gushing forth like a destructive volcano. He realised he was talking out loud to himself, and his hands were gesticulating wildly: "Here's my mother's rapist returning under the title of Sayyid to rape the village and the country. Here they are, back once again. The alliance of criminal murderers. History repeats itself. Shit repeats itself. What's the point? What should I do? I have to do something!"

He saw in the bottom of the valley that dogs had gathered to fight over some carrion. He spat at them, continuing his ascent and his questions.

Tariq and Qisma stayed there for a moment, watching him in silence as he moved away. Then they kept going, but there was a dryness in Tariq's throat and tears were forming in Qisma's eyes.

Later, when they were on the road again, Qisma told Tariq that Abdullah was a very good man, very much afflicted and wronged. He was extremely like her father, and she loved him on account of the strength of her father's love for him. They were alike in their silence, their endurance, their goodness and their misfortune, which had not vouchsafed them to take a single breath in freedom nor determine for themselves the course their lives took.

"We are all alike," Tariq commented. "We resemble each other. And at the same time, we are all different from each other. The solution is that we are alike in our acceptance of our differences."

Qisma said she was thinking about Abdullah a lot and wanted to do something for his sake so he would live the rest of his life in a better way and taste some pleasure or happiness. She was thinking of getting him married, for example. "And you have to help me persuade him!"

Tariq told her the story of Abdullah's love for his sister Sameeha, and he confessed to her details that her father had not mentioned. He told her, "I will confess something to you alone. This is the first time I've spoken of this matter out loud, even though it never ceases to resound painfully within me, making me feel bitterness and guilt towards Abdullah and my sister Sameeha. I'm the one who convinced my father to refuse their marriage. Yes, I, and don't ask me why. I was young. I was an ignorant child." He did not tell her, of course, about his psychological motive at that time, which he had never forgotten on account of the betrayal it led him to commit.

It pleased them that they were in complete agreement and they decided that their first goal, as soon as they returned from Baghdad, would be to arrange the marriage of Abdullah and Sameeha. Tariq even suggested that they put on one large joint wedding for the four of them. They found themselves more eagerly committed to sharing each other's thoughts, and they agreed on most things. Among other things, they said, "Yes, life must go on – patching the cracks, mending tears, gathering what has been parted and putting in order, as far as is possible, what has been scattered. Life must go on."

During their conversations, which continued for long stretches of the road, at petrol stations, in roadside restaurants and through inspection checkpoints, Qisma informed Tariq of another matter she had resolved within herself, and she asked him to go with her as she took care of it during their time in Baghdad. "I want to change my son's name," she said.

"And what will you name him?"

"Ibrahim."

Tariq was silent, as though taking a long drink of water. Then he commented with an enormous satisfaction, "My God! Despite all the conflagrations and wars. How many Ibrahims have walked and will walk this land of the two rivers, ever since the original Ibrahim, the forefather of us all!"

Somehow, this optimistic positivity that Tariq always expressed in his thoughts and attitude made Qisma's spirit nervous. It was as though he did not feel what she felt, or did not see what she saw: this complete destruction up and down both sides of the road; skeletons of cars and smashed military equipment; collapsed buildings and houses; these dejected military checkpoints that punctuated the road every half-hour with sandbags, blocks of concrete, and rusty fences; the unwashed faces of policemen and soldiers, fear and control mixed in their eyes, their baggy clothes inspiring pity, transforming them into animate clothes racks draped in rifles, pistols and bayonets; columns of American military vehicles, their weapons aimed at the civilian cars passing by them at a distance; neglected fields on all sides, wrapped in their thirst and a dejected withering; and columns of smoke rising in every direction.

Nothing but destruction, and if Qisma turned her gaze inward, she came across a destruction that was equally severe. Didn't Tariq see all of this? Didn't he feel it? How was it possible for him to turn everything into an advantage? Specifically, to his own advantage? It was something that troubled her and shook something of the confidence she felt inside, especially when her thoughts came back to her father, the sacrificing and sacrificed Ibrahim.

She touched the head of her child, sleeping in her lap, as a drumbeat of questions began rattling in her head: Which drop of sperm produced him? Who will he be like? Like his father, her husband? Like the insane President? Like herself? Like her father? Or like this Tariq, in whose protection this little one will flourish?

They were halfway to Baghdad when she felt all these thoughts combine into a chaotic jumble, a mix of salty, sour, sweet and bitter. Stones ground together in a kettle of pus that boiled in her belly. Dust, blood and smoke clouded her vision and constricted her breath to the point of fainting. A wave of nausea rose from her stomach. She felt such a violent desire to vomit that she suddenly cried out, "Stop. Stop! I want to get out!"

MUHSIN AL-RAMLI is an Iraqi writer, poet, academic and the translator from Spanish to Arabic of many literary classics. He was born in northern Iraq in 1967 and has lived in Madrid since 1995. He obtained his Ph.D. in Philosophy and Letters from the Autonomous University of Madrid in 2003 with his thesis *The Traces of Islamic Culture in Don Quixote*. Now he works as a professor at Saint Louis University, Madrid Campus. He writes in both Arabic and Spanish, and is a well-known figure in the world of Arabic literature.

His novels *Dates on my Fingers* and *The President's Gardens* were longlisted for the I.P.A.F., known as the "Arabic Booker", in 2010 and 2013, and he was a finalist for the Sheikh Zayed Book Award in 2016 with his novel *The She-Wolf of Love and Books*.

Much of his writing is based on his own personal experiences, including his service as a tank commander in the Iraqi army during the Gulf War. His brother, the writer Hassan Mutlak, was hanged in 1990 at the age of twenty-nine for an attempted coup d'état, and he is considered by many in his country to be the Lorca of Iraq.

LUKE LEAFGREN is an Assistant Dean of Harvard College, an Arabic teacher and translator and inventor of the StandStand standing desk.

A New Library from MacLehose Press

This book is part of a new international library for literature in translation. MacLehose Press has become known for its wide-ranging list of bestselling European crime writers, eclectic non-fiction and winners of the Nobel and *Independent* Foreign Fiction prizes, and for the many awards given to our translators. In their own countries, our writers are celebrated as the very best.

With this library we mean to make the books you would not want to overlook harder to overlook. The landscape for literary fiction in translation is expanding; we will go on looking beyond our shores and making it possible for readers to share in the most exciting and most renowned international writers.

Join us on our journey to **READ THE WORLD**.

PUBLISHED IN 2017

1. *The President's Gardens* by Muhsin Al-Ramli

TRANSLATED FROM THE ARABIC BY LUKE LEAFGREN

2. *Belladonna* by Daša Drndic

TRANSLATED FROM THE CROATIAN BY CELIA HAWKESWORTH

3. *The Awkward Squad* by Sophie Hénaff

TRANSLATED FROM THE FRENCH BY SAM GORDON

4. *Vernon Subutex 1* by Virginie Despentes

TRANSLATED FROM THE FRENCH BY FRANK WYNNE

5. *Nevada Days* by Bernardo Atxaga

TRANSLATED FROM THE SPANISH BY MARGARET JULL COSTA

6. *After the War* by Hervé Le Corre

TRANSLATED FROM THE FRENCH BY SAM TAYLOR

7. *The House with the Stained-Glass Window* by Zanna Słoniowska

TRANSLATED FROM THE POLISH BY ANTONIA LLOYD-JONES

8. *Winds of the Night* by Joan Sales

TRANSLATED FROM THE CATALAN BY PETER BUSH

9. *The Impostor* by Javier Cercas

TRANSLATED FROM THE SPANISH BY FRANK WYNNE

www.maclehosepress.com